About the author

Allison McKay was born in Derbyshire and now divides her time between Suffolk and the South of France. She studied English, History and Creative Writing at Nottingham Trent University, and has published articles and poetry in local magazines and compilations. She has worked for most of her adult life in the advice sector, and currently works with older people in sheltered housing whilst continuing to write in her spare time. This is her first novel.

NEEDS MUST WHEN THE DEVIL DRIVES

DEDICATION

For Sam and her pink pen, this would have
never have been written without you.

Also for the *good* people of Campagnac, Tarn, France.

Allison McKay

NEEDS MUST WHEN THE DEVIL DRIVES

AUSTIN MACAULEY

A CIP catalogue record for this title is available from the British Library.

ISBN 978 1 84963 044 3

www.austinmacauley.com

First Published (2011)
Austin & Macauley Publishers Ltd.
25 Canada Square
Canary Wharf
London
E14 5LB

Printed & Bound in Great Britain

DISCLAIMER

This novel is a work of fiction. Names and characters are the product of the author's imagination and any resemblance to actual persons, living or dead, is entirely coincidental.

Chapter 1

Twenty-three years ago yesterday, my Mother met her husband over the wall of the sprawling uphill cemetery. She stood on the pavement, he leaned on the handle of a spade next to the green council mower with paint peeling near the blades. Use of either depended on the passing of seasons or the passing of trade, namely death.

At the little infant school, where I was in no means a little infant, I attended daily in Wellington boots or t-bar sandals, depending on the weather. The teacher asked one day what our fathers did for a living. Mine was dead, but, instructed that I should accept this new version, I tried.

She hadn't quite married the grim reaper, more a six-foot-four balding man in blue denim overalls who dug graves in a grey plaid shirt. She had seen him on our many journeys to and from the school where she daily dragged me by the hand, leading the conversation about the class guinea pigs and the price of postal orders and registered envelopes at our little local post office.

I bought sherbet dabs; she bought stamps.

I'd noticed him as we passed by in that period between the *Collins Big Book of Monster Stories* – I liked the ghouls best, green with red cracked eyes – and the opportunity of having arctic roll for tea. These were the things that then engrossed my mind far more than keeping my eye on what my Mother was up to, it was these things that kept me absorbed for years.

It was only later, as I chewed on the corner of a clear plastic box that held a mock silver horse shoe with pink confetti bells for luck, that I realised she'd married him and I had a new father.

In those interludes of understanding, that grew closer and closer as the years passed and I developed, I reflected on the idea that there was always a place on the horizon that looked like home. A tree silhouetted bleakly on the landscape caught in the corner of your eye, the certain way the sun sets over the hills, the passage of a river cutting its path through the winding of a valley. That certain something that reminds you of the past and comes to hook you back to the place you once belonged.

From under the bed, draped with the pink and slightly threadbare counterpane, I looked up at the spitfires from the newly made Airfix kits, the freshly coated plastic paint smell hanging in the air. My Brother's bedroom held many delights and dangers, especially when vacant. Under his bed was a cornucopia of things never dreamed of in my own room: old and empty glue packets, gobstoppers half sucked and gnawed and a small pile of magazines called *Boyz Own Story*.

I had Rupert Bear wallpaper; it was peeling off in the corners and had Badger Bill striding across the landscape of the walls ninety-three times – I counted – each time with a wheelbarrow and an empty flower pot.

My Brother's walls were purple; he'd chosen the colour and painted them himself in one evening. The sounds of 'Black Sabbath' reverberated through the house as he applied each new coat; to me he seemed very grown up.

A year or so later, after my stepfather had a win on the 3.45 at Kempton and a divvy up of the trebles and accumulators each way with prepaid tax, my Brother's grown-up world became all the more detached from my own.

It was decided our house would be made bigger by building an extension. It had two rooms upstairs, three if you counted the airing cupboard, and making the house bigger meant we were to have a bathroom. At last we had entered the seventies, albeit in the latter half of the decade. Life perforated slowly into my little piece of the world and, as I grew, my acknowledgement of its far-from-swift pace became more and more noticeable.

My Brother moved out of the expanding family nest, like a reversing cuckoo, into the shed at the top of the yard.

I know that living in a shed sounds too far from the truth to be reality, but it was by no means a £99.99 shed from selected home improvements outlets. It had, in the past, held much more than a mower and some blunted garden shears.

The shed had been my own place of dreams. Inside, it smelt of tea from long-thrown-out crates, cigarette ends and geraniums. Long before I was born, it had been the village shop, built of long lengths of thick pine and painted, year in, year out, with dark green paint.

'Clarke's Family Shop', right above the door, embossed on a heavy iron sign, was flanked at one end by a 'Craven "A"' cigarette sign and at the other by 'OMO – the best for your whites'.

Passing motorists temporarily stopped here for that quarter of tea or the odd pound of sugar that people had run short of. The locals bought their weekly necessary buys: soap, bread, flour, yeast, milk, sometimes fresh potatoes grown in the fields to the far side of the village, eggs from the chickens and cheese from the milking nannies. When I stood behind the counter I was transformed into my paternal great-grandparents, the severe-faced Victorians I'd seen in old family photographs, standing proudly, measuring out two pounds of Quaker Oats from the sacks stored in the big back room.

When my Brother moved into the shed, life began another change. My fantasyland of shopkeeping and budgets was over and I was bankrupted from the family business, never to return. The smells changed from tea to the over-powering aroma of stale beer, spilt on the worn-smooth wooden floor and emanating from musical instruments he made with bottle tops and old boots on sticks. The chinking of nails burrowing their way through the metal of the bottle top, then into the old rotten broom handle, lulled me to sleep for many nights, until the time came when the hours of darkness fell into silence. A silence that would prevail long after the shed was vacated by its final resident.

Chapter 2

My first day at school began with a note apologising for being late, a faithful if not hurried promise from Mother that she'd collect me at a quarter past three, a reassurance that if given salad for dinner I only need eat what I could and a small tartan bag, one side advertising the Bay City Rollers, the other the Wombles. She deposited me at the door of my classroom, offered my hand to the teacher and hurried away.

I was four and a half, my Mother was thirty-six, and it was already half past nine.

I delved my hand into the first sandpit of a new education as my Mother arrived at the gates of the red-brick factory that stood opposite our house. The factory yard seemed to stretch up as far as the heavens. At the bottom she pulled out her new blue overall, slipped it on over her old green blouse and snapped the fasteners shut. Her first day too.

The factory made plastic. Things made of plastic that is.

Granville worked the extruder, a big, white space-age tunnel of a machine which ground plastic pellets into shavings and heated them into liquid before pressing the cooling substance into its final form. It churned out mile after mile of plastic-coated wire and string, technically labelled 'Sisal', which was then wound into lengths by: Batty Betty, who worked the winding machine – people said she had a slate loose; then Nelly, who put the newly wound clothes line into stout plastic bags and sealed the top with a clip – she had iron-grey hair (I thought she looked like the Queen Mother, apart from having a missing front tooth); Dot, with the help of Dawn, who was in love with Barry Manilow, weighed and bagged 'Percy Thrower' plant ties and stakes – Dot had gout, the Doctor reckoned from too much good living; and Gladys, who ran the catalogue – she arrived at work each day laden down with parcels and packages and taught my Mother the art of making up green-and-red pan scrubs, the kind you see in the kitchen section of hardware shops.

Soon Mother became as proficient in the art of plastic knitting as Gladys, who had stood at the same bench for the past twelve years. She praised my Mother.

'Maureen, you catch on sharp like.'

And she did. Sometimes.

When I visited them after school, I dawdled up to the factory yard through the field behind, counting the cars and horses that belonged to the gypsies – or so it was said. I'd never seen a gypsy, in spite of spending enough time looking for swarthy men with gold earrings and women with headscarves and bags of pegs. I kept a weather eye out for their caravans as well, though I never saw one of those either.

On my walk, I also wondered what I would learn inside the great red-brick building today. My education was twofold, school and factory, both important in very different ways.

Gladys showed me the groove her steel-heeled shoes had made in the rubberised cover on the concrete floor. She pointed it out, and in warning tones, hushed and for my ears only, told me, 'don't ever end up in a place like this little 'un. You'll be here forever. There's a big world out there, things I've never seen. You go and see 'em for me, eh?'

I said I wouldn't and that I would, though I had no idea what these things might have been and certainly didn't find out for years.

She told Mother and me stories, stories kept for after school. They made her laugh. Gladys was good company, and she didn't laugh often.

Anecdotes about the packers that worked downstairs in the oily corners of the big, red-brick, damp building, and how, if Mother was careful and learned from them, each evening she could slip a few clothes lines into her shopping bag before clocking out, then flog them on to the neighbours.

'Needs must when the devil drives,' said Gladys.

Mother believed the only devil that drove to our house was the milkman in his electric-powered float, calling each Friday evening for his weekly money. Every Friday the bill went up and up and the time we spent behind the sofa hiding from him became longer and longer.

Eventually, with the well-given advice and the not-so-well-earned money from pinched clothes lines and plant ties sold at weekly intervals to the neighbours and women in the hairdressers, the devil again took on his human form and the bills got paid.

Our time behind the sofa lessened and was restricted to Saturdays only, when *Doctor Who* visited the screen of our black-and-white television and the Daleks threatened our existence.

Chapter 3

The factory changed so many things.

In December, after she'd paid into the works' social club week after week, I was ushered to the factory Christmas Party held in the canteen, along with all the other workers' children and relations. Then, after jelly, cake and seeing Santa, we were all bundled on to a coach for our trip to the local pantomime.

I sat with a girl called Joanne and ate fruit gums from sticky boxes passed around the bus at regular intervals; I picked out the green ones.

In the theatre, a woman dressed up to be a man strode around in thigh-high leather boots and beguiled my eyes. Whilst the action happened on stage, Mother sat with the other workers in the theatre bar, drinking gin with Nelly and Dot, talking about Englebert Humperdink and the last time they'd been out dancing.

For my Mother, it had been a long time.

In the years before she met my stepfather, Mother had been completely my own. Weekends were spent visiting Grandma and walking her dog along the quarry tops, me picking wild flowers, collecting pebbles that caught my eye and holding buttercups up to my chin. Grandma and Mother walked and talked as they had for years, all subjects covered, from Granddad's motorbike to the cost of living.

Granddad's motorbike was a bone of contention, as indeed was the price of life.

Saturday teatimes were a sacred time before returning home on the bus that toured every limestone-built village on its route.

I mused over the banana and sugar sandwiches I'd been given for tea, not wanting to eat them, yet not wishing to appear ungrateful or rude.

Mother busied herself in the kitchen.

Grandma, with the *Matlock Mercury* folded to the sports page, at the kitchen table, waited for the football results.

East Fife - three, Forfar - four.

Hibernian Athletic - nil, Celtic - two.

The pools. Wonderful columns of crosses that dreams were made of.

Once I'd received a letter from Grandma signed with her full name, Sarah Rebecca Brown. Mother read it to me. Grandma had won the weekly pools draw; she was giving me the money when it came through.

In my mind's eye I could see all the things I would buy.

A washing machine for Mother: one that had an electric spinner so she wouldn't have to mangle the sheets on a Sunday morning or boil-wash the whites in the copper in the back yard.

Petrol for Granddad's motorbike: he wasn't allowed to ride it these days – too expensive – and he loved that bike.

New knitting pins and a Hoover for Grandma: one that 'beats as it sweeps as it cleans'. She'd said her old carpets could do with a good beating.

A Bionic Man doll for me: I would be able to see for miles through its bionic eye and hear all my Brother's secrets through its bionic ear.

And nothing for my Brother: we were on bad terms after he broke a copy of 'Itsy Bitsy Teeny Weeny Yellow Polka Dot Bikini' over my head. It was supposed to be a joke. I don't remember it being that funny.

When the cheque came, it was opened with trepidation, the moment of fortune.

Please pay the bearer – me - the sum of £3.54 only. My plans were somewhat curtailed.

Mother and Grandma didn't always get on. Sometimes weeks would pass when they didn't even speak to each other. Then there were times that they got on so well they became inseparable. My Auntie Joan, in later life, said that my Mother was so like her own that they basically couldn't stand the sight of each other even though they were as close as a mother and daughter could be. It was as if one knew exactly what the other thought and what they were going to say.

When they fell out it was mostly due to me or my Brother, and later the treatment I received from my stepfather. Grandma didn't always appreciate the fact that my Mother had different attitudes to childcare and upbringing from her own, never failing to make her opinions known.

One afternoon, in the middle of a miserable autumn day where the sky was as grey as a battleship, Grandma had been talking about my Mother's inappropriate choice in men - and the weather, repeating her favourite impending-storm saying several times: 'Bit black over Bill's Mothers'. My Mother visibly prickled as she picked up her coat and said, 'I'm off outside for half an hour, going to chop up some more logs for the fire, we're getting short.'

Grandma started to argue, telling her she couldn't just walk away if she didn't like the sound of the truth. Mother had to be told about that man she seemed sweet on. But the words fell on deaf ears. The only replies that came were the slamming of the back door and a silence which descended over the house.

I looked at Mother through the window. She was swinging the chopper high over her head and cursing under her breath, her mouth was moving and I could imagine what was coming out. I pulled on my green woolly cardigan and black Wellington boots and went out to join her. According to my Mother, there had to be a reason to be somewhere. I understood that even then; my reason came with the carrying of the wood basket and the picking up of the sticks as she chopped. She seemed to appreciate the gesture, smiling for a few seconds before going back to her chopping and grumbling.

'Bloody woman won't leave off.' Splintering sounds crackled from the large log she was breaking down.

'She thinks she can swan in here and tell me I don't know how to manage, telling me who I can and can't see.'

The log split, shattering into several small splinters and one larger chunk which dropped onto the floor with a crash.

'Well, she'd better give it a rest or I'll be telling her where she can go.'

She stopped and wiped her sleeve across her forehead, brushing off the perspiration and small bits of sawdust gathered on her face. About to carry on with the job at hand, she was halted as my Brother raced out of the back door, closely followed by William, the Jack Russell Terrier. Bill, as I called him, was a thorn in Mother's side. He'd been my Father's dog and only seemed to take to men. I don't think he really liked women; certainly he didn't like my Mother. Bill tore across the garden, my Brother in close pursuit, bringing down the carefully mounded late potatoes that had been set a couple of months previously. Mother stood aghast at the destruction of her crops, stunned into silence, if only momentarily.

'John, you come here now,' she bellowed. 'What the bloody hell do you think you're doing with that daft dog? We need those potatoes for winter. We can't afford to be losing them because of your stupid clumsiness.' She waited for him to reply. An answer did not readily come.

'Well, aren't you even going to say you're sorry? You're such a naughty little bugger,' she chastised, raising her hand to give him a slap on the backside. Just as she swung her hand, she was thrown off the mark by Grandma shouting for her to pack it in. She missed my Brother's backside completely, ending up smacking her hand against the chopping block, with a swarm of expletives.

Finding this extremely funny he started to rock about with fake laughter until Mother, with the most anger in her face I've ever seen, raised her arm again and side-swiped my Brother across the face.

He stopped laughing immediately, standing there shocked until the tears started to seep from his eyes. He ran to Grandma and buried his head in her apron, sobbing.

'Yes, you little sod, and you'll get another you won't forget in a hurry if you laugh at me like that again.' Mother's hand burned with the pain of the slap, but it didn't hurt as much as the anger and shame she felt rising in her face.

'Well, you look as guilty for that as you should my girl,' chided Grandma. 'It's about time you controlled that temper of yours. You can't just lash out at a kiddie, no matter how angry you are.'

Mother looked incredulous. She reached up and took off her glasses, waving them at Grandma.

'You see these glasses, Mother? You did this, chucking Dad's football boot at me. You hit me on the head so hard the optician said it had damaged the optic nerve, so don't come the sanctimonious Mother routine with me. You aren't as good as you make out and if I have a bad temper it's only you I have to thank for it.'

Mother's tirade at Grandma clearly shocked her and she stood quiet. The only sounds heard were the softening sobs from my Brother as he realised the importance of the row that was going on between them.

Mother continued. 'And I tell you what; if you don't like how I bring up my kids you should know I took the example from you. There's a bus due in ten minutes back to Middleton. Why don't you go and get on it.'

With that she turned her back and took another petulant swipe at the chopping block.

Grandma did indeed get the next bus home.

After she'd gone, we went inside again, my Mother, my Brother and me. He wasn't talking and I babbled incessantly to fill the void. I talked about my rabbit and how I thought a rat was gnawing at the legs of her hutch. I wondered if we should put it on bricks and would that be safer. Mother didn't answer, but I carried on talking, regardless. It was always better than the uneasy quiet.

I became very adept at filling in strained silences over the years, and at the same time very scared of the ones in which I found myself. Certainly, in any argument where my counterpart refrained from speaking it became my duty to fill in the gaps, usually with apologies and pleas to end the fracas. Sometimes this worked and others it didn't, but it did always end up with me being on the losing side, acquiescent, but at least not voiceless.

I prattled on and Mother slung things around in the kitchen, opening drawers and sweeping the contents of the worktops into the already overflowing space. Years later I had the unfortunate job of helping her clean out those drawers because she remembered leaving her Co-op card in there and now wanted to collect her divi. At the time. I cursorily asked how long it was since she'd seen it; she wasn't sure but thought it was five or six years. I found it eventually, sandwiched between a *Woman's Realm* knitting pattern dated 1983 and a hire purchase agreement from Britons furniture shop for the sale of a table and four chairs. They were long since chopped up and on the bonfire heap. She was a hoarder. Mostly she hoarded in fits of temper.

During the silence I tried to fill that day, she cleared and I retreated into the front room, playing quietly with my farm set.

I arranged the pigs into size and colour: Gloucester Old Spot and babies, big pink pig and babies and little yellow pig with one leg missing. She'd been found in the garden covered in dirt, but had definitely once been pink. My Mother decided she was far too dirty to get clean with mere water, and plonked her into a cup of extra thick bleach. She went in pink and came out yellowy, her leg now so wobbly it had to be amputated; one quick snip with the scissors and yellow pig was a tripod.

I heard Mother clanking around in the saucepan cupboard and then the tin opener started to chew its way around the top of a can. Beans on toast: standard fare for meals at angry moments or when she was sad, too tired, short of money or any other reason that could be thought of. We always had a huge stock of beans. It never fell under a standard fifteen tins; they were essentials according to Mother.

When the toast had been crunched in a more comfortable atmosphere and the television had been turned on, we settled down to watch the afternoon episode of *Crown Court* with a cup of tea and several digestive biscuits. Mother had calmed and so had her temper. Beans never failed.

The biscuit tin was bestowed upon me and I started to root around in the bottom with the crumbs to see if there were any bits of coconut rings left. Mother tutted and gave me one of those looks which I could only equate to Paddington Bear – a hard stare. Then the back door opened and she let out a big sigh, almost as if she expected new arguments were about to start.

24

'Are you there Maureen?' rang out the voice from the kitchen.

She raised her eyes to the ceiling and replied as pleasantly as she could.

'Where else am I likely to be?'

Granddad Sam was in the kitchen. He'd come ready for working his evening shift at the quarry. He was a blaster by trade and sometimes he'd take me for long walks round the quarry tops and point out where the explosive needed to be put in order to blow the largest section of limestone from the face. He'd worked there all his adult life. I asked once how much stone he'd blown up over the years and he pointed to the very bottom level of rock way down below. Down there the lorries were being loaded for their journey up and onto some distant location where a housing estate was being built, or where the stone was going to be ground down and mixed into the tarmac that covers the roads. He said he'd begun at that level years ago as an apprentice, blasting ten-tonne lumps of stone. He slowly moved on to blowing the sides of the quarry, then to being the most qualified blaster at the site, dynamiting thousands of tonnes in one explosion. He blew a rock face, checked his charges for the next blast, set them out, then had a cup of tea whilst the stone was cleared. It was a job for life. Now he was nearly at retirement age. Sat at the back of the garden puffing on his un-tipped Woodbine he told me he dreaded the thought of not working, he simply didn't know how to fill his day.

'It's no good little 'un, I shall have to get myself a hobby.'

He never had the opportunity for a hobby; within three months of his retirement it was discovered he had lung cancer. He'd had a cough for a couple of months previous to the diagnosis but assumed it was just breathing in a lifetime's worth of quarry dust. Little did he know. By the time he found out the truth it was too late, almost six months to the day after he retired he was dead.

This day though he was in my Mother's kitchen, pit boots on her clean kitchen floor, snap bag slung over one shoulder, sandwiches and slab of Grandma's Madeira cake hidden inside.

'Has she told you to come down here Dad?' Mother asked.

He shuffled awkwardly from one foot to the other and came out with it.

'Well, yes she has. She said I wasn't to unless I wanted, but you know what your Mother's like; if I hadn't come there would be hell to pay. Came down on the motorbike. Nice day for a ride out and I never like to miss the chance to take the "old girl" out on the road.'

Granddad loved his old motorbike. It had more welding than true metal but it was a 'Norton' and had a proud heritage, or so he told me. He'd won it in a card game in the quarry and had hung on to it for nearly thirty years, never telling anyone what he'd bet against the bike. People used to say he loved that bike more than Grandma, though I knew there really was no competition; he was devoted to his wife. 'There'll never be another woman like her,' he told me frequently.

'I saw her one afternoon; she had the loveliest brown hair I'd ever seen, and I could have drowned in them eyes. At least until she told me off for staring! It was then I realised Sarah was the one for me. There's never been anyone else that's come close. Mind you, I've never looked. We've had our rocky patches, no more than anyone else's, but we've been happy and got five bonny children to show for it, eh.'

He was happy and would do anything for his wife. So there he was, in my Mothers kitchen, wary of the temper of this first daughter of the family, only too aware that it had the same ferocity as his wife's and came just as quickly.

'So, what's up our Mo? Mother says you're in a nasty mood,' he said tentatively.

My Mother again looked up at the ceiling and blew out another sigh.

'No, I'm not in a nasty mood. I'm just fed up with being told how to do things and not being given a minute's peace for myself. Some bugger's always got to put their nose in, and I'm sick of it, that's all'.

He nodded and seemed to understand; he'd felt it enough over the years himself.

'And another thing, you can tell her when you get back, I'll go out with anybody I choose if I like them. She won't be picking a man for me, she didn't when I married the first time and she won't now.'

I didn't know what she meant but Granddad obviously did. Before he got the chance to open his mouth and say she hadn't really made that good a job of her first two marriages, the back door opened and in came Grandma, closely followed by Auntie Joan.

'Well this beats all doesn't it?' Mother muttered to herself. 'It's like famine or feast here! Like Piccadilly bloody Circus it is!'

She turned her back on the new entrants, winked at Granddad and said sardonically, 'I expect you'll be wanting a cup of bloody tea now you're here.'

She turned and smiled. Grandma smiled back, if a little sheepishly, pushing a bag with half a cake in towards her across the worktop.

'And don't skimp on the sugar,' Grandma replied.

The argument passed over a bit like 'Bill's' black rain cloud, bestowing a quick shower that was forgotten again once the sun had appeared. The battle was forgotten, but to Grandma the war over my Mother's choice of men was only half way through. In her view, Mother had messed up once already with my Brother's father; she'd always thought he was no good. Then she married my Dad, which was ill-fated, only lasting five years before he died. Grandma told my Mother in no uncertain terms at the time that she was daft to marry a man so much older than her. She'd had no choice but to let her get on with it.

Chapter 4

The matter of the women in the family choosing unsuitable men was obviously still playing on Grandma's mind the next afternoon as she tended her herbaceous borders. Her garden was an extension of her family, she loved and tried to nurture it in the same way she cared for her children. Plants were being thinned out ready for summer, weeds were being pulled up and any seedlings which stood a good chance of growing into healthy specimens were transplanted into a space of their own where hopefully they would thrive.

Whilst she planted and pottered, I helped her as much as I could and Grandma talked incessantly. Granddad said she liked the sound of her own voice but I think looking back that she just liked to tell stories. She was from a long line of women beginning generations back in the Ukraine who told tales about their past in an attempt to make sense of their current situations and thoughts, passing on the things viewed as important. My Grandma was no exception, storing up myths and titbits and stories she'd been told as a child, regurgitating them at moments when it seemed they were relevant or helped to look at a problem differently, or simply just to fill a gap in time. Sometimes I would ask for specific stories, other times she would just pull one out of the library in her mind and launch into it. I liked her to tell me about the past. Her eyes would almost glaze over and take on a strange look when she harked back to that place. She recounted tales of her great-grandmother and the generation beyond that. The tales had been passed down and probably embellished along the way, but that's the nature of stories, like Chinese whispers they grow, changing organically and taking on a life of their own.

As we tended the ground she told me the tale about her great-great-grandmother Isabella, who'd seen an angel. Before

28

I uttered 'really' in amazement at the claim, she began her tale at a pace.

It was at that point that Isabella realised she was going to witness something out of the ordinary, something she would need to remember. Then the figure was gone. She thought she had seen an angel, a great bird with white wings, a woman taller than any man she'd ever seen, with a pure white dress, looking almost like a swan. But as the seconds passed she wasn't sure.

She picked up her pail and pottered back to the house to sit by the hearth and watch the bread rise. Her daughter sat opposite and peeled the potatoes for that day. Unphased by the apparition, she pondered and let the thoughts fly into the fire and burn up with the branches and sticks. She was a woman who had many visions. Visions were everyday things to her, quirks of the imagination to remind folk of things that were important. Outside, the young fir trees waved straight in the breeze, dancing slightly, offering perches to a family of young doves that called to each other in hushed tones and gave comfort in their song.

The crackle of dead leaves, not wishing to detach from their branches as they caught the glare of the fire, lulled and coaxed her into her mid-morning doze. The air filled with wood smoke and the rising waft of yeast filled her nostrils, reminding her of the past. She sat and watched her life pass slowly, through half closed eyes. Later in the day the bread would be baked and flour would need to be milled for the next morning. Soup would simmer on the open fire, potatoes cooking down into a soothing, thick broth with barley and herbs collected from the hedgerow. She had little money but taught her children from an early age to share what they had and this generosity would be returned to them threefold. All that mattered was not to harm anything and treat all with the respect they would wish to have returned.

She, in a time when thick meat stews and goulashes were the norm across their country, had become a vegetarian; her pigs and the old cow became her pets. Tenacity of spirit had brought her to the age she'd become; hers had not been an easy life, some would call it an existence, but not her. She'd tended the red soil alongside her Mother and her Mother's Mother whilst her husband fought in a distant war. They expected him to return one day.

When that day finally did arrive they'd grown so used to not having him around his role in the family had all but become redundant. He sat on the porch in the mornings and read. Sometimes he would sing to himself with closed eyes, long wooden pipe clenched softly between his teeth, occasionally allowing the tears he always felt to seep out and run unattended down the cracks and crevices of his face.

One day he'd sat on the porch as usual, seeing his wife and daughter off into the fields with a small smile and a big wave of his solid hand. When they returned, he'd gone, not gone in the sense you might think, just taken up his cap and pipe and disappeared, never to return.

Isabella carried on her life much as she had before, occasionally leaning on her spade and scanning the horizon, looking for his return before going back to her tilling with a troubled frown. She carried on with routine and softness, picking the caterpillars from the cabbages and moving each one tenderly to other more tasty plants, watching and waiting for them to emerge as butterflies.

He never did return. Grandma told me Isabella thought of him often but never missed him. It was the way of her world: nothing belonged to anyone, it was only lent for a while and when that time was up, freedom had to be given, like the caterpillar emerging from its chrysalis into a beautiful creature that took flight and was nobody's possession.

Once he had gone she deferred her judgement to no one. Never one for convention, she made sure her family, her garden and her home flourished as she had, on an abundance of love, freedom and a meat-free diet.

She had three daughters, all married by a decent age. Rabatzii, wed at seventeen to a close family friend, now lived some miles across the valley. She visited only occasionally. Ramona married at eighteen and moved a little way down the road. My Mother's great-great-grandmother Angelina had waited for the right man to come along. And waited a long time.

At thirty she met her husband to be, a passing tinker who sharpened knives and scissors and followed the flight of the distant geese as a pointer for which way to travel. He believed it was as good a way to choose a path as any.

They were married under an old oak in the local village square as tradition had it. The priest, in his long black gown, blessed the couple with the longevity of the life of the tree. She hadn't expected him to settle in one place: there was only a finite need for sharpening and shaving metal from well-worn tools in their village; he needed to work and, more importantly than that, to keep moving. He returned intermittently, settling for a few weeks, giving up his profits to the household, before hitching up his cart again and wandering off into the distance.

The last time she saw him was a few months before her baby was born. Almost as if he had fulfilled his purpose he'd gone off into the distance, grinding and sharpening tools, clinking a slow romantic tune as he went. As with many of my family's men-folk, he did not return.

Soon after the visit of the woman who Isabella thought could have been an angel, the baby was born.

She knew it was to be a girl, had been shown by the angel; no predictions, no dowsing, she knew. The baby was born in the height of winter, the blue light of the sky reflecting on the new snow. Crystals formed against the thick window panes, patterning them with frost inside and out, artists' cold fingers holding brushes of ice and painting their beautiful murals on the glass. Snow had fallen steadily for three days, large perfect flakes, settling, preparing a bed for yet more snow. On the side of the hill the only visible landmark was the dome of the church breaking into the sky. A red and gold onion dome placed on a plate of perfect blue white.

Life flooded her tiny cheeks in front of the flaring fire. She was wrapped tightly in a blanket of soft wool, knitted by a past grandmother and handed down through the family from Mother to daughter, imprinting spirits of babies from generation to generation. Angelina wanted to call the baby *something warming, a fiery name to ward off the cold and inflame hearts. But Isabella knew differently; she will be a wanderer, she told her daughter as the baby opened her eyes and gazed unseeing around the room. She will be a wanderer and her little eyes will see the world as it is and as it can be.*

She had her way. The baby was named Alauda after the skylark, and indeed she learned to wander, to trust her instincts and know the right path.

Angelina attempted to distract the child from its wayward leanings, trying to dilute the wild streak she clearly had, by teaching her the names for special dishes and tempting sweetmeats. But as she grew and learned these things she was also learning from Isabella. Herbs to heal, how to make liquor, what the song of the birds meant and when the approach of a stranger warned of danger. The child had her eye fixed firmly on the horizon, the point where the track traversed the hills and disappeared. Winters came and went and she grew, her hair lengthened and became ever brighter red, curling madly and tangling in bushes and briars. Angelina despaired, believing the child would have birds nesting and raising their young in there.

Alauda hoped that they would.

Grandma had a habit of stopping halfway through a story when something distracted her, almost never going back to where she'd broken off. It was frustrating for the listener; eventually I came to the conclusion it was because she could tinker with the stories, adding or taking away the bits she didn't like or think were effective. I never heard any more of the story of the angel but stored it up in order to add to it myself as the years went by.

Chapter 5

As I grew older I became inquisitive about my Father. Nothing was ever said to me about him, Mother thought I was too young to understand and as I grew she seemed to hope I'd forget. Silence on a subject, however, spoke volumes and I imagined all kinds of horror stories. How he had entrapped her and made her marry him. That he was nasty and rough and kept her chained to the kitchen sink, metaphorically, like those stories I'd seen portrayed in afternoon films where women sweated over hand-washing until their fingers cracked and bled from water and soap. Finally my Grandma mentioned him and a door had been opened and left ajar. A chink of light now illuminated the way to asking about what kind of man my Father had been, how they'd met and why I'd come to be.

She stood there for a few minutes and seemed to be staring blankly into space, so much so that I thought she hadn't heard my questions. I was summoning the words to ask again when she started to speak.

Over the next few years she told me bits and pieces, details thought reasonable to recount to a growing child. Some days she would talk for hours, others it was just a word here or there. I put the parts together like a jigsaw and stored them up in my memory. As the years passed I added more details, padding out the bones of her account with things learned from listening in to conversations I wasn't supposed to hear, reading letters I wasn't meant to find and adding two and two together to make one complete picture.

Eventually I was able to replay it all like a film in my head.

Imagine the cinema. The lights go down and the women in the front row rustle their paper bags of pick and mix, gluing their dentures together with liquorice toffees and chocolate éclairs. There's an air of expectancy and, as light appears on the screen, a silence descends around the auditorium. Music starts and the picture rolls. Its grainy black and white, narrated by someone who sounds distinctly like me.

The film runs like this: by the age of seventeen my Mother had never had a boyfriend; she'd never even really looked at a boy. Auntie Joan was on her fourth, even though she was a couple of years younger, and my uncles seemed to go through streams of women, one after another. Mother had too much to do to be bothered with boys, or so she said. She had wanted to go to college on finishing school and train to be a market gardener but that was one of those dreams which involved having money to make come true. Grandma and Granddad only had just enough to make ends meet, never mind send their eldest daughter for further education. Bitterly disappointed, she'd accepted the necessity and got on with life, taking a job in the textile mill down the road where Grandma had worked as a young woman and my great-grandmother had worked before that. My Mother didn't much like the job. She wanted to nurture and plant, instead she learnt to thread and knit. But at least she had her hobbies.

Monday and Friday evenings she went to band practice with the Wirksworth Quarry Band. She was a member because of Granddad's job in the next village's quarry. The quarries were like vast scars across the land, as if some huge hand had taken a knife and carved out large rough chunks from the ground. They were all linked by a sense of community, but if they continued to gouge at the rate they were these days the link would become a physical one as well as one of neighbourliness. Mother played the cornet; she'd started to learn after joining the Methodist Sunday School. Grandma wanted her to go, thinking my Mother could do with a bit of religion. That's what she told her but Mother knew better. She'd heard Grandma tell old Mrs Metcalf that she needed a bit of time to herself, with all the children to manage and Granddad to look after as well. After all he was like having another infant at times! Mrs Metcalf told Grandma she should farm them out a couple of times a week to get a bit of peace. It was advice that was taken.

My Mother's farming-out was done firstly at the Sunday School and latterly the band. Auntie Joan played out at her friend's house on the Sunday afternoons and had her tea with them. Uncles Bill and Ralph were old enough to fend for themselves. They turned out for the local football team where Granddad, after his Sunday morning lie-in with Grandma, joined them. The only one left in the fold was Uncle Roland; he slept in on a Sunday. Being the eldest and in part-time employment, with a naval career beckoning, guaranteed certain privileges.

Overall, Mother didn't mind her Sunday morning placement; it gave her a sense of freedom in a way she hadn't felt before. And at least she didn't have to share this time with her Sister, seeing as everything else she had was as much Joan's as her own, through necessity as well as a lack of physical space and money. Sunday mornings alone were very precious to her. The cornet playing came quite quickly after she signed up for Sunday School; they were recruiting trainee band members and she fancied having a go.

The only problem became the need for an instrument. She hadn't wanted to play the cornet at all but had designs on the tenor saxophone, all brass and shiny valves. She returned home on the third dinnertime of her Sunday School education full of excitement at the prospect of her ensuing musical career, asking Grandma whether she could join the band. Grandma said she could if that's what she wanted to do, secretly thinking that would be another couple of hours a week of peace and quiet whilst she was out at band practice. Mother then asked if she could have a saxophone. Grandma drew in her breath sharply and replied to her.

'I tell you what my girl, you don't half come home with some ideas. Where do you think we'll get the money for one of those? If we saved up for long enough then we could happen afford a triangle or a pair of cymbals for you, what do you think?'

Grandma was half smiling, but the look of disappointment in my Mother's eyes was enough to wipe the smile off anyone's face.

'I tell you what, why don't we see what your Dad says when he gets home? We'll sort something out.'

Mother was none too convinced and had given up all hope when, the next evening, Granddad returned from work with a broad grin on his face that could have lit a room. At the dinner table he announced to everyone, 'the lads at work are having a whip round to try and buy you an instrument for the band Mo. I don't know how much we'll collect but we'll see what we can get second hand and you never know, eh!'

Grandma scolded him under her breath, murmuring about not being charity cases and not wanting folks' pity. Granddad heard and nipped it in the bud with some force.

'Now it's not charity Sarah. The lads love my kids like their own and wouldn't you give a few shillings if one of theirs were wanting for something? So we'll hear no more about it. They're doing it from the good of their hearts. Mind, they did say Mo, that when you got good you had to join the quarry band. It could always do with a new face.'

No one knew how much they would raise but my Mother was as pleased as she'd ever been about anything. They were going to give the collection until the end of the week then Albert was going to take the bus up to the music shop in Buxton to see what he could get. Albert was the oldest of the quarry men that Granddad worked with. He was nearly at retirement age but full of life, telling everyone he only felt forty-five never mind sixty-five. He knew about instruments, about brass bands. He'd grown up in a musical family and even though he didn't have a tuneful bone in his own body he did know what was good and what should be passed over. She didn't care if it was second hand; the saxophone was to be hers. That night, and for several after, she went to bed with an excited feeling in her chest.

By the time the last shift of the week had ended Mother was on tenterhooks waiting for her saxophone to appear back from Buxton with Albert. Granddad had come home after his usual pint of mild in the Wheatsheaf pub at the top of the dale, chuffed as he sat down at the table, and told Grandma how much the lads had raised.

'Seven pounds, ten shillings and sixpence. Not bad from twenty-five blokes is it? Even old Cloughy gave some towards it and I've never seen him put his hand in his pocket for anything.'

He was clearly proud of his workmates and their generosity towards his eldest daughter. Later, he told my Mother how the box had been brought over from the site for him to count up; he couldn't believe his eyes at how much they'd raised and, tough as he made himself out to be at work, he admitted to shedding a tear.

About two hours after Granddad had arrived home and tea had been eaten and cleared away, there was a knock at the kitchen door. Albert had arrived.

He had a hard, black music case in his left hand and a paper bag with a book of sheet music in the right. Granddad let him in and sat him down at the kitchen table. The music case was set down in the middle, taking pride of place next to a pile of cooling fruit scones that Grandma had just got out of the oven. While they waited for my Mother to come down the stairs, Grandma split open a scone, spread it with a knife-load of butter, and cut Albert a piece of Cheddar to go with it. She had the kettle boiling and was ready to do the honours with the teapot.

Mother appeared at the bottom of the stairs, wearing her nightclothes under the oversized woollen cardigan that had been a cast down from an Aunt who lived close by but was at least three sizes bigger. She was clearly excited to see what Albert had brought back and sat down in anticipation at the table, not knowing what to say, where to look or who to look at.

'Uncle Albert, thank you for doing all this for me. I don't really know what else to say, but thank you.' Albert wasn't her real uncle at all, but all of Granddad's workmates were called 'Uncle' by the children of the family. The quarry men were as much Granddad's kin as his own blood. They faced danger together and looked after each other, through happy times and adversity.

'Well Maureen, it isn't quite what you wanted. The shop had saxophones which weren't good enough to buy: too much wear and tear and damage. Then the good ones were out of reach. So I got you this instead.' He flipped the front of the music case open and revealed a brightly shining brass cornet. 'It's got new valves and I managed to get a mute thrown in and some sheet music for you to practise with.'

Mother was shocked at the change of plan; she wasn't even sure what a cornet had looked like until then, never mind what sound one would make. It was beautiful to behold, more than beautiful, but it wasn't a saxophone.

'The cornet, Maureen, is a fine instrument,' continued Albert as if he knew she wasn't sure what she was looking at. 'Lovely brass tones and very different from the sound of a trumpet. It's quite rare to find such a good one for this price. Not a scratch on it and as clean as a whistle. Have a look.'

The horn of the cornet caught the light; suddenly the disappointment of the case not containing a saxophone dissipated and she started to fall in love with the beautiful instrument. She saw the reflection of her face in its neck and the way the valves glistened under the power of the electric light.

'Go on, have a blow,' encouraged Albert, grinning widely at her.

'Go on Mo, give us a sound at least,' pushed Granddad.

Having worked up enough courage and fighting against the fear of not being able to get the instrument to make any noise whatsoever, Mother raised the mouthpiece to her lips, took in a huge lungful of breath and blew as hard as she could. The noise that belched from the horn was such a shock she nearly dropped it. Grandma spilt her tea in her saucer and the canary, which had been asleep for at least an hour with its beak tucked into its fluffed-up chest feathers, fell off its perch with a bemused squawk.

'Well, there's no doubt she can blow the thing Samuel!' Albert said, laughing.

Granddad, hooting with laughter at the chaos the cornet had caused, patted my Mother on the back and said warmly, 'go on, take yourself off to bed love. You can have a proper play with it in the morning, then you can start your lessons with the band.'

So she joined the Sunday School band as a junior member and began her lessons. She practised scales and started learning to read music; eventually understanding it and slowly mastering one piece after another. Some months later she was fitted with her band uniform. It wasn't as plush or well cut as the one she progressed to once she'd joined the quarry band, but she was very proud to walk out and play carols alongside the Salvation Army in Wirksworth market square. Albert stood at the back of the crowd with Bill Green and watched. Occasionally he would join in with the chorus of a rousing carol, but mostly he concentrated on her playing.

Two days later, Bill Green, the leader of the quarry band, arrived unannounced on the doorstep, much to Grandma's annoyance. Grandma was in the middle of stuffing the turkey with sage and onion from a large bowl and didn't want a dirty quarry man in her kitchen tramping white limestone dust all over the floor.

He had brought Mother an early Christmas present: the offer of joining the quarry band. Only as a junior second cornet, but it was a start. Grandma softened towards his entry into the house without invite when she found out why he'd come, shouting Mother in from the back yard where she was helping Granddad chop up sticks to keep the fire going over the Christmas holiday. They both came inside wondering what the sudden fuss was about.

Granddad clapped Bill on the back and poured him a mug of pale ale from the keg that had been newly brought home from the pub by Uncle Roland. This was Roland's contribution to the festive celebrations to come.

Bill took the mug, had a swig, and started to tell Mother why he was in their kitchen at this time of night. She was astounded by the offer, feeling she'd only just got to grips with the instrument and didn't think she was good enough to join a proper band. The prospect was incredibly exciting.

'Yes please,' was as much as she could muster before promptly bursting into tears. Later she explained to me that it was because she had hoped for this more than anything and when the opportunity came she was overjoyed yet utterly scared of making a mess of her chance. She knew she could play but didn't really rate herself that accomplished when compared to the experienced cornet players who marched with the quarry band.

Grandma, uncharacteristically, gave her a hug and told her she just needed to try her best, put her all into it, practise hard and she would get there.

'He wouldn't have asked if he didn't think you were good enough, my girl. It's not pity he's giving you; they want you there because you can play. Now don't be so daft. Put the kettle on, we'll have a cup of tea and then we can measure you up for your new uniform.'

So play she did, getting better and better as the months progressed. She attended her music lessons and each morning before leaving for school – the secondary modern up on the hill looking over the town - played her scales and practised her mouthing. Grandma called it the morning wake-up call to the troops. It got everyone in the house up for work or school and even though Auntie Joan complained bitterly about losing her beauty sleep, she was impressed with Mother's devotion to her treasured cornet.

Grandma told her she looked a picture in her uniform: dark blue serge with gold braid around the wrists and on the shoulder epaulets. Mother said she felt incredibly privileged to step out of the front door onto the street with her fitted jacket and skirt, and her smart-yet-sturdy flat leather shoes. She was particularly proud of the cornet case she carried.

She marched with the quarry band every Saturday and Sunday during the summer months, playing all the bandstands and market crosses throughout Derbyshire. These were the Dales brass competitions, where the local bands competed against each other for the title of best band in the County; frightening to a young girl. The pressure to perform well was immense. She once said the best bit of advice was given to her from the trumpet major one day when she was having a problem following the music for a new piece that had been put into their marching score.

'If you do it wrong Mo', he said, 'just keep going. If you don't show you've cocked it up then no one listening will really notice. It's all about front. Just keep on going.'

She used this piece of advice throughout her life and tried to pass it on to us children as a good way of being.

Chapter 6

When the time came for her to leave school she was in for a disappointment. Apart from playing her cornet, the thing she most wanted to do was become a market gardener; she'd grown veg under the watchful eye of Granddad since being a little girl and certainly had an aptitude for it. Her onions and cauliflowers were entered in the local show and she'd been commended for them both. The certificates took pride of place next to Uncle Roland's naval credentials and Uncle Bill's mechanics examination official diplomas; all decorating the wall in fine brown wooden frames over the fireplace in the kitchen. But her dreams to become a market gardener were not to be fulfilled. She came home one afternoon full of hope, with a handful of forms to sign up for the Marketon College horticulture certificate. She had visions of a future where one day she would run her own gardening business and bring in a good wage to help the household.

Grandma looked at the forms and frowned as she scanned down the pages to find the cost of the three-year course. She knew even before looking at the prices that this was a dream that they couldn't afford to give their eldest daughter. She waited until Granddad got home to break the news; this was her way. Grandma told herself that her daughter understood things better when they came from him, but it was actually more a case of not always wanting to be the one who said 'no' in the house.

So, after Granddad returned from work he washed the dust off his hands and face, changed into his clean shirt, then sat down in front of the fire to tell my Mother how it was.

'Maureen, you know that we've always wanted the best for you, don't you?' He didn't give her a chance to reply. 'And I know you want to make something of yourself and be a proper gardener, but honestly duck we can't afford it for you, not this year anyway. It's such a lot of money. At this time we don't have it to give you, what with all the others needing new shoes, Ralph growing so quick and going up to the Grammar, all the money that'll cost in uniforms and kit…'

Mother nodded, deep down she'd known, it was no surprise. Though bitterly disappointed and crying once outside in the safety of her own company and neat rows of growing produce, she accepted the decision. There was no choice but to. Granddad told her not to give up hope, there was always the next year or the one after, and if she could save a bit of money herself in that time then maybe together they could afford to enrol her on the course. She wasn't entirely comforted by the thought; particularly as Grandma then came out with the alternative career path she had in mind for her daughter.

'Anyhow my girl, all is not lost. I went down to Masson yesterday afternoon and asked if they had any jobs going. There's one for an apprentice loom minder and threader. The foreman has put your name down and says if you turn up at seven on Monday week you can start. That's good isn't it?'

Mother didn't think it was but couldn't say anything, knowing she had to work and bring a wage into the house. Yet she'd set her heart on something better than this. It seemed her future was now mapped out and it wasn't the one she wanted.

Masson Mill could be seen for miles along the Derwent valley, its tall chimney looming up into the sky and blowing out clouds of steam high into the air. Steam made in leviathan-sized boilers that in turn powered the mechanism to run the giant water turbines. The smell of the vapour tainted the air for miles. Mother had told Grandma years before, when she was a little child, that she thought Masson was the workhouse. She'd read about them at school. The Master had told them how lucky they were not to have been born fifty years earlier because they might have been unfortunate enough to have ended up in one themselves. Masson and its looming nature scared her. Grandma told her not to be so fanciful and daft, the mill had been purposely built by Arkwright to produce high-quality cotton using the power of the river Derwent. Still, it did look imposing. Even today I could see what she'd meant: all dark red brick and painted black iron windows, very stark and unforgiving.

Mother reckoned that if you half-closed your eyes and stared at the windows for long enough you would see workers from the past staring back at you dressed in the flat cloth caps and collarless shirts which were standard wear then; I often tried to see them but never did.

The day of her incarceration, as she termed it, began to loom a bit like the chimney; wherever she looked she could see signs of it approaching. When she was out in the town helping Grandma with the shopping or taking Granddad's slips to the betting shop, she didn't seem able to avoid seeing the Masson girls. In the mornings they were stood in unruly masses waiting for the bus to come and take them to work. Evenings found them arriving back in the market place, full of the chatter and gossip of the day. They stuck out in their navy blue twill overalls and inside the factory wore matching hats so their hair didn't contaminate the cotton in any way.

She was to work with these girls or, if not these girls, then some very like them. The hordes of them all together frightened her. She tried hard to catch their eye if they glanced her way, smiling her warmest smile. Sometimes she'd get one back, at others it was more of a confused questioning stare at who this girl was that kept looking at them.

When the dreaded Monday morning came around Mother got up with a heavy heart, not even finding it in her to play a scale on the cornet. Grandma knew this was a bad sign and to combat it had set about fixing her up with a workmate to take her to the mill. A friend's daughter was coming to pick up Mother at seven o'clock, walking her to work and escorting her back at night until she got used to it. Mind you, she was less than thrilled with this prospect, especially when she found out the girl she'd been set up with was none other than Mary Metcalf, someone she'd avoided since her first day at school.

Mary was three years older than my Mother, though less mature and actually seemed several years younger. People nicknamed her Hairy Mary, not just for the way it rhymed but also because the abundant hair on her arms was as black as coal. It looked peculiar, contrasting with the fair curly hair framing her face, waves which were almost white in the sun. The difference in colours seemed somehow wrong. Mary had never been liked at school, possibly because of her hairy arms but more likely because of her Mother's views on religion. Not that Mary shared them, but mud sticks; at least that's what Grandma reckoned.

'Old Mother Metcalf was a right one, had been all right before that bang on the head down the market hall. She was waving her placard, one of those barmy things written with red paint, 'The End is Nigh' or 'Women of the World Unite' or something, when she dislodged a crate of Spanish onions. It fell on her head with such a thump, onions rolling all over the place, knocked her straight down onto the concrete floor. Out cold so they say, for five minutes or more, and then when she did come round she couldn't remember her name or where she was. The ambulance driver passed the placard back to her but she didn't even know it was hers.'

Mary's Mother Hilda was a big woman, in stature and size but also in spirit, appearing to be absolutely fearless. She'd been taught how to stand up and be proud of herself. Her own Mother had been brought up in London, growing up with the ideals of the suffragettes. She'd stood shoulder to shoulder on the protest lines with other women who believed there should be more to their lives than being in the shadow of men, wanting their own viewpoints heard and to make their own way in the world. Hilda had been taught the importance of sticking up for herself as a woman, about how crucial it was to fight for what she believed in and to always be upright and strong. Unfortunately her mother had died far too early, lessons were unfinished and Hilda had muddled through her later teenage years without her much-needed role model. She sought out a replacement, eventually looking to the Pankhurst Sisters for continuing inspiration, from then on carrying a newspaper clipping of them in her purse. Whenever she felt dispirited or cornered by an insurmountable problem she took it out and tried to think about what they would have done in her place. When she returned from the hospital with her unwanted placard and a waft of onions about her, she opened her purse to see if there was anything in there that would explain who she was. Even though she'd been told her name and brought home by a strange-looking little man with protruding nasal hair who said he was her husband, she tried to gain more knowledge about herself by looking inside. The purse didn't really tell her anything. She tipped out the change and looked at the bills and receipts, including the clipping, then cast it all into the dustbin without realising its prior significance. Hilda changed beyond recognition, though wasn't aware she'd changed at all, just tried to get along with her life as best she could. But the Mother that Mary had grown up with had disappeared. She was left facing a blank canvas that, to her horror, started to be filled in by the influences of those Hilda came into contact with.

Hilda became impressionable. It was almost as if that bang on the head had ridded her of all former ways of looking at the world, dispersing the morals and codes she had previously lived by. She became a complete sponge. The Conservatives came to the door with election leaflets and she was swayed their way; another knock and she was swayed towards Labour. When the local elections were over she had her attention taken by the Unitarian chapel's need for a new roof. She worked hard, pulled into every venture that came along until she tired of each new cause. She was searching for something to make her life complete. Then along came the Mormons.

She first met the Mormons when they came to the door early one spring afternoon. Hilda had been up to her elbows in flour baking for the church bazaar, all monies going to the roof fund, though her husband Charlie thought that proceeds actually lined the pocket of the vicar. She let them into the kitchen, sitting them down in the spot which was furthest away from the flour dust. Anyone who came to the door was welcome in Hilda's house: every stranger was just a friend she hadn't yet met. All were invited in and made to feel at home, Mormons being no exception. After apologising profusely for the mess, she put her last tray of buns into the oven, wiping her hands on the tea cloth before brewing the couple a pot of tea and sitting down to talk to them. Charlie wandered in halfway through their chat, raising his eyebrows in despair at his wife pouring over scripture leaflets, then wandered out again muttering about some 'barmy bloody cause or other'.

The couple in Hilda's kitchen were well dressed but not overdressed, with impeccable manners. The woman was called Jenny and spoke with a strange accent that Hilda later discovered was American, though it was very soft. The man, Brian, she found out had been saved by the Mormons whilst on a day trip to Skegness. He had meandered down the sea front eating an ice-cream wafer and been lured into the church tent. He said he'd gone in mostly to have a few minutes sit down and a respite from the sun, though once inside he'd liked what he heard and been very much taken by the woman at the front with the lovely warm smile and face of an angel. This was Jenny. Brian had fallen for her and under the spell of the Mormons at the same time. He joined their cause there and then and started to see what he'd missed all the previous years of his life. Eventually he told Hilda he'd given up his job handing out the miner's weekly pay packets at a colliery in Yorkshire, there was more to life than that and he decided to follow the Lord. He had a calling; it came to him whilst he sat splitting a shilling into pennies at his counting table. Brian now followed the Lord, and Jenny, much to his relief, had decided to follow Brian, living on subsistence from the Mormon Church, working as missionaries for God. He added that they were both very content and wanted to share that happiness around, helping people like Hilda find joy in the Lord and live a good and wholesome life.

Hilda took it all in.

She read the pamphlets again, feeling she had finally found something to wholeheartedly give her life to, agreeing to go along to their prayer meeting on the following Sunday in Bonsall Village Hall. After they were gone, leaving behind washed tea cups – Hilda had never known any visitor to wash up in her house before – she remembered the buns rising in the oven. It was too late; some came out slightly burnt, others hard as rock cakes. Shrugging her shoulders, she cast the blackened ones into the iron dustbin outside the back gate, packed the rest into a sturdy tin and added a note inside.

Dear Vicar, please find cakes for the roof, I hope they may bring in some money for your fund. I won't be seeing you this Sunday, I'm going to join the Mormons. Hilda.

After leaving them on the doorstep of the church, she closed the gate behind her and never looked back. Neither physically nor metaphorically.

That was the start of the problem for Mary. Before, people had viewed her Mother as harmless, some thought she was a bit easily led and daft, but nice with it. The Mormons changed that. Hilda became almost radical in her beliefs. She was vociferous in her certainty that there were two deaths in this life of ours: the physical death and, more importantly, the death of the soul. Two deaths to suffer and two deaths to be saved from. To her, mortality was a state in which everyone had to prove their worth; people were to aspire to become more God-like. Souls were in a perpetual probationary state whilst on earth and, during this waiting period, had to do their best to be better. Hilda believed in good for good and evil for evil, an eye for an eye and a tooth for a tooth. She was Old Testament through and through, believing in plagues upon evil nations and floods to wipe out wrongdoers. When the quarry had a land slip and part of the side of the blast face fell down on the men below, she appeared with the worried wives and friends to state her beliefs. When no one would listen she returned home and wrote out one of her makeshift placards: *We are all buried in this life, but God will let us out of our fiery pit if we ask.*

It didn't go down too well. When one of the quarry men was dragged out three days later with a crushed leg which he later lost in hospital, Hilda testified to the surrounding crowd. She told everyone that God had saved the man; his leg was clearly evil and had to be given to save his soul. The wife of the ill-fated quarry man wasn't so sure. After giving Hilda a severe telling off and a few home truths, she broke down in tears of shock.

Hilda did herself no favours. She was belligerent, knowing what was right, and that was all that mattered. She would be saved and it was her duty to rescue as many mortal and spiritual souls along the way as was possible.

People started to say she was mad. They avoided her in the street; if she was on one side of the road, they crossed to the other. When Hilda walked Mary to school, singing rousing hymns and marching along to the beat of the tune in her head, other mothers laughed nervously and kept a discreet distance. Their children stared and pointed, laughing openly at Hilda but also slyly at Mary. Hilda was oblivious; Mary, unfortunately, was not.

Hilda drove her husband Charlie insane, at least that's what he told her frequently. More than once he'd found himself in such a temper he had walked out of the house rather than stay and listen to her ranting. Many times he'd scooped up Mary and taken her off to his own mother's for the afternoon. Sometimes afternoons would grow into weekends and, on rare occasions, stretch into a week or more.

When they returned, Hilda often hadn't even noticed they'd been gone. She had used her time well, thanking Charlie for giving her the time to get out and evangelise people in the streets. Mary was just seven years old and even at this age aware of the way people would look at her Mother. When they went down to the market on a Saturday morning to buy their weekly vegetables Hilda carried pockets of pamphlets to hand out to people. It didn't matter if she knew them or not, sometimes it was better if she didn't; it was then less embarrassing for Mary when they pushed the sheets of paper back at her Mother or turned away and pretended they hadn't heard. Mary often spent her time pretending that she hadn't heard Hilda either and had nothing to do with this zealous woman at all. Sometimes people would comment piteously on Mary's plight; Old Dutton, the fruit and veg man, once said to his neighbouring stallholder how sorry he felt for her: 'Poor soul, I feel that sorry for that little lass. It was bad enough when her Mother was mad on women's rights, but since she had that bang on the head she's been a right bugger. She never gives up. She thinks she's saving your soul. I've told her straight, my soul's all right as it is, Hilda. I can save it myself if it needs saving. Still, she takes no notice. Like water off a duck's back. Still, as I say, it's that poor little 'un I feel sorry for.'

People avoided Hilda and in turn started to avoid Mary. Friends whose Mothers used to take pity on her now tugged their daughters away when Mary came close to them at school-leaving time. It was the fear of the Mother tagging along that put them off the child. Unfair as it was, she took the brunt of her Mother's views, eventually turning into a very lonely girl. She retreated into herself and then into the house, where she spent time in another world, a world of books and the local municipal lending library. By the time she entered her apprenticeship at Masson she was probably the best-read girl there, not that that cut any ice with the other girls in the weaving shop. She was odd and that was that.

Anyhow, eventually she started to grow on my Mother as they walked to and from work each day. Mary still turned up on the doorstep each morning even after Mother had settled into the factory routine, met her workmates and got into the groove of mill life; Mary was persistent in her pursuance of a friend. My Mother realised that Mary had a good heart. Mary once missed half a day's pay in order to take a hedgehog home that she'd found dehydrated on the path across the fields on the way to work. The poor thing was half starved and so thirsty it could hardly get up on its little legs. She scooped it up and tucked it inside her coat despite it spiking her skin and giving her a spate of fleabites all down the left side of her rib cage. She got the little creature back on its proverbial feet again and fed it up on Hilda's best minced beef. A lot of the other girls on her shift laughed at her for losing money over something so daft as a hedgehog, but Mother didn't join in. It was then she realised Mary actually cared about things other than lads and money.

They started to spend time outside work with each other. On the nights when Mother wasn't at band practice or out performing, they went to the pictures down in Matlock or occasionally the local dance, neither girl being particularly interested in meeting the lads that also went there. Grandma heard that people were starting to talk about them. She tried to broach the subject, but Mother told her that folk could think what they wanted; she didn't care and neither did Mary.

My Mother had never really had a best friend; there wasn't the time, what with Sunday School, the church band, the quarry band and looking after Uncle Ralph when Grandma was out at work. Mary had never had the opportunity to make any friends during her childhood due to Hilda's dogmatic behaviour. For a while they became inseparable.

Chapter 7

Then, without looking and certainly without trying, my Mother met Peter Starr and things inevitably started to change. She met him on the bus; he was the driver of the number 26, Bakewell to Derby, passing through Wirksworth at twenty past the even hour. It was usually late. This should have been a precursor to how he would behave in the future, but Mother didn't notice. Dressed in her band uniform, with cornet and music bag, she got on the bus, putting the money onto the tray as he looked her up and down and said admiringly, 'give us a tune then love.'

Mother smiled. She was shy with men then, not knowing how to behave. She blushed and stuttered as he restarted the engine, then made her escape up the aisle and sat down.

As they drove along, the bus winding its way through the villages, she became aware of the sensation of being watched, causing her to glance up and see that the driver's rear-view mirror was trained upon her. Shyly glancing away, she continued to feel his eyes upon her. Once the bus reached her stop she breathed in a sigh of relief, scurrying off behind a large woman with a pushchair and loudly screaming toddler.

In the village hall she safely took her place between 'Big Bert', who played first cornet, and Marie, who played the tenor horn. Practice went well. They wended their way through the popular classics and the local favourites, then attempted their first run through of 'Rhapsody in Blue'. Harry Thompson was a Gershwin fan and, as he was the bandleader – 'Director of Music' was what he actually liked to be called – what he decided went. The band weren't fond of Gershwin – too modern-fangled, at least that's what 'Big Bert' reckoned, but still they played it. Mother liked it but kept her mouth shut. She was still the youngest in the band and didn't feel it was wise to go arguing against the likes of Bert.

The band's engagements for the next month were set and then it was time for home.

Mother walked back to the bus stop with Marie, who only went as far as the next village then changed and caught another bus up to Fritchley from Bull Bridge bottom. She would still be home much earlier than my Mother in spite of the more complicated journey.

They stood at the stop together and waited for the 26 to come back from Derby. It was never full of an evening: no one wanted to go up to the villages after dark; there was nothing to go there for. Living in the top of Derbyshire was no life for a young woman. There was nowhere to go and even if there had been there was no way of getting back again as the buses all stopped at eight o'clock. Six o'clock if you were in the really tiny hamlets tucked into the limestone hillsides.

Mother hoped with all her heart that the driver would not be the same man who had taken her down to band practice. She felt nervous and a little threatened by him but wasn't sure why. As the bus turned the corner she was dazzled by the headlights and crossed her fingers inside her mittens.

The 26 drew to a halt at the stop. Marie clambered on first, paying and getting halfway down the aisle before Mother had even climbed onto the first step.

'Come on my girl. There's no time for daydreaming tonight. I've twenty daft women to pick up in Idridgehay from the bingo in half an hour. I'll be lynched if this bus is late,' bellowed the driver.

She jumped onto the bus grinning and paid her fare with a flourish before rushing down the aisle, more than relieved to see that the drivers had changed shifts. She bumped down next to Marie and started to chat on about band practice and 'Big Bert's' taste in music. The girls laughed to themselves and she felt at peace.

The bus made its way down the narrow lanes, surrounded on both sides with the dry stone walls and crumbling boundaries that the middle of Derbyshire is famous for. In a way she found them comforting. Those very stones were once blown from rock faces not unlike the quarry where Granddad worked and his father had worked before him. As the bus rumbled closer to Middleton Top the colour of the weathered walls changed slowly from grey to white due to the blasting dust and incessant lorries that trundled up and down Cromford Hill. They picked up tonnes of rock and took it across the country where it was ground into road stone, ending up lining the lanes of distant counties that had no quarries of their own.

'Mo, did you hear about that house on the hill again? The front gable got smashed in by one of the quarry lorries. They reckoned his brakes failed a third of the way down and he couldn't do anything to slow himself. He just ploughed straight into the side of the house. Such a speed he were going, folk are surprised the house is still standing. Mind, it's a one-in-four hill isn't it? I'm only surprised that more accidents don't happen down there.'

Mother nodded in agreement. She'd heard the tale; Granddad had told them when he came back from work at teatime. He was upset about it as he knew the driver and how disturbed he was to have lost control of his lorry in the way he did. He told them how his friend had been so distraught he actually broke down in tears on the side of the road when he saw the devastation his lorry had caused.

By the time she'd related this to Marie, her friend's stop had arrived. She went to the front of the bus as it slowed, turning and smiling at my Mother before appearing to get into a furtive conversation with the driver. As they came to a juddering stop, Marie looked back down the aisle and giggled, pointing her out to him. Mother didn't know what to make of it, but as the bus pulled past a waving Marie she was mouthing something that looked like a name.

After the bingo women had got on, paid and sat down, the bus started to make its way up the winding hill roads to the two stops in Middleton. First stop, the cemetery entrance; second stop, the market place.

As the 26 pulled down the hill towards the market place Mother worried about what was going to be said when she was ready to get off. She stood up in the aisle and started to make her way down to the front, pleased when other passengers did the same; very relieved that she wouldn't be on her own.

As she reached the front the driver held out a piece of paper and gave it to her. On it was a scrawled meeting place for the next day and it was signed 'Peter'. This, she twigged, was the other driver who had taken them to band practice that evening. She took the note, muttering a quick thank you before the driver pulled the bus into the stop and said, 'he were fair taken with you, young 'un. All break at switch-over point he never stopped going on. He even offered to take my shift for me so that he might pick you up again on your way home. I couldn't let him mind – have me bingo girls to pick up and one of them reckons one of these days I'm on a promise.'

Mother didn't know exactly what this woman had promised him but she was sure it must have been incredibly important for him to miss out on going home early. She got off the bus slightly dazed, weaving across the market place and up the slight rise to the back gate, stuffing the note in her music bag so as not to provoke any questions later.

Supper was out on the table for her: bread, cheese and a piece of Madeira cake. Grandma brewed a pot of tea for them both and Mother went on to tell her about the music they'd played, about Gershwin and 'Big Bert's' hatred of more contempory pieces. Grandma laughed. She wasn't surprised to hear it. After the second cup of tea Mother decided to get to bed as she had to be up sharp in the morning. She and Mary were going in an hour earlier than normal. All the girls on the shift were in order to get through some work that had started to pile up. Mother didn't mind, an extra hour's overtime was always useful.

Up in the bedroom shared with Auntie Joan she took off her uniform and hung it up in the wardrobe. Half the space was hers and half her Sisters. The uniform was a matter of dispute as it took up a lot more room than anything else; all the other clothes ended up squashed and needing re-ironing in order to be worn. The arguments the wardrobe caused could be mistaken for the start of a new world war sometimes. My Mother didn't often buy new clothes; she made do with what she had or occasionally sat and sewed herself a new dress with the help of Grandma. She didn't often add to the congestion in the cupboard, though the same could not be said for her Sister.

At least this night Joan was asleep and Mother did her utmost not to wake her. Once she was in her nightgown and had put out her clean overall and underclothes for the morning, she sat down on the bed to dry and polish her cornet. This was a job she did with devotion each time she came back from a band practice or concert. Without drying out the buttons and horn, the cornet would start to clog up inside and the valves would stick. After putting the instrument away she took out the scribbled note again and this time read it properly, having been too embarrassed at the bus stop, wanting to get away home as quickly as possible.

It read: *I'm sorry I don't know your name to address this note properly, but I would like to know it and know you as well. Would you consider meeting me? I'll be at the Matlock Regent on Saturday evening and will wait outside for you at half past seven. Please come, Peter.* In brackets it said his last name, *Starr.*

She read it over and over, put it away in her bedside drawer, then got it out and scrutinised it again. Eventually she fell asleep, the note crumpled up on the bed next to her.

Morning came and Mother was rudely woken by Joan wafting the note under her nose in a state of high excitement.

'Eh our Maureen, who's this Peter then? Where did you meet him? Are you going to the Regent then? I'll come with you if you want to go.'

Mother stirred from her bed and grabbed the note from her Sister. She rubbed the sleep out of her eyes and stared at the screwed-up message again.

'I don't know if I'll go or not. I was going to the pictures with Mary and I don't want to let her down. I met him on the bus; he's a driver. I don't know anything else about him and I don't know if I want to.'

With that she picked up her clothes and overall, put them on and rushed downstairs.

Chapter 8

Four days later, after much anxiety and band practice, the choice between the pictures or the Regent had to be made. Mother walked down to Mary's and told her she'd decided to go and meet Peter, although she wavered about the decision on finding Mary all dressed up ready to go and see the latest film. She hated disappointing her friend, feeling her heart grow heavy in her chest on seeing the look of sadness flit across her face. However, the appeal of the unfamiliar was stronger than any desire to stay with what she knew and, after all, before leaving the house she'd spent the best part of an hour trying on one outfit after another. Eventually, Joan took pity on her and lent her one of her dresses. Mother wore it gratefully, though admitted feeling uncomfortable, worrying she was going to spoil it. She eventually left the bedroom with a makeover from her Sister and a warning not to 'ruin that frock'.

When the bus rounded the corner into Matlock, Mother got off a stop earlier and strolled through the park. She was a bit early and didn't want to appear too eager, so stopped by the boating lake to watch a young lad trying to launch a hand-made boat that was tipping violently to one side. As it finally sunk and disappeared under the murky surface of the water she walked on towards the front of the Regent. The queue was already starting to stretch around the side of the building but because she didn't have her glasses on – Joan said they didn't go with the frock – she couldn't actually see whether Peter Starr was there or not. Feeling flustered and uncomfortable and needing something to do with her hands she crossed the road, calling into the little corner shop which was just about to close.

She stood at the counter fiddling around with the clasp on her purse whilst trying to make up her mind which packet of cigarettes to buy. The shopkeeper stared obviously at his watch and let out a huge sigh, jolting my Mother into a decision.

After paying for the first box of cigarettes he pointed to, she fled the shop, leaned up against the wall outside, opened the packet and lit up. On drawing a mouthful of smoke into her lungs she collapsed into a fit of coughing, so much so that her eyes started to water, making her mascara run down her face. She tried to recover her composure but, still coughing, with eyes streaming, she heard a voice that sounded vaguely familiar and felt a handkerchief pushed into her hands.

'Hello there, you came then. I was beginning to think you'd stood me up.'

It was Peter, and through her subsiding coughing she managed to smile and say hello. After confirming that she looked like a panda, they adjourned to the coffee bar on the corner near the Regent entrance. Mother visited the 'ladies' and tried to repair her make-up while Peter went to the counter and bought two frothy coffees and a jam doughnut. When she came back he said he thought she might need something sweet to make her feel better. She did.

The next time he spoke Mother noticed he had badly stained, uneven teeth which looked sharp at the bottom. Assuming the yellowing was from nicotine, she fumbled in her pocket and offered him one of her cigarettes; he took one and smiled. This time she noticed he had a curling upper lip and when he wasn't smiling his face set into something of a snarl. Still, as she'd learned from her relationship with Mary, you shouldn't judge someone on their appearance or expressions so she dismissed her observations to the back of her mind. A few years later, on remembering those first impressions, she wished she'd taken more note of them there and then.

She started to like Peter. He was compelling: he held doors open for her, he pulled out seats in cafés so she could sit down and he treated her as if she were the only woman in the room. No one had ever made her feel quite so special. His charm offensive began to work.

Chapter 9

Thirteen months later, after many nights out and frequent cheap presents, she finally met his Mother and Sister Ruby. They seemed decent, kind people who made her welcome. She was surprised at how much bigger and more comfortable their house was in relation to her own home.

Mary was sceptical; something about him just didn't sit right. There were no concrete grounds on which to base her suspicions but she did make it known she didn't think he was genuine. Isn't that what a good friend should do? Mother didn't take the criticism well and it was then she realised she had fallen in love with him. It was a feeling which had been growing but still shocked her when she had to acknowledge it.

When Peter announced his intention to ask Granddad if they could get married she was both thrilled and felt sick at the same time. Grandma was of the same opinion as Mary; there was something about him she didn't trust; but after seeing that her daughter was unmovable on the issue of Peter, Grandma had given up, just continuing to grumble at Granddad and Joan on the quiet.

'There's something about that man that just isn't right. He gives me the creeps; seems too good to be true. I don't know what it is but I get the impression that he's no better than he should be. Nothing like your Garth, Joan. Now he's a decent lad, no corners and nothing hidden. What you see is what you get. I've told your father he's to tell Garth he can have your hand in marriage when he asks, which I know he will soon. But that Peter; now that's another thing altogether. But what can I say? Your daft Sister is smitten and there's no moving her.'

Grandma maligned him as she stoked the kitchen fire ready to prove the bread for next week. Joan nodded in agreement and carried on sipping her mug of tea. She had her doubts about Peter too but hadn't said much about him to my Mother. They both seemed to know it was a subject which wasn't up for discussion. Joan was worried though; she'd seen the way he looked at her when he came round, the admiring glances she caught when he was in the room. Nothing more than that had happened and she felt stupid after telling Garth that she'd caught him looking at her.

'That's the way blokes are duckie. You're a pretty woman and he's noticed. Don't worry about it. I'd knock his block off if he ever did anything more than look. Just take no notice. There's nothing to worry about; he knows you're spoken for.'

Two weeks later, after much scrubbing of quarry dust from his face and hands and dressing in his best Sunday suit, Garth plucked up courage to ask for permission to marry Joan. It was readily given; she had a ring on her finger and was pleased as punch. So were Granddad and Grandma, getting the best china out for high tea. Mother started to think it must be her time soon.

Peter pursued her relentlessly as if he scented that she was ripe for the picking. He even called her his 'little plum' in private. Mother liked this pet name; it made her feel special. As the weeks went by his goodnight kisses became more passionate and his hands wandered around her body as they embraced. She didn't dislike the feeling and one Saturday night as they stood at the garage waiting for the last bus home, she gave in to his desires. She didn't really know what she was giving in to until she found herself let inside the bottom deck of a stationary Derby bus in the depot. Peter always had his depot keys with him, 'just in case', he said. Mother didn't know in case of what, but later she began to wonder if he used the parked-up buses as a home from home when he had women to entertain and nowhere to go. Her breath was apparent in the cold of the bus and she shivered. Peter took this as excitement; she was, in fact, frozen.

Mother was totally smitten. On telling him that she loved him he simply smiled and squeezed her thigh. She took the lack of verbal agreement to mean that he felt the same, becoming oblivious to everything other than how wonderful she felt.

Joan started to quiz her about when they were going to name the day. 'Not really thought about it,' she answered, but this was far from the truth. She'd thought about nothing else, sincerely hoping he would ask her to marry him soon, in the meantime just continuing to wait, crossing her fingers that eventually he would come up trumps.

In the end he did, but not without a massive push from my Mother herself, who was now desperate, needing an answer and some reassurance quickly.

After several weeks, when her monthlies seemed to have stopped completely, she approached Grandma in a dreadful state, worried and frightened about both what was happening to her and the lack of progress on the marriage front.

After Grandma calmed down she started to think about practicalities.

'Well my girl, you've done it this time haven't you! You've been sleeping with that Peter and I don't suppose he's taken any precautions.'

Precautions? Mother didn't know what Grandma meant and though she tried to spit out all that had been happening, couldn't manage it through the tears.

Grandma continued, softening her tone at the distress my Mother was obviously going through.

'Well, how long is it since you last bled? It might not be that you know, but I think it will be. I have a sense of it and you look a bit different to me. I remember my face changed when I was in the family way. Your Dad said I had a wise look about me. I told him it was more an annoyed look but he didn't seem to know the difference. Mind you it wasn't long till he did!'

Before giving Mother a chance to answer, she went off again.

'Well, I suppose that if you are, you are, and there's no point worrying over it now. What's done is done. But if you aren't young woman, then you need to start bloody well taking care from now on and make sure that great lummox gets it in his stupid thick head that no daughter of mine is going to be led down the garden path and not be looked after properly. It's his duty and if he can't be careful with you then he'll have to be taking the consequences.'

Mother nodded, still sobbing uncontrollably, knowing Grandma was making sense and already trying to understand the fears inside herself. She was starting to worry about what to do if Peter didn't want her because she was pregnant. The very thought of it made her so distraught she could hardly breathe. Grandma took a breath for her and started to set out a plan.

'The best thing we can do now is wait and see. It'll be our secret for a few days. We'll give it a week then me and you will go down to Dr Jennings at the surgery and see what he thinks. Can you keep it quiet that long Maureen?'

Mother nodded and blew her nose on a duster picked up from the mantelpiece; Grandma was about to shout at her error, but taking pity instead, suggested kindly: 'Shall we have a nice pot of tea and a piece of that Battenberg cake I've been saving for your Dad's pack up?'

Grandma didn't wait for an answer, but carried on clattering around with the cake tin and boiling the old tin kettle on the range as Mother sat staring into the fireplace at the glowing embers of her fate.

Mother calmed down and they started to talk about Joan's forthcoming wedding, what needed doing, when they should bake the cake and what Joan should wear. In the middle of all this planning Grandma suddenly harked back to their previous and much more one-sided conversation.

'Whatever happens our Maureen, you'll never be on your own. Little 'un in tow or not, you'll be loved.'

Then she carried on with Joan's planning, almost as if the words hadn't been said at all. Mother smiled a weak smile, suddenly convinced that whatever happened in the future it wouldn't be as bad as she'd been imagining. She had her family, a home, and that was all anyone could want.

Mother carried on as normal, seeing Peter, though wary of getting too close to him. He didn't understand why and thought she was behaving weirdly, getting angry with her, though he backed off when she told him she couldn't be physically close because of 'women's problems'. It didn't need elaborating and he didn't ask questions. She was safe, at least for a while.

On the way to band practice Mother visited Mary. She wasn't seeing as much of her as she once had or liked to; knowing she was neglecting the friendship made her feel awkward. Mary, though, was the same as always with her, overjoyed and chuffed as ever that she'd come round and spent a little time with her best friend. Life was never easy for Mary and she missed Mother desperately. Conversation flowed, words came as easily as ever between them. Mother told Mary about Joan's engagement to Garth, what was being planned and asked her if she would come to the wedding as her guest. Mary grinned broadly before a frown crossed her face as if she'd considered something which made her uncomfortable.

'Mo, don't you want to go with Peter? He is your boyfriend after all.'

Mother jumped at the mention of his name then blurted out all her fears, her possible pregnancy, his lack of commitment and the worries she had about his character. Before the end of the tale she broke down, so Mary put her arms tenderly around her shoulders and hugged her, trying to comfort her best friend in the only way she knew.

'Look love, it'll be all right, if he doesn't want you then someone much better will. You've got a good family, you've got me, you've even got my mad Mother and me Dad. We won't let you down, but don't go thinking the worse until you have to.'

'Who else will want me if I'm stuck with a baby?' She sobbed harder and clung onto Mary's neck.

'You're lovely Mo. You deserve much better. He's a very lucky man to have you and if he doesn't see that then he's a bloody fool. There's plenty of men out there that would take you and a baby on, you see if there's not. You're patient, kind, warm, clever and funny. Any bloke would be proud to have you.' Mary was getting upset at her friend's lack of self-esteem. Mother could tell because the colour in her cheeks started to rise and the crack of her usually steady voice was audible.

She clung closer to Mary's neck; taking comfort in the warm, compassionate feelings and the knowledge that at least she had one person in the world that understood her. Mother never had a close relationship with her Sister or any of her Brothers and Peter wouldn't give her the feelings of safety and security she needed unless he was turning on the charm and wanted something in return. Mary's unconditional affection encouraged a sensation of being extremely fortunate, always having someone to turn to when others let her down. Releasing the burden made her feel lighter, relief flooded over her and she relaxed back onto the settee, resting her head.

The front door slammed shut and in marched Hilda warbling some obscure psalm or other at the top of her voice. Spreading the word of the Lord had gone well today. She was pleased to see Mother and gave her a cheery squeeze of the cheek.

'Well my dears, shall I make us some tea?' She clattered into the kitchen and started to warm the pot, shouting to Mother and Mary, 'do you fancy a chip butty? I do. Saving souls makes you right hungry!'

She didn't wait for an answer, was already peeling potatoes and singing 'What a Friend We Have in Jesus', tapping out the melody with a well-worn heel on the flagstone floor.

There was no chance now that they would be able to continue their heart-to-heart; Hilda was on the loose filling all the rooms with her singing and noise. She no sooner had deposited the chips down in front of them than she was out in the yard clobbering the hall runner with the carpet beater, sending clouds of quarry dust up into the air onto the next-door neighbours' clean sheets. Their complaints didn't stand a chance over the noise of her rhythmic thumping and singing of the twenty-third psalm, however out of tune.

An hour later, Hilda scooped up her pamphlets from the toppling stack of religious paraphernalia on the sideboard, stuffed them into her shopping bag and rushed out of the door, shouting as it closed behind her: 'Tell your dad I'll be back later on. I'm going down into Matlock to do the ministry; them heathens down there need me. Make sure you lock the door if you go out, our Mary. Be good; I know you will be…'

Mary spoke quietly, 'well there won't be anybody home, at least 'til me Dad comes back from work. What are we going to do with you then, eh?'

Mother shrugged and burst into tears again, unsure of what she felt, her mind awash with contradictory emotions, beliefs and questions. Instinctively, Mary put her arm back around her shoulder and slowly the swirling, splintered thoughts in her head started to settle.

'Why don't we wait, eh, see what happens. You might not be having a baby, and if you are then you can think again and decide what to do. You need to talk to Peter, tell him what you want from him... But be sure of one thing: I won't let you down. Just be brave, eh?'

Mother nodded dolefully and, as if a panacea for all problems, got up and put the kettle on. In the kitchen, she leaned against the stove and furrowed her brow in thought, deciding that she must speak to Peter as soon as possible, try and sort out something for them both, especially if she was going to have their baby. Mary came into the kitchen to see how she was, noticing her worry lines and matching them with her own, nodding in agreement with her plan.

The very next day Mother set out to track Peter down, but on finding he wasn't at the bus terminal asked Gerald the foreman if he was out on route. He answered without thinking, telling her he was on his dinner break and had gone to Evelyn's house to help mend her sticking door. Evelyn was a nice woman, the wife of Jim Smith, who drove the late shift up into Crich and through the dales. Jim never had any time for maintenance in the house and Peter was handy with his tools.

At Evelyn's house Mother couldn't see anything of either of them, though thought she heard his voice inside, recognising his shallow laugh. After knocking and shouting through the letterbox there was no more sound and she went home, presuming she was mistaken and deciding to wait for Peter in their usual place that evening.

A few years later the truth surfaced: he was with Evelyn that day and the little blonde girl she wheeled proudly around the town was actually not Jim's but Peter's. No one was any the wiser at the time of her birth.

Wisdom was overlooked where the other births were concerned as well. It turned out that he had more than one child around the Derbyshire villages, the bus route mapping out the children he fathered. Like a sailor and his ports, he had a woman at each turn-around point.

Back then Mother was oblivious to Peter's antics, as were many women.

Chapter 10

When she and Peter met up that evening he charmed her as usual, relaxing her enough for her to blurt out the worry that she might be having his baby. Initially he was stricken with panic, going cold and distant, planning his getaway until she mentioned she'd already told her Mother and talked it over with Mary. This eye-opener miraculously made him think again.

'Well my lovely little plum pudding, I suppose we'd better wait and see what happens. But if by next week we find that you're having a baby, then we'll go and see your Dad and ask if we can get married. It's the best thing to do; we can't have the little 'un born a bastard can we?'

So the date was set.

The next weekend Peter rushed to Woolworth's in his dinner break, bought the first ring he saw and the arrangements were made. Along with the family, Mary pretended she was pleased, agreeing to be bridesmaid. A month later at Wirksworth Registry Office they were married before the reason for the haste became too apparent.

Afterwards people kept telling my Mother with a smirk that they would never forget her wedding day. Certainly that was true, though it wouldn't be the romance and joy of the occasion that they would remember.

She arrived at the registry office with a proud but dubious Granddad a couple of minutes late, as was the tradition, only to find Peter sat out on the wall with a pint of mild and a fag in his hand - the registry office was right next door to the County Tavern and the temptation had been too much.

The ceremony itself should have been uneventful; it had purposely been kept simple so as not to drag on for too long. But eventful it certainly became. The registrar had a glass eye. Neither Mother nor Peter could tell which one of them he was looking at when asking them to make their vows; he became increasingly agitated as they hesitated or failed to answer in the required places. At the point in the service where he asked the wedding guests if they 'knew of any lawful impediment' why the couple shouldn't be married there was movement on both sides of the room.

Auntie Joan stopped Grandma from pointing out that her future son-in-law was 'a wrong 'un', and Peter's mother had to be physically restrained to prevent her from telling all and sundry her son had been trapped by a woman looking for a sure-fire way of getting a good husband.

Standing at the front, in the off-white, more yellowing, dress she had borrowed from Grandma's second cousin, Mother was blissfully unaware of the palaver going on behind her.

Once the register had been signed the party decamped to the pub next door. The top-floor function room had been booked for the reception only a few days before; originally it had been intended for a wake but the family had a fall out and all celebrations of a long and happy life were off. The intermingling of wedding frills and funeral bouquets provided quite a contrast.

The groom's family took up residence on the left side of the room, barricading their stronghold with a row of carefully turned backs, whilst the bride's family group took umbridge at the snub and vowed they wouldn't be going 'across there' if they were paid. Bemused friends, neighbours and band members shuffled around in the middle of the divide, unsure of which way to turn or where to sit, until it was time for the cake to be cut and the speeches to be made.

Great Aunt Jessie had made the cake in a hurry, a two-tiered affair covered in white Royal Icing. Jessie's husband had opened the oven door before the sponges were properly cooked and the smaller one had sunk in the middle. Not one for wasting anything, Jessie decided to do a timesaving rescue, filling the dent with an industrial sized dollop of icing. It looked right to the eye and once the plaster bride and groom were on top there was no way of telling there had ever been a problem.

Unfortunately, as the room began to warm up, so did the icing. By early evening the wedding figurines were tipping sideways and starting to sink like a pair of climbers falling into a snowy crevasse.

It was a disastrous day by anyone's standards. The only guests who had a genuinely enjoyable time were the hordes of under fives, showing off their fancy new outfits, eating packets of salted blue-bag crisps and skidding across the polished parquet floor.

It wasn't the marriage Mother had imagined but, with her Grandmother's wedding ring jammed on her finger and her last name changed to Starr, at least she felt she was now secure.

Unfortunately little did she know. She also didn't know that on her wedding day her husband of three hours had managed to slip into the cleaner's cupboard unnoticed for a bit of a drunken fumble with Elsie from Bowdens Bakers.

He carried on unnoticed through Mother's entire pregnancy.

She went through the next five months fairly easily, getting bigger, as did her bottom drawer of things for the baby. Grandma knitted and sewed and Granddad put his carpentry skills to work, building the unborn child a cot. It was beautiful by the time it was finished and, though Grandma complained and grumbled about the noise and sawdust, she was astonished at the quality of the work, proud as punch at the look of wonderment on my Mother's face at the unveiling, when the cloth was pulled from the crib.

As time grew closer to the birth, my Mother started to worry more and more about where they were going to live as a family. There was nowhere at Grandma's house for the three of them; there was barely enough space in her and Joan's room for their beds and clothes, never mind the cot, the baby and Peter; it was impossible. There was also no way that she, Peter and the baby could go and live at his parents' house. Ruby had the biggest room and she wasn't about to give it up. Besides that, Peter's Dad gave her the creeps. She told Grandma about how his eyes followed her around the room, how she'd once been cornered in the kitchen. He put his hand on her shoulder and had it not been for Ruby coming in she wasn't sure what would have happened next. Grandma was all for going up to the house and sorting out Peter's Dad once and for all, but Mother wouldn't let her, thinking it would just make things worse.

So they were left at stalemate. My Mother felt that Peter wasn't that bothered, that he would be perfectly happy to stay at his home and she stay at hers with Grandma. Mother didn't want her family separated but couldn't stand up to him; Grandma, on the other hand, could.

Peter came round for his tea on the next Sunday; they'd been married nearly four months. Grandma had baked fruit and cheese scones and made a trifle with the last drop of sherry saved from the previous Christmas. The table looked grand, set out properly, and at half past four they all sat down: Grandma, Granddad, Mother, Peter, Uncle Ralph, Uncle Bill, Uncle Roland, Auntie Joan and her fiancé Garth. There wasn't a lot of room around the table, particularly with Mother's stomach taking up the place of two people. Elbows clashed and Ralph giggled; he had a daft sense of humour. Mother reached over to cut a piece of Red Leicester, but being heavily pregnant and slightly off balance, dropped the cheese into the top of the trifle. Ralph was in hysterics. It looked like a floundering goldfish lodged in the cream. Soon he had them all laughing and when Mother had fished out the cheese, smearing the cream down Ralph's face in retaliation, everyone was enjoying themselves.

The men of the house had the job of washing and wiping up while Mother made a pot of tea. Grandma started turning over in her mind what she wanted to say to spur Peter into action about sorting out a home for her daughter and the forthcoming new generation.

She eventually called him away from the draining board.

'Pete.' She shortened his name, being over-familiar to annoy him, 'I want a bit of a word with you my, lad.'

Grandma sat down in the front room and after a couple of seconds he walked through, still with the tea cloth he'd been using in his hands.

'What are you planning to do about our Maureen and the baby then?'

She gave him ample time to answer but the only attempt he made in reply was one cough and a feeble shrug of his shoulders.

'Well, that's no way to carry on is it? You've got to sort out a place for your family to live. That's what they are now, family. When that baby is born you'll have even more responsibilities to manage. You'd better realise you're going to be a father. Doesn't that mean anything to you? It's about time you got your finger out and got on with it. It's not as if you don't earn enough to manage getting a little house. You can afford the rent, I know you can. You should stop messing about.'

Grandma eventually stopped to draw breath and Peter took his opportunity to speak, clearly rattled by her outburst. The look on his face was almost one of anger.

'Look, Mrs, I know you mean well, but Maureen is my wife now and I'll decide what to do and when to do it. I have plans to get us somewhere to live, it's just not going as easily as I thought it would. It doesn't mean I haven't been trying. I don't need you telling me how to behave and about my responsibilities. I know what they are and I'll do what I feel is best when I think its right.'

He was becoming increasingly agitated with Grandma; she hadn't taken her eyes off him as he spoke and he was clearly finding it uncomfortable being in that kind of spotlight. He carried on, his voice getting louder and his face redder.

'I'm the man of our family and when we get somewhere to live I'll be the one who says what goes in our house, certainly not you. It's about time you stopped interfering. We'll get a house when we get a house. There's no point in going for the first place we find; it's got to be right'.

He stopped and stared straight at Grandma, almost goading her into making the discussion an argument. She wouldn't bite.

'That's all right then isn't it? Just make it soon,' she replied sarcastically, getting up and walking away in disgust.

Two weeks later, he found a home for my Mother and their yet-to-be-born baby. It was a mobile home. Mother was not altogether happy, but when Peter reassured her it was only a temporary measure until the council gave them a house down in Wirksworth, she put up with the move.

The few bits and pieces she'd managed to put together were ferried down to Whatstandwell in Uncle Ralph's car. Grandma thought Peter couldn't have found a place further away, or at least one that had fewer bus changes, if he'd tried. She told Mother this frequently. On the day Grandma walked her to the bus stop for the last time, heavily pregnant, bags bursting at the seams, she felt the need to tell her again.

'That husband of yours couldn't get you further away from us if he wanted to. I think he's trying to keep us away. I know you won't tell me even if you think I'm right, but I know you my girl, I can see you're worried. Just you make sure you keep enough money in your purse to get the bus home if you ever need to.' With this bit of sound advice she forced a pound note into my Mother's hand. 'Just you keep that safe. You might need it some day.'

Mother tucked the money into the zipped compartment of her purse and that's where it stayed for nearly the next eighteen months.

Chapter 11

Mother settled into the caravan. She got into trouble for calling it that as it said 'mobile home' on the tenancy agreement; Peter liked to point it out as if it were a status symbol. Each time she mentioned the 'C' word he jabbed his finger under the title on the rent book, making her read the words over and over, getting angrier and angrier the more mistakes she made. Initially Mother thought he was playing a game and giggled, but she soon gathered from the look on his face that it wasn't a laughing matter.

This was the first time she realised that her new husband had the potential to be nasty.

Mother continued to get bigger; everything took longer and was more of an effort, with her stomach getting in the way. Shopping was an ordeal, puffing and panting with the bags, struggling up and down the steps of the bus and lugging them back to the caravan park.

Peter didn't come home some nights, telling her he was doing a late shift followed by an early one the next morning and it was easier for him to stay at his Mother's or his mate's near the bus garage. She would spend those nights curled up on the pull-down bed, reading magazines or knitting clothes for the baby, quite happy on her own and, if the truth were told, almost preferred it.

Mary occasionally managed to get down to the caravan park to see her; it was hard for her to do, but she tried to visit at least once a week. The company was important for them both as Mother had had to give up work now. She couldn't manage the bus ride or being on her feet all day, the machinery was too heavy and the cotton irritated her skin. Grandma said that often when a woman was heavily pregnant they got very sensitive to things which had been normal and everyday.

When Mary arrived Mother's spirits rose. Mary brought things for the baby that her own Mother had found as she was going round on her mission to save the souls of mid-Derbyshire. They were often obscure items such as a battered old saucepan that Hilda thought was just the right size to heat up the baby's bottles. My Mother was actually going to breast feed, but she appreciated the thought. Mary mostly brought things for her: a magazine, a bunch of flowers, a quarter of liquorice allsorts. She appreciated these treats; feeling like someone cared. When Mary was gone she had her magazine to read, keeping her mind occupied, her allsorts to chew on, satisfying her cravings, and the flowers to look at, brightening her day. These were the most important things for her. She told Mary they made her feel loved.

Mother wasn't sure who she was any more, only knew she was huge, overtired and extremely alone in the world, a world that started down by the river near the furthest caravan and finished a short bus ride away in Ambergate at the local shops. The only time she felt like a real person was when Mary was near, chatting about the girls in the mill who she missed dreadfully, about Hilda's latest exploits and day-to-day life in the villages. The pregnancy and her current abode made her feel removed from the world, as if she was the only person that existed.

'Do you know, yesterday I went for a walk – well more of a waddle – and I never saw a single solitary soul, not all day long. When the paper lad turned up with the *Evening Telegraph* I was so pleased to see him I invited him in for a cup of tea,' she told Mary with a cynical laugh, but the laughter only covered up the misery she really felt.

Soon the paperboy became one of her best friends.

In fact, if it hadn't been for him she would have gone into labour and had my Brother all on her own. It had started quickly, the contractions coming much faster than expected, the pain so intense that even though she tried to make it to the phone box to call an ambulance she didn't make it any further than the next-but-one row of caravans. There was nothing to hold on to and, frightened of passing out, she made her way back so slowly she felt she would stop dead, eventually managing to get back through her own door and collapse on the settee.

The contractions were increasing in fierceness, gaps between them becoming closer together; in between she got up and gathered the things together for herself and the baby. Would she ever manage to get to the hospital? The thought of having her baby alone was terrifying to the point of making her rigid, then the contractions started again. After the most intense pain ever experienced, she sobbed so hard she didn't hear the caravan door open and the paperboy walk in. He coughed nervously to try and make himself known.

'Mrs, are you all right?' he got out before my Mother went into another spasm of pain.

The paper lad dropped his bag, spewing *Matlock Mercurys* across the floor, and bolted out of the caravan, leaving the door wide open to the world. Halfway across the park he could still hear her crying out and it seemed to spur him to run faster. There was no one around the site that he could turn to so he just kept going, out onto the main road and up towards the closest building. The Derwent Hotel was only just open for business. Apart from the usual three old blokes at the bar who wandered in as the doors opened and staggered out at the time of closing, it was empty.

The landlord looked stunned at the sweaty little lad tearing into his lounge bar, disturbing his regulars and knocking over the pile of beer mats. He'd stacked them carefully ready for Janice the barmaid to lay out on the tables when she finally turned up. She was always late.

'Eh now, where's the fire lad?' he said in a comic tone. 'I can't serve you yet, come back when you're older eh!'

'Mr, can you ring for an ambulance? Mrs Starr in the caravans is having her baby and she looks right bad. She's all on her own.'

'All right lad, calm down, I'll ring for one now. You and Old Joe nip back to see if you can help her and wait there 'til the ambulance comes, eh. Take this tot of brandy. She might need calming down a bit.' He pulled down a nearly empty bottle from the optic, handing it to the paper lad, who turned on his heels and ran at full pelt back to the caravan park, with old Joe in slow pursuit.

When he got back to the caravans it had gone quiet; the wailing had stopped. He came to a dead halt outside the door, worried at what he was going to find inside. After a deep breath he stepped in and sighed with relief at my Mother sitting quietly on the settee; she'd picked up his papers and put them back in his satchel.

'Hello lad, I'm sorry I frightened you; it's gone off a bit now, at least for a while. Have you rung for an ambulance?' She was very tired but managed a weak smile to reassure him.

'Yes, the pub man has rung through for one. He sent you this.' He held up the brandy bottle. 'Do you want a bit? He reckons it might help you feel calmer?'

She shook her head and replied, 'I don't think I'd better, my waters have broken. It won't be long now. I don't want the ambulance men to think I'm a drunk, do I?' She laughed shallowly then rubbed her belly, 'It's starting again.'

Old Joe finally puffed his way into the caravan, red in the face and short of breath; he'd clearly hurried as fast as he could manage.

'You all right Mrs? Bill from the pub has rung for an ambulance. It should be here soon.' With that he plonked himself down on the arm of the settee and mopped his sweaty head with a rather grubby handkerchief. 'If you aren't having that drop of brandy, I could do with it. I've not moved so fast in years!'

Mother pushed the bottle over to him and sank back into the cushions, clutching at her stomach and moaning audibly with pain.

In the distance, sirens could be heard, the wail wafting in and out of the trees as the vehicle sped along the main road, getting louder as it got closer, eventually silencing as the wheels of the ambulance trundled and churned over the wet grass of the caravan park. The paperboy went out to wave it down, stopping it directly outside the still-open door. All across the site fellow residents had come out of their homes to

76

see what the rumpus was about. As Mother was helped into the ambulance she became aware of the faces watching her, people she had never set sight on before.

Years later she imparted the following words of wisdom: if something was to go wrong, no matter how private it seemed at the time, someone would pop up to witness your downfall. I found out she was right on more than one occasion.

Chapter 12

She didn't manage to get as far as the hospital. The ambulance driver had decided she was too far gone to get to the maternity unit in Derby and started out the other way, heading toward the Darley Dale Cottage Hospital, a scaled-down version of the Royal Infirmary in the city. The other medic sat in the back with my Mother, willing her to hold on, hoping with all his might that she would manage the journey. He was a trainee and had never in practice helped a woman go through labour. About three miles from the hospital they came to a screeching halt in a lay-by; my Mother was giving birth and certainly wouldn't manage to get any closer to the maternity ward than she was.

An hour later, there she was in the dimming light of a November evening, lying back on the strapped-in bed of a mud-spattered ambulance alongside the A6, with a baby boy in her arms. The paramedic who helped her deliver was wiping perspiration from his brow and humming 'Congratulations' under his breath, as much for himself as for her. It was nearly the end of his shift. Just Mother and baby to drop into the cottage hospital where they would be checked over and admitted, then he could go home and get a well-deserved pint at his local.

'What a day, eh missus! We'll get you to the hospital and billeted up, then we'll be leaving you. Someone will get in touch with your husband and tell him the happy news,' he said cheerfully whilst packing up his few bits of medical kit and wiping away the greater majority of the blood from the bed.

'You'll be lucky!' Mother replied as she started to drift off to sleep clutching the baby. 'I never know where my bloody husband is from one day to the next, so I don't expect the hospital to have much luck in finding him.'

She finally succumbed to her eyelids wanting to close; the ambulance man lifted the crying baby away, talking in soothing tones to get him to settle. The other driver started up the engine and moved out into the road. It was bonfire night; across the hills of Derbyshire little beacons were lit and the occasional firework whistled across the sky, lighting up the half-light of the darkening evening with flashes of gold and silver.

'Look little lad, fireworks for your arrival. It's not everyone that gets such a welcome.' The baby looked up at the ambulance man and gurgled.

Across the valley and beyond the next hillside, Peter Starr was looking through the bedroom window of the terraced house he had just spent the afternoon in. He was buttoning his trousers.

'Tell you what, girl, I know I'm good but you didn't have to arrange a firework display to thank me!' He laughed to himself; he always found his own jokes funny. The woman behind him, half asleep in the crumpled sheets of her own marital bed, groaned at the jibe and turned over to ignore him.

Mother had nothing with her apart from a copy of the *Matlock Mercury* which the paperboy had thrust into her hands, her packed bag getting overlooked as she was hurried into the ambulance. The auxiliary nurse had tried to take the paper away and throw it in the rubbish cart, but Mother was having none of it. It stayed on the bed with her, her only possession in the sterile little ward, the one thing to connect her and the baby with the outside world. Then Grandma and Joan arrived.

They brought nappies, endless great piles of folded, pressed terry nappies; Grandma plonked them down on the bed.

'Nappies,' she said.

They brought a blue bobble hat, a white cable-knit cardigan, a soft cotton baby suit, a little stripey vest and a red-checked blanket.

'Hat, cardi, baby grow, vest, blanket,' she said.

They brought two sterilised, plastic feeding bottles, a large tub of formula, a pleat of cotton wool, unperfumed baby bath, talcum powder, and a comb and bar of soap for my Mother.

'Bottles, formula, cotton wool, bath stuff, talc, comb, soap for you,' Grandma said.

Mother smiled warmly, very glad to see her Sister and Mother.

'Tell you what, Mother, it's like the Generation Game here now you've arrived. I expect you'll be sitting a bear down on the bed and telling me, "cuddly toy, cuddly toy" in a minute.'

They laughed with her, especially when Joan whipped out a carrier bag, passing my Mother a small yellow bear with a brown furry face and red bow tie.

'Cuddly toy,' said Joan, and they all howled with laughter.

The hilarity did not last long, ending when the Matron walked through the ward and glared at my Mother.

'Mrs Starr, you will wake the other babies with your caterwauling.' She glared at Joan and Grandma before turning on her immaculately cleaned black lace-ups and marching out of the ward.

'Well, that's told us hasn't it?' Grandma said. 'Silly old sod she is. Where's that baby? Give him here, what you going to call him then?'

Mother lifted my Brother out of the cot beside the bed and passed him to her own Mother, her first grandson. She was already smitten.

'I'm thinking of calling him John: that's the young paper lad's name. I don't know where I'd have been if it hadn't been for him, really I don't'.

And so John it was. Peter hated it, wanting Eric, after his father, but John stuck and Eric became his middle name.

The bell for the end of visiting hours rang, Joan and Grandma gave the baby a peck on the cheek, stroking his head and gazing lovingly at his pink and still quite wrinkly little face. My Mother smiled, blowing them both kisses as they turned and waved from the entrance to the ward. She breathed a sigh of relief as they disappeared out of sight, grateful for the visit and gifts but glad they had left, being so very tired. She yawned, staring into the cot and pulling the little blanket up around my Brother's back, wary of closing her eyes in case he woke up and needed feeding. Now Grandma and Joan had gone, the worry started to manifest in her mind; how would she manage to look after him? Would she cope and what would Peter think of his son? That is, if he ever turned up to see him. That thought, combined with being exhausted, set off the tears and she started to sob, the sounds getting louder even though she tried to muffle them in her pillow.

Matron was beginning her round and on hearing the noise marched down the ward towards my Mother's bed. Mother heard her coming and started to cry with even more volume.

Matron, uncharacteristically it turned out later, took pity on my Mother and sat down on the corner of her bed, pulling a highly-starched handkerchief from her uniform pocket, passing it across, where it was gratefully received. Mother dried her eyes and blew her nose.

'Now, Mrs Starr, I'm going to take the little Starr away to the baby unit and you're going to get a good night's sleep; that's all you need. You'll find tomorrow it'll all be much better.'

'Matron, has my husband rung up after me? I'm worried about him. He must know I'm in here by now.'

The matron shook her head in reply, saying, 'I'm sure he'll be in tomorrow to see you and his new little boy. Don't be worrying about it. It's been a long day and you just need a rest. It'll all look better after a good night's sleep.' She stood up, smiling as warmly as she knew how, before picking up my Brother, his blanket streaming behind him as she walked swiftly off down the ward and through the swing doors.

Chapter 13

The next day, as Matron had assured, she did indeed feel a little better and brighter in herself. My Brother was brought back, spending the day gurgling, feeding and sleeping. All seemed to be going well, though she was aware that the day was passing and her husband had still not appeared. Granddad had been in on his way to work and Uncle Ralph had driven down with a very flustered and excitable Mary, who cried and hugged my Mother so tightly she nearly suffocated her. Still Peter hadn't turned up.

She watched the wall clock, counting through the hours. Minutes ticked by, the large black plastic second hand passing round the face, pointing to time's departure. The ward filled up over the day. Women with brand new babies swaddled up in colour-coded cellular blankets were wheeled into the empty spaces, permeating the silence with cries and chatter. As the afternoon visiting hours began, excited fathers coming to see their new offspring added to the cacophony. Mother felt like scooping my Brother up and hiding away. When the orderly came around with the tea trolley she asked if he would mind pulling the side curtain across; it was easier not to be seen than be judged as the sad woman in the corner with no visitors and obviously no husband to cluck over his first child. Once the curtain was drawn she busied herself with changing the baby and feeding him his bottle. She was proud of her little lad and focused all her attention on him, at first so absorbed she hadn't heard the commotion start in the corridor outside the ward. Now she became aware of the raised voices of the nurses. Babies startled by the ruckus started to scream and their Mothers tried to calm them using hushed tones interspersed with guarded curses and tuts.

She listened to the chaos from the other side of the curtain, beginning to recognise one louder voice above the sounds of families bonding.

'Now look here woman, I'm going to see my wife and baby. I know I've had a drink but I'm not doing any harm, just wetting the baby's head. You'd do the same if you were me. Now, where is she? I can't see her anywhere. Maureen...' he started to bawl out across the ward. 'Mo, where are you?'

He appeared around the curtain with a large burly nurse attached to his elbow. In his right hand he had a bunch of the most wilted looking roses she had ever seen and, in his left, about a quarter of a bottle of whisky. The rest of it, she assumed by the potency of his breath, he had drunk.

'Been wetting the baby's head have you?' she spat at him. 'It looks like that's what you've been doing all night. Couldn't you even have gone home, changed your shirt and had a bit of a shave? You look like you've been pulled through a hedge backwards.'

Her words were lost on him; Peter was leaning over the side of the hospital cot and stroking his son's downy head. She felt a sudden softness for him, and the fact that he had chosen the pub over her had almost been forgotten until he started to heave, eventually throwing up in the waste paper bin. The rising stench of sick and drink brought all her gripes and insecurities back. After he'd recovered enough to stand up straight and wipe his mouth, Mother decided it was time he heard a few home truths.

'Now, listen here Peter. I've been in this hospital for nearly two days, but if it wasn't for that little paper lad at the caravan site I'd never have got here at all. You're useless to me as you are, bloody useless. You've got a family now and you've got to pull your finger out, start being a proper husband to me and a father to young John, do you understand?'

Peter stood aghast at the flow of anger coming out of her mouth; she had never really stood up to him before and it knocked him sideways, for a moment at least. He might have been quiet, but she could sense his mind thinking over her demands, albeit fogged with drink.

'Well, I don't know what you want to be calling him John for. I wanted to call him Eric after me dad, but you seem stuck on that bloody ugly name. I know what you're saying about me not being here for you. I was working and didn't know he was here 'til late on last night. Was out on the buses all day, did a bit of extra overtime to buy some bits for the baby and these for you.' He gestured to the limp roses lying on the bedside cabinet. 'I'm sorry that I didn't get here before. I got caught up with the lads from work. They are so happy for us. I couldn't get away and it's rude not to accept a drink bought for a celebration. I'm sorry, I'll be better from now on.'

Mother looked sceptical as he delivered the pre-planned but slurred speech, but by the time he'd finished she was falling back under his spell again, believing his carefully chosen words. He took the smile on her face as a sign it was safe to carry on in his own particular way. And that was exactly what he did.

Chapter 14

Peter floated in and out of my Mother's life when the mood took him, but at least for the first three or four months he was attentive, supportive and seemed to take on the mantle of father figure and husband to the best of his abilities. It didn't last.

She started to settle into an apparently normal married life, getting on well with bringing up my Brother. Grandma said she took to it like a duck to water. She was kept busy caring for the baby, sorting out the caravan, cooking Peter's tea when he was on the right shift and rising early to cook his breakfast on the other. She was pleased with the way she and her husband appeared to be getting on. They had their little spats but largely he seemed to stay considerate, being around when he was supposed to without prompting. Once he even bought her a bunch of flowers, not wilting this time; Mother was so surprised she was speechless.

He'd been on days for the first month after the baby was born so that he could be around to help in the evenings, and with feeds and changing during the night. It impressed Mother that he'd gone to work and asked for a shift change so he could be of use.

When she was wheeling my Brother down the high street in Matlock a few months later, on her way back from the baby development clinic, she met up with one of the other drivers' wives, Shirley Cox, who was herself heavily pregnant. Shirley told my Mother how much she was looking forward to getting rid of the bump; it made her so tired. Mother enlightened her to the fact it didn't get any better once the baby was born, it just changed to a different type of tiredness.

'At least Jim will have a month of days when it's born; that does make it a bit easier. I bet you felt the same when Pete had his month off shift didn't you? I know that firm is useless at the best of times but at least they give 'em a bit of leeway when they have a new kiddie,' Shirley said in all innocence.

Mother agreed, but as soon as the words had sunk in knew that Peter had lied to her, telling her he'd gone in and asked for a shift change to help out, how he'd had to beg the boss to get him to say yes. She felt he'd led her up the garden path. What difference would it have made if he'd just told the truth? Had he made it up in order to get in her good books and receive a tick in the perfect husband box to save for later when he wasn't being one? She didn't know what to believe but the deception started to gnaw at her. He'd been on earlies for the past week, driving the Derby to Matlock route. When he came back later in the day she would tackle him about her concerns.

She sat him down, put his tea in front of him, poured his usual glass of pale ale and asked about his day, as always. She listened dutifully to him moan on about the pensioners, how long it took them to get on and off and how they could never find their bloody bus passes.

She laughed at what he said. It wasn't entirely the right thing to do; he was touchy, feeling he was having the rise taken out of him. She had to be careful not to make him feel mocked as he seemed to have a problem knowing when someone was laughing with him, not at him; it made him difficult to live with.

'I saw Shirley Cox in the town this afternoon. She's right big now, I think she'll be dropping that baby sooner rather than later,' she paused and Peter grunted as a kind of reply. She continued to talk, 'Anyway she said that her Jim was having his month of day shifts as soon as she had the kiddie, told me the firm gave every bloke the month on days when they had a baby. You cracked on that you'd got a special favour because you asked the boss. Why did you do that Peter? There was no point to it. I would have thought as much of you for being here no matter how it'd come about.'

He listened to what she was saying in silence, then pushed his half-finished dinner away from its place setting and stood up.

'Are you calling me a liar? I go out of my way for you lady, more than any other husband would. I'm stupid to look after you the way I do. Folk at work tell me that. I'm laughed at for running about after you and that baby. Well, I tell you what; this is where it stops; no more. If you can't appreciate me then this is where it ends. I won't have the likes of you calling me a liar, especially in my own bloody home.'

With that, he turned, picked up his wallet and walked out of the caravan. Mother was knocked for six. She hadn't expected him to be contrite in being found out, but the depth of aggression took the wind out of her sails. It was the start of things to come.

Pub closing time came and went and still Peter hadn't come home. She locked up the windows and door; he would have his key. She checked on the baby. He was sound asleep and showing no sign of stirring so she got into bed and lay in the dark worrying about where her husband was, listening intently for any noise outside the van. Each sound was magnified by worry. Eventually she fell asleep, although it was a very fitful, uncomfortable night.

Morning came and she woke up alone; he hadn't returned. She got up and lifted the baby out of his carrycot, changed him and set about getting herself dressed to go up to Grandma's house, trying to keep busy, taking her mind off her errant husband. The paper lad delivered the *Morning Echo*, had his daily cup of tea and helped her wrestle the pram out onto the frozen grass. He waved goodbye and she set off.

The day passed uneventfully and Mother returned cautiously to the caravan. Peter hadn't been back. He was due home for his tea but she didn't know whether to bother cooking any or not. She decided she should; it saved arguments, and if he didn't appear then it could always be warmed through the next day.

He didn't turn up.

The dark, moonless evening drew in and the curtains were closed tightly against the icy drafts; the baby was bathed and readied for his cot. He got off to sleep quickly and she set about knitting a few rows of the jumper she was making him;

it got very cold in the caravan park and if they had to sit out winter she needed to ensure he stayed warm. It was just about time to get herself ready for bed when the caravan door flew open and her wayward husband bowled in, knocking into the table.

'Hello wife. I'm back. Is there any tea for me? I'm right hungry; drink always gives me an appetite,' he slurred.

She turned and reached for the dinner made earlier, boiling a saucepan of water and putting the plate on top. It was the only way of reheating food, but took a long time to get anything properly hot. Heat directly under plates tended to dry out gravy or sauce.

Peter frowned at the pan of water, then at my Mother.

'I don't want that warmed-up rubbish Maureen. Do us a bit of bacon will you?'

It wasn't so much a request as an order. She decided it was easier to get on with it than argue, not wanting him to go off out again. He already smelt like a brewery. She knew he was drinking his way through the week's housekeeping and thought it wiser to feed him then coax him to sleep, hoping this would nip any spat in the bud.

She got the frying pan out and put it on the stove, clicking the gas bottle to heat up the fat that was already congealed in the bottom. Grandma had brought her up not to waste anything and this fat would be good for at least another couple of breakfasts and a plateful of chops before it needed cleaning out.

Peter was leaning on the worktop and she could feel his eyes burning into the back of her neck. Bacon in pan, she turned and smiled warily at him. He shot a leering smirk back at her.

'Eh Maureen, I don't half fancy a bit.'

'Well it will only be a couple of minutes, Pete. Get the bread and brown sauce down and I'll make you up a couple of sandwiches.'

He was loosening off his belt and unbuttoning his trousers, letting her know he didn't mean the bacon. He started to move towards her and she sidestepped away from him; this was the

88

last thing on her mind, but he didn't give up. Brandishing the fish slice whilst protesting about the bacon burning, she caught his breath; it smelt of beer and stale fags. Still he came closer. She pushed him away and pleaded, 'Peter, I don't feel like it. It's late and you stink of drink, the baby has only just gone to sleep and I don't want to wake him. You just have your bacon and wait until the weekend. I'll get Mother to have John. Happen we can go out for the evening eh... What do you think?'

He didn't answer. She assumed her plea had been heard and he was doing his trousers back up, but when she looked again it was clear that wasn't the case. He came at her and pushed her against the sink, the edge of the unit digging into her back as she struggled to get away. But there was no chance for that; he had her by the hair with one hand and held her steady with the other. Any movement caused intense pain. She started to cry out and tried to push him away again. He was having none of it, turning her round and forcing her over the sink. A couple of punches in the kidneys and she gave up the struggle. It knocked the wind out of her and she couldn't even cry any more, never mind tell him to stop. He drunkenly finished, collapsing onto the bed, and was asleep within seconds.

When Peter woke in the morning, for him it was as if nothing had happened. But my Mother hurt; her kidneys ached and she was sore. She shied away from him when he came near her in the caravan, but because it was so small they were never more than five feet apart. She couldn't bring herself to speak; there was nothing to say.

Peter talked for the both of them, telling her about his shift, what he was on for the next week, what he wanted for tea and that he needed his best blue shirt pressed for Sunday because he was going out with Jack and his mates from the depot. They were going to Derby in the evening for a stag night but he wouldn't be back late. He made himself a sandwich for dinner at work, bounced his son around for a couple of minutes and got up to go, opening his wallet and putting a couple of pounds down on the worktop for housekeeping. He went over and tried to kiss her cheek, Mother turned her back on him.

She heard the door open and the words 'frigid bitch' come out of his mouth as it closed again. He was gone. She picked up my Brother, hugged him close, and sobbed.

He returned at teatime again. Pretending that all in the garden was rosy, she attempted to be civil when it came to him going out to the pub. He came to kiss her goodbye and she tried her best to be warm. She'd spent all day thinking about what had happened, starting to blame herself, not able to work out why he had behaved that way and deciding it must be her fault. She thought about being called 'frigid', knowing he was experienced whilst she was not at all, having only ever been with him. She felt she wasn't a proper woman, didn't let him have what he needed and that was why he went out so much to drown his sorrows, to blank out the missing bits, to forget that she was a useless wife. She didn't want to be a useless wife, she wanted him to love her. Most of all she desperately hoped that what had occurred the previous night would never happen again. She would have to try harder.

When Peter came back from the pub, Mother was waiting for him with an open beer poured into a glass. He drained it in one and went to the fridge for another, but she hadn't been out to buy more cans, couldn't manage the heavy shopping and pram, feeling too sore and bruised. He wasn't best pleased.

'Why haven't I got more beer in then? I gave you money this morning. Couldn't you be bothered to go out and get me any? God, you are soddin' useless sometimes. I really don't know why I bother with you, bloody fat cow.'

It was said with such venom that she edged back from him. He continued to chunter on under his breath and then fell silent, sitting at the table, lighting up a cigarette and puffing on it malevolently, blowing the smoke down his nostrils like an angry dragon. Mother had got into bed, lying rigidly quiet, scared now, waiting to see what his next move would be.

He sat there for a while, silent and brooding. Eventually he stood up demanding, 'well, if I can't have beer, can you at least give me a cup of bloody tea woman.'

Mother obediently got out of bed and walked past him, putting the kettle on the gas ring and lighting it. She picked up a mug from the drainer and put a couple of spoons of tea into the pot without looking at him, but knowing he was watching everything she did. The kettle boiled, she poured the water out, bent for the milk, tipped a little into the bottom of the mug and replaced the bottle back in the fridge door.

She stirred the tea and poured it out, putting the mug down on the table in front of him, still not giving him eye contact.

He grabbed her by the wrists then pulled her face down to his level forcing her to look at him.

'I think you'll find that you should warm the pot before you put the tea in', he hissed, 'and if I ever go to get a beer out again you'd better make sure there's one there waiting for me.'

His face was white with anger as he spat the words at her. Feeling the venom in his voice she tried to pull away but he raised a hand, slapping her hard on the top of the arm. His fingers curled into a fist, she closed her eyes and physically shuddered. He let go of her in disgust, pushing her away.

'Just fuck off to bed you miserable specimen of a woman. Get out of my sight; you make my stomach turn'.

Mother did exactly as she was told.

The next morning was a repeat of the previous one; he again acted as if nothing had happened, wittering on about what he was going to do during the day – a couple of hours overtime after his shift as he had to take the number 35 bus into the Derby Depot to get it serviced and MOT'd. It was his turn to do a few maintenance runs in the next couple of months, starting today; he couldn't help it.

'I thought we could happen take the little 'un out on Sunday before I go to the stag do. You don't have to if you don't want; make a change though, eh? And I will have a few extra quid in me wages this week. Up to you, though.'

He carried on chattering to himself, playing with my Brother and his rattle. The baby started to scream. He picked him up to try and quieten him but it only soothed him for a couple of minutes. Having had enough of his paternal role, he passed him over to my Mother, who still hadn't said anything about his offer. It was clearly annoying him that she hadn't jumped at the chance to be in his company, so he thought he'd have another go.

'So, do you want to go on Sunday or not?' he barked at her and set the baby off crying again.

She looked at him, the first time she'd looked him square in the eye since the happenings of two nights ago. Not able to bring herself to speak at first, she just nodded. Then after a few seconds' thought, decided she should say something before he got angry with her again.

'Where do you want to go then?' was all she managed.

'Well, I thought we could go to Marketon Park if it's not wet and then to my Mum's for our tea. We've not been up there in a while. She'd like to see John, see how he's changed. That'll be a nice day out won't it? If it rains we can think again,' he paused as if mulling over his plan. Then he opened his mouth to continue.

Mother butted in quickly to answer him. Now she had started to speak it was if the floodgates were open and the devil himself couldn't stop her.

'That'd be nice. Shall I make us a picnic to take? I could make a cake, one of those rich fruit ones you like. Mind you, it'll be heavy to carry. And some sandwiches and crisps, a bottle of pop and some beer for you. Yes, it would be a nice change.'

Peter was getting irritated. She could see him twitching and moving around in the chair, tapping his left foot, it getting faster and faster in tempo. Before she started to speak again he stood up, face full of anger and eyes black as coal.

'Don't you ever cut me off again when I'm about to speak, woman or you'll know about it. And will you shut that bloody kid up; he's getting on my pissing nerves.'

Turning his back to Mother, he slammed his hand down on the tabletop.

'And another thing: if you don't behave yourself in the next couple of days then you won't be going anywhere on Sunday. I don't want to take any bugger that disrespects me out for a nice day. So bloody well think on.'

Not understanding what she'd done wrong, she calmed the baby and went over to Peter to put the situation right. Edging towards him she tried to smile and look reproachful at the same time, but wasn't very successful; he looked at her with pure hatred. Suddenly scared of him again, she started to back away, but there was no retreat. He had his hand across the space between them faster than she could move, grabbing her by the arm and pulling her towards him with a sneer. She screamed out. His spare hand jabbed a fist into her stomach, winding her, abruptly stopping the desperate cry and leaving her struggling for air. He let her go and she sank down onto the bed, instinctively pulling herself into a ball for her own protection.

'Just think about that one before you start disrespecting your husband. I'm the man here and I say what goes. You just bloody well remember that.'

He grabbed his coat, slung it over his shoulder hostilely and crashed out of the caravan.

She was left alone again, sitting on the bed and crying desolately. My Brother joined in and the noise carried on until he fell asleep and Mother ended up in a silent stupor. She stared out of the window, watching the rain pouring down over the hills and the mist rolling in to cloak them all in a coat of misery, much like the way she felt. Empty hours went by until my Brother woke and started to scream for his bottle; it ripped apart her cocoon of silence and jolted her into action. After feeding, changing and dressing the baby in his thickest sleep-suit she got the pram ready, securing him in it and rushing out across the caravan site. The boggy ground swallowed the wheels as she struggled across the grass onto the pavement before hurrying up the hill towards the bus stop.

Just ahead of the last turning she made a sharp right instead, all but runnning down the slope towards the local off-licence. She had decided to do as he said.

Inside, dripping wet and soaking the counter with her umbrella, she asked for six cans of pale ale, twenty Woodbines and a box of matches. Pushing the beer into the carrying tray under the pram, she paid for her shopping and wheeled the baby outside. It was still raining heavily but across the hills the sun was weakly trying to push through the clouds. Normally she'd have stood and watched, hoping it would dry out the valley below, but today she was eager to get home and clean the van up; the mats needed a shake to knock the dust out and a hang on the line to air, the piles of clothes needed washing and ironing and the furniture could do with a polish. She wanted a little bit of normality back and a clean caravan. Mostly she wanted Peter to be pleased with her, happy to come home to a comfortable little haven, for him to be calm and for them to live peacefully. She was scared that if she didn't make the effort life would keep getting worse.

The rain didn't stop all the way home. She got back to the van and left the pram under the awning, lifting my Brother out and carrying him inside. He was still slumbering peacefully so she had carefully to unwrap him from his sleep-suit and put him in his cot before setting about cleaning the cupboard fronts. The kettle went on the gas and while it was boiling she wrung the dirty water from the cloth and carried on scrubbing manically.

The cupboards soon shone, the van stank of bleach and disinfectant, and the windows were running with steam from the forgotten kettle which had nearly boiled dry; there was just enough left for a mug of tea. She picked a tea bag from the caddy – lazy tea-making according to Peter; he liked his to be made from fresh leaves and brewed properly, tea bags were for 'sluts and idle bastards', that's what he reckoned. At this moment Mother didn't care, they were her secret, hidden right at the back of the cupboard where they were safe from view.

She sat down with her tea and sighed. The beer and cigarettes were on the worktop across from the cooker; the Woodbines tempted her. With the cans away in the cupboard and one in the fridge - it was only little and wouldn't fit any more - she picked up the cigarettes and opened a drawer to put them inside, but then hesitated, peeled off the plastic wrapping, pulled one out and lit it. She hadn't smoked since the day she met Peter for their first date. This came back as she took her first drag and coughed heartily but, not sure if it was the fags

94

or the memory, it didn't stop her taking another drag and coughing again, smiling wistfully to herself.

After she'd finished her tea and stubbed out the cigarette, burning her thumb in the process, she started to pick up the clothes from the awning ready for ironing. John was still asleep, so she got the board out and whilst the iron heated through put the clothes that needed a press into piles and stacked up the towels and tea cloths. Peter liked to have a sharply ironed tea towel hanging on the rail, not that he ever picked one up to use it.

The first item on the ironing agenda was Peter's best shirt for the stag do on Sunday. Mother pressed the collar, cuffs and epaulets with the steam on full, then set about the shirt tails and fronts, lastly the sleeves, spending a full ten minutes before hanging it up on the padded hanger taken from her wedding dress. She didn't think she'd need the dress again so had put it in a box and stuffed it under the bed; the hanger would be good for his shirt: it wouldn't mark the shoulders. She hoped he would notice and be pleased.

She worked her way through the rest of the ironing, put it away and started on the tea. John woke up halfway through peeling the vegetables, so she fed him and let him sit in his high chair with a washed potato to play with. She'd bought some stewing steak a couple of days before and started it off browning while chopping up the onions; they were strong and made her eyes stream, so she stood with a teaspoon in her mouth, the bowl of it placed under her tongue. It was an old trick Grandma had shown her and it worked albeit for the saliva that ran down her chin.

The piecrust was rolled out, the braised steak and onions put into the bottom of the bowl with some thick gravy, chunks of cooked potato went on top and it was all covered with a layer of pastry. Everything was done with the utmost precision. It looked good and she hoped Peter would be home in time to eat it before it went cold; it was never the same reheated.

She made some extra gravy and opened a tin of mushy peas. The door chime jangled and in he walked, just as the pie was due out of the oven. She smiled, in a way glad he was home, at least he hadn't gone straight to the pub. It was a relief.

'Just in time for your tea love. Hope you're hungry; its meat and potato pie, just as you like. There's a beer in the fridge if you want one, or I can put the kettle on. I bet you're tired aren't you?'

He put his bag down on the floor and moved over to where Mother was standing. She shied away from him, worried he might start on her again, but he simply smiled and held out his hand, open-palmed as if to say there was nothing to fear. She hesitated before taking it.

'Look Mo, I'm sorry I've been awful with you over the last couple of days. I don't know what's been wrong with me. I know I hurt you, I'm so sorry. I know you probably hate me, but I won't do it again. I love you Maureen, I do.' He started to cry.

Mother was shocked by the admission and display of affection; he'd never cried or shown any real emotion in front of her before so she just stood and looked at him, almost hypnotised. This was the first time he'd actually said he loved her; it came out of nowhere, she was stunned. After a couple of bewildered seconds she let go of his hand and picked up the oven gloves instead.

'Come on love, let's say no more about it and have some dinner, eh? Shall I put the kettle on?'

He nodded, sitting down at the table and fiddling with his fork. Mother was aware of him watching her, scrutinising every little move, waiting for her to make a mistake before pouncing. It made her nervous. Her hands shook and she dropped the knife she was going to cut the pie with; it skidded across the lino, coming to a stop near Peter's foot.

'Talk about butter fingers. Sorry love, I don't know what's wrong with me today,' she said, retrieving the knife and putting it down on the draining board.

'It's me; that's what's wrong with you. I've made you a bundle of nerves, haven't I? I'm so sorry. Please try not to worry. I can't tell you how sorry I am. I promise you I won't do it again. Do you think you can forgive me?' Peter begged.

His face looked crushed with the shame of what he'd done and his eyes pleaded for another chance.

'Yes, it is what's wrong with me. I'm frightened even to breathe too heavily in front of you, just in case you turn. I know you say you won't do it again, and I want to believe you, I do, but I'm terrified it will all start over at any moment... How do I relax and be myself when I don't know if I'm waking up with Dr Jekyll or Mr Hyde each morning?'

She doubted she should have been this forthright and stood looking back at the sink, waiting for him to react, convinced that he would, trying to steel herself for the blows which would surely follow.

Mother trembled in the heavy silence, fearing it would never end, until her husband spoke again.

'I can change, you know. I've never hit a woman before and I'll never hurt you again. I'm sorry I've made you scared of me; you don't need to be. I will change and I will make it better for you, I swear.'

'Well, let's just have our tea and try and forget about it, eh? Come on, can you help me get the pie dished up?' she asked reassuringly, passing him the knife and serving spoon whilst stirring the peas in the saucepan.

The plates were filled and placed on the table, and steaming tea mugs set down next to them. She and Peter sat down to eat; he dragged the high chair over so John was sat in between them, pulling a bit of pie crust off his plate, blowing it and giving it to him. The pastry went straight up to his little mouth.

'He's not on solids yet Peter; you'd better take it off him before he chokes, love,' Mother said with a smile.

Peter prised the pastry away from the baby and gave him back the potato.

'I can't wait for him to be toddling about. I've started paying into the works' club so I can get him a Derby County football shirt. And I'm looking forward to having his feet measured for his first little boots.' Peter was quite animated, making Mother laugh.

'You'll have to fight my dad off on that one; you know how barmy he is about County. What with him having that trial period years ago, I know he was only on the second team, but he was so proud. Bless him.'

'I suppose I'd better let him get the boots then, but it'll be me that teaches him how to kick a ball though. Why did your Dad pack in the football?'

'Well, it were all to do with a match he was playing. This chap on the other side kept trying to bring him down. He was fast me Dad in them days, and they reckoned it wouldn't be long 'til he was up for the first team, but this chap wouldn't leave it alone; kept running at him, tripping him; brought him down as he was heading towards goal. Ref didn't see it, though. Dad all but knocked the other bloke down he was that angry. Got a yellow card for it; lucky he wasn't sent off. Mind you, he wasn't long on the pitch; got a free kick, but as he went for it the bloke tripped him again. Well, my Mother was across that field like a whippet. She whacked that other player over the head with her umbrella with such force that he fell flat on the ground and couldn't get back up again. The ref was furious. He waved a red card at Mother and she wasn't even playing, then when she waved the brolly at him he sent Dad off as well. That was the end of his football career with County. He was so embarrassed when the scout from Sheffield Wednesday came round he gave him short shrift and sent him off with a flea in his ear, telling my Mother that he couldn't face going through it all again. She begged him to try but he said he couldn't play for another side: his heart belonged to Derby and that was it.'

Peter had eaten virtually all his dinner whilst Mother was telling her tale; he finished his mouthful of pie and burst out laughing.

'That Mother of yours, she's a bugger! I've such a picture in my head of her with that umbrella, she could frighten the daylights out of a team of blokes, that one! She told me in no uncertain terms what she thought of me when we were going to get married. Like I said, she could put the fear of God into anybody.'

Mother chuckled, nodding her agreement, and they finished their meal in a comfortable silence. To an outsider it looked like any scene of domestic bliss.

The evening passed off peacefully. Peter had admired his shirt for the next evening, commenting about how nicely ironed it was. Mother was thrilled he'd noticed.

Peter put John to bed and settled him before opening a can of beer and pouring it into two glasses. Mother didn't really like pale ale but she sipped at it thinking she should, not wanting to rock the boat, particularly as it was sailing on an even keel at this moment.

She listened to him talking about his day, about what his Mother was going to make for their tea tomorrow. He thought it was to be a sherry trifle for pudding and was chuffed: it was his favourite. Most other people didn't put jelly on top of the custard; no one made a trifle like his Mother. She didn't argue with him.

She yawned. It was half past ten; she'd had a busy, funny, tense old day and was tired. Peter noticed and smiled considerately at her.

'Go and get yourself to bed love; you've had a bad few days. I'll just have a cigarette, then I'll come too. I'm tired as well. We'll have a nice day tomorrow, make up for a bit of the mess lately.' He squeezed her hand affectionately as she got up and moved towards the bed.

Mother slid under the blankets and settled down, relieved, soon asleep, not even feeling her husband get in beside her.

Chapter 15

Sunday came and went and was a pleasant day. She'd secretly dreaded it all, but had been surprised at how enjoyable it turned out. Peter bought her an ice-cream with a flake in the park, they fed the ducks and ate a picnic at lunchtime. Even the visit to his Mother's had been bearable. She usually found them a bit full of themselves, talking about what they had, what they were going to get and how much it cost. But today they were only interested in her, the baby and how they were doing.

When they caught the last bus home she felt almost happy; something she hadn't experienced for a long time.

They got back, put the baby to bed and had a cup of tea. She was careful how she made it just in case he was watching, but he just accepted the mug and drank it gratefully. They went to bed in peace again.

Mother only closed her eyes once she heard Peter breathing deeply next to her. She relaxed, realising he was asleep.

The new week began: late shifts on the Derby to Matlock via Crich route for him and a tranquil week for her. Wednesday, Grandma came down for the day and Peter made her almost welcome in the caravan, even making her a drink. After he had gone to work, Grandma couldn't help but comment on Peter's uncharacteristic behaviour.

'What's come over him then our Mo? He were almost nice to me. Is he after something or happen he's feeling a bit under the weather, eh!'

Mother laughed, making no reply, conscious not to draw attention to what had happened the previous week, before his effort to be different. She didn't need it brought up again, not wanting to pick at the scab on a freshly closed wound.

That wound would open again without help before too long.

A fortnight later Peter was still coming home straight from work without going drinking; even buying her a bunch of daisies from the market one evening. He was attentive and helped around the caravan, washing pots and wiping up after John when he was sick, even changing his nappy occasionally. One afternoon after an early shift he arrived back at the park in a cheerful mood and decided to take the baby out for a walk. It seemed like a breakthrough.

'Eh love, I'm thinking of taking John out in the pram. I thought I might wander up to Crich and show him the trams, what do you think? It'd do him good to have some fresh air and I wouldn't mind a bit of exercise myself. Sometimes I feel like all I do is sit in that bloody bus, looking at the fields and never being able to get out in them. Bit like being in a moving zoo cage, I suppose. Anyway, what do you think?'

'Yes, it must be tiring for you all day long. It'd do you good to stretch your legs.' She was puzzled, because he'd never shown any interest in walking in the countryside before now. Still, he seemed to be mending his ways.

'I was thinking as well, maybe you could take yourself off to Matlock Bath while I'm gone and go to the hairdressers or something. There's a bus in twenty minutes. I know you haven't had any time for yourself since he was born. Would you like that?' he put his hand in his trouser pocket, pulled out a couple of pound notes and passed them to her. 'Will that be enough?'

'Love, that's more than enough. I can have a perm and colour for that and there'd still be enough left to bring some shopping home.'

'Well, why don't you have that done, eh? You don't have much for yourself and I haven't been spending it lately. I'd like you to have something nice.'

Mother walked across the room and gave Peter a kiss; he looked happy at her reaction and set about getting John's bits and pieces together while she got her coat and put the money in her purse.

'Right then, I'll be off to the bus stop. I was thinking I'd get something nice in Matlock for our tea, maybe a bit of steak or chicken, would that be all right?'

Peter smiled, giving her a squeeze on the arm and a quick peck on the cheek.

'That'd be lovely. I'll look forward to my tea now; probably fancy it by the time I've been up to Crich and back!'

She laughed, agreeing with him; then picked up her bag and went out, experiencing a strange sense of freedom; it wasn't something she was used to. She hadn't been out of the caravan without my Brother for months and felt strangely alone, as if she'd left something important behind.

She caught the number 35 and settled back into her seat, watching the trees as the bus meandered its way through the valley towards Matlock Bath.

Three hours later she was back where she'd started, except now with a curly perm teased and shaped until it was perfect, making her feel glamorous and stylish, like a new woman. She also had a small plastic bag of stewing steak, mushrooms, onions and a bottle of stout. Thinking in the hairdressers about what to make for their tea, wanting it to be special, she'd decided upon a steak and ale pie; Peter would like that. He wasn't back, so she took the opportunity to work on the meal in peace, peeling the onions and frying them in the saucepan, cutting the steak into chunks and dropping it in, cooking it just enough to seal in the flavour. As it started to brown, she added the mushrooms, let them soften a bit, then poured in the stout. The smell of beer was overwhelming and it momentarily reminded her of Peter's breath when he used to come home from the pub drunk; she shuddered and put it out of her mind.

The pan continued to simmer, the stock grew thicker and the wafts of alcohol lessened as it cooked down. She started on the pastry, making it a rich crumbly consistency before rolling it out and lining a deep dish. While it was in the oven baking blind she sat on the settee waiting for her husband to come home. But when there was no sign she decided to have a cup of tea and one of her hidden cigarettes. She opened the door to let the smell out; Peter didn't know about the secret smoking, wouldn't like it. She hoped that what the eye didn't see the heart wouldn't grieve over.

She sipped and puffed, enjoying her five minutes' peace and quiet. Finishing her tea and stubbing out her fag, she set about filling the pie and placing the crust on top.

Peter and John still hadn't appeared so she put the pie in to bake and cleaned up the flour and pans.

Half an hour later she heard footsteps and wheels coming towards the van door and assumed it was her family back, but the polite knock told her it was the paper boy with his bicycle.

He came in and put the evening paper on the table.

'Somert smells nice Maureen; makes me hungry. I hope my mum's made something nice for our tea. What you having?'

He sat down and grinned at her. They'd been firm friends since the birth of John, his namesake. He was the only one she had in the area and relished his visits even though he only stayed for about a quarter of an hour. She fetched the biscuit barrel out of the cupboard, passed it to him and got a glass of milk.

He was always pleased to have this little break, a lonely lad that liked having a bit of attention; it made him feel like someone was interested in him.

The papers came every afternoon about the same time, apart from Sunday. He wasn't comfortable on the days Peter was around, never staying longer than to take a biscuit, say a cheery hello, deliver the paper and leave quickly. Today he was happy to stay.

They chatted about his day at school and what he was doing on the weekend; some Saturdays he went to the football with his Dad and big Brother or he helped his Mum around the garden. From being a little child he'd had a patch of his own and grown flowers. He and Mother talked about the shrubs and planters she would have in her garden if she had one, designing the borders on scraps of paper. Often when he'd gone off to deliver the rest of his round, she sat and closed her eyes, smelling the perfumes coming from the tea roses she'd planted in her mind and watching the imagined lavender bushes blowing in the slight summer breeze.

Mother saw John out and watched him pedal merrily off down the pathway. As he disappeared from sight she saw her husband wheeling the pram up towards the park gate. She waved, noticing how red in the face he was, as if he'd marched up the steep hill at full pelt. So she nipped back inside and put the kettle on, then went back to wait on the steps of the van.

She was excited about Peter coming home, wanting to show off her new perm and for him to compliment her. Checking herself in the window of the caravan door made her smile; she was pleased with the transformation. It was the first time she'd had her hair done since before John was born.

As Peter got closer to the van it became obvious the baby had been crying for some time, his little face was puffed up and red around the eyes and cheeks. His Dad was virtually scarlet, looking angry and heated, sweat dripping down his brow, making Mother feel slightly apprehensive.

'This little sod has been crying for the past hour, wailing like a bloody banshee. I could have clocked him one in the end; nothing I could do would stop him, nothing. A woman in the pub thought he might be teething. I've felt round and can't find anything. I rubbed a bit of whisky on his gums to see if it helped, but it didn't make a lot of difference. So much for my peaceful walk, eh!'

'Poor little mite,' Mother began. 'Did your Daddy put something nasty in your mouth? No wonder he screamed, he's not old enough to be teething yet, not by a long chalk. Did you tell the woman how old he was? And what were you doing in the pub? I thought you were looking at trams. He's probably got colic or something. It's gripe water he wants not whisky! Oh well, not to worry, he's quiet now at least.'

She had picked up her son, busily peeling off his baby-grow and undoing his nappy, already realising he needed changing and this wasn't making him too sweet of temper. Peter pushed the pram under the awning, climbed in through the door and threw himself down on the seat. He saw the teapot was ready, water boiling on the stove, so he decided to brew it himself. Mother was busy cleaning up the baby and talking quietly to him, tweaking his toes with her fingers. He was soothed now and smiling up at her wriggling his foot, making her laugh.

'Naughty Daddy, eh John? Didn't think to look at your nappy. Still it's all right now isn't it? All clean again. Do you want to go back to Daddy and show him what a cheerful lad you are now?' she said, picking up my Brother and turning towards Peter. He was pouring the tea into two cups ready for her to come and sit down, looking at his baby with contempt.

'Don't bring that little bugger to me; I've had just about enough of him for one day. I can't believe all that palaver was about having a dirty nappy; he's spoilt, that's what he is. You want to leave him with a dirty arse for a bit every day; we wouldn't have this complaining then. Christ, you pander to him Maureen. You don't want to be so soft'.

She looked shocked at his suggestion and stared in disbelief.

Seeing she wasn't very impressed, he tried to make it better. 'Look, all I'm saying is he needs to learn from an early age that he can't have it all his own way. You'll be saddled with a Mummy's boy if you're not careful. He needs toughening up, that's all.'

Mother was astonished, unable to get over the idea that he would leave a baby, his own baby, to sit in a dirty nappy on purpose in order to teach him not to complain.

'For God's sake Peter, he's a baby, only a baby. We have to look after him. You wouldn't want to sit in filth, and if you did you wouldn't be happy about it, would you? Well, would you?' She didn't give him a chance to answer. 'He's a baby; he doesn't understand that he's upset your little private time in the pub. He only cried because he was uncomfortable. You'd be the same. I bet your Mother never left you sat in a dirty nappy, did she?'

He didn't say anything, just pushed her cup of tea across the table and smiled.

'No of course she didn't. She was a good Mother, always kept us clean and well fed. But you knew where you stood with her, you knew where the line was and you didn't cross it. I'm sorry. I wouldn't make him suffer; he just made me that mad. I could no more hurt him than I could hurt you.'

Realising what he'd said, he gazed down at his hands, ashamed.

Mother got up from the table and turned her back on him, putting their son in his cot and sighing loudly. All the pleasure she'd taken in anticipation of him coming home had dissipated in the last sentence he'd spoken. She suddenly felt cold, remembering how scared he made her feel. The good work he'd put in over the last few weeks was washed away in a few ill-chosen words.

'Don't you want this tea, love, its going cold?' he said to her back.

She didn't reply, didn't want to talk to him, just wanted him to be quiet and leave her alone.

'Don't ignore me Maureen. I asked a question. Do you want this bloody tea or not?'

She turned around, staring straight at him though her eyes looked beyond his shoulder, not daring to meet his glare, not wanting anything from him at all. Eventually she spoke.

'No, I don't.' It was short and to the point. She'd started to turn her back again when she caught sight of him picking up the cup, hurling it in her direction. In the split second before it found its target, he shouted, 'look at me when I speak to you, bitch. Here's your fucking tea.'

It hit her on the side of the face, the cup rebounding and smashing on the floor, where it broke into three pieces. Tea splashed onto her cheek, but most of it landed on her right side, soaking through the fabric of her blouse and down onto her skirt. Two seconds later the baby let out a loud cry of shock, turning into pain; some of the tea had hit him square in the face. Mother gasped in horror and ran towards his scream, pulling him out of his cot and rushing him to the sink. She wet the dishcloth and tried to soothe the burning, but his delicate skin had already turned red in patches, matching the blisters starting to appear across her own cheek.

Peter stood detached from the scene he had created, watching it all unfold in front of him until he became aware of the smell of pastry and distinct aroma of cooking beef. His stomach rumbled; for a second he forgot how dismayed he was.

She put cream on the baby's face and across his hand where he'd been caught, settling him down. The cream had taken the pain away and the rich tea biscuit offered had given him something to take his mind off the shock.

Turning to her own face she saw skin turning red and bubbling up into tiny blisters. She could feel the pressure building inside each one as they started to fill with protective liquid.

Knowing Peter was standing watching her, she was aware of him crying, though could hear no sound. It was as if he were in another room where she could only see him through a window and he couldn't have any effect on her. All that had happened in the space of the last five minutes seemed like a silent movie, something she'd watched with herself in the starring role. However, as she put her hands up to cream her cheek, the pain was only too real.

Mother blanked Peter out completely, feeling nothing for him as she tended her scald in silence. Slowly she became aware of a noise in the background, a murmuring. She turned to see Peter holding the baby on his hip, talking to him. Seeing the two of them together - John with splashes of pink across his cheeks hidden by cream and Peter with tears streaming down his face - made her feel physically sick. She wanted to snatch the baby away from her husband and run as fast as she could, to get away from both him and the caravan, but she didn't dare, was scared she wouldn't get far enough, that he would hurt the baby even more than he already had.

Eventually John started to grizzle again, the noise breaking through the wall of silence that had built up between his parents.

'Give him to me Peter; he wants his Mother,' she demanded, stretching out her arms. When he was safely back in her embrace she turned away from her husband and set about re-dressing the pink patches on the baby's little face, continuously aware of Peter watching her.

He started to talk again. 'Look, I'd never hurt that baby; you know I wouldn't. I wouldn't hurt a hair of his head. You know it was an accident. I'm sorry, it'll never happen again. I was so wound up and you were taking the mickey out of me. Before I knew it I'd thrown the cup at you. I know you won't forgive me, but I will make it up to you. I'll show you.'

He sounded desperate but Mother again retreated back into silence and didn't allow his words to affect her. She continued with her care of John; washing off the old cream, dabbing his face dry with a cloth, then carefully adding more ointment whilst singing softly under her breath. He had the lid of the tub to hold and was busy trying to get it into his mouth. It was eerily quiet. She stood holding John, wondering if Peter had got fed up and gone out of the caravan, listening for his breathing. But the only sounds she could hear were her own heartbeat and the baby mouthing the lid. Realising he was sat on the settee watching her, she turned around and looked at his eyes; they were unbelievably cruel. It was the first time the thought had come to her, but now she'd noticed she couldn't understand why she hadn't seen it before: he had cruel eyes. Cruel eyes and a cruel nature.

Mother walked towards the door with the baby in her arms, going to let some cool air into the caravan to enable her to think a little clearer. Peter started to speak again but she remained in her own impermeable world, not catching what he said. Reaching for the clip which kept the door closed, she pushed it; it stayed closed. She tried again, shoving harder; it wouldn't budge.

'It's locked,' he shouted. 'I've locked it. You aren't going anywhere, not now, not like this. You're staying in here and we'll put this right.'

She was trapped inside the small, cramped space with a man she hardly knew and didn't want to know; her world had become limited to a twenty- by eight-foot caravan and she needed to break out, escape to a life beyond the perimeter fence.

'Just open the door Peter, open it. I need some fresh air. It's so hot in here. Please just open it up. I'm not going anywhere, I just want some air that's all, just some air'. She began to weep uncontrollably and with each sob the baby started to get more and more agitated in her arms until he was screaming. The caravan was filled with the sound of anguish and turmoil; it echoed around the room and rattled through every pot and pan on the draining board. Infuriated, Peter wasn't going to listen to it anymore.

He slung his coat on quickly, taking the key from his trouser pocket and opening the door. As Mother made her way forward to step out, he pulled her back by the arm, pushed past and slammed the door behind him. Before she could get there, the key turned. She was locked in.

He stomped away across the field, Mother's cries ringing out in vain, reaching his ears, but he still kept going. The lady from three caravans down was outside pegging out her smalls, watching him stride angrily towards her. As he drew level he stopped for a second.

'Is there something I can do for you, Mrs? Have you seen enough or is it a photograph you're wanting? Fucking nosy cow.' He spat the words at her then physically spat in her direction. She was shocked, dropped her pegs and rushed back into her van, slamming the door shut.

Peter laughed to himself and started to march on. With each step away from the caravan my Mother's voice was a little quieter, and as he reached the end of the field he couldn't hear her at all. Pleased with himself, and smiling with satisfaction, he set out through the site entrance with purpose; he had a few quid in his pocket and was going to get a drink.

Chapter 16

It became clear no one was hearing her desperate pleas, and even if they could they weren't going to help: it wasn't their business. So she surrendered to her incarceration, distracted by the need to calm the baby. She sat in the ensuing silence and watched him sleep, the marks on his face now only slightly noticeable, unlike her own blisters, which burned and felt like they would possibly scar. The window was open slightly, that was as far as it went; the park owners had fixed them on security settings so they couldn't be wrenched wide enough to get an arm through. No one could get in and no one could get out. She was a prisoner in a 1950s Jubilee Butterfly.

She looked through the kitchen drawers in the faint hope of finding a screwdriver to take the window from its fixing, knowing it was unlikely: Peter wasn't one for handiwork. The knives were all far too big to fit into the counter-sunk screws in the frames, so she gave up and sat down for what seemed like an age. The caravan was deathly quiet and it was nearly dark outside. The breeze coming in through the windows was getting wintry and she realised she was cold. The cool air helped the blisters on her face but when she reached over to the baby and touched his hands she decided it was time to shut them and pull the curtains. Sitting in the darkened caravan she lit one of her precious cigarettes. There were only a few left in the packet and she made a mental note to go out as soon as possible and buy some more. The smoke curled around her fingers and made patterns in the gloomy air, mesmerising her for a while until the cigarette had virtually burnt away. She took a last drag and stubbed it out.

She got herself into bed, fully clothed; no desire or inclination to get undressed, just taking her shoes off and throwing the covers over her, falling into a fitful sleep.

The next morning came around and there was still no sign of Peter. She tried the handle just in case he'd returned unheard and unlocked the van door out of kindness, but realised it had been a stupid thought; there had never been much kindness in her husband and there was no reason to think he would start showing any now.

She got John out of his cot, thankful he was such a good baby; apart from when his father tormented and upset him or he was poorly, he hardly ever cried. He took his bottle and a bit of mashed apple stewed the day before, eating them happily, gurgling and smiling at his Mother as she talked to him and tickled his feet. His face had cleared completely now; there was no sign of the trauma he'd undergone the night before, making her appreciate how marvellous human skin was, how it was resistant to water, how it healed itself from cuts and bruises and changed colour in the sun. Would he be a little boy that easily tanned? Certainly his curly blond hair was darkening into a light sandy brown, suggesting that he would. She pulled one of his curls downward, watching it spring back; he gurgled and raised his hand to try and grab his Mother's large fingers. She let him catch her and sat there with his tiny hand wrapped in her own, feeling safely insulated with her child but starting to worry how long it would last.

Morning turned into dinner time and she felt pangs of hunger, not having eaten since the previous day, deciding she should at least try and find something. There wasn't a lot in the cupboards. Today would have been shopping day, but this shopping day was going to be different; today she was going nowhere unless her husband came home with the key. She cut herself a piece of the pie cooked the previous day and ate it cold.

She listened to the one o'clock news on the radio, the usual doom and gloom; somewhere bombs had gone off and several people had been killed, the stock markets had gone up and down overnight, the weather was to be clear with chances of rain in the evening; not that it mattered to her, she wasn't going anywhere. Leaving the radio on for company and a bit of background noise, she played with the baby again and changed

111

him for the second time, humming along with the tunes she recognised. In an odd way she was having quite a pleasant day despite being caged, and wondered if this was how it felt to be imprisoned all the time. It was a daft thought; she wouldn't have steak and ale pie to eat or a radio to listen to.

Towards teatime she began to wonder whether Peter intended to come back at all, whether she would be stuck in here with John until they both starved to death. Being confined wasn't such a pleasant feeling anymore.

She tried not to panic or get upset again. John would pick up on it, so she sat calmly and waited instead. The paper lad would be here soon; at least he'd be able to help, though only the Lord knew how.

Sure enough, the wheels of his bike came to a stop outside the caravan and footsteps came towards the door. He tried it and found it closed. She climbed onto the settee, craning out of the gap in the window to call to catch his attention.

'I'm here. I can't open the door. Peter's taken both the keys and he's fastened me in. Can you see if you can get it open for me?'

'Hello Maureen, how long have you been stuck in there then?' He reached up and passed the paper through the window. She grabbed at his hand, desperate for him not to leave.

'I've been in here all day, me and the baby, we're trapped.' She was embarrassed by her predicament. 'It was a mistake. He went off to work this morning and picked up my key. He had his own in his coat and didn't realise it. I don't know what time he'll be back but I can't stay in here 'til he does. Can you get someone to come and unlock the door for me? Maybe Mr Knight the site man is about; he should have a spare.'

The paper lad rushed off towards the entrance to the caravan park, just near the road where the bridge crossed over the river. It would take him a couple of minutes to get there and back, leaving Mother praying that Mr Knight would be there. Sometimes he didn't bother going into his office at all but would sit by the river and fish for hours instead; it was a slow business managing a caravan site. Apart from general repairs and mowing the field occasionally there wasn't that much to do. Before the paper lad returned she had time for a quick look at her face to see how bad it looked and, not wanting all and sundry knowing what her husband had done, time to conjure up a good excuse.

She tried to wait patiently, putting the kettle on to make a pot of tea for anyone that wanted it, staring out of the window watching for any sign of life. With a sigh of relief she saw the paper lad and Mr Knight, who at the best of times could be described as portly, wandering across the field towards her, disappearing from sight around the closest row of caravans then reappearing yards from her own, as if in a magician's sleight of hand trick.

'I'll have you out of there in a jiffy Mrs,' shouted the proprietor, swinging a huge bunch of Yale keys towards the door.

She felt expectant as she waited for the door to open even though she knew exactly what was on the other side. It was the same feeling as opening her stocking on Christmas morning as a child, knowing there would be an orange, an apple and some nuts in the bottom, but still wanting it. She heard Mr Knight puffing and panting outside and the chinking of keys as he tried each one in turn in the lock. The door handle turned; not the right key. He tried another, and another after that. She could hear him muttering to the paper lad and hoped he wasn't complaining about her. She moved closer to the door to listen.

'I've asked Mrs Knight more than once to label up these keys, it'd only take an hour or so. Will she though? Will she buggery! Too interested in listening to the Light Programme or knitting to be bothered with the important things in life. Says I should do it. I'd like her to tell me when I have the time to be doing that as well as everything else I do here; bloody liberty that woman takes, I'll tell you.'

He carried on grumbling, the keys clanking together as the door was tried each time, until after several more attempts it swung open as if the magician had theatrically shouted 'Open Sesame' in true pantomime style.

The rush of air that flowed into the stuffy caravan was like the most expensive perfume she'd ever smelt: fresh and heady. She couldn't wait to get outside, but patiently turned and relit the kettle, politely asking if they would like a cup of tea. Mr Knight refused the offer – he had to get down to the entrance and close the overnight gate as it was nearly dusk. She thanked him profusely, telling him it would never happen again, sorry for putting him to any trouble. He smiled at her and said not to worry her pretty head about it. She felt a great sense of liberation though doubted her head was that pretty with the blisters currently residing across half her face. The paper lad came in as usual.

'I'd better not stop for a cup of tea today Maureen, I'm a bit late now, what with all this. My Mum will have the tea on the table by the time I'm home. I don't want to be late, she hates her food going cold.' He was looking at her, clearly wondering how she had ended up with those marks across her cheek. 'What's happened to your face? It looks really sore. Is it a rash?'

She was taken aback by his sudden question and for a second fiddled with the teapot, not knowing how to answer, chewing over her reply.

'No love, it's not a rash. I had a bit of an accident with the kettle last night. Don't ask me how I managed it but the top flew off and it sprayed boiling water up at me. It's lucky it isn't any worse than it is; clumsy clot, me, eh? Mind you, it hurt. It'll be a while before I forget to put the lid on properly again.'

He seemed to swallow it, or at least not ask any more. He jiggled the toes of his young namesake saying he should get off and finish his round before it got too dark.

'Thank you so much for getting Mr Knight for us. I've had a bit of day all in all; I'm glad its over. If you hang on for a couple of minutes I'll walk out to the road with you. Thought I might nip up to the shop in the village before it shuts up for the night. I need a few bits and pieces for tonight's tea. I couldn't get out to get it today. Well you know that!'

Aware of chatting away as if she hadn't seen another living soul for years, half excited and half embarrassed, she felt both free and a liar for concealing the mess she was in. It wouldn't be the only time lies covered up the truth of her existence.

The baby was wrapped up and in the pram as quickly as could be managed before she pulled on her coat and followed the paper lad across the field. He was talking about his garden again and how the vegetables were coming on; she listened attentively, drinking in every word in case she had to spend another full day without hearing a human voice. At the end of the path they went their separate ways. She was alone again.

At the shop she bought a few bits and pieces for the food cupboard, some milk, another packet of secret cigarettes and a pack of batteries just in case the radio went dead. She realised how much of a sanity saver it had been and couldn't face sitting in silence waiting for Peter to come home. Now free, her thoughts focused on what to do if he did indeed decide to come back. She was in two minds about whether to pack up all she could carry and go home to her Mother or stay with her husband and sort things out. After all, John needed a father and, foolish as it was, she still loved him. Thinking about what the love between them meant made her more unsure and confused; the only thing she concretely knew was that she was frightened for her future.

Chapter 17

Taking her time walking back, she scanned the dusky blue scenery as she went, listening to the birds and watching them return to their roosts for the night. Across the darkening horizon, a formation of geese flew in a perfect chevron, honking as they passed overhead, low enough for her to see the way their wings caught the wind. She stopped and watched them, showing them to John, holding his hand up to point at the sky, hoping his gaze might follow his arm. She didn't know whether he'd spotted the birds or not but wanted him to see all there was in the world, far more than she ever had, to go further, travel the globe, hoping he would have the chances she hadn't.

As she rounded the corner to the caravan park, she could see a light on in her van and wondered if she'd left it on by mistake in the rush to get out. A silhouette moved in the window and it slowly dawned that Peter was waiting for her.

She stood watching, transfixed by the shadowy shape, until the baby startled her by beginning to cry. Jiggling the pram, she made the decision to tread softly towards the caravan until she could make out her husband in the kitchen standing staring out of the window, peering into the night. He couldn't see her approaching as the light inside was stronger, so they were masked for a while; only when the pram wheels sounded on the hard, foot-worn ground did he know they were there.

Peter swung open the caravan door and looked directly at her. She froze.

'Are you coming in then? I'll put the kettle on.'

Mother didn't answer him, simply felt compelled to follow as he turned to go back inside. In the caravan she stood unsure of what to do as he busied about filling the kettle, putting the cups out on the table as if the last two days hadn't occurred.

'Are you hungry? My Mother has sent one of her fruit cakes down for us. I picked it up this morning. She sends her love and a kiss for the little 'un. I didn't tell her what happened, it's our business, nothing to do with anybody else. How did you get out? I am sorry I took both keys. Who got you out? Did you tell them what happened?'

He was clearly panicked that somebody might know what he'd done the night before.

She sighed.

'Mr Knight let me out. He has a key for all the caravans. The paperboy got him to help me. I couldn't stay in here any longer, I was going crazy not knowing if you were coming back or if I'd be stuck in here all night again. It didn't take him long to let me out, I just said you'd picked up my key as well as your own: it was an accident. They don't think anything different. You don't have to worry; no one's any the wiser.'

She sighed again and looked at him in despair.

'Look Maureen, I didn't mean it; it was an accident with the tea. I know you don't believe me but I was angry. I know I fly off the handle sometimes; I was just that het up. You weren't to blame. I shouldn't have locked you in, taken it out on you, but I just felt you were going to leave. I know I shouldn't have done what I did.'

Mother didn't reply, had heard his apologies before and was starting not to believe him or the excuses. He didn't seem to notice the lack of response and carried on with his monologue.

'I won't do anything like that again, I swear to you. Just try not to wind me up anymore, eh? I don't want to be angry with you, I don't want to hurt you; you must know that. Lets start again, eh. What do you think?'

She nodded and sighed once more, still feeling trapped, willing him to shut up, not wanting to hear any more. He seemed to take her silence as an agreement, but all she wanted was a quiet life.

True to his word, he didn't do anything like that again, finding other ways to show his cruelty and slowly grind her down. She started to feel she deserved what was happening to her; being treated like a skivvy, the beatings and the foul language. Whenever he hit her, he told her in no uncertain terms it was because she drove him to it; it must be her fault, she didn't treat him properly. In between the blows he would list her defects. She was:

1. Useless in bed.
2. A shit wife.
3. A bad mother.
4. Fat and ugly.
5. Always in his business.
6. A bloody awful cook.
7. Lazy around the house.
8. A drain on his hard-earned wages.

The list continued to grow; it was no wonder she felt worthless.

She had no one to talk to, no one to tell her what was happening wasn't right. The paper lad had been banned from calling to see her in the afternoons; Peter had cancelled the deliveries. When he found the paper lad was still dropping in anyway, he chased him off with a vicious warning.

'Don't be crawling around my wife. I know you're trying it on with her. I'm not bloody having it. You come back round here again and I'll break your soddin' legs.'

Understandably, her young friend didn't return.

Life continued week in, week out, in the same way. Every day she strived to be better, to keep Peter happy, but it made little difference. Each new morning she would try harder and fail again, perpetually repeating the pattern.

Evenings witnessed the birth of a new bruise or scratch, they were well hidden below the neckline. No one saw them apart from herself or occasionally Peter when he caught her unawares and forced himself upon her. After the first couple of times she'd stopped struggling, ending up worse for wear. It was easier to lie back and let him get on with it. He, after a drink, called it making love, but there was no love involved on either side; she, seeing the hate and contempt, kept her eyes tightly shut while he was on top, not opening them again until he'd gone. More often than not he went to the pub after he'd finished, walking merrily with a spring in his step, leaving her lying there rigid, waiting for the feelings of nausea to fade.

Occasionally, Grandma turned up at the caravan bringing cake and a little gift for John. My Mother would be uncomfortable with her there, ironing the same tea towel three times; fidgeting all the while, anxious he'd come home. Grandma sensed she was uneasy. The atmosphere was strained but she didn't know why.

'Our Maureen, what's wrong with you these days? I come all this way down here on two buses to see you and the little 'un and it feels like you don't want me here. Is there something up?'

'No Mother, nothing, I promise you. I just feel a bit under the weather that's all.'

'You aren't pregnant again are you my girl? It's too soon to be having another one, not in this poky caravan. You can't swing a cat in here, never mind looking after two kiddies and that great ox of a husband of yours.'

'No Mother, I'm not pregnant; I make sure that doesn't happen, I tell you. I just don't feel all that well at the moment. Now just leave it will you.'

'Well, I'm bound to be concerned; I'm your Mother after all and I do worry about you.' Grandma did leave it. Her questioning stopped, but the worry didn't.

Chapter 18

Three weeks later Granddad appeared on the doorstep uninvited, about to knock when a bang from inside set the baby off crying. Peter was bellowing and swearing at the top of his lungs making the glass in the open window shudder. Underneath the sound of crashing and breaking crockery, angry threats to kill my Mother punctured the mildness of the late spring air. Footsteps came towards the door. Not wanting to get involved in a domestic dispute, Granddad quickly nipped around the side of the van and took cover, planning to sit tight until the coast seemed clear before sneaking off home again and pretending he hadn't heard anything. The neighbours were taking the same view, drawing curtains and closing windows, unwilling to acknowledge the disturbance on their doorsteps.

The door burst open. Peter, seething with temper, barked his demands at the terrified woman standing at the kitchen sink. Granddad heard it all.

'You fucking bitch, one of these days you'll learn that I want my dinner on the table when I come home and I want it hot; none of this cold rubbish you think I want. And you have the nerve to tell me it's good for me. I'll tell you what's good for me, and if you know what's good for you then you want to watch you do proper dinners from now on or you'll feel the back of my hand again. So just you think on.'

He slammed the door with such violence it was a miracle it stayed on its hinges, then veered off across the grass jangling the loose change in his pocket.

Granddad processed what he'd seen and heard; now understanding why Grandma was constantly worrying at home. He wasn't sure how to react until he heard his little girl crying inside the van. He tapped gently on the door, but the sound of weeping kept coming, forcing him to knock again, louder and more insistent this time. Silence. He stood waiting tensely for any minute sound, holding his breath. More silence. He could wait no longer and called through the barrier between them.

'Maureen, it's your Dad, open the door. I heard what was going on. Come on, love, let's have a cup of tea, eh and talk about it. You know you can tell me anything.' He knocked again.

Behind the door she stood glued to the spot, hearing her Father outside, wanting to let him in to help sort out the mess that had accumulated in her life over the past months, but was ashamed and frightened he would think her a failure.

'Come on Maureen; open this door. I can't be stood here all afternoon; your Mother will be wondering where I've got to. I heard what he said to you. I've got an idea what's going on; I've met men like him before, you know. Your Auntie Pearl was married to a pig of a bloke. He nigh on killed her one day. I don't want that happening to you. You and that little lad are all that matters, now let me in.'

He waited anxiously for another couple of minutes before trying the door for himself; it wasn't locked. He pulled it open and stepped inside. Mother stood staring at the floor, too embarrassed to look up.

He went over and put his arm around her shoulders. 'Come on lass, let's get that kettle on, eh?'

Lifting her head slightly, she met his gaze and the tears started to flow again. Seeing his big gnarled hand on her shoulder, ingrained with limestone dust from years in the quarry, made her suddenly feel safe. It wasn't something she knew with her husband.

The tears ebbed away as he led her over to the settee and sat her down, pulling a hanky from his trouser pocket and passing it to her. It was crumpled but clean and she took it gratefully, smiling weakly. Granddad filled the kettle, lit the gas under it, and picked up John, who was whimpering and pulling at the bars on his cot. He nestled into Granddad's neck. Mother smiled, but a little brighter this time.

'He loves his Granddad. Look at his little face. I'm sorry I didn't let you in, I couldn't seem to manage to get to the door; it was like I was rooted to the spot. You know I'd never ignore you Dad.' She pushed her hand through the front of her hair, wiping it out of her eyes, inadvertently exposing the blemishes above her elbow.

'Maureen, what's that mark on your arm?'

The smile slipped from her face and she looked down at the ground again.

'It's nothing Dad, just a little knock where I walked into the cupboard door that's all; it doesn't hurt'.

He didn't swallow her explanation and pulled her sleeve up to have a better look, realising there were actually four little bruises in an arc shape, with another slightly larger one five inches beneath. It came to him: the span of four fingers and a thumb: Peter's hand.

'Did he do this to you love? Has he been hitting you? I'll kill him if he has. No man is going to hurt you my girl; just you tell me now. Come on Maureen, spit it out.'

'No, it's nothing. I told you, it's nothing. I just knocked myself on the cupboard that's all. Let's leave it. He hasn't hit me.' She wasn't altogether lying; he hadn't hit her. He had punched her, slapped her, thrown tea over her, raped her, burned her with a cigarette end and kicked her a few times as she lay on the floor trying to protect her face from his boot.

Granddad looked at her, wide-eyed and disbelieving.

'Well, if that's what you say then I'll have to believe you, but you mustn't let him hurt you. Think of John. It's no way for him to be brought up, seeing all this. How do you think he'll grow up, eh, twisted like his Dad? That's no way. You just think about it. You know where I am, where we are. You just come home, eh?'

She nodded. 'Where's that tea then?'

They drank their tea, the uncomfortable silence intermittently broken by John's contented gurgling. Granddad pulled on his jacket and made for the door.

'Just remember love, you can come home. There's always a place for you there.'

And then he was gone.

Chapter 19

Mother sat back down and lit one of her hidden cigarettes. Each time she had been out on her own she'd picked up a packet of fags, but hardly smoked any of them; the little stockpile was reassuring. They were her secret, getting moved around the caravan and hidden in different places so that Peter wouldn't come across them. Her favourite hidey-hole was under the sink where the wheel arch sat. He wouldn't do 'women's work', so would never look there. Near the pin which dropped the axle there was a gap big enough to get her hand inside, a gap with just enough room to stash five packets of cigarettes.

Thinking about the secrecy made her feel pathetic and underhand. Why couldn't she leave the packet out on the table and have one whenever the mood took her? She should be able to offer him one and know he wouldn't take them all when she wasn't looking. Or worse, take them even if she was.

Watching the smoke swirl gave her time to ponder about what to buy from the supermarket with her shopping allowance, if Peter had indeed left her any. She wanted to buy fish but knew that would cause a row because he didn't like it; thinking like this made her realise how pathetic she'd become.

She couldn't leave her fags out, buy a piece of cod or have an evening paper. Going into the village shop for a quarter of pear drops was impossible since he'd pushed her into the window nearly smashing the pane; the shop woman had scuttled out worried about her plate glass and he was sweetness and light to her, saying sorry, offering to pay for any damage, telling her that my Mother had slipped and stumbled. She'd been charmed by his explanation, big smile and apologies, saying there wasn't any problem or need to worry. After she'd gone back inside again he sneered at my Mother, chiding, 'Clumsy fucking cow you are. You'd better be bloody careful. If I were you I wouldn't go in there again. She'll be watching you from now on; probably thinks you're a drunk!' Then he laughed at his own cleverness.

Well, she wasn't him but she didn't go in again, feeling too ashamed. Slowly but surely her world was closing in on all sides. Not that it had been much of a world to be begin with, but at least it had been free and full of laughter.

She was stuck. What was it her Mother said frequently? 'Caught between a rock and a hard place.' It wasn't somewhere she enjoyed being.

So she carried on trying. Trying hard to manage, trying to stay out of trouble and trying not to irritate him. It was physically and mentally exhausting; to get through a day without being punished for her failings was impossible. Breaking point was looming like a huge, sodden cloud waiting to burst.

Chapter 20

The inevitable evening came one Friday when she had slogged diligently over a nice tea: setting the table, making it look welcoming; he repaid her by returning from work over an hour late and stinking of drink. She could feel the irritation in her head growing stronger and stronger. It was like a mass of angry bees crawling around the inside of her skull, not quite swarming but getting ready to take flight. There had been enough sorrow and grief, month upon end of blaming herself, and now the bees had come to make a nest in her head; and all she felt was a rising sense of anger towards him.

Throughout the day, she'd slammed doors, broken glasses, tripped over John's toys, picked him up when he was crying and burned her arm on the oven. One more thing, she thought, and she was going to go over the edge, could feel it coming. The edge was a mystical place Grandma had talked about when Uncle Ralph brought old bits of carburettor into the kitchen to clean, and when Granddad had boil-washed the whites in an attempt to help, putting them in with a pair of black socks, colouring them all an obvious grey.

'Samuel, you're pushing me to the edge I tell you now.' He knew he had and went out for an hour or two while she clawed her way back from the precipice, waiting until everything was fine again.

My Mother's edge seemed to be luring her closer and closer. She didn't know what would happen if she fell but couldn't see a way of moving back from it either.

So Peter was home again. He banged around the caravan, kicking off his shoes, leaving them where they fell for her to pick up and put in the awning where they were supposed to be. He slung his sandwich box out of his work bag; cake crumbs fell all over the table and onto the floor. She begrudgingly swept them up, tipping them into the sink and turning the tap on to wash them down. Swearing under her breath she turned her back on him and started serving up the tea. The peas jumped off the plate as she spooned them on, making her laugh to herself as she scooped them out of the washing up bowl covered in foam, deliberately dumping them on Peter's plate. She didn't care any more; in fact the little bit of rebellion made her feel in control and the bees hummed their approval. The cottage pie was slopped onto the plate and banged down on the table in front of her husband.

He looked at the meal with disgust.

'What the hell is this muck, woman? And you needn't think I'm eating those peas. I saw what you did. Well, aren't you going to apologise? I've been out working all day for you and this is what you serve up. Is it any wonder I get angry? You're just bloody lazy, that's what I think, and where's my fucking knife and fork?'

'In the drawer like always. Where else do you think they are? Oh no, sorry, you wouldn't know would you, as you've never washed them or put them away. Well, find them your bloody self. You're the lazy sod here, not me. And if you don't want to eat it then bloody well don't, I don't care.'

She had shocked herself, feeling proud for standing up to her husband, almost powerful and, even better, it seemed to have shut him up. He didn't answer back in words but by petulantly pushing his plate up the table and glowering at her.

She sat down opposite him and started to eat her tea, her outward calmness not portraying the terror that coursed through her body. Her cottage pie was placed nicely on the plate and the cheese on top was perfectly brown and crispy.

'Why doesn't mine look like that? Saving the best for yourself as usual, eh, greedy cow. I'm the man of this house; I should be getting the best tea. What do you do all day? Play with that baby and cook up foul meals. Well, I want that plate of food and you can have the one that looks like shit.'

Mother carried on eating, ignoring his words. He leaned across the table and made a grab for her plate; she moved it sharply away and carried on with her mouthful of food, watching him out of the corner of her eye. His face was getting

126

redder and redder, the snarl she'd grown accustomed to was starting to spread across it and his breathing was becoming more rapid.

'Give me that dinner now. It's time you started doing as I say before you feel the back of my hand, lady.'

'Go on then. You can't hurt me any more than you have already and you aren't having my bloody dinner. I'll throw it out the window first.'

He stood up at the table, the chair scraping back across the floor and smacking the cupboard, making the baby scream. In the disharmony, the thudding sound of his fist against her face was lost. It wasn't lost on her, though; she felt the crack of her cheekbone as it split under the skin and the slow trickle of blood start to run down her face. It was the first time he'd ever hit her above the neckline.

'Think about that the next time you go against what I say.' He laughed and turned his back on her.

She held the tea towel up to her face and stemmed the blood, feeling it soaking through the cotton, warm and sticky under her fingers. The stain was growing quickly but she didn't cry, didn't want to cry. She felt stronger at that moment than she ever had and was determined he wasn't going to see her surrender.

'So, do you want your pudding now?' she spat at him without waiting for a reply, pulling the plate of apple crumble from the oven and slamming it down on the table.

'That's better, woman; looks lovely that does. It's not that hard to be nice to your husband is it?'

'Well, it's a case of having to, isn't it?' she replied with disdain, not looking at him, carving up the crumble. The blood on her face was dripping onto the side of the worktop and trickling down the front of the cupboard. She wiped it off with the tea towel, smearing it into a red mass.

He impatiently picked up the spoon, waiting in readiness for his pudding.

'What do you mean by that?' His face was reddening again.

She didn't answer, simply placed the bowl in front of him.

'Custard?' she asked impersonally.

127

'What do you mean by that?' he asked again. 'What do you fucking well mean by that?'

'I suppose I mean I'm only doing this because I have to. No more, no less,' she enlightened him, tipping the custard onto his plate, not caring if he wanted it or not.

She turned away again and put the crumble dish down in the sink, aware that he was on his feet and coming up menacingly behind. She stood waiting for him to lash out again, not needing to wait long. He hit her hard on the back of the head and a darkness floated across her eyes; she felt faint and tried to steady herself against the side of the sink. He was talking again but it sounded far away, fuzzy, and she didn't have the strength to tune into the words. He pulled her around to face him. The side of her head was covered in blood and he winced at the sight.

'You might well pull a face, Peter; this is what you've done to me. This is what you've brought me to; this is what we've become. I'm only here now because I haven't got anywhere else to go. If I had the chance I'd be off like a shot. You'll never mend your ways, I know that now. You've had your last chance, and the first one I get, I'm off, and you won't see us again. Neither of us. I promise you that.'

'You're going nowhere, you bloody bitch,' he threatened, pulling his fist back and punching hard in the pit of her stomach. She doubled over, winded and in intense pain; the bees in her head had started to swarm now. 'And you won't be taking my son anywhere, either. He belongs with me and I'll bring him up to be just like his Dad.'

The swarm started to buzz around furiously now and she could no longer control their flight. The saucepan on the side was suddenly in her hand without thinking; raised above his head and bought down heavily before she knew what was happening. He fell backwards, more from the shock than the pain, falling into the chair and staring at her for a few seconds before sobbing like a child who'd lost his favourite toy and knew full well it was gone for good.

'I'm sorry. I've never meant to hurt you. I know that I have. I won't do it again Maureen, I won't, I won't. Listen to me. I'll never hurt you again.'

'No, you won't ever hurt me again. You will never have the chance. You've had your last opportunity, that's it, over.'

Mother staggered back towards the sink and poured a glass of water, tipping it into her mouth. It felt soothingly cold. She tasted the blood and spat out what she could, turning to face him again. He was bawling, hunched over the table, muttering under his breath. She could pick out the odd word, sorry, repeating over and over again. Where once she would have softened, now her heart hardened. Any love harboured in there had now gone, died completely. She was free of him at last.

With this newfound sense of freedom, she turned away, picked John out of his cot, and started to sing him a lullaby, trying to comfort him. He'd been crying unheard for such a long time that the soothing sound of his Mother calmed him quickly and he started to go limp in her arms. She rocked him slowly, putting him carefully back into his cot once he was properly asleep

Peter leaned in the doorway smoking a cigarette, mulling over the family meal, not noticing as she walked coolly over and lifted her right hand, pushing him swiftly in the back. He stumbled out onto the grass, shocked by her sudden move. She hastily closed the door and locked it, making doubly sure he wouldn't get back in by lodging one of the kitchen chairs under the handle.

He rattled the door ferociously, swearing and demanding to be let back in, making her heart thump against her ribs like a thousand butterflies trapped in a jar, desperate to escape the noise, wanting to cover her head and hide so she couldn't hear him any more. The banging and hammering carried on for nearly an hour then suddenly it went quiet. She strained to hear, paralysed like a rabbit caught in headlights, as if her movement might invoke him to start trying to get in again. Creeping slowly over to the door, she put her ear to the frame.

Nothing. No movement, no sound, nothing.

Convinced he'd gone, she let out an immense sigh of relief. She hadn't taken a single breath in the last anxious minutes.

She reached under the sink and pulled out a packet of cigarettes. The smoke made her cough until her eyes watered;

the salt ran into the split skin on her cheek and made her wince. The pain gave a stinging reminder of what a bloody mess her life was in. She took another drag, and instead of coughing, found herself laughing and crying hysterically, uncontrolled, like her existence.

She sat and smoked one cigarette after another, starting to think about what to do next. She had no home, no job, no money, no family near, no friends, no husband worth mentioning, no hope and only one option. There was, in point of fact, nothing to think about and nothing to decide. She would have to go home to Middleton, take John, go back to her Mum and Dad and be safe.

With fresh purpose, she picked up a pen from the table and an old bus company envelope – ironically the only paper she could find – and started to write:

Peter

I've taken John and gone to my Mother's. I am not coming back, I've left the things I don't want, you can do what you want with them. Don't bring them to me, I don't want to see you or them again.

There is no point in going over old ground, I don't hate you, I'm long past that. In fact, I don't feel anything for you, I certainly don't love you anymore. You've killed that. You have hurt me so much and you will never have the chance to do that again; I won't let you. So I am saying goodbye. Don't try and follow me. When I can get round to it and can afford it, I will be getting a divorce.

Maureen

She checked it through a few times, the lump that came to her throat subsiding a little at each read. The words conveyed her indifference and didn't need changing; it said what she wanted, no more and no less.

It took the next four hours, until it was totally dark outside, for her to pack all she could carry. The sum of her married life in one holdall, two carrier bags and a pram basket. She was ready for the off.

Smoking another couple of cigarettes, she sat musing about the practicalities of the trek to her Mother's. It was already too late to get a bus up to Middleton. Instead she wondered if she dared go to sleep for a couple of hours then get up early for the first bus. Exhausted, her eyes felt like they were burning in their sockets, but she couldn't settle in case Peter returned and the nightmare started again. Her guard couldn't be let down for a minute in case he found a hole in her resolve and convinced her he'd be better this time, be a proper husband. She couldn't let that happen, had to be strong, and to be strong she had to stay awake.

She thought about the concept of home, coming to the conclusion it wasn't the place where someone lived but the place where they felt safe and loved. For her, it wasn't there in the caravan, it was a bus ride away in her childhood home.

All the time lost with her family over the last few years preyed on her mind. No words could express how much she'd missed them. The only expression that came being the tears rolling unchecked down her cheeks.

The last three years and how they'd changed her passed through her mind. She reminisced about the band, how she missed her cornet and the pleasure it had given her, wondering if she could get it back from the pawnshop. She'd traded it in for a couple of pounds a number of months before, when she didn't have any money to buy baby food or essentials for the week. Peter wasn't giving her any housekeeping and she couldn't cope. The cornet was the only thing worth any money; either that or her engagement ring. She'd checked how much she would get for the ring but it wasn't as much as the cornet; the pawnbroker examined it through his eyeglass and declared it paste. The first thing she would do when she was on her feet would be retrieve her beloved cornet.

She smiled as she thought about Mary. They hadn't spoken for such a long time, not since John was tiny: Peter had frightened her off. Mary had told Mother he had tried it on with her but she hadn't believed it and virtually threw her out of the house. Knowing she had a lot of making up to do, she hoped Mary would forgive her mistakes and they could start again somehow.

She worried about how she would manage to get herself, John and all the belongings she'd packed onto the bus back to Middleton – how she was physically going to manage it or get there with no money in her pocket. Wandering around the caravan, she searched the places where there might be an odd copper or two, finding a few pence in the kitchen drawer and just over a shilling in the housekeeping pot: about enough to cover the journey. It didn't feel right to use her free bus pass on this journey as she was leaving her driver husband. She tipped the bit of change into an old purse found in the back of a drawer, not used for all the time that she'd lived in the caravan park, unneeded as she had never had anything much to put in it. Grandma had given her the purse on her eighteenth birthday, putting a penny inside for luck, a blessing so that it would never be empty; it hadn't worked. She smiled fondly at the memories it brought back, stroking the brown hide and taking in the leathery smell. Inside the front pocket were a couple of old receipts for clothes: things for her wedding night; she remembered shyly paying for them and the fancy bag they were put in. She'd been so nervous. Would she look attractive and sexy or foolish and silly, turning Peter off? He didn't notice. The clothes were long gone, but the image was still fresh. She cast the memory from her mind and the receipts into the dustbin. The inside pocket was zipped shut and she struggled to free it; something was caught in its teeth. Tugging at it she wondered if this was the reason she'd stopped using it in the first place. The teeth started to move, and opened it a little way, just enough for her to get her index finger inside and wiggle the stuck object around a little until the zip finally moved.

Inside lay the totally forgotten pound note Grandma had given her on the day she moved away from home. Her Mother warned, 'Keep it safe. One day you might be glad of it!' That day had finally arrived. The money would be used wisely; it would be so much easier to get a taxi instead of struggling with the baby, the pram and her bags on the bus. Also, none of the drivers could rush back to Peter and tell him that she'd gone.

Chapter 21

Light started to filter through the caravan curtains and the birds began to sing: morning was coming. She looked down at the two empty fag packets and overflowing ashtray and realised the whole night had passed in meditative contemplation, cleansing the wounds in her soul.

She collected up her bags, fishing out a coin for the phone box. She took one last reflective look around the van then turned and stepped out with conviction, locking the door and leaving the key hanging there. Walking out on a glorious morning that was turning into a beautiful day, she never looked back. This life was over; today was the start of a hopeful new one.

Nobody was around as she wandered through the rows of vans; it was still far too early. Mother liked the feeling that she and John were on their own in the world and nothing was going to intrude. She stopped a row away from the home she'd walked out on, gazing at it for a few seconds, thinking it looked no different from the other caravans in the park, at least not from the outside. She wondered whether behind each of the curtained windows anyone was living a life like she had. Wondering about her neighbours was all she'd ever done, never having been able to make friends with any of them; they had avoided her once the peace-shattering arguments began. It made her sad to think about it, she had never been given a chance.

She trundled the pram slowly over the field, the bags she couldn't carry stacked on top. The field hadn't been cut recently, Mr Knight had been 'busy' on the riverbank; the trout were biting well. It was a struggle when the wheels got caught in the tufts of long grass: the added weight didn't help and by the time she reached the phone box she felt like she'd already pushed the pram half way to Middleton. She rang for her taxi;

there weren't many firms in the area and the drowsy voice at the other end said there'd be a half-hour wait.

Out on the pavement she propped her bags against the wall and sighed, relieved they'd made it this far, but only too aware there was still a great deal of trauma to get over and the huge mountain of a new life to scale. She knew she couldn't just slot back into being part of the family again; it wouldn't be an easy return. On one hand she was filled with trepidation about being greeted with disapproval and a chorus of 'I told you so', on the other she was excited to be going back where it was safe and they could relax for a little while at least. The journey had started, she'd struck out on her own and even though it hadn't worked she made a solemn promise to build a better life for the two of them from now on. Still, a little while back in the nest wouldn't hurt.

She lit another cigarette and leaned back against the wall, waiting for the car to appear, sure that the first one to come down the deserted road would be her taxi. She listened to the silence and felt as if she could hear for miles. Disappointingly, the first engine she heard wasn't for her at all, it was the 6 a.m. Matlock to Buxton service bus. As it passed, the driver slowed down and she willed him not to stop for her; he didn't, he merely raised his hand and waved as he lumbered by. She was more than happy when a blue ford with 'Allen's Taxis' emblazoned on the side turned the corner.

The driver instantly noticed her swollen face and the bruise starting to bloom under her left eye.

'Crikey Mrs, I hope the other bugger came off worse! Are you all right?'

Flustered, Mother instinctively tried to pull some strands of hair across her cheek to hide her shame, blurting, 'There was no other bugger; it's not what you think. I tumbled and caught my face on the door, that's all; I'm just clumsy. Nothing to get your knickers in a twist about.'

Put in his place, he packed her bags and folded-down pram into the boot and she and John clambered into the back of the cab.

It was a good journey. John was content to watch the scenery go past and the driver was happy to ramble on, passing on tales of his exploits of the night before and the fares he'd taken home on the late shift. She was glad he wasn't expecting any answers; it meant she could sit and gather her jumbled thoughts. Before the taxi came everything had seemed a little unreal, like a bad dream that would fade in the morning, but the journey through the rugged landscape opened her eyes and focused her mind. She wasn't dreaming, it wouldn't go away and her flight was only too real. She thought about the sermons heard at Sunday School, back to the Exodus, wondering if the Israelites had felt the same apprehension about going home after all their years in captivity. She smiled wryly; at least she didn't have to walk.

Deep in thought, she barely noticed when the car turned into Middleton. The hill leading up to Grandma's house was lined with little two-up, two-down limestone cottages; dwellings covered with the dust from which they were built, as if they had been given an extra coating for good luck. The people who lived there regularly cursed the limestone lorries: the windows were only transparent for a couple of hours after they'd been freshly washed, clothes couldn't hang out on lines and the amount of dust they had to shift from their ornaments and floors would fill a small bucket each week. Mother though, was pleased to see the dust: she'd grown up with it, remembered her father saying how it lined the lungs of everyone that lived around here; limestone wasn't just in their blood.

The taxi drew up on the pavement outside the green wooden gate that marked the entrance to Grandma's and the driver helped unload the bags and pram. She hitched John up onto her hip and held him there whilst she paid, then watched the car reverse and drive away.

Straining her arm over the top of the gate, she pulled back the bolt. Beyond she could hear Grandma in the kitchen talking to Auntie Joan. She was baking; Mother could hear the rolling pin travelling across the tabletop followed by the sound of a knife cutting spare pastry from the edges of a pie dish. Normal everyday sounds that made her feel comfortable. She pushed the gate open and wheeled the pram inside.

'Hello Mother, it's me and John, can we come in?' she called out.

Grandma appeared at the open kitchen door. One look at her daughter's battered face and the amassed bags on the path told her all she needed to know.

'What the bloody hell has he done to you? That's a right mess. Have you had anybody look at that? Ralph'll nip you up to the hospital; it needs a stitch if you ask me'.

Unable to hold in the emotion any longer, the words overflowed as she broke down: 'I've left him; it's the last finger he'll lay on me…'

They both sat and listened as Mother related the story to them, Joan sniffing into her hanky as she realised the strain her Sister had been under and Grandma listening in horror, shaking her head every now and again. After three pots of tea, the truth was out, the bags and pram stowed away and John set down in the front room, placated with some toys and a ginger biscuit.

Mother and John moved back into her old bedroom. Granddad made a put-up bed for John. He settled well enough in his first proper one, although he was too small for it, lost in a sea of blankets. Joan went to stay at Garth's house. It was seen as acceptable to sleep in the spare room as they'd been engaged for nearly two years. Marriage wasn't far away and she was happy to go.

Peter heeded my Mother's warning and never attempted any contact, leaving her able to settle into a quiet family life again with only a few hiccups along the way. Like the one when his Mother came banging on the door shouting about wanting to see her grandson and Grandma calmed her down by force-feeding her tea and sponge cake. They worked out a plan for when she could come round and see John, taking him for walks to the park and trips to the milk bar for ice cream. It worked well until she stopped turning up for her once-a-fortnight appointments without a word. One day Joan cornered Peter's Sister Ruby on the market as she was buying three

136

pounds of King Edwards and a cabbage. She rushed home to tell them what she'd learned.

'Ruby says that her Mum won't be coming up here anymore because Peter's got a new woman on the go and he won't have Maureen's name mentioned in the house. She says this woman doesn't even know he has a little lad with Maureen and so he's laid the law down his Mum isn't to set foot in this house again. Says he just wants to forget the past and start again.'

Grandma spent the whole of the next hour chuntering about how she couldn't believe someone would abandon their grandchild because their son had told them to.

'Well, I can't get over that, I really can't. That woman has no backbone, that's all I can say: no backbone at all. Can you credit it, eh?'

Mother sat quietly questioning why a man would lie about ever being married, with a child, making no comment until she was asked what she thought by Joan.

'What do you think then our Maureen? You must be really upset by it all?'

She wasn't. But answered her Sister anyway, 'Well, all I can say is poor bloody cow.'

This set Grandma off again in a torrent of fury.

'Don't you be feeling sorry for her. I wouldn't give up my grandchildren for no one, not for my sons or anybody, not ever. Poor cow, my arse; she should stand up for herself. Like I say, no bloody backbone.'

'No, I don't mean his Mother. I think poor cow for that woman that Peter's hooked up with. Little does she know, eh? Poor bloody cow. And as for his Mother not wanting to see John anymore, well it's no loss really: he's got one Grandma that loves him. He's better off without that family, I know I am.'

Soon after this she and Grandma went down to Wirksworth one morning to redeem the precious cornet from the pawn shop. Having it back would be a sign that life was returning to normal. They looked amongst the old gramophone records, unwanted wedding gifts and discarded family heirlooms, but were too late: it had been sold three months previously. The man behind the counter said he'd got a very good price but this was hardly any consolation. Bitterly disappointed, they made an appointment with the solicitor in his austere office on the market place to start divorce proceedings. My Mother had started to do a few hours again at Masson whilst Grandma looked after John; she put the money aside to pay for the legal fees, citing cruelty and adultery as her grounds for separation. Peter didn't contest it; if he had his new girlfriend would have found out he already had a wife. Mother was offended at the ease with which she could be discarded, but thankful nonetheless. She didn't ever want to see him again.

Chapter 22

Two years passed, the months blurring into one another. John was almost school age before she knew it; he'd been going to nursery class each afternoon to get him used to being away from the family he'd grown to love. Although he was happy to go, he was far happier coming back. When he wasn't at work, Granddad spent time with John, showing him how his motorbike engine worked and where to plant charges in a rock face in order to bring down the largest sections of limestone. It was like having a son again, a little person for him to teach the important things to, the things which mattered in life. Grandma constantly tutted.

'Samuel, that lad doesn't need to know about your bloody old bike and blowing up bits of rock, he should be in the garden digging up worms. Christ almighty, he's only four!'

It was easy living back at home for Mother, safe and relaxed with no real worries to contend with. Occasionally she thought back to the morning she left the caravan park and the promise made to herself about finding her own way in the world, but life was so cosy and comfortable there that she'd grown complacent. She should be starting afresh, making a new home for herself and standing on her own two feet. It was another two and a half years before she found a way to do it.

Mother waited patiently to find the right moment to lay out her plans and reasons. She knew Grandma would be reluctant to see them go. The response she expected was duly given.

'Our Maureen, you don't have to go you know. We like having you both here. We had a long time when we didn't see the little 'un at all and I don't want to go through that again. If you do leave, make sure you don't go too far; I want to be able to come round and see you and John. Your Dad loves that little lad. It's done him the power of good to have him around, so just think on, eh?'

With this plea in mind she started to try and find somewhere to live, trekking out each day with a newspaper to look at the houses and cottages for rent in the local area. In those days flats didn't exist and, with a child, she had to find something big enough for them both but small enough for her budget. Grandma teased at the time they would both have fitted into one room, they had so little stuff.

Mother made a list of the things she had to furnish a house:

1 pair of long curtains.
(Flowered)
1 pair of short curtains.
(Plain blue)
1 kitchen table and 2 chairs.
(Including one that wobbled because it had one leg slightly shorter than the other three)
1 two-seater settee.
(Second-hand from Mrs Myrtle's 'Nearly New' shop in the high street. The settee stood in Granddad's outhouse under three old flour sacks borrowed from Alsops Bakery in Crich. Granddad had his weathered fingers in many pies and always knew who to ask for a favour. He knew the bread man who delivered around the local villages and occasionally they would get a couple of free misshapen Hovis loaves.)
1 double divan bed.
(Without drawers)
2 single camp beds.
(Made from dark green canvas, each side having two long metal poles which slotted together and attached to rectangular bed ends. One of the beds had a damp patch where it had stood in the outside lavatory and been dripped on. There was a crack in the roof tiles, Granddad was supposed to have fixed it but it was low on his list of priorities.)

Bedding.
(Went with the three beds)
3 large boxes of kitchen utensils.
(Including a large enamel colander with chips in the rim, its dark blue undercoat showing through the creamy white top)
Plates, knives and forks.
(All odd, no complete sets)
Numerous wooden spoons.
(Mostly with burnt handles)
Kitchen knives.
(Blunt)
Aluminium pastry cutters.
(That stacked inside each other like metallic Russian matryoshka dolls and fitted inside a large plastic mixing bowl in the shape of a 'Homepride' sauce man's bowler hat. The main part of the bowl had eyes and a smiling mouth etched into the plastic)

These were the bare bones of my Mother's life, all she had gathered together since leaving her husband. But at least they were her things. No one had given them to her, no one could take them away and she didn't owe anybody anything. There wasn't a lot but there was enough to start building a new life and she was immensely proud.

She made a list of the other things she'd eventually have to buy, keeping it in her handbag, occasionally adding items and crossing others out as they were acquired or no longer deemed necessary. It was a long list.

Grandma promised her net curtains from Jennetts market stall when she knew what size her windows were. Mother would tick them off the list if she ever had any windows to hang them in.

Granddad sat with my Brother, continuing his 'education', while she set out armed with a paper to try and find the right place for them to start again. She returned on five consecutive days with no luck. One house was too big, one too small, one was beautiful and she would have loved it but it was far too expensive, and another was damp with mould growing up the bathroom wall and a musty smell in the kitchenette. My Brother was prone to asthma and, though it was a good size, Mother couldn't subject him to living somewhere that would end up making him poorly.

The last place would have been perfect, but the landlord wanted far more than a week's rent to secure the tenancy and she certainly had no intention of going down that track with him.

By the end of the third day she came home in a state of despair, having visions of being stuck with her parents for years, sharing the little back bedroom in Grandma's house with a teenage John. Much as she loved her son this was not something she wanted to think about.

Then, on the fourth day, she appeared back in the early afternoon, overjoyed but flustered, reporting that she had not only found a house but also a job to go with it in one fell swoop.

She had gone on the bus to Ambergate. Her free bus pass was invaluable, meaning she could get about to wherever she wanted, giving her the freedom she valued, particularly as she had been a prisoner in the caravan park for so long. This was a perk she'd kept from her marriage to Peter. In fact the only perk she'd had in the marriage at all.

Ambergate was as far as she could go without moving John from the little local school in Middleton. At the offset he'd hated going all day, would rather have been with his Granddad, but eventually he'd made friends and settled. The days of rushing up to the Headmistress's office every afternoon to sort out his crimes and misdemeanours were gone; she didn't want to unsettle him again.

On that fateful day she'd called into the garage to look at the village notice board and buy a quarter of peppermint creams to keep herself going until she got the chance to have some dinner. There were a couple of 'house to let' cards pinned up between the adverts written by teenage girls offering

142

their services as babysitters and cards for second-hand motor mowers. She spent a few minutes staring at the notices, taking out a pen to write down the number of a house up for rent, when the counter assistant came over and asked if she needed any help. The card looked like it had been there for some time.

'Well, I wouldn't bother writing that number down my love. The man whose house it is, well, he left it in a right old state. The last tenant had rats under the sink and the owner wouldn't even bother to get the vermin killers out from the council. He's a bit of a bad 'un if you ask me.'

Deflated, Mother sighed and mentally noted the warning.

'Mind you, my dear, it does depend on how you're fixed at the moment,' the assistant continued.

Her name was June, a stocky, blonde lanky-haired, cheerful woman in her early fifties with a twinkle in her green eyes. There wasn't anyone in the shop and the road was quiet so June put the kettle on and Mother started to warm to her over a mug of tea, discussing what had happened over the last few years and how she'd ended up trawling around villages looking for somewhere to live.

June explained why she wanted to know how Mother was fixed. There was a job going in the garage service station and the best thing about it was that it came with a house.

The owner was moving out and semi-retiring, hoping to have a bit more time to himself and concentrate on beginning a garden. He was relocating to a modern detached house he'd had built up on the hillside overlooking the river. It had a large sunny garden plot. For years he'd longed for a place where he could sow cucumbers, build a glasshouse to grow tomatoes and perhaps plant a grape vine. He'd never had the time, space or money before his Mother had died and he inherited the family home. It wasn't worth much, but along with his own savings he managed to claw the money together to have his dream home built and now he only had to work half the week in the garage. He was a very happy man.

That meant there was a vacancy going in the garage for someone willing to work hard, who had a nice way with them that the customers would like and, most importantly, was happy to live on site.

June had already decided that Mother fitted the bill.

'What do you think then Mo? Do you think you could manage it? I can ring Bill up for you now. The job's only been up since last night so there won't be anyone in the queue before you.'

'I'd love it. But do you think I could cope with working here?'

'Course you could, my love. I've no doubt about that. Why don't you nip round, have a look and see what you think? Here's the key. Go on, pop off with you and I'll ring Bill while you've gone.'

So, with key in hand, she started to cross the forecourt towards the house, eager to see inside, not quite believing her luck. These things happened to other people, folk she read about in the Sunday papers, like pools winners blessed with good fortune. They never happened to her.

Chapter 23

It was a red-brick, detached house with white painted window frames, a peacock-blue front door and a rickety wooden fence around a little front yard. She would have to get that fixed up as soon as possible. Inside, the rooms were completely bare, making it easy to see where her bits of furniture would go and what was still needed to fill the empty spaces. To her delight she thought the curtains she had would fit the windows without having to be altered. The place had a homely feel; she could imagine the fire blazing in the grate and the smell of baking wafting through from the kitchen.

She'd never worked in a garage or shop before, but with June's support she was sure it would be easy to pick up. The house coming with it was an absolute godsend even though it lowered the wages. If she could pick up another few hours a week somewhere close by then this would be the answer to all her problems. The new life was tantalisingly close; so close she could already picture herself living it. She started to panic about whether Bill would give her the job, hoping the image wouldn't fade and disappear like the spot on the telly screen when it was turned off.

By the time she got back to the shop an old van had pulled up in the car park and a balding middle-aged man in oily overalls started to walk towards her. Bill was here.

Mother nervously followed him into a back room stacked with boxes and packages. She sat between a box of soda crystals and a case of anti-freeze, telling Bill of her willingness to put her all into the job, that she would do overtime if needed, and how, given training, she would gladly learn to operate the petrol pumps and manage the fuel deliveries. He was impressed with her eager enthusiasm.

Twenty minutes later the job and house were hers. The picture on the screen was now bright and in focus.

Now the only difficult issue was how to get her belongings over there in time to start a week on Monday. It was not going to be easy to achieve as there was no way she was going to get a two-seater settee onto a bus, not to mention the other things.

Granddad called in favours; he knew all kinds of people with all sorts of transport. That same day the bed and settee were dropped down to the new house by the bread delivery man in his lorry, ending up covered in crumbs and smelling like a stale crusty bloomer. The boxes of kitchen things and camp beds were taken down to Ambergate in the back of Eric's car. Eric was Granddad's mate down at the quarry. Inordinately proud of his car, he was desperate not to get it scratched by Mother's unruly kitchen implements. Granddad persuaded him into running the errand with the promise that he would get cheap bodywork and a cut-price service once his daughter had got her feet under the garage table.

Six days after she had been given the job, everything was installed in the house.

On the seventh day she rested.

Sunday evening came; Grandma washed the tea plates and packed up a Madeira cake into a 'Tea Time Assortment' tin. They christened the newly attached sidecar of Granddad's motorbike by getting my Brother strapped into the seat with the cake tin balanced on his knees. Mother rode pillion.

Grandma was worried about three generations of her family on what she thought was a death trap, warning, 'Samuel, you'd better be careful on that soddin' bike, bloody rickety old thing. If you go and kill yourselves then don't you come running to me!'

Grandma packed my Mother a bag so that they had a few bits to tide them over until she could get some shopping done. There was a pint of milk, half a pound of butter, half a dozen eggs, a small brown loaf and a tin of beans for my Brother's breakfast before he went to school. As the bike careered through the lanes her thoughts turned to getting the shopping after she'd finished her first day at work and John had come home: such simple thoughts that most people would dismiss as unimportant. But not to her. They were a sign she was on her way.

As Granddad pulled up on the forecourt the bike jerked to a halt. The cake tin bounced off John's knee into the footwell and unceremoniously spilt its contents; luckily, Grandma's cakes were of a very solid consistency. Mother pulled off her crash helmet and fiddled in her handbag for the front door key. Glancing up at the windows of her new home, she smiled to herself; things were about to change.

Mother worked with June for the first three weeks, learning how to use the till and press the buttons to release the petrol when a customer picked up the fuel nozzle outside. Next came filling the shelves and when and how to reorder new stock for the shop. Most importantly, she was trained to check the before and after measurements on the massive underground tank which was filled up weekly. She was shown how to use the dipstick to look at the levels of stored fuel and advised never to let the petrol go below four feet because this would only last a full day and a half of normal consumption. If it got this low then a phone call to the petrol company was urgently needed and they would deliver the next day. Years later she told me how she woke up in a cold sweat night after night having dreamed she'd let the petrol tanks run dry. Cars were queuing for miles, standing in lines all the way to Derby and beyond, irate drivers hanging out of windows, protesting and shaking their fists.

Weeks later she realised that as long as the tanks were checked morning and night then that nightmare would never come to pass. She started to enjoy her job, and after the third week was left to run her shift on her own. There was a crossover time about half past two each afternoon. June would come in ready for a three o'clock start and Mother would put on her old bobbly work cardigan and be ready to leave. If they weren't busy then the two of them would have a chat over a mug of tea. June made light of her errant husband and his most recent antics, but Mother noted she looked drawn when she spoke. Sometimes her laugh sounded a little hollow and put-on making Mother think she was hiding something behind the humour. Mostly, though, they gabbed about local news and gossip picked up from people who came into the shop each day.

She began to meet people and feel part of a community. The house was now considered home. She no longer worried about being the new girl in a new place – didn't have time. Instead her mind was occupied with village trivia; who said what, who was seeing who, if Mrs Edward's bunions were playing up and whether Mr Jones' Labrador was going to respond to the ointment the vet had prescribed for its gammy leg.

Occasionally Grandma would go down on the bus and cook liver and bacon for their tea with an apple pie for afters. She would fetch John from school and get him out of his uniform into his everyday clothes, saving Mother time.

My Brother would help her make the pie, rolling the pastry out thinly and putting it over the topping in the dish before going around the edge with a fork to seal the two layers together, using the blunt edge of a knife to cut off the spare pastry. Whilst the pie cooked in the oven, Grandma cut vegetables into uneven chunks to be simmered, singing to John while she worked:

'I'm a rambler, I'm a rambler from Manchester way
I get all my pleasure the hard moorland way
I may be a wage slave on Monday
But I am a free man on Sunday.'

John learned the chorus and joined in rapturously after each verse whilst sprinkling small fists of flour onto the pastry board and rolling pin. He liked the song. It made him laugh, particularly the verse that went:

'I once loved a maid, a spot welder by trade
She was fair as the rowan in bloom
And the blue of her eye matched the June moorland sky
And I wooed her from April to June.
On the day we should have married
I went for a ramble instead,
for sooner than part from the mountain
I think I would be rather than dead'

It tickled him because he thought the idea of a woman being a spot welder was stupid. Women didn't do jobs like that. They worked in schools and hospitals as teachers, nurses and cleaners; they toiled in factories and stacked shelves in Woolworths. He had read 'Janet and John' in his class at school and the implied roles of men and women were already taking shape in his young mind.

'Grandma, you wouldn't marry a woman who was a spot welder would you? John offered this question up then burst into laughter.

'Well lad, first off I wouldn't be able to marry a woman at all. Women don't marry other women, they can't. Only men can marry women. But there's nothing wrong in a woman being a spot welder. It's a perfectly good job. I wish I'd learnt a trade when I was younger, then I might have had a different life and I wouldn't be stuck here with you making pies!' she chuckled.

'Well, I don't think its right that my wife could be a welder. What would I do when she was out welding things – stay at home and look after the children and do the washing up? That's not right. I'm not doing that. It's stupid talk that song,' he retorted petulantly.

Grandma told him that he should never marry anybody, whether they were a cleaner or a spot welder, if he didn't want to give up everything to be with that person. She was now being very serious and that made him laugh even more.

She didn't think her spurned advice was funny so gave him a clip around the ear for his cheek.

'Maybe you'll remember that my lad, if nothing else.'

Shocked by the sudden stinging in his ear, he stopped laughing immediately. It wasn't funny anymore.

Feeling guilty, she reached into her 'special items' drawer for a sugar mouse and he took it gingerly. Once it was in his mouth he forgot his throbbing ear and she forgot he'd ever angered her.

Chapter 24

Life continued at speed for Mother. Hectic days blended one into another until she'd grown accustomed to the pace, but finding her purse always empty she was soon on the look out for another part-time position to add to her income.

She scoured the job sections in the local *Mercury* and *Belper News*, looking for something nearby with hours that fit those at the garage. This proved not to be an easy prospect, but after a number of weeks pouring over the papers and ploughing through the small ads she found something that would fit: school crossing warden at my Brother's school, uniform provided, including wet-weather gear. Afternoon shift only. Perfect.

She made her application in person the very same day, bustling up the hill to the Council offices in Matlock. By the time she reached the top she had a red face and was sweating profusely, needing to sit on the wall for a few minutes and eat a Minto to calm her nerves. Mother had a theory, telling people on day trips and coach outings, even strangers at bus stops after proffering a bag.

'A Minto a day keeps you sane. No matter how hard life is, a Minto's harder. By the time you've sucked it enough, your problems are smaller, just like the sweet.'

It made no sense, but seemed to make all the sense in the world. Later I too would endorse the theory. She smelt of Mintos pretty much all her life. When the dentist warned her that her teeth were rotting and he thought it was due to the intake of confectionery consumed over the past half century, she shrugged her shoulders, paid her bill and went outside to unwrap a mint.

Recovering from the exertions of the hill, known for miles around as heart attack heights, she pulled up her coat collar to hide her orange garage overall and strode into the building. An hour later she had another new job, one hour a day.

She was spending the money already. The small extra wage from the council was completely unspoken for in the household budget, meaning she could save for some of the things she fancied for herself and the house rather than just pay bills. The first thing she'd buy would be a new set of saucepans, even though there had been pans left in the house.

'You never know what people cook in their pans or how well they clean them afterwards. I bet there's been kidney in this one,' she grumbled, peering into a big silver saucepan. 'I can't stand kidney or them that eat it.'

Grandma told her she was far too finicky for her own good.

'You shouldn't look a gift pan in the mouth.'

Mother laughed and leafed through the pages in her mail order catalogue to see what she could afford. In the years to come, what we couldn't buy from a catalogue wasn't bought at all, from clothes and shoes to twin-tub washing machines. Pay so much a week and, what with the interest, by the time the item was paid for it had long since died a death. Life's needs began and ended within the pages of a club book. It started with the pans.

Her working hours as a lollipop woman increased as she started to supervise the after-school clubs. The time that my Brother spent at school increased with it, much to his dismay. Discipline and rules weren't for him. He spent as much time outside of the classroom as possible, purposely cheeking the teachers to escape lessons or taking far longer than he should have to run errands. But even then he had a certain roguish charm which meant he got away with far more than he should. His disgust at having to hang around the school three-quarters of an hour longer than necessary each day, so his own Mother could show his arch rivals and their parents across the road, was written all over his sulking face. This was not a happy lad.

Each day he pleaded with Mother to pack the job in and find something else that didn't involve his school. She turned a deaf ear, a skill she would find very useful in the future.

He was embarrassed at the sight of her standing outside the school each day in a an orange coat with a big stick; that he couldn't play with his mates in the way he wanted, suspecting the ever-watchful 'weather eye' was on him.

To some extent it was.

Grandma had her doubts about my Brother. She'd spent enough time with him to witness his unpredictable mood swings.

'That lad of yours takes after his Dad,' she said astutely.

'Don't say things like that Mother, you couldn't wish that on any bugger,' came the reply.

'Well, you can hide your head in the sand my girl. But you mark my words, he's got a bad streak he has and I won't be far wrong.'

It wouldn't take many more years and Grandma, inevitably, would be proved to be right.

Chapter 25

Mother continued her twin jobs, becoming acquainted with more and more people at school and in the village where they lived. Some people she liked immediately, quickly calling them friends; some she didn't like at all, avoiding their presence like the plague. Ad some were merely tolerated, only spoken to when caught in the queue at the Co-op.

She took the bus into Belper every Friday to do her weekly shop, and used the main post office to cash her family allowance, buy her stamps and pay her club book. Try as she might, she just couldn't take to the couple behind the counter, trying to be sociable but finding them condescending. They weren't keen on the working class, looking down their noses at her standing there in her lollipop woman coat. Once she heard them talking to a loud-voiced plummy woman about the lower classes and how it was their duty to try and educate them through politics. From that moment on they fell into the 'plague' category, but had to be tolerated because she couldn't buy TV licence stamps anywhere else. She was working class and proud of it.

Mother couldn't abide snobbery and, worse than that, couldn't stand Conservatives with a big 'C'. Especially when they were on her doorstep.

Two weeks before the local government elections Mother hadn't been in from work long when there was an official-sounding knock at the front door, interrupting her as she tried to sort the washing. She unceremoniously dumped the armful of underpants and handkerchiefs down on the floor, wiping her hands on her pinny front and muttering under her breath, 'bloody people. Can't they see I'm busy? I bet it's some bugger selling something.'

On the other side of the door stood Mr and Mrs Ashford, Brian and Angela; or Brian the postmaster and Angela the local

Tory councillor. Mother dubiously said hello and wondered why they were on her doorstep this late on a Tuesday evening. Brian pushed a pamphlet into her hands. She scanned the front very quickly: 'Vote Conservative and keep your local Council safe'.

She turned the booklet around in her hand, held it back out and, despite being annoyed at their arrival on her doorstep, said in her politest voice, 'no thank you.'

Brian said slowly and quietly in best his best postmaster manner, 'now Maureen, the Council are counting on you to put your ballot in the box. Can we depend on you to vote the right way and elect your Conservative candidate?'

He had a tone she found patronising, rubbing her up the wrong way.

She glanced at the smiling Angela before turning back to Brian. With an equally calm, measured voice she made sure her reply was totally understood the first time.

'Thank you for the leaflet and your invitation. I will be voting, but to be honest I would rather cut my bloody hand off then vote for you lot!'

The colour rapidly drained out of Angela's face. Brian coughed, trying not to choke, managing to spit out, 'Good day to you then and thank you for your time.'

It fell on deaf ears. The door was already closing behind Mother as she returned to her washing with a look of satisfaction on her face, giggling to herself. She remembered something she'd heard on the radio in the garage about how to make friends and influence people. Well, she hadn't made any friends there. In fact the next time she bought a stamp the atmosphere was decidedly frosty.

She heated up the copper, inherited from Bill. It was a tall rectangular boiler which held six buckets of water and plugged into the electricity. It boiled rather like a kettle, except a lot slower. An hour and a half and a lot of shillings through the electricity meter later, the water was hot enough for the soap powder to be added. The whites went in first, then coloureds, towels, and lastly my Brother's socks, which smelt strong enough to knock out an army at twenty paces. Mother called them his secret weapon.

Working through the household chores she thought about the characters she'd met since her move, thankful they weren't all as pompous as Brian and Angela.

All kinds of people, from young to old, came into the garage. There were my Brother's school friends, who lived in the village, although there weren't as many of them as he'd have liked, most living closer to the school. Only a handful of them lived in the surrounding lanes and neighbouring hamlets. My Mother served them 'Liquorice Laces' and 'Black Jacks', occasionally popping in free chocolate-covered toffees whose wrappers had been torn or peeled away. This made her extremely popular in her role as benefactress of the sweet tooth.

Then there were the adults she met in the garage. Thursdays brought in the old folk who went to cash their pensions next door at the sub-post office inside the little shop before coming to the garage to buy newspapers and the odd packet of cigarettes. The garage and the shop had an unwritten agreement: the garage wouldn't sell ice cream or bread and the shop reciprocated by not stocking papers or fags. It meant that neither had to compete against the other, keeping them both afloat.

At exactly half past ten Mrs Evans would come in to buy her *Matlock Mercury* and *Derbyshire Times*, regular as clockwork. They were supposed to be delivered by the paperboy at teatime but Mrs Evans always came in long before there was a chance for them to be dispatched. Even so, she always put two shillings in the paper lad's Christmas box to say thank you. She said she couldn't wait for the papers to come; the lure of the gossip and the births, deaths and marriages were too much for her.

'One of these days my name will be in one of those boxes,' she grinned toothlessly. 'I want to make sure I see it first!'

My Mother smiled back, unsure whether she was serious or meant she was going to get married, give birth or be found deceased. It couldn't be birth, as Mrs Evans was seventy-six if she was a day. It wouldn't be marriage; she already had a husband she couldn't stand and wouldn't want another one. It

155

was most likely to be the last option. She shrugged her shoulders and decided to take no notice.

Joe Else would come in about eleven with most of his pension still intact. By half past six that evening his pocket would be almost empty. He bought a book of stamps and paid a couple of pounds towards his gas bill arrears in the post office, before moving on to his main shopping: two loaves, a Victoria Sandwich, two tins of beans, one tin of potatoes, a packet of dried fruit, a bag of flour and half a dozen eggs. He then shuffled on to the garage where he brought his essentials: two hundred un-tipped Woodbines, half an ounce of hand rolling tobacco, three packets of fag papers and a bag of humbugs. Always the same shopping. He counted the money from his battered wallet and added up what was left: his allowance to spend in the local pub, the White House, just down the road. By teatime that day he would have a couple of quid left to see him through to next Thursday and a blinding headache to see him through to Saturday morning. Before leaving the garage and hauling his weekly staples back to his prefab, he opened his bag of humbugs, took one out and put it in Mother's hand.

'There you go girl. Have a mint on me.'

He wasn't the wisest of old men but he had a certain charm.

Then there was May. May Clarke. She came in each Thursday dinnertime and paid off her paper bill, a *Derby Evening Telegraph* each evening and a *Sunday People* on the weekend. Occasionally she would buy a *Matlock Mercury*, but only if she fancied what was on the front cover.

May loved to stand and have a chat. She'd been used to seeing June over the past year or two and initially was a bit put out at seeing someone new behind the till. She spent a few minutes browsing the magazines and eyeing my Mother as she pushed the petrol pump buttons and took the money from the customers.

She studied my Mother's face with great interest, then switched her attention to the condition of her hands.

156

Eventually she marched towards the counter and said tersely, 'good morning young woman. I am Mrs Clarke from Belford. When I get to know you a little better you might be allowed to call me May. I will let you know when that is. Until then I have come to pay my paper bill. My name is under 'C' in the ledger.'

Taken aback somewhat, Mother coughed and tried not to laugh as she made a mental note to mention this overbearing woman at shift changeover. She found the ledger, ticked the payment off Mrs Clarke's bill and took her money. May waited while she wrote out the receipt, then took it, folded it in half and placed it in the back of her purse. Before turning to leave she said more gently, 'well, it was nice to meet you Maureen and I shall see you again next week.'

Mother said goodbye cheerfully, unsure what to make of the little five-foot-two woman with the commanding voice and imposing manner, puzzling over how she'd known her name. At some point she would no doubt find out.

Weeks went on and May continued to come in every Thursday to pay her paper bill. Mother served her each time and was polite and friendly. May started to relax in her company, talking about her garden, how she was growing potatoes and onions in the top section and raspberries, strawberries and blackcurrants at the bottom. She presented her with a jar of jam made the previous year and banged it down on the garage counter.

'There you go lass. Have this for your tea. I bet that lad of yours has got a sweet tooth. I know mine always did.'

Mother nodded and thanked her, a bit taken aback by the sudden act of generosity.

'Yes, my Wilfred,' May continued. 'He was a bugger. He'd go off in the morning on his pushbike; a half loaf of bread and a pot of jam and off he'd go, all day, mile on mile on that bicycle. He always told me his favourite bit of the day was when he leaned his bike up against a wall and sat down for his dinner: chunks of bread smothered in jam. Said the sugar gave him extra energy.'

Mother laughed, then wasn't sure she should have, anxious in case she'd offended her. But May laughed back, a little laugh that turned into a real laugh, a laugh that brought a glow to her cheeks and a sparkle to her grey-green eyes, deepening the creases underneath. May regained her composure and took in a breath.

'You and your lad; why don't you come for your tea on Sunday? Nothing fancy like. I'm making a cake and there'll be a baked ham and bits. Mind you, you'll have to put up with my Jack; he's a funny one. The neighbours say he's dour. I've never thought so but you'll have to make your own mind up, eh.' She said all this without expending the breath she'd taken in the first place.

My Mother was even more taken aback now. She held the jam in her hands and stared at the label, both surprised and touched by the offer.

'Thank you Mrs Clarke, that'd be lovely. I'd like that. I'm sure John would like it too, he's a glutton for cake.'

'I think you can call me May now, Maureen. Don't you?'

My Mother smiled. She'd been accepted.

'We shall see you on Sunday then, about three o'clock?' And without waiting for confirmation May turned and walked out of the garage.

When June heard about the invitation she was incredulous, exclaiming, 'well, in all the years I've served that woman she's never once invited me for a cup of tea, never mind cake with her and Jack. Crickey, Mo, you are honoured!'

Mother got the impression that June was equally stunned, May didn't take to many people and they debated why she had become one of the chosen few.

Chapter 26

Sunday came around quick enough; it was Mother's turn to work the half-day. She busied herself around the shop and restocked the refrigerated cabinet with pork pies and cheese slices until it was time for her shift to end. At one o'clock she nipped across the forecourt and prised John from in front of the telly for their excursion to Belford. She dressed him in his best sweater, made by Grandma in grey double knit wool unpicked from Uncle Roland's unwanted cable cardigan. He hated it when he first put it on, standing with his arms out at right angles like a scarecrow. Grandma told him to stop being stupid and Mother smacked him sharply on the legs, but he still complained; it made him itch and he wouldn't put it on. Twenty wears later he had given up and wore it with a resigned gloom. Today, when he reached May's house, he forgot the mysterious itching, having been given a slab of yellow crumbly Madeira cake in one hand and the lead to Bill, a rather portly, rambunctious Jack Russell in the other. He wandered around the garden, munching on the cake, struggling not to drop any while having his other arm pulled out of its socket. Mother was introduced to Jack – not the Russell outside, but May's husband.

Initially described by May as being dour, he gave Mother a different first impression. He was a tall, slightly built, white-haired man with glasses. The combination of freckles across his nose and the greenest eyes she'd ever seen led her to ask, 'Jack, did you have red hair when you were a young man?'

He smiled mischievously at her and replied in his soft Hebridean lilt, 'however did you guess that young woman?'

May laughed and chided him gently, 'Now then Jack, don't you be sarky with Maureen,' before explaining to Mother, 'You'll get used to his ways eventually. I know I have!'

She picked up a gilt-edged frame from the top of the Welsh dresser.

159

'These are my grandchildren, our Wilfred's kiddies: girl called Joanne and a boy called Andrew. That's the exact same hair colour Jack had when I met him all those years ago.'

Mother took the photograph, peered closely at the two young red-haired children and joked, 'I bet you saw him coming didn't you May?'

May let loose her infectious giggle and replied, 'he always looked like a Belisha beacon to me; I could spot him for miles in a crowd. Mind you, he did look handsome in his army uniform. That's when I first saw him, on a parade through the town. The whole battalion of the Sherwood Foresters regiment, boots gleaming. When they fell out they were supposed to be talking to potential new recruits. I made a bit of a beeline for him I'm ashamed to say.'

Jack winked and teased, 'I thought you were only interested in finding out how to enrol with the Foresters! It wasn't until you made that cake a couple of Sundays later and gave it to me for the barracks that I realised we were walking out together.'

'Funny how things happen,' May reminisced, 'He went off to the front in 1917 and I thought it'd be the last I saw of him. We said we would get married if he came back. It seemed like a big 'if' then; we were only nineteen and young and bonny-faced. With all the lads that had gone to war and not come back, I didn't pin my hopes on him; at least I tried not to. Then, in his own particular style, like the bad penny he was, he rolled back up again in the December of 1918, two stone lighter, all skin and bone. He'd proved me wrong and we were married in two months.'

'She still makes a good cake,' Jack quipped, cutting a big slice of Madeira and passing it to my Mother. The afternoon went well; after a couple of hours my Mother and Brother were packed up with half a cake, six thick slices of ham, another pot of blackberry jam and an invitation to come next Sunday if they wanted. She did, and even John didn't mind.

Several weekends passed in a similar fashion. John's sharp edges softened, at least for a little while. A chunk of Angel or Madeira cake and a boisterous Jack Russell would always make a day with the neighbours more bearable.

Chapter 27

Weekdays started with the problem of dragging John out of bed. There was a definite timetable in the morning that needed adhering to in order to make sure he got on the 8.10 bus. Mother was like the sergeant major, drilling her battalion of one unwilling soldier, trying to get him to march in time and not fall out of line. He wasn't one for structure: reciting times-tables and learning the scales on a recorder were not for him. He was only interested in life when he was on summer holiday from school and could fire his catapult at Mrs Braithwaite's Ginger Tom, or pinch the apples from the tree in Mr Cooper's back garden. When Mother came home in the afternoons he wasn't forced to do anything more than slouch around the house or lounge in front of the telly pretending to be The Lone Ranger. For those idyllic six weeks there was no strict timekeeper clocking his every move.

My Mother had become a stickler for time: never late and, if there was a choice, liked to be more than early. On the rare occasions she ever caught the train she checked it was the right one at least twenty-seven times and was on that platform half an hour before it was even due in.

Years later she blamed this obsession with punctuality on the cautionary tale of her Grandmother missing the works bell and forfeiting her wages.

My Mother had never met her Grandmother; Eliza was the first of the line to have been born outside the Ukraine and had died in an unfortunate accident before she was born. The horse-drawn trolley bus she was riding rounded the corner too fast, at too much of an angle, and tipped over. Eliza was on the step ready to get off at the corner of Jessop Street; she had been to the chemist for a bottle of Sloan's Liniment for her husband's bad knee. He had twisted it the previous day making a sliding tackle in the local football league. Eliza never got home that day and her husband never got his liniment. The strange thing was that when he went to identify her body, the casket was open and there was an overwhelming smell of camphor. He thought it was a new kind of embalming fluid until the undertaker asked if he wanted a simple burial – cheap – or a full service burial – not so cheap. Apart from the lining of the coffin and the handles, the main difference was the issue of embalming. The realisation that his wife had already been embalmed with Sloan's Liniment influenced his decision and he went for the cheaper option.

Anyhow, Eliza had indeed once been locked out of Masson Mill for being late. The bell had ominously tolled 8 a.m. as she ran down the road, her dinnertime sandwiches clutched in her hand. As she charged round the corner the great wooden gates swung closed and the inside latch clicked into place. The gate was used by the maintenance workers who mended the weavers' looms and winding machines and unravelled the water weed from the mill turbine. This was not a job for the faint hearted, mostly because of the putrid smell, but also because young Billy Sullivan had lost two fingers when the wheel freed quicker than he bargained for.

Eliza banged and hammered for what seemed like an age until the works foreman, Eric Adkins, opened the gate, showing his disapproval by sternly frowning at her and questioning why she was late. The story went like this: Eliza's Mother, Alauda, went to work for 6 a.m. at the Derby Road Doctor's Practice, where she cleaned the surgery and dispensary, then swept out and made up the fire in the grate in time for Doctor Morley to see his patients. She usually left her six-month-old son sleeping with his father who had just finished a night shift at Stevenson's Wire Works, but this morning the baby had woken early with colic. Not wanting to keep her husband awake she'd left Eliza trying to pacify her Brother. An hour of 'Wind the Bobbin Up', face-pulling and gentle rocking later, he still wouldn't settle. Worrying about her own fast-approaching clocking-in time, she decided to race down to her Mother's work place and hand him over. Running down Gorsey Bank with the baby screaming his lungs out woke up the whole of Wirksworth; by the time they arrived, he was distraught and she wished she was deaf. Eliza dumped the baby on her Mother and, with a mouthful of the doctor's cherry cake – a very rare treat – noticed it was already ten minutes to eight. There was no way of getting back up Gorsey Bank then down Green Hill to Masson in ten minutes, not even if she ran as fast as a greyhound chasing a rabbit, so she took the direct route across old man Stenson's meadow. This was a field full of blackberries in late summer and a herd of cows with the occasional bull for the rest of the year. Eliza didn't like cows, had hated them since one had charged her when she was picking blackberries along the fence as a child; she'd dropped her rag doll in the rush to get away and the cows had trampled it into the mud. This time she successfully avoided the herd and, looking up, saw the mill was now in view and there was still a minute or two to spare. However, those minutes ticked away when she tried to hurdle the stile into the lane, getting snared on the barbed wire. Her skirts were ripped and she'd snagged her stockings.

She managed to condense the sorry saga into four breathless sentences for Mr Adkins' benefit, even trying to impress upon him how much she despised cows, hoping he would take pity and allow her back into work. She raised her tattered skirt slightly to display her ripped stockings. The foreman's face went from pale with shock to scarlet with embarrassment, changing colour like a traffic light. The only ankle he was used to seeing was his wife's, and he didn't see that very often; it wasn't seemly to be looking at another woman's legs.

Eliza took a breath, not that she had a great deal of breath left, and finished her tale.

'The bell was clanging and I ran as fast as I could Mr Adkins, but I didn't manage it; the gate had just shut.' She'd started to cry now. 'Will you let me in? I've never been late or missed a day at work before. I've never had a day off sick even when I've been proper poorly.'

The foreman laid his hand on her arm and said in a consoling voice, 'I'm sorry young Eliza but rules is rules.

163

Happen next time you'll think twice before you make yourself late. Now you get off home and we'll see you tomorrow, eh?'

He turned sharply and disappeared back through the gate from where he'd appeared five minutes earlier.

Eliza vowed from that day onwards to get up that extra bit early, then if she had to run another mercy mission there would be time to do it without ever being late for work again. In fact, she was never late for anything. She drove her husband mad with it, demanding he was equally early for everything they did together, even if it meant standing out in a downpour waiting for the music hall or pub to open. Once she'd died her husband reverted back to his old ways. He'd been chivvied along by his wife for so long that when she was no longer there he couldn't even get up for work on time. He'd have been late for his own funeral if it was left up to him.

My Mother had inherited her mania for timekeeping from Grandma, as if it had been passed down the maternal line from Eliza.

She would drag my Brother up each morning for school, packing him off for a wash before setting about the food for tea. It was all done with military precision and meant the meal would always be on the table at exactly 5.30 every evening. She timed it to perfection. Potatoes were peeled and left immersed in a pan of water ready to light; the tin of stewed steak was waiting on the worktop; apples were cooked in the morning and left to go cold, primed for putting under a piecrust. My Mother always thought that pies were best made with cold fillings and tinned meat was the salvation of the working mother. Anything to not waste precious time.

She was a good cook then, even with her dependency on canned provisions, though as she aged she acquired some interesting culinary techniques, learning to overcook everything. Christmas morning was the best time to see these dubious kitchen skills at their best. The turkey went on at half past six closely followed by the vegetables, though on a low light. By midday, the traditional time for Christmas lunch in my Mother's house – though she always called it dinner – the carrots disintegrated when they came in contact with a fork,

164

the potatoes all but mashed themselves in the pan and the cauliflower developed a distinct pink tinge. Greens, though, remained the brightest of shades. She swore by a pinch of bicarbonate of soda in the water to keep their colour, though the taste was certainly not one of cabbage or sprouts.

Christmas, however, was a special occasion, when monotony was pushed aside by rich food, long-saved-for gifts and the odd drop of Harvey's Bristol Cream. Today, though, was just the start of an ordinary working day for Mother and another dismal day at school for my Brother. After he'd eaten only a couple of mouthfuls of Shredded Wheat, and pushed the rest around the bowl for as long as possible, it was time for Mother to walk him to the bus stop. He lagged behind, scuffing the sides of his shoes down the pavement edge as he trudged along. It was a usual Thursday.

May came into the garage for her bits and pieces at eleven o'clock, as always. She was her usual self and full of tittle-tattle, chatting to Mrs Mason about the fish she had got from the mobile delivery van that travelled around the little Derbyshire villages each Wednesday. She told her she sometimes thought the fish was a bit stale, but the bit of cod she'd had the night before was as fresh as if it had swum onto the plate by itself. Mother could tell May was in a good mood. She would usually only give Mrs Mason the time of day and no more, saying she had a whiff of mothballs about her; she couldn't be doing with that whilst trying to pick her boiled sweets for the week.

When the garage rush had cleared, May came over to the counter where Mother was busily stacking boxes of matches into their specific compartment on the shelf. Try as she might she couldn't keep her home as ordered, especially since John had brought home a scruffy mongrel that had outstayed its welcome at his friend's. They had both been abandoned in some way: John by his father, the dog by its owners. My Brother sensed a kindred spirit; Mother just sensed trouble. The ensuing mess was driving her to distraction: 'I just can't keep that bloody house clean, what with John leaving his mucky finger marks everywhere and that dog moulting all over the carpet and peeing in the kitchen. Making me bloody hairless it is!'

May laughed sympathetically at her plight, then the smile faded, replaced by a solemn air.

'Put the kettle on Mo, I've something I want to ask you about.'

Mother knew immediately that something important was in the air and came back to the counter with two steaming mugs, looking quizzically at May as if to prompt her to carry on.

'Mo, when something happens to me, and it will, I'm getting on in years now, I need you to promise me something.'

Mother replied with a cautious smile and encouraged her to go on.

'Well, I will if I can. Mind you, you'll have to tell me what it is.'

May continued, if a little hesitantly.

'When I go, will you look after Jack for me? He's like a baby bird. I do most things for him; he can't even cook an egg never mind manage a house. I know it's a big thing to ask, but will you look after him? Then I can die with peace of mind, knowing he'll be taken care of.'

Mother looked puzzled, unable to grasp the full motive behind the unexpected request. She spoke slowly, as if measuring her words.

'Well, I don't know how much help to him I'd be. I don't really know him very well, do I May?' She paused, then answered her own question. 'I suppose I'll have to make more time to get to know him a bit better, but don't you be worrying about things like that; you'll be around for a good few years yet.'

May looked as if a weight had been lifted from her shoulders. With a preoccupied expression she patted her friend's hand, swigged down her tea, turned tails and left the garage.

Three weeks later, around about half past nine, the door of the garage burst open and in flew Jack, clearly out of breath. He was unkempt; a wild, lost look in is eyes. Mother knew straight away what he'd come to tell her without him even having to speak, but speak he did in rambling, broken sentences.

'She's gone Mo. She didn't feel right well last night and said she had a pain in her arm. I told her I thought it was wind, but she did look a bit funny, a bit grey... I said I'd go to the phone box and call for the doctor. She wouldn't have it, though; said she'd be all right after a good night's sleep. She had this awful cough. It had been getting worse over the last week and it were making her tired. She couldn't get a good night's sleep or nothing. Mind you, she wouldn't rest even though I begged her to, was baking all day yesterday, told me she couldn't be leaving me without a cake for Sunday. I told her I wasn't bothered about a cake, but she wouldn't have it. Then last night before bed she said I was to come to you when she'd gone and you'd know what to do...'

With that he fell silent and looked away as the tears started to trickle down his face.

Actually, Mother didn't have a clue what to do, but a promise was a promise. She rang up Bill the garage owner and told him there'd been a death in the family. It wasn't really lying; they'd become almost that. She locked up the garage, turned off the pumps, and they started the sombre, heavy-hearted walk back to Belford.

When they got there Mother fully expected to see May in her high-backed armchair, knitting in her hands, smiling as she did each Sunday. Instead, there was an empty space. The chair was in the garden; Wilfred had set fire to it and was morosely watching it burn. Mother had never met May and Jack's son, but he seemed to know who she was and that she was there to help.

Inside, the house was spick and span. Wilfred had tidied up and cleaned through in the time that his Dad had struggled to the garage and back. He said it had given him something to do whilst he waited for the funeral director to come and take his Mother's body to the chapel of rest in Belper. The doctor had been already and pronounced her dead. He mumbled again he was just waiting for the undertaker; in fact, he repeated this sentence several times as a kind of lament.

Three weeks later the funeral was over and the dust had settled. Life laboured on as normal. Well almost.

167

My Mother spent most of her time going backwards and forwards between Ambergate, Middleton and Belford. When she wasn't in the garage or on the school crossing, she was on her feet or travelling between them. The only time she ever got to sit down or catch her breath was on a bus seat.

One Tuesday teatime she arrived flustered at Jack's house, laden down with his shopping for the week; crabby child in tow. John was moaning about walking all the way to Belford when he'd had a hard day at school. Mother chastised him for his whinging.

'What are you on about lad? I've been up since six, done a shift in the garage and the lollipop run as well. And I've done the shopping and walked here without mithering on. You don't know you're born!'

Jack was sitting in the front room smoking his pipe. He'd heard all their conversation as they came down the front path and it confirmed his suspicions; she was overdoing it, worn out, especially with the extra running about after him. He frowned and went into the kitchen to put the kettle on. He'd baked a cake using one of May's old recipes; no one had her touch and it had come out a bit flat and biscuit-like. Nevertheless, he cut three chunks, giving the biggest bit to John to keep him quiet.

'Thank you for getting my messages from the shop Maureen, you're very good to me'.

'What does he mean "messages" Mother? You only got bread and milk didn't you? Nobody gave you any messages to bring for Jack did they?' butted in John.

'John, it's Mr Clarke to you, and messages is Scottish for shopping, that's all. Nothing for you to be worrying about. Now eat your cake and there's pop in the fridge if you want a mug.'

Jack chuckled and took a bite of his cake.

'It's a bit chewy this. Supposed to be sponge, but it's more like a flapjack. Hope it doesn't pull your teeth out,' he laughed again. 'Come and sit yourself down for a minute lass, I have something to ask you.'

168

She followed him into the front room, leaving John stuffing cake into his mouth quite happily. She flopped down on the settee and yawned.

'I'd better not sit here too long or I'll be asleep. I've got to get me laddo home and bathed for school. The nit nurse is coming tomorrow and I can't be sending him with that bird's nest he's got on his head at the moment. She'll think I don't look after him and then I'll have the school inspector on the doorstep. He gets me into enough bother as it is, little bugger!'

'I think you're doing too much, running back and forth for me with all that work you do. I've been thinking. You can say no if you don't think it's a good idea, but as I say, I've been thinking that happen you should come and live here with me. Save on running about so much and maybe then you can pack in the job at the crossing. You won't have so much to pay out; there'll be no bills for you here. Anyhow, I'll understand if you don't think it's a good idea. You think on it.'

Mother was flabbergasted; hadn't seen it coming and didn't even begin to know how to respond. Her head was swimming. He, on the other hand, had obviously given it a lot of thought. It couldn't be brushed off lightly, but jumping in with an answer, whether it be positive or negative, wouldn't be the wisest thing to do. She needed time to think, so, after having a tidy round and putting his tea on the stove, told him carefully.

'I do appreciate what you said Jack. I'll think about it and tell you tomorrow. It's a big decision for both of us; you should have another think about it as well. What with you getting on in years you might not want a mad eight-year-old running around moaning all day long. Let me tell you, he gets on my nerves and I'm nearly forty years younger than you. Then there's that bloody dog; that'll be two you'll have. Think on, you might have changed your mind by tomorrow anyhow. You let me know if you have, eh?'

With that she patted Jack's arm affectionately, gathered up her coat and son and set off for home.

All the way back John jabbered on about Simon Partridge's Dad's new car, but she didn't hear a word, was too absorbed in her own thoughts, pondering the move and whether it was wise. Plus points: certainly she could do with the rest, and not having to pay any bills would be useful. Perhaps she could even save up a little money. Minus points: what would the neighbours say? What would the family up in Middleton think? She could imagine what her own Mother would make of it and would rather not dwell on that prospect. It all spun round and round in her head with no let up until sleeping on it seemed the most viable option.

Except she didn't sleep and the spinning didn't stop. What would May think if she was looking down on it all? How would John react to the upheaval? He would have to move schools if they went to live in Belford because it was too far to walk him before getting on the school bus in Ambergate. If he didn't change schools she'd have to get him up even earlier, much earlier and it wouldn't be worth putting him to bed at all, what with all the morning palaver. Then there was her Mother. Grandma was already scathing about the fact that she ran after Jack so much. In her eyes, Mother should be sticking to her own family, not chasing around after someone else's. Moving in would have Grandma teetering on one of her 'edges' again.

Morning came around in its own inevitable way and Mother started another day bleary-eyed and weary of the world. She hauled John out of bed, pulling the sheets and blanket with him as he fought to stay in it, then rubbed a wet flannel across his face in an attempt at a cat's lick. He protested no end as he was force-fed his Shredded Wheat, continuing his grievance all the way to the bus stop. She gladly shoved him onto the bus and went back to the garage for another shift of relentless pensioners and never-ending petrol customers complaining about the weather. There was just time to stuff down a cheese and beetroot sandwich before donning her lollipop overall and charging off to her next job. The crossing shift was done in driving sleet, the sky the colour of an anvil, then a miserable, whining John was rounded up before they caught the bus home again. John bleated on about what he'd been made to do at school and that Steven Pratt had got new boots for his birthday; at least he wasn't waiting for his mother with freezing feet. She leaned against the window, drifting in and out of listening to him until the gritty sound of sleet hitting the pane lulled her off to sleep. Six miles passed until the bus jolted to a halt, waking her with a start to find John still creating about boots. Mother stumbled off and pulled herself together as the icy cold bit at her cheeks on the way down the lane. June waved cheerfully as the pair of them approached.

'Mo, you look worn out girl. You should pack that other job in. You'll work yourself into the ground. Get yourself a rest and put your feet up for a bit, eh?' June shouted after her as she disappeared into the house.

Inside she spooned some tea into the pot. As she waited for the kettle to boil, she fiddled with the pans of pre-peeled vegetables. Sitting down with her tea, she lit a cigarette and puffed her way through it, realising she only ever smoked when a problem needed to be solved; it usually helped her come to a decision, although after the stresses of the day that decision was already half-made without the aid of nicotine.

'Mother, are we going to Belford tonight? I have to make a cake in cookery tomorrow and I thought I might be able to borrow a recipe from Mrs Clarke's book. Do you think we could go? We have to take our own recipe and I know you haven't got any cookery books. Grandma would help me but I won't see her 'til it's too late. So can we?'

Mother was surprised by John actually asking to go to Belford and decided she should take the opportunity to see Jack whilst the going was good.

After tea they set off and as they walked she quizzed John about what he thought of Jack and the cottage, even whether he'd like to live there.

'I like the garden; I like the dog and the room to run about. Jack's all right, I don't always know what he's saying but I like his pipe. I'd like to smoke a pipe. Can I smoke a pipe Mother?'

'Well, you might one day, but not yet. You're far too young to be smoking anything, never mind a pipe. But you wouldn't mind too much if we ended up living there then?'

'I wouldn't mind living there but then where would Jack live? In our house?'

'No, we'd be living there with Jack. We'd share a room, me and you. We'd have a bit more money living there and I wouldn't have to work up at your school anymore. I wouldn't be so tired all the time and you wouldn't have to get on the bus so early. What do you think?'

'It sounds all right to me… What sort of cake can I make out of Mrs Clarke's book? Have we got any currants at home?'

And so it was decided.

Chapter 28

They moved out of the forecourt house and into the cottage in Belford, from relative space to being slightly squashed into a tiny farm worker's cottage. She enrolled John in the local primary school, Long Row, which sat at the bottom of a long, steep flagstone street that seemed to stretch up to the heavens.

It was a much larger school than the little primary he had attended in Middleton, the classes were bigger and the teachers didn't have as much time for each child on a one-to-one basis. John didn't know any of the other children and each morning brought a more intense battle than ever to get him to go. Mother tried to convince him he would soon make new friends; he eventually did but they weren't the sort of friends she would have liked. They were the rough boys that lived on one of the top estates, lads that pinched from shops and threw stones at passing trains. John felt he'd found his niche; Mother felt she'd found a load of trouble. After a few weeks of believing he had settled, official school envelopes started dropping on the mat. She found out he'd been given letters to bring home but they'd never got there: they were thrown over the river wall or stuffed in a hedge on the way. The teachers realised they weren't getting to their intended recipient and started to use more efficient measures:

Mrs Starr, one read,

John has been very disruptive in his class over the last two weeks. He has not been undertaking his homework in the specified manner and, in fact, has not handed in anything he has been asked to do over the last week at all.

It is assumed that you are not aware of these matters, therefore could you come into school one evening this week and have an informal chat with John's form teacher, Mrs Frost, about these and other concerns.

Yours Sincerely

Mrs E. Coop
Headmistress.

Mother carefully read the letter twice then thrust it at Jack. They both shook their heads in despair.

'I'd better go down there tonight hadn't I? Find out what's been going on.'

'Do you want me to come with you Maureen?' Jack answered.

'No, I'll go on my own. You shouldn't have to put up with his performances anymore than you already do, little bugger. Honestly, I can't trust him out of my sight for more than two minutes.'

So, when teatime came around, she walked thoughtfully to the school. All the way she chewed over in her mind what she was going to say to Mrs Frost, then chewed it again. How would she explain John's behaviour? How would she deal with him when they got home? Would a week with no telly make him see sense?

At Long Row she waited apprehensively outside the classroom for the children to finish lessons and file out. The bell rang and twenty-three scruffy kids surged into the playground, shouting and hurtling towards their Mothers and the ice cream van which was parked opportunely outside the gates. Mrs Mazza wasn't one to miss the chance for a profit; when it was too cold for cornets she could always sell sherbet lemons and treacle toffee.

John had belted out with them, busy playing karate kicks with a boy from his class, unaware his Mother was standing under the veranda watching him. He headed for the gates, shouting loudly how he was going to break his friend's head like a brick. She yelled out to him; he stopped dead in his tracks and turned, face falling when he caught sight of her. He started to walk reluctantly back.

'What are you doing here Mother? You're not going to start working at this school now are you? It's bad enough me having to come here without having you here as well.

174

'Don't you be so cheeky. I'm here because I've had a letter from the school about your behaviour, so I'll have less of your lip my lad. You come and stand here. There'll be no more Kung Fu tonight. We've got to speak to Mrs Frost about it all.'

His face fell even further still and he stood sullenly next to her.

The door to the classroom opened and Mrs Frost emerged carrying her cherry shoulder bag and a pile of Ladybird books. A kindly faced, full-figured woman of about forty, she clearly wasn't expecting any visitors and looked a little perplexed.

'Oh, Mrs Starr, you should have knocked. There was no need to be standing outside waiting, especially in such awful weather. Come on in and we'll have a little chat. Mrs Coop told me she'd written to you; sit yourself down. Would you like a cup of tea. I'm sure I could get someone to rustle us up a pot?' she said, in a soft, well-spoken voice.

'I'll have one Mrs Frost,' chirped in John.

Mother was embarrassed by his remark. 'Have I not told you to stop it with your cheek already once today. Apologise to your teacher. No, I won't have a cup, thank you Mrs Frost, I have to get back to get Jack and this little pest their tea.'

'Oh, is Jack your husband Mrs Starr? I quite understand, I won't keep you here for longer than necessary.'

'No, he's not my dad. He's an old bloke we live with,' piped up John again. This time Mother just glared at him and let the comment go.

'Anyway, it's John's behaviour, Mrs Starr. He's been very vindictive towards his classmates recently and has also been missing school: registering first thing then disappearing with James Burkett. His Mother has also been called in to have a chat. We've tried to contact you about this before but I assume you haven't been getting the notes.' She paused. 'Has she John?' she asked accusingly.

John said nothing and sat squirming. Being caught out had never crossed his mind.

'Well, I don't know what to say Mrs Frost, I really don't. I never had these sort of problems with him when he was up at Middleton School. I don't know what to do with him. Can you think of anything, because I'm at the end of my tether?'

'Well, perhaps if John promises us both that from now on he will do his homework and not skip lessons, then we'll say no more about it. He isn't a bad child and can be quite clever when he puts his mind to it. But I do have to tell you John that if you carry on in the way you have been then the school inspectors will have to be called and it won't be just you that's in trouble. It will be your Mother as well. I'm sure you don't want that, do you?'

John shook his head and carried on staring down at the floor.

Mother prodded him in the side and appealed to his better nature: 'So, will you promise then? Promise that you will do your work and pull your socks up from now on, eh?'

He nodded and mumbled: 'I promise and I'm sorry.'

'We'll say no more about it then. Thank you for coming in Mrs Starr. It's been nice finally to meet you. If you have any more problems with this young man then you come in and have a chat and we'll have that cup of tea.' Mrs Frost smiled warmly and Mother and John walked out of the classroom, one hopeful for her son's education and the other hopeful he'd done enough to still get his tea.

On the way home she was quiet, deep in thought and walking purposely; John almost had to run to keep up with her: any buses were long gone. Halfway back she stopped and hung over the dry-stone wall which overlooked the Derwent. She pulled a twig from a dead tree leaning dangerously over the river's edge, threw it into the fast-flowing current and watched it float downstream until it was out of sight.

'See that river lad. That's like life that is. And that twig, that's just like you and me. We have to go with the flow, have to learn to live with what cards we're dealt. It's no use trying to pretend things don't apply to you. We all have to follow the rules and that's how it is.' She'd carried on pensively studying the water whilst she spoke, but now turned to look him square in the face.

'Clean them glasses, lad. You'll be able to see things clearer. Just make sure you stick to the rules from now on and everything will go fine for us both, eh?'

John was mystified by her little monologue and pulled off his glasses, looking puzzled; they weren't dirty. He squinted quizzically at his Mother, but wiped them on his shirt-tails anyway as if to appease her.

'She's nice that Mrs Frost. You've got a good teacher there. You just behave from now on and, as she said, we won't say anymore about it.'

They headed off down the lane again, but this time she let him keep up. He'd been forgiven.

Chapter 29

Several weeks passed with him behaving well. There were a few hiccups at home: temper tantrums and throwing things around in their shared bedroom. But, to her knowledge at least, he'd stayed in school and largely done all the homework he'd been set. Mother was under the illusion she was getting somewhere.

Then the problems began in earnest. One afternoon he asked if he could have a ride round on Jack's bicycle; he was tall enough to reach the pedals and capable enough to ride on his own. Jack agreed, but only if he stayed around the village. After all, they didn't want him up on the estate causing bother with his mates.

He went back on his word and was gone for hours. When it began to get dark, Mother started to panic, pacing the floor cursing and constantly twitching the upstairs curtains. He appeared back an hour later with his left trouser leg ripped and his glasses broken, though the bicycle had fared better than he had, only suffering a snapped chain. It was an accident: he'd been showing off to his mates, demonstrating his 'Look, no hands!' technique when he lost control, skidding on the wet road. Mother was livid. He'd been on that estate even after promising faithfully not to go, and she ordered him to bed without any tea. If he couldn't be trusted then he couldn't have his egg and chips.

The next morning he limped down the stairs, eyes red from crying. Mother softened when she saw the pieces of gravel embedded in his left knee, spending the next hour painstakingly picking the bits out with a pair of eyebrow tweezers and a rag dowsed in disinfectant. At some point, Jack had come into the room and told them that unless they were careful the police would come round to see who was being murdered, the screams were so loud. He bought John a bar of

Nestlé's milk chocolate to see if it would lower the decibel level, but it didn't; it just muffled the noise as he screeched between half-chewed mouthfuls.

The accident was forgotten after the last gravel piece was plucked out and a large washable bandage slapped over the wound. Jack's bicycle was repaired and in his stoical Scottish way he simply shrugged his shoulders and said not to worry.

By the end of the month, John had smashed a school window with a cricket ball, bunked off two afternoons on the trot, got sent to the headmistress for swearing and spitting in the playground, and was caught by the lady who ran the sweet-shop with his trouser pockets stuffed full of pink bubble gum pieces which stunk the house out once he took the paper off and stuffed them into his mouth. The police were called in and he and James Burkitt were hauled off to the station to be chastised for their crime.

Police Constable Barraclough brought John home in a police car; he was sat defiantly in the back, strapped in by the seat belt and locked in by the door. The police were taking no chances with this hardened criminal. The car drew up outside the gate and Mother scurried out to meet it. She was mortified, particularly as the Booth twins and their Mother, who lived up the lane, were standing at the bus stop waiting for the 4.50 to Ripley, taking the entire shameful scene in. The whole of Belford would have word of this within the day. The policeman let John out and reprimanded him further about his behaviour, then drew Mother to one side for a quiet word.

'Mrs Starr, John needs taking in hand now before he gets any worse. I know he hasn't done that much wrong in the grand scheme of things, but its bubble gum today and robbing mail trains tomorrow. You need to rein him in.'

With that he took off his helmet, got in the car and drove off, leaving Mother fighting back tears on the pavement, wondering how strong a rein she would need.

She did her best, keeping him penned in both for punishment and observation. He was dispatched to bed there and then, the shouts of how he would now be staying in his room both before and after school following up the stairs. He could only come down for his meals then go back to his room until he found a way of controlling himself and behaving in a proper manner. There would be no privileges, no exercise periods, just solitary confinement. To add insult to injury, he would be taken to and from Long Row, the only fifth-year boy escorted in by his Mother. Two days was all he could stand; on the third day she summoned him for tea and he didn't appear. After several increasingly angry calls she stamped up to the room. He wasn't there; he'd climbed out through the window, slid down the drainpipe and disappeared. She assumed he'd be back when his stomach started rumbling and, sure enough, three hours later he reappeared. Only he didn't get cottage pie and cabbage; instead he got the backs of his legs smacked so hard it left the imprint of her hand on his skin. He stood firm, adamant he wouldn't cry.

'That didn't hurt. You can't hurt me. I'll do what I want and you won't stop me.'

So she smacked him again. It still didn't make any difference. He stared rebelliously with his bottom lip trembling and legs stinging, but he was determined not to shed a single tear or utter any apology.

Two days later, he missed school again. Mother's presence was requested once more at Long Row to meet with Mrs Frost and Mrs Coop. They wanted to discuss John's truancy, his smoking in the playground and where he might possibly have got the cigarettes.

'Do you allow your son to smoke at home Mrs Starr?' enquired Mrs Coop in a very measured and precise clipped voice.

Mrs Coop was a slight, immaculately turned out woman who managed to look down her nose at people despite being only five-foot-three. Straightaway, Mother could see why John didn't like her, but she answered the question nonetheless.

'Of course I don't. He's only eight years old for goodness sake. I don't know where he got them from and I don't know what to do with him at the moment. He's being nothing but trouble and causing row after row. I will of course tell him that he mustn't do it again, but it doesn't seem to make a lot of difference what I say. He just does the direct opposite.'

Mrs Coop nodded in acknowledgement and Mrs Frost mumbled something about him being a very disruptive influence in class. Mother felt completely inadequate, as though sitting in front of a judge and jury, wishing a very large hole would appear in the parquet and swallow her up there and then.

She decided to pack him off for a week in Middleton to see if seven days with Grandma and Granddad would get him back on the straight and narrow. However, only a few peaceful days had passed when Grandma arrived back red-faced on the doorstep, with a triumphant-looking John clutching his bag and coat.

'I can't be doing with him our Maureen. Three days I've had him and he's been nothing but bother. He's broken the gate swinging on it, thrown a brick at next door's dog and nearly crowned it, and pinched all his Granddad's Mint Imperials and pigged them down. Freshest breath in bloody Derbyshire he must have. And that's just the start of it. I don't know what's wrong with him. Your Sister reckons he's possessed by the devil, your Dad thinks he is the devil and I haven't made my mind up yet. But I tell you this: he wants going away somewhere where they can put him back on the right path because I'll be buggered if I can do it.'

Mother was beside herself, too angry to speak to her own son. Jack tried to reason with him, man to man, but despite his determined effort the words fell on uninterested ears; John stared insolently into his eyes before hammering up to his room, slamming the door behind him.

He was still not out of short trousers.

'Jack, what's he going to be like if he carries on like this when he's eighteen? I just don't know what to do with him. He frightens me, and what's more I don't even like him very much at the moment and he's my son. I'm beginning to think he is his Father's son after all. Do you think that badness runs in the blood?'

'I don't know about that Maureen, I really don't, but I do know someone who might be able to help. If you think it's a good idea I'll go and have a word with Percy Roberts. He was a friend of mine in the army and went on to work in a school in Bolsover, a school for lads like John. He should know what to do. What do you think?'

She nodded, though without conviction, no longer believing anything could redeem her child. The next day Jack donned his tweed jacket, strolling off to see his old friend and returned with a bunch of dahlias for Mother, a cake for their tea and some striking news.

Mother hadn't come back from the garage yet so there was enough time to put the tea under a spotty cosy and set the cake out ready for cutting. He was pleased with it; an old Derbyshire variant of fruitcake and one of his favourites. Since May had passed on he hadn't been having the full selection of cake he was used to. He pinched a currant out of the crust, popped it in his mouth and smiled fondly, remembering how May would shout at him for picking at the Dundee before it was even cold. This was a nice bit of cake, but it would never live up to her standard.

The door handle rattled, interrupting his reminiscence. In drifted Mother, her garage tabard hanging out below her anorak. She smiled warmly at Jack, taking in the sight of freshly brewed tea and the cake waiting on the table; it was a good feeling to have someone caring to come home to.

'So, how did you get on with your friend then? Was he in when you got there? It's a long old bus ride to Bolsover if he wasn't there. That looks a lovely cake Jack. Cut us a piece love, I'm famished. It's been one thing after another today. What with worrying about John I haven't had a minute to even have a sandwich never mind sit down to have a cup of tea with it.'

He cut a large chunk of cake and put it down in front of her.

'There's a lovely bit of fruit in there. Did you get it in Bolsover? I bet it was from that bakers up near the castle.'

'Well, if you let me get a word in edgeways, I'd tell you all about it,' he gently ribbed her. 'Yes, I got the cake from that bakery. Old Percy had a slab. We had it with some cheese at dinnertime and it set me off wanting more. Makes a change

182

doesn't it? Anyhow, he doesn't work at that school any longer. He retired two year ago. Shows you how time flies. His son William, young Bill, is one of the year heads and he rang him up and had a word. Bill popped up to his Dad's and, to cut a long story a lot shorter, John can start a week on Monday if you're in agreement. They'll give him a uniform and wash everything so he doesn't need much; some clothes for the weekends, whatever personal bits he wants to take and a very small amount of pocket money. We were lucky really, a lad just left because his parents have moved up north. That's why they could offer us a place. But it's totally up to you. We don't have to take it'

Mother had only expected Jack to come back and tell her they could go and look around, maybe put his name down, never imagining for a minute that her John could be in a boarding school in under a fortnight. He'd never been away from her for more than a few days in the eight-odd years since he'd been born. She munched on her cake, regretting that it had ever come to this, wishing there was another way.

'It'd be for the best Maureen. The more I think about it the more I know we're doing him no good. It's not that you haven't tried. There's only so many hours in the day we can keep him in and I don't know what to do any different. He hasn't changed. What do you reckon? If you can think of another way to make a difference then we'll try that instead.'

'Well, I don't know Jack, I don't. I can't keep failing with him or either he'll be in prison or I'll be in the nuthouse. I suppose it's the only thing to do. At least we can try it and see.'

After the initial refusal to go and a few days of pleading and begging for one more chance, John accepted his fate in a resigned stony silence. Mother wasn't going to be swayed by his empty promises and started to pack his belongings with a determined air. The draining atmosphere in the house lingered on until the day Uncle Ralph came to pick him up and take him and his luggage to Bolsover. He wouldn't be returning home for thirteen weeks; it sounded like an eternity to Mother. She could already sense the impending void in her life. Bitter to the last second, he got in the car and stuck two fingers up at her; she could finally let out a fortnight's tears as the Austin Cambridge drove out of sight.

Chapter 30

For the first couple of weeks after his departure Mother missed my Brother terribly, constantly expecting to catch him in the kitchen with his hand in the biscuit tin or hear him giggling at *Captain Pugwash* on the telly. Gradually, though, she relaxed, starting to enjoy the time she had to herself now there wasn't an unruly child to keep under surveillance. Days became much easier: no tantrums, no rows and no mess, but these private thoughts made her feel guilty; a Mother should miss her son.

Evenings could now be spent sitting out in the garden; it was staying lighter longer and there was a subtle warmth in the air. She started to look after a plot of ground underneath the high wall near the bus stop, planting potatoes in neatly mounded rows and tending them daily. Runner beans were sowed against six-foot garden canes; onions, beetroot and curly kale were set, and each evening she took the watering can and sprinkled rainwater from the butt onto each area. It reminded her of being at home when she was younger and of her ambition to become a gardener. True, she wasn't quite where she'd hoped, but as she stood back and admired her neat patch of ground she thought that life could certainly be a lot worse.

The feeling of being at peace with herself only lasted a few weeks. One evening she was stood leaning on the handle of her Dutch hoe admiring the abundance of brassica seedlings poking out of the ground, when she heard footsteps and voices above her at the bus stop. It was old Mrs Booth and her two daughters, Sandra and Diane. They were identical twins. Mother couldn't tell the difference between the two so she never addressed either of them by their first name; it was a clever tactic. Sandra lived in the lodge at the entrance to the cemetery. She had to walk the boundary each evening and lock up the gates, checking for any damage or problems and report them back to the council. For that she had reduced rent at the lodge and cut-price fares on the council-run bus services. Diane lived with her Mother up the lane: she and her husband and teenage son. They had reduced rent as well, a handy sweetener for having to put up with Mrs Booth twenty-four hours a day. Mother didn't like Mrs Booth very much; she was like the village bloodhound, always sniffing out a juicy morsel of tittle-tattle. Mother huddled against the wall and kept quiet. She didn't want them seeing her or interrupting her peace, and certainly didn't want to participate in the scandal-mongering hobby the three of them seemed to waste their time on. Unfortunately their voices drifted over the wall in the still evening air.

'Well, I don't think it's right really. She's only been dead six months and already that woman is living there with that bloody lad of hers. Talk about jumping in the grave as quick. Where is that bus? It's always late,' grumbled Mrs Booth.

'It'll be coming in a minute Mother,' replied one of the twins. 'You know it's always late at this time. It's driver changeover and that adds on a bit. It'll come when it comes. At least we know it's not gone, eh?'

'Well, she's no better than she should be that Maureen. I'm not one to talk,' stated the other twin, doing the opposite, 'But it's no surprise that people are wondering about what's going on is it? I'd be ashamed if I was her, living over the brush with someone old enough to be my own Dad. He must getting on for seventy now, isn't he Mother?'

'He's sixty-seven; the same year as Mrs Salt, that's how I know. Anyway, it'll all come out in the wash I suppose. The bus is here. Come on both of you, we don't want to be missing it now do we? First house at bingo is calling!'

With that they clambered up the bus steps and Mother slowly let out the breath she'd been holding in whilst they gossiped above her. The 124 pulled off, leaving her silently trying to collect her thoughts, being both angry at them and worried that people were misinterpreting her relationship. All her life she'd been plagued by what people thought about her and just when she thought there was nothing to blabber about, someone came along and invented something. People were talking about her without knowing her circumstances or what went on behind closed doors; her bond with Jack was honest and innocent. She was not ashamed of it but had naively never recognised it could be misconstrued.

She put her tools away, locked up the shed and went into the house, crestfallen. Jack was pottering in the kitchen, the kettle was just starting to steam, and he was cutting some home-baked bread. One look at Mother and he knew there was something wrong.

'What's up Maureen? You look like you've lost a pound and found a shilling!' he quipped.

'Oh, it's nothing; I'm just fed up with people talking about me. If it's not one thing it's another. I had all that rubbish with Peter, then the trouble with John at school and now folk have started on about me living here. Anyone would think I was some kind of scarlet woman. The likes of Eileen Booth, they never wait to find out what's really going on. She would rather make up things and embarrass folk going about their everyday lives. I don't know why she doesn't mind her own business, I really don't.'

'What has she said now then? That bloody woman does nothing but wrong to folk, sticking her beak in wherever she can. I've never had anything to do with her. May used to put up with it but would always tell her to shut her clack if she got too much. Anyhow, what's she said now?'

Mother repeated the spiteful conversation heard over the wall, telling Jack of her humiliation and disappointment in human nature. He shook his head; to him there was an obvious solution that would allow her to walk with her head held high again.

'Well lass, there's nothing for it. You'll have to marry me, then no one will have a reason to say anything. We both know there's nothing wrong with us, but if it keeps them quiet and makes you happier then that's what we'll do.'

Since her experience with Peter, Mother now believed you should only marry a man that gave you butterflies and made your heart beat faster, like in the films she'd seen on a Sunday afternoon. Jack didn't do any of those things but he did offer security, kindness and comfort; would be someone to rely on. She came to the conclusion that butterflies and missed heartbeats were irrelevant. By the time John came home at the end of term my Mother had been remarried for a month.

Neither my Grandma or John were exactly over the moon when they found out, but it was too late to change anything: the ink was already dry on the marriage certificate. Grandma begrudgingly learned to live with it, though being denied a big hat and a new frock for the wedding was never forgotten. My Brother couldn't come to terms with it, believing Jack had only sent him to boarding school to get him out of the way, clearing the path for a covert marriage. His behaviour worsened. Though my Mother was initially happy to have him home, she was happier still to see him go back a fortnight later.

The next year continued in the same way for John. At school, where they knew how to deal with him, he was no better or worse than any of the other boys, was just one of many miscreants. At home, he was a single delinquent force that they couldn't cope with. It seemed to Mother that he used the school holidays to cast off the shackles, cross the boundaries and push them to their limits. He made her cry more than smile and she started to dread the times when he would come home. Jack couldn't handle his behaviour, saying he wished his stepson could stay at school all the time. John raised his blood pressure, and he frequently had to resort to his angina pills to stop the pains in his chest.

John wound up the pressure another ten notches when he came home on summer break and Mother dropped her bombshell. He would have a Brother or Sister by Christmas.

The baby wasn't planned. Mother hadn't expected to have a physical relationship with Jack, but had grown to love him; it was a natural progression for her to share a bed with her husband even though in years he was so much her senior. They were both surprised by the pregnancy but soon grew accustomed to the news. She grew as well and as her stomach started to show knew she had to tell people; this would give the village grapevine something more to prey on.

John was livid, unable to speak to Mother for over a week; he wouldn't speak to Jack either, but this was nothing out of the ordinary. When he did finally open his mouth again it was to Grandma. He sneaked off one afternoon on Jack's pushbike eager to let the cat out of the bag. Five words and she charged onto the next bus, turning up to give her eldest daughter a much-needed piece of her mind.

'Maureen, he tells me you're having a baby, is that right?' She didn't stop for the answer. 'It's bad enough that you married a man as old as your own father. That's not right in itself, but this takes the biscuit. You can't control the son you've got never mind bringing another kiddie into the world. How are you going to manage with another one? Before it's grown up its Dad'll be dead and gone. It's not right. Do you know, I despair of you sometimes. That Peter was bad enough but this! Crikey, I thought I'd brought you up sensible, but I'm beginning to wonder, honest I am.'

'Well, I am pregnant as it is. Not that it's anything to do with you.' Mother was angry. 'And don't you dare compare that evil man to Jack. He was bad to the bone. And yes, I wished I'd listened to people who knew better before I married him, but I didn't. I married Jack because I wanted to. Anyhow, yes, I am having a baby and that's all there is to it. If you don't want to know your grandchild when Christmas comes then that's your choice, but it'll be loved and it'll be cherished, and even if Jack goes before it's grown up it'll have me.'

Two pots of tea and a packet of custard creams later Grandma had lost the strength in her anger: blood was blood after all. The baby would need a knitted matinée jacket and bootees. Two weeks before Christmas Mother gave birth to a seven-pound girl with a shock of bright ginger hair. Jack cooed proudly over his new baby before handing her gently to her Grandma. The youngest granddaughter, with pale skin, green eyes and red curls, appealed to her at a level she didn't quite understand. Was it the sense of the familiar, the reminder of ancestors long-gone?

Chapter 31

John hated his little Sister on principle; nothing about her appealed to him.

Jack was the most overjoyed of the amassed group around Mother's hospital bed. He had a daughter, something he'd always secretly wanted but never managed with May. May had rheumatic fever after Wilfred was born and, though the doctors never said, she couldn't have any more children. Now he was sixty-eight years old and had the little girl he'd always longed for. For the next four and a half years he doted on her.

And that little girl was me. I now understood exactly how I'd come to be, how my Mother's life had unfolded; the twists and turns it had taken on its path to the present. I am certain I now know more about my Mother than she would ever have wanted me to know. From here her story would intermingle with my own. I come from a long line of women who, down through the years and across miles of vast lands, had struggled to make their way in the world, documenting their lives in myths and legends. I would be no exception, having my own tale to tell from now on.

I was my Dad's haven in the world. He wandered around the garden with me as a baby and pointed out the flowers. As a toddler he took me by the hand and walked me along the riverbank, picking me up and carrying me on his old shoulders when I got tired, pointing out the swans and wading birds as he meandered along the path. As I got older he read to me, sat on the settee, his protective arm around my tiny shoulders.

Wherever I was in the house or garden he was never far away, like a guardian angel. Until one day, he wasn't anymore.

I was four years old when he died. It was January and the wind was howling around the house. It wafted through the gaps in the windows where they didn't fit properly; years of bad weather and drying out in the sun had warped the wood

190

and twisted the frames. I sat on the carpet in front of the roaring coal fire, the wind billowed down the chimney making the flames dance in the grate and leap out towards me.

I was playing with my Duplo bricks, constructing a house. It was red and white stripes with four black corner stones and black window frames, but the doorway was simply a hole. I'd lost the plastic door; it had fallen down the outside drain when I was building an extension to a former Duplo palace out on the doorstep the summer before. The neighbour's cat, which had been sitting with me, started to nudge the bricks about with her paw; before I could stop her, half the house was across the yard and the door was down the grate. The brick set was incomplete from then on, but I managed without the door, consoling myself with the thought that cavemen never had them but it didn't stop them getting on with their lives.

I spent a lot of time and energy building; once my creations were finished I never wanted to break them apart again. It was as if the houses, farms and offices I snapped together developed lives of their own and I couldn't bear the idea that these could be broken apart.

When he was home from school my Brother took great delight in wrecking what I had spent many hours building; this seemed to be his role in life: wrecking things, physically and metaphorically.

This particular day he achieved his pinnacle of success in terms of destruction. He once again borrowed my Dad's old pushbike and pedalled off with strict instructions to stay within a five-mile radius of the cottage. Surely in that small area he would come to no harm?

After riding around for barely an hour he was bored, feeling restricted by the imaginary pen he'd been given to stay in. Having seen the road sign for Nottingham he decided to cut through the invisible boundary and cycle over there; after all, no one would be any the wiser.

And he would have been right. Except that halfway there, on the Woodlinkin bypass, the sudden rush of wind from a passing cattle truck unsteadied him and he veered to the right. Not able to regain his balance, he wavered into the path of a green Ford Anglia that couldn't help but knock him flying.

He was very lucky, or so the policeman reported when he came around to the cottage in the early afternoon to tell my Mother and Father

When he told them that John had broken his right leg in three places and it was quite a nasty injury, Mother's face paled and the look of fear was acute. But, on finding out he'd be all right once he was plastered up and brought home from Nottingham Hospital, the colour flooded back and she remembered he'd defied their explicit orders in the first place.

'He won't be so lucky when I get hold of him. A broken leg'll be the least of his problems. I told him no further than five miles but he won't take a blind bit of notice of anything I say. He wilfully disobeys me at every turn. I'll be glad when they take him back at that school again. It's only a shame they can't keep him there all the bloody time.'

The policeman left Mother with a kindly pat on the shoulder and a phone number to call the hospital. She was seething, completely oblivious to the state that my Dad was working himself into.

'It's all my fault. He could have been killed today up on that bypass. It's such a fast road and folk don't take notice of cyclists the way they ought. I should never have let him take that blessed bicycle, I shouldn't have. I'm lucky he only has a broken leg and I don't have his death on my conscience.'

'Don't be stupid Jack; he's his own worst enemy. You know that lad will do exactly what he wants when he wants and nothing will stop him, certainly not you. If you hadn't lent him the bloody bike he would have taken it anyhow. You know he would.'

My Dad knew she was right, but by now he was so het up he'd started to redden in the face and had trouble catching his breath. He had a strong sensation he was going to faint so he threw himself down heavily on the settee. The intense gripping pain started in his chest as he sat frantically trying to gulp in air. Panic-stricken, Mother tried to calm him, but it was no use: the pains were getting stronger. From my seat on the Duplo-strewn carpet I could see his lips turning a distinct shade of blue.

Clinging to the sideboard, it took every last ounce of what little strength he had left to haul himself up. Desperately rubbing his chest, he reached blindly into the corner cupboard for the heart tablets that went under the tongue when he had twinges. They would usually work within minutes, suffocating any pain and leaving him tired enough for sleep.

As he picked up the little glass bottle the pain in his chest reached its climax; he felt hotter and hotter, as if his racing heart was going to explode at any second. As he unscrewed the lid a final agonising wave of pain crossed his upper body; he let out a last rasp before slumping back on the settee. From my place in front of the hearth I watched his life cruelly fade away, now-forgotten bricks scattered all around.

I was transfixed by his face; it had been contorted with pain but was now softening and returning to normal. His eyes were closed. He looked like he was in a peaceful sleep, but those eyes would never open again.

Mother was beyond distraught, feverishly trying to shake him awake. His head lolled to one side, his grasp on the bottle had loosened and it fell to the ground, landing next to the wall of my newest creation, pills mixing with building blocks on the floor.

Years later Mother would tell me I was too young to remember him dying, but I did. The scene had been imprinted in my mind in painful technicolour. When I recounted the story in vivid detail the colour drained from her face again. I had watched my own father die and couldn't forget that moment, though I could blank out the rest of that day.

I haven't, however, managed to push the day of his funeral from my mind; not that I understood what a funeral was back then. All I knew was that he wasn't there, replaced by lots of strangers dressed in suits with black ties, crowded into the tiny cottage. A couple of men were wearing kilts; it seemed funny that men wore skirts so I was removed to the kitchen to stop the strangers hearing giggling in the midst of all the solemnity.

Even though I had been a witness to everything that happened, I didn't understand what death meant, not then. It was all a blur of people coming and going and long silences.

Mother tried over and over to spell out that my Father wouldn't be coming home again until it slowly dawned that something awful had happened.

The spelling wasn't clear enough and I cried myself to sleep every night repeating pitifully.

'I want my Dad,' again and again until exhaustion took over. It lasted for weeks, yet each night he never answered my call, never coming to tuck me in or tell me whether the owl ever married the pussycat.

I asked Mother where he was and she tried her best to clarify it on the day of the funeral, telling me he had been laid to rest now and we could visit him in the next few days. It pacified me enough to leave the questioning alone. However, three days later, when she took me to a mound of newly dug soil in the cemetery and explained that was where he was resting, I didn't believe her. Why would anyone have a rest under a pile of cold wet earth? It didn't make any sense.

For days after that I couldn't speak to her. I thought she was lying. I didn't speak to anyone else either; they were all in on the conspiracy. I sat in the front room holding on to the woolly panda with the missing eye; no one could prise it from my arms. It was the last present my Dad had bought me. I thought if me and Jimmy sat quietly for long enough and I was a good girl, Dad would come back home and everything would be all right.

Mother was at the end of her tether, considering getting the doctor as a last resort after bribery, toys and teatime treats had failed. I heard her talking to Mrs Clayton from next door. She'd called round with a jigsaw for me; one hundred pieces of cartoon elephants with cream buns. I thanked her half-heartedly, put it down on the floor and went back to cuddling the panda.

'I don't know what to do with her Bridget, I don't, honest. She doesn't want to speak and I can't interest her in anything. I even tried to give her Arctic Roll for dinner today. All she did was chase it round the plate with her spoon until it melted, then it got left,' Mother told her despondently.

'It's early days yet Maureen, and it's only ice cream after all. Just give her time. She'll come round. Perhaps you all need to have a break from here and try and get back to normal. Have you thought about going up to your Mother's for a few days? Might do you good and take her mind off her Dad not being here. What do you think, eh?' Bridget Clayton was a matronly woman with an ample bust that had sagged to join her equally ample stomach, making her look like a large rosy apple. She spoke to my Mother in soft even tones. 'You go down to our house and use the telephone. See if you can organise it, eh? I'll stay with the little 'un.'

Mother nodded and ten minutes later she reappeared and thanked Mrs Clayton for thinking of us.

The rest of the afternoon she busied herself with packing enough clothes and shoes for a year, never mind a weekend, explaining we were going to have a little holiday for a few days up in Middleton. I told her I didn't want to go; how would my Dad know where we were if he came back? She ignored it, so I asked if we could leave him a note.

That evening me, a one-eyed panda, Auntie Joan, Grandma and three suitcases were crammed into the back of Uncle Ralph's car. Mother and John sat in the front seat, him squirming on her knee, complaining that at nearly fifteen he was far too old to sit on his Mother's lap. Grandma had decided that my Mother should go for a rest; Mother had decided I should go to forget and John had decided that he should go and relieve the village off-licence of several bottles of cider.

In the eyes of my Mother I did seem to forget. On the surface I returned to normal, chattering and playing as I had before my Dad's death, but deep inside something had irrevocably changed. I no longer wanted to build anything. The Duplo had been consigned to the bottom of the toy box and there it stayed, as if tainted with a bad memory. I never mentioned my Dad again and in return neither did she, until he became a hazy image that only became clear when I poured over old photos. It seemed my recollections of the short time we had together were solely constructed from the grainy snapshots, much thumbed and dog-eared. I kept one of the pictures next to my bed, until one day Mother put it in a drawer because she swore his eyes followed her around the room.

Chapter 32

For the next four years Mother and I, and sometimes John, spent a lot of hours traipsing back and forth to Middleton, staying with Grandma. Most weekends we were there; it felt as much my home as the little cottage nestled in the Derwent Valley.

The bus rides home were akin to a roller-coaster, labouring up a steep hill one minute before hurtling into oblivion down the other side, jolting abruptly to a halt at each stop. In between hanging on for dear life and keeping a tight grip on her belongings, Mother would tell me stories. They were usually taken from the Ladybird books I brought home from school and carted along to pester her with; *The Little Red Hen*, *The Elves and the Shoemaker* or *The Three Bears*. The tales became so familiar that I could already recite them to the teacher at reading time just by looking at the pictures and recalling the words Mother had uttered as we trundled along. Miss Bunting, my teacher, had me marked down as a miniature genius, to be able to read a book from cover to cover without hesitation at only four and a half years old was seen as being something prodigious. In the years to come it became my duty to let the education system down gently, my status as child prodigy sinking slowly with it.

Sometimes Mother told me about the people she had known at school, about her Father and about sitting on the pavement chewing tarmac in the war, waving at the soldiers passing by in convoys. Then there was the time she and Auntie Joan had carried a tree on their backs through the heavy snows of 1947. I loved to sit and imagine the eight-foot frozen snowdrifts that coated the landscape and obscured the roads. They meant she and her Sister had to walk upon the old crumbling limestone walls and rock solid hedges in order to get the tree back to fuel the kitchen fire. I was enthralled by the dangers they would have faced if they'd fallen from the heights and disappeared into the tundra like Captain Scott.

These were the best kinds of stories.

Over the years she would tell me moral tales, Bible stories learned at Sunday school embellished with added twists, and fables about lazy foxes that couldn't be bothered to go out and catch their own supper.

Once she recounted a cautionary tale heard on the radio. Betty, who everyone at work thought was a little on the tapped side of barmy, liked to listen to the afternoon plays on Radio 4. This one was a story about a sad, deserted atoll, a place that was once benevolent, abundant and kind; an island that trusted men to do their best by it.

Long ago, in a past that is shrouded by mist and blurred by memory, there was an island far away in the east. On this island the trees grew into tall dense forests where plants filled the hillsides, sweet-scented magnolias bloomed vibrantly and the song of birds rang out from every branch and nesting place.

Birds had flown for miles to land in this magical paradise. Their migration becoming renowned in ornithological circles, their flight plans mapped and the routes they had swum plotted. They were happy on the island. In no time at all they'd lost the use of their wings; why did they need to know how to fly? Here they had no reason to catch their food in flight: the island soil teemed with life, the clever microscopic world of the insect continued to flourish as it had for thousands of years, providing enough for all to feed.

The birds had no desire ever to fly away again.

Occasionally the volcano would bellow out its ominous warning to the sky.

Then one day patterned canoes came silently across the ocean.

The yellow-eyed moon bird saw the men paddling towards the shore. She called across the fertile valley floor to tell her neighbours in the high green forests of the curious sight. Far across the volcano crater the story rang out: strangers had landed on their beloved home, and everywhere the panicked song of the birds was heard shrieking across the land.

Soon the visitors were established; they had found a place without owners, a new realm they could call their own. They built wooden camps to live in with their families and children. They constructed log bridges to scale the rivers. They cooked their food with firewood from the home of the yellow-eyed moon bird; each man chopping and taking as he saw fit.

Homeless, and with tears in her yellow eyes, the small flightless bird scurried across the island to the crater of the volcano, seeking deliverance and the advice of the Goddess.

The men, leaning on the handles of their axes and spades, had intently watched her escape and, thinking she might lead them to food, had followed her. In the belly of the volcano they came across the great grass altar that the many colourful birds had weaved for their benevolent Goddess.

They wondered in awe at this feat of beauty and devotion and it was decided that their own Gods could not be ignored. So the stonemasons began to carve and add altars to their own deities.

But their Gods were greedy Gods.

Hemelsin, the bringer of fruitfulness, demanded a great stone fortress with carved heads to epitomise his significance.

Next, Samrekinna, the God of strength. He commanded statues of stone to uphold his great virtue, proving his might and imprinting his macho face on the island the men had taken for their own.

The men listened to the words of their priests and holy men.

The men listened to the advice of their elders and betters.

After much consultation, the men took the words and advice of those that should have known better and conceived a plan.

They began to carve. The artists tapped and pummelled the stomach stone of the volcano into heads and bodies, pillars and architraves, columns and arches.

The architects decided upon the place where the stones were to be set. The builders went out into the remaining forest groves and pulled down the last of the trees and foliage.

Seven years later, Hemelsin had his fortress, towering over the bare landscape, looming where once tall trees had sheltered the land with their canopy of leaves and branches.

Samrakinna had his statues: great heads staring out to the ocean, warning off all seafarers, scaring away the roaming shoals of dolphins and the sea birds which followed in their wake.

The building and sculpting was completed, monumental and reigning supreme over the island.

The men stood back and looked at their achievements. They stood back and admired their skill and hard work. They stood back and rubbed their tired eyes in order to take in the magnificent sights they had created. They were euphoric, at least for a short time.

They were left with very little to sustain themselves and soon came to realise that though their efforts brought forth fine results, there were no more trees. Without the trees they had no wood, no wood meant no fire, no fire meant no warmth or food. The birds had no homes and without their natural habitat, they slowly died. Bleached skeletons rotting on the barren ground, scorched on the dead red earth of the island.

The men had been foolish; their boats had decayed, left neglected on the shores. What little was left was too rotten to even burn on the fires. The men could no longer sail away.

All they had left was stone and fortress, lifeless land, starvation and certain death.

After a few short hungry weeks, the men were all gone, bones becoming one with the earth, enriching the dead island, which anticipated its certain rejuvenation.

The island waited. Once again the volcano bellowed its lonely warning into the sky.

Mother sighed when she'd finished the tale, wiping a porthole in the steamed-up bus window and peering out into the rain. She stated emphatically and in no uncertain terms.

'You see, the moral of that story is you should never trust a man. They'll take what you have and think they're making it better, but in the long run they'll ruin it. Never trust 'em.'

Chapter 33

Three weeks later, on one warm June morning, my Mother remarried. She gave good advice but, I learned later, never took it.

She wore a long, tiered, lemon-yellow frock and carried a white plastic handbag; it matched her white patent shoes.

He wore a slate-grey suit and a Derby county tie. Fifteen years on, the suit still fitted him, though the tie was no longer in club colours.

He moved into the house and everything changed. Crossroads Motel at 6.30 p.m. closed its doors to me; Shughie McFee had put down his cleaver. Channels were switched over. Evening news. Silence. The weather. Complete and utter silence. At least this was only a few minutes long. Saturdays were the worst. Saturday afternoons 12.45 to 3.45 to be precise. Horse racing. Quiet in the house.

Mother went to bed to read and doze. Mills and Boons with covers bent backwards, spines splitting. She told me she had to get her romance somewhere. I was left to my own devices.

My devices were all held in a little six-foot by six-foot bedroom. I avoided the front room, couldn't bear the silence. It was bad if his horses lost. It was worse still if they won; he was happy then and when he was happy he became dangerous.

I was always prone to wander at will and, even as a little child, appreciated the freedom to investigate mysteries like the back yard of the pub or our next-door neighbour's shed. When she married him the door to this wondrous outside world became somewhat barred to me. I had to ask to leave the house and permission was only given when the mood took him.

Saturday afternoon in a small village was no fun; life was quiet, too quiet. In Belford, in real classification terms no more than a hamlet, there was only my imagination to fall back on.

There were no children to play with, no parks and no specific places to go. Our village had twenty houses, a factory, a pub and a phone box for the living, and a sprawling cemetery stretching up from the valley floor to the top of the pine-clad hills for the dead.

The twenty houses were off-limits, having no children to warrant a visit. The factory was no use: minors were banned by employment law, and I was far too young to go to the pub, sit with the locals, smoke fags and gossip. There was the phone box, but I had no one to call then; there were only so many times I could phone the operator and tell him I'd dropped my hair band in a puddle.

I was left with the cemetery, its weaving pathways scaling up the side of the valley.

I learned many things in that quiet serene place, such as the names of trees and flowers. The more unusual trees had rectangular metal signs giving their Latin and common names along with the approximate date of planting. I was particularly fond of the Chilean pine – Araucaria Araucana, or monkey-puzzle tree, with its huge odd-angled branches of individual prickly spears. When the wind blew hard enough, browning spikes fell groundwards, landing in the peaty pine-covered soil. Year's worth of needles and grass cuttings had built up on the ground making it spongy and bouncy underfoot. Near the vast, criss-cross-marked trunk of the tree stood a tiny Victorian grave marker shaped like a shield seen in a coat-of-arms on mugs and plates in National Trust shops: the sort of shield that depicts a family crest, connecting a lineage to the Royalty of the past, however tenuously. The commemorative inscription was half obscured by years of debris but the date of 1823 and the first name Emmeline were still visible. Its dark-red enamel was peeling in the place where the surname would have been. Emmeline. I couldn't even read how old she'd been. I swore to her that one afternoon I'd come and unearth her plaque and show her the light of day again. I meant it. I wanted to know more about this Victorian woman. For all I knew she could have been a girl the same age as me; could have been my friend. In the friendless world I was in, she already was.

Much of my childhood passed there, gazing in awe at Mother Nature and contemplating the lives of folk long gone. Roaming among the dead was a lonely existence for anyone; friendships were very one sided, but I wandered because it was in my blood.

As a tiny child my Mother held my hand and we wandered together through the same cemetery to lay bunches of flowers on the bare clay earth of Dad's grave. I still didn't believe he was there resting but, if he was, what would he want with a handful of pink and white carnations? He never liked cut flowers. After this we would meander up into the woods to watch the Derwent River sneak its way through the valley below. We peered through the leafless trees and haze of cold winter mist, making out the lanes that snaked past our little cottage and the smoke rising from the chimney stacks of the neighbouring houses.

We talked then, my Mother and me, both talked and both listened.

She spoke about how life had changed for her, about the things she'd done as a child, her dashed hopes and the ends she now had to meet. The cemetery reminded her of the finality of death: her best friend Mary had passed away in childbirth without her ever trying to rebuild the bridges of their friendship, bonds that had been broken by her first husband. Looking back, wistfully, she wished she'd made more effort, impressing upon me the importance of not having any regrets in life.

On our way home we ambled back down the zig-zagging paths of the cemetery and looked at the gravestones; big old Victorian alabaster monuments, elegant gargantuan angels looming over greying tombs, enigmatic faced and beautiful. I liked to look at the Hall Family graves; fair-folk, entertainers and showmen for generations. Their plots stretched as far as the eye could see. One in particular fascinated me; it had carousel horses carved into the headstone, manes flowing and nostrils flaring, as if in full flight across the marble.

Even then Mother had knowledge of the graves and the cemetery at an exemplary level, knowing the things that would engage a tiny child's mind.

Ezra Hall, showman, had been put in the ground with a covering of coins from the mourners so he had the entrance fee to heaven's fairground and enough money to maintain his extravagant lifestyle. I was amazed at all that money buried beneath the dark sodden earth, asking if Mother thought it was still there and could we dig it up. She said no, it was a long way down and we didn't have a spade.

Occasionally on these walks I would ask her awkward questions. Sometimes she would answer quite candidly, other times she would ignore the query completely and move swiftly onto an unrelated subject. It was a way to draw me off the scent when she felt uncomfortable.

'Mother,' I asked, 'why was my Dad so much older than you?' A simple question, I thought.

'Do you know, when I was carrying you, me and your Brother were walking up here and I found a dead swan. It was still beautiful, even though it was dead. Its mate sat watching me, about ten foot away, head down in misery. I sent your Brother back for a shovel; it took him ages. While he was gone I talked to the swan's mate, tried to tell it I was sorry. But how can you make a bird understand that, eh? Anyhow, I buried her and laid a flower on the earth to mark the place. Do you know, that swan, her mate, it still comes back every year?'

Of course I knew it came back. I'd seen it in the cemetery. Now I knew what it came back for, though I think I'd always intuitively known, sensing its sadness in the beat of its wings and whisper of the wind as it flew.

I listened attentively to the story and stored it up in my mind. Years later I set down her tale, more or less as it had been told. I put pen to paper during the morning I was supposed to be packing up Mother's effects to send to the charity shop; she'd been dead for a few weeks, but her voice was still very much alive in my head.

Back through time they fly, the swans, straight-necked and perfectly balanced on the wind. Never looking down, only straight out to the horizon for fear of being lured to the ground by the green pastureland; tender shoots that would disappear quickly. Hundreds of miles to the west, when they did land, it would be for a purpose, to pass on a spirit, and one day that spirit would come to be seen in the sparkle of a girl's eye.

Minutes flow, hours pass, time marches.

It was reported that on the south coast of England small flocks of swans, Whoopers, Bewicks and Black-billed Hooters, were crossing the sea to over-winter, to paddle the flowing streams, disturbing the bottoms and dredging up riverbeds. Usually they would fly a matter of hours into the countryside and land on a flat plain where they would tend to their feathers, re-oiling them and letting the breeze flow through their wings without lifting them for flight.

Local news stations reported that some swans were flying to the centre of the country. This was unusual and after days of monitoring the final pair of swans were found to have landed in one of the most landlocked counties of England.

Celebrated visitors, local ornithologists, and the plain nosy flocked to photograph them, to gaze at what the miracle of flight had brought, to write about it in local papers and filter the news through to the nationals.

It was reported that the pair of furthest-flown swans had somewhat unusual traits. Definitely a pair, it was discovered that both were female. They nestled their long necks together and called to each other in muffled, contented tones: tired, but happy from flight.

Their journey ended, they'd arrived at where they'd been drawn.

When the photos taken for papers and journals across the land were developed and printed, the unusual traits became all the more obvious. The slightly smaller of the pair had pure white eyes, no visible pupil at all; not blind, she was alert and reacted to all there was to be seen. From one angle the other seemed the same as all swans, but on turning its head the distinction became apparent. This bird had the reddest of left eyes, pure glittering scarlet; it viewed all with suspicion, almost looking angry.

Solitude encroached on the pair, their celebrity worn away. As with all things which at first seem alien, they became commonplace and accepted.

Red-eye though, had begun to ail. Her mate, clearly concerned, never wandered more than a few feet away.

The smell of the air changed to look towards the depths of winter. Ice crystals formed into sheets, icicles like daggers draped from frosted willows.

Red-eye had stopped eating and was content to merely to rest her long neck with its now ruffled feathers on the back of her mate, waiting for the breaths finally to end. Slowly they stopped altogether in the dark of the still, moonless night.

Her mate had known there was no more, but waited until the new morning to bare witness to the pain that echoed through her proud white breast.

That cold morning, walking the same path as she always did each day, a very pregnant woman strolled with her bespectacled little boy. It was almost Christmas; he was excited, she was weary, looking forward to shedding some of the weight she was carrying.

That day she found a dead swan, eyes closed, lifeless.

Sending the boy back down the hill to borrow a spade, she sat sorrowfully next to the body and carefully stroked its cold but still-so-soft head, at the same time rubbing her stomach, trying to ease some of the tension and burden.

She waited.

She wrapped the swan gently in the old shawl she'd been wearing and listened for the boy's return.

Moments later his feet crashed up to the place where they'd parted. Taking the small hand-spade from him she began to dig, watched attentively by her child and suspiciously by the swan's mate who stood back warily, hissing a low warning.

Eventually, as the hole grew deep enough, the woman lay the swan gently inside and slowly covered her with the cold dark soil. Once the ground was levelled she broke a sprig of holly with the brightest of red berries from a nearby tree and placed it on the grave. She turned and walked away, not

206

*looking back, not letting her boy look back, until they were far
enough away for him not to disturb the scene.*

*At the grave the single swan lay; her neck stretched prone
against the new soil: its beauty juxtaposed against the harsh
reality of what had happened on that day.*

*Afternoon turned to evening and the dark of the night
began its creep across the hills. The swan took her flight into
to the sky. She would return.*

*She flew higher, a single elegant silhouette against the
rising of the moon, her wings beating out an uninterrupted
melody. She swooped low over the house of the woman who
had given such kindness and heard the cry of a newly born
soul. The child was born.*

Swan baby, the woman thought.

*She was born with the palest skin, almost translucent
white; the brightest red hair matching the flecks that appeared
in her left, as yet unfocussed, eye.*

*Each year on the child's birthday, the pale-eyed swan
returned to the grave of her mate.*

*She sat beside the patch of ground that was now covered
with grass and decaying leaves. The tiny flowering plant the
woman had taken to mark the place was slowly opening.*

Within hours the swan left.

*The child, now growing, gazed up at it as it made its way
into the sky. She shed tears without knowing the reason why,
didn't understand but knew the lone swan would always return
to wait; it was the saddest thing she'd ever felt in her little,
innocent life.*

*The child was strangely attracted to the spot. Each year a
mystical single rose bloomed from the grave. The child waited
to see it open its tiny head to the sky, blooming its red vibrancy
against the white of the snow. Each year the same as the last.
December the fourteenth. By the next day the flower was gone.*

*The child watched the shortest of life spans; birth,
existence and death played out in a single day.*

*The lone swan flew away from the scene, effortlessly
beating her large perfect wings.*

She would always return.

Beautiful stories like that didn't come along too often. Instead of being filled with graceful swans and winter landscapes, my mind was usually occupied with how I could get Mr Buckley to let me have a go on his tractor or whether there were fairies behind the milking shed; I'd seen the toadstool rings in the early morning dew. After my stepfather stopped allowing me so much freedom I had to spend much more time trapped indoors.

Chapter 34

At mealtimes my stepfather ate slowly, each mouthful apparently needing to be chewed exactly forty-two times to break down properly in the gullet. He'd read this in the *Readers Digest*, delivered monthly to our house. I liked the pictures, trying to get first look at it because all too soon it disappeared into the outside toilet, where it became first reading matter, then toilet paper. He liked to save money after he'd absorbed how the funnel web spider caught its prey.

After the main meal was over he would leave his pudding on the table. Mother would cover it with a plate to stop the flies settling. There it sat until at least teatime, congealing slowly; by then it would be stone cold and have developed cracks like the San Andreas fault line. He wasn't the only one studying the *Readers Digest*.

This was my first and foremost grudge against him in those days, when time was still my most pressing pre-occupation; he ate far too slowly. My Brother compared him to a ruminating tortoise. So, after two more than healthy helpings of blackberry and apple crumble, I still had to wait for what seemed like hours to leave the table.

If I accidentally tapped the handle of my spoon in time with his chewing I was judged severely for my error.

More often than not he seemed to find it difficult to distinguish between accident and purpose. The taste of summer fruits and the salt from swallowed tears did not, in general, mix well together, but this still happened each day. I stood at the sink, up to the elbow in soapsuds, my back to him, crying unseen because I'd long realised that tears didn't soften his outlook or lessen your crime. You were guilty and that was that.

Grandma swore he was no good. She voiced her beliefs out loud to my mother, sitting like a head of state on our leather-effect settee.

'It'll be no use crying now lady,' she reproached. 'You've gone and set yourself up for a life of right misery. And you with two children to bring up. I'm telling you, I don't like him. He'll be no good, and I'll not be far wrong.'

But, as we all found out, Mother did like him, no matter what. He was her husband and that was that; she was sticking by him despite the tears of her child and the warnings from Grandma.

'For better or worse,' she'd said lovingly to him on their wedding day. I thought it would be more worse than anything else.

'Until death us do part,' he'd replied smugly. I hoped it would come sooner rather than later.

But it didn't.

It took him three years, almost to the day of their anniversary, to start his reign of terror over me and my Mother, but in very different ways. To begin with, though she clearly loved him, she didn't seem all that bothered whether or not he was around. She'd managed on her own for over four years, taking a part-time job at the plastics factory when Jack had died, and doing everything at home from decorating and plumbing to setting potatoes. She'd ensured the upkeep of the cottage and provided sumptuous feasts for the table. At that point she was both financially and emotionally independent, coping with anything that life threw at her.

It turned out that Batty Betty at the factory was a big follower of Marx and Engels and, on the quiet, a backroom feminist. In her first week, Mother was given training on the clothesline winding machine; Betty also gave her a sermon along with it about the de-skilling of the workforce, explaining how doing bits of a job was not good for a person. It meant they would eventually be programmed into thinking they were unable to complete a job from start to finish, becoming unskilled and depressed about their place in life. Betty saw clothesline winding in exactly this way because they only ever cut lengths and never knew how to craft a finished product.

'If it weren't for me meetings in the evenings then I'd go round the twist, Mo,' she joked.

Mother was too polite to say that most people thought she was round the twist anyway. She coughed instead, then asked, 'what meetings do you go to Betty?' Genuinely interested in answers to questions she posed, Mother believed in giving everyone a chance to have their say.

'Well, on a Monday I go to the local traditional singing group. We do old weaving songs mostly. I'll teach you one later. I like a good sing-song. Tuesday, me and Ernie go to the Labour club. Not that we vote Labour. No, they hire it out to the South Derbyshire branch of the Revolutionary Communist Party: much more my cup of tea... then Wednesdays I stop in and have a clean round. I do downstairs, Ernie does up... there's enough to do in life without mithering about dust.'

She never got any further than Wednesday, as Granville rolled up with a push-cart load of new clothes-line. It came in big card barrels, like huge rain butts full of white plastic-coated string, a couple of miles at a time.

Betty's viewpoint on life made an impression on my Mother. She thought about Bertha, the old lady next door to her own Mother. When her husband died she'd been left without knowing how to pay the gas bill at the post office; didn't even understand how to fill in the payment slip. Grandma had to drill into her how simple it was over a pot of tea. Poor old girl, Mother thought to herself, vowing never to get to the point where she couldn't manage things on her own; she would always be independent. But, by about three years after she'd married, Betty's words were fading, independence was being eroded, and my stepfather was cultivating his very own Bertha.

He slowly made himself indispensable, starting to chip away at her armour bit by bit, taking away little duties. He commandeered the vegetable patch; she ended up moving indoors and being relegated solely to cooking the things he now grew. When she cut up carrots and cauliflower for tea he insisted they were boiled until falling to pieces; nothing was properly cooked until it turned to mush. That's what he thought and what he thought went. One day I caught her muttering, 'I wonder if this is what Betty meant about being de-skilled in the workplace?' Her friend's words weren't completely forgotten, but the desire to keep the peace was stronger than the need to exercise her free will.

Mother started to read. I went to the library to get my weekly supply of books from the array in the children's section, climbing a creaking staircase and emerging at the top in another world; a world of literature and facts and bright colours and light. She wandered downstairs and picked up novels of a romantic nature. I read Enid Blyton, dreaming of Claudine at St Clare's and being her friend and confidante, getting involved in all the shenanigans she was mixed up in. She read Mills and Boon, dreaming of being swept up by a knight in shining armour, riding off into the sunset and living happily ever after.

Mother picked up Catherine Cooksons and Barbara Cartlands, going on what the picture on the front showed rather than the words on the cover. If it had a snappy title and a good picture then she took it home. She withdrew into a fantasyland of romance and flowers, where she was wooed and wanted, wined and dined, adored and desired. In such a short time her reality had become very different. Sometimes as I lay in bed at night listening to their arguments about racing pigeons and money matters, the raised voices, threats of divorce and tears would float up the stairs. I wondered if she regretted her decision to marry again.

Chapter 35

The day they married was a momentous one for me in all sorts of ways, not least because I finally managed to get rid of the red-and-blue polka-spotted party dress that necessity had forced me to wear for the previous two summers.

I'd worn it when Miss Bunting had given the class a Christmas party, and it had its last airing at the end of term before we all moved up into Miss Clumber's class.

Now I had a new dress, a new teacher and a new 'father', though I would not call him that. Life was always full of change.

Miss Clumber was my new teacher. She was young, with short, cropped, dark brown hair. Mother said she looked like a lad, from the back.

'Mind, she looks like a lad from the front as well until she opens her mouth. Rum old do that one.'

I didn't really understand that.

'She's almost fashionable for 1970', Victoria Gilbert said cattily. She knew everything there was to know about fashion in 1976: her Sister Jane got *Look-In*, and Victoria was able to read the fashion tips a week later. She'd swapped her tartan socks for glitter and sequins two whole months before the trend came to our attention.

Miss Clumber had a yellow car. 'French thing', my Mother said scornfully. Victoria Gilbert said it looked like an upside-down pram, and if you asked her it wasn't safe. No one ever did ask her, yet it was surprising how she always got her opinion heard.

Last of all, Victoria Gilbert said cryptically that Miss Clumber wasn't married. She lived down the next street to them and her Mum was on speaking terms; they'd shared a bottle of Mateus Rosé in the back garden one evening. Most folk drank beer then; Mrs Gilbert had ideas above her station.

According to Victoria, Miss Clumber lived with another woman. She clearly meant more by this statement than I or any of my friends understood.

My new dress was in a Spanish-style, with two lacy tiers and a top that could be worn off the shoulder.

In the playground we no longer played hospitals, farmers or elastic, and the big ship had finally sailed over the 'Ally Ally O' and was long out of sight.

At home I wore my dress in the conventional on-the-shoulder style, but at school, in the playground, I found my niche as a toreador's moll. I flamencoed my playtimes away to the sound of wooden castanets borrowed each day from Mr Dilks, the music teacher. He liked to encourage our enthusiasm for new musical styles. Mr Dilks had one of those moustaches that crinkled like a hairy caterpillar under his nose and a beard that trapped bits of his lunch, keeping the morsels hidden for hours.

I prized those castanets as if they were the crown jewels, watching them intently as they clacked together in my fingers. It was the same way Grandma prized her pools coupon and intently watched Dickie Davies on those Saturday evenings in front of the telly, hoping to win enough to buy her own crown and sceptre.

Those playtimes were something to treasure. There was a freedom I'd not felt before. I was empowered by the rhythm of those little wooden instruments and the feeling of daring as I cheered on Neil the toreador in his grey, ill-fitting school shirt and tatty black trousers. He dived and teased the bull on to its impending death on the dull asphalt playground floor.

Each break time we picked out the bull using three criteria:

The bull should have long brown or black hair.

The bull should have a loud and imposing
voice to enable it to roar and bellow.

The bull should be able to run fast, but not
so fast that it was unable to be caught.

On the odd days Victoria Gilbert was off school we were known to make an exception.

As if a catalyst, that dress led me to many changes. I thought about them each night as I hung it up on its metallic hanger to air. Mother thought I'd become so obsessed with the garment she'd only ever be able to wash it at weekends.

'You'll be breeding maggots in that frock if you're not careful,' she despaired.

But maggots or not, it was amazing the effect a change of clothes could have.

My Mother had worn a yellow dress and now she was married.

My Mother's husband had worn a Derby County tie and now they were on the slide, glory days over.

And I had begun to wear my Spanish-style dress and things started to change, at least at school.

The dress led me to gain a popularity I'd never known before. Each playtime I entertained and amused my new followers on the castanets. In that dress, and with my newfound confidence, I followed my blue-eyed bullfighter around the side of the school canteen where no teacher would see us.

Behind the red-brick building, near the bins which overflowed and spewed rubbish on the ground like confetti, my first not-so-romantic encounter took place. It was here, pressed up against the damp wall, I felt the buckle of Neil's belt in my stomach. I realised that no matter what dress I wore or how newly confident I was, my days as toreador's moll were numbered. The matador was not for me.

For me there was Miss Clumber.

In the chilly autumn mornings that followed, the traffic noise seemed to echo louder and louder, car stereos blared and horns honked as I obliviously danced my way to school with a head full of thoughts of the day to come; of the desire to speak with Miss Clumber, if only about the class nature table. I was now allowed to walk to school on my own, mainly so Mother could get to work an hour earlier and add to her weekly bonus from the factory. I was left ten-pence on the side in the kitchen along with with a hurriedly written note that said simply 'bus fare'.

I promptly pocketed the money and walked to school, crossing the road at the point where she could see me from the factory window, looking as if I was going to the bus stop. Once out of sight I would skip off and wander the mile and a half to school. The money was saved in a pot under my bed, slowly beginning to grow, put away until I could afford a new Abba record or maybe a trip to the cinema on a Saturday morning with one of the girls from my class. It was a slow investment strategy and slightly underhand, as I couldn't explain to Mother exactly where the money was appearing from.

Still, the thoughts of my burgeoning nest egg made the walk to school much more fun. I listened to the car radios as they passed, seeing if I could sing the rest of the lyrics after the vehicles had gone and the stereo sound had been lost to the breeze.

Chapter 36

Each morning the same battered white transit van flew by with the radio blaring out. It was my Brother, though I didn't recognise him at first.

His driving had long been a bone of contention with Mother. She didn't trust anyone to drive her anywhere, only taking the bus when necessary and never wanting a lift, even when the rain was pelting down like stair rods. She would struggle down the road soaked through, blue factory overall sticking out below her anorak and umbrella battling against a wind which either wanted to rip it from her hands or carry her off like a slightly overweight Mary Poppins. John drove too fast, my irritated Mother told me, 'He'll come to a sticky end that Brother of yours... I've told him but he never listens. I may as well not waste my breath. Remember that morning he gave us a lift to your Grandma's? Round that bend near Middleton Top like a madman, nearly killed us he did... never again.'

Years later, over a mug of tea, John told me how he used the white transit van to work the markets. I sipped the tea slowly; carefully avoiding the chip in the rim, wishing it could have been coffee.

Each morning he packed his bags and boxes with hairspray, deodorant, shampoo, spray for athlete's foot, make-up and the cheapest, most pungent perfumes. 'The punters love 'em,' he winked.

He worked two stalls: one for make-up, the other was cleaning products. He spread his time between them, clambering over the great boxes of squashed soap-filled pads and cut-price packets of toilet rolls used as a demarcation point.

'Rob's', the stall said, in big handwritten letters. 'Quality and quantity guaranteed to brighten your day'.

He'd renamed himself when he left home, cast aside the name he'd been given as a baby and taken on a pseudonym. He thought it suited him better, giving him a clean sheet as he tried to leave his past behind.

He started a stall and became a businessman, trying to be respectable, as much as he could be. He told me it didn't always pay to be too straight. Certainly the customers came flocking.

He had his regulars.

On Tuesdays old Mrs Castle bought her disinfectant and bleach for the week. She cleaned at the local butchers. John's bleach was poor quality but so were her wages.

'Cheap bleach for a cheapskate. I tell him it's more expensive than it is,' she admitted to him.

My Brother gave her over-inflated receipts for the things she bought.

The girls from the nearby school wandered past each dinnertime. They tried the tester lipsticks; some were green in colour but when applied changed to an odd deep pink which shone in the bright sunlight. They sampled the eye shadows and mascaras and fingered the oddments in the 'anything for twenty pence' basket.

Occasionally, one of them would buy something.

His customers seemed to love him and he in turn loved their wallets. It was like a game of skill getting them to part with hard-earned cash or pre-order things for their next shop and still have them believe they were getting a bargain.

Every now and again his customers changed roles and sold him their valuables for a well-needed injection of cash. He traded things that were cheap and would sell quickly, such as televisions, radios, and once even an electric food mixer from the hands of a desperate husband who needed the money to put on a dead cert in the 3.20 at Redcar.

'Not bad for three quid,' my Brother crowed, and promptly sold it on to a very happy customer for double the money. 'Not bad at all'.

John's life had become a conveyor belt of selling, restocking and arguing with 'Bloody Hamish', the Scotsman from the next stall who sold chocolate seconds and sweets by the pound. In the slack periods, he daydreamed his moments away.

On the days the rain poured down and his customers stayed inside, avoiding the weather, John brought his van round to the side of the stall and dozed in the front seat until some brave woman ventured out in her plastic rain hood, running across the concrete paving slabs which shone like silver. Sometimes if the rain was hard enough he would get his flask from the cab, wipe out the spare cup with a cloth from the oddments bin and give her a sip of his whiskey-laced tea, warming her up and rewarding her exertions. He offered a free tea towel to dry her glasses when she got home; it was this 'kindness' and lukewarm tea that gained him yet another regular customer.

On the days when the sun shone and the warmth began to melt the eye shadows in their plastic boxes, he would put on his dark glasses and gaze out from behind the lenses into the distance. He watched the young men as they passed by, smiling to himself as their pale skins began to turn brown under the glare of the sun. When they looked his way he wondered if they were watching him too.

Periodically they were. A couple of exchanged smiles later and he had a date for that evening.

At half-past-two each afternoon, earlier if it was wet, he would repack his leftover stock into the van and travel home.

In the traffic jams that built up with clockwork regularity outside the gates of school at last playtime, he would often put on his hazard warning lights, jump out, and cross the road to talk to me. To begin with, I hadn't really known him, but eventually we re-established our relationship and were on good, if secret, terms.

Some days he would give me ten pence for sweets, warning me not to let on where the money had come from.

Apart from once, I never did.

One afternoon I returned home, full of the things I'd done that day, pockets bulging with the bounty found in and around the public toilets near our top playground, plus a bloodied, once-white handkerchief and a shiny new ten pence piece.

We regularly climbed the wall at dinnertimes; escaping the school grounds in the hope our exploration would bring us new and more useful discoveries. Neil and Gary over first, then me hauled up by my wrists, so that each evening it looked as if I'd undergone brutal Chinese burns.

Our first expedition was always to Mrs Mazza's sweetshop.

She was a large, dark, curly-haired Italian woman who had supposedly emigrated to England during the Second World War to escape Mussolini. This was a fact well known in the school yard community; sometimes the boys in our class would ask about the tanks and bombs she would have seen. Her answer was usually that she didn't speak good enough English, thus getting out of the wearisome discussion. It almost always worked.

I had my doubts about Mrs Mazza.

They had a whole fleet of ice cream vans, one to park advantageously outside each school in the town. In total there were five. The oldest and most decrepit rattled down the steep hill to our gates at 3.15. You could hear it coming a mile off, rumbling over the big flagstone cobbles and warbling 'O Sole Mio' out of tune over the surrounding houses.

'That van looks like it came out the Ark. I'll be surprised if she doesn't run some kiddie over soon; bound to have faulty brakes,' so prophesied Mother on the Friday evenings when she met me from school and I demanded a 'ninety-nine' with strawberry sauce. I didn't always get it; it depended on my Mother's mood and whether we needed to invest in washing powder.

'I've never seen 'em off the road, you know. Their eldest, Ted, he mends 'em when they break down, and he's no mechanic. Just you wait and see.'

My first doubt didn't stem from the poor maintenance records of the fleet but rather from the fact that Mrs Mazza actually had a perfect command of the English language. I'd heard her swearing at her sons one morning when they'd forgotten to plug in the vans to charge up overnight.

Secondly, I doubted that they could possibly have driven five ice cream vans over the Alps, even to escape Mussolini, especially as there were only three of them at the time: Mr and Mrs Mazza and her ageing Mother. She sometimes sat in the back of the shop knitting up baby clothes and muttering under her breath at the children who came in for halfpenny chews. Old Mother Mazza didn't look as if she could possibly see over the steering wheel of an ice cream van, never mind drive one up a mountain.

Lastly, ice cream vans ran on electricity. Where would they have plugged them all in?

On our illicit missions from the playground we brought liquorice Black Jacks and pink and yellow rice paper Flying Saucers that stuck to the roofs of our mouths, making our eyes run when the sherbet escaped.

Almost beside the school's top gate were the old red-brick public toilets, smelling of stale urine and 'Izal' disinfectant. They'd stood in the same place for over a hundred years, built by the owners of the great, vermilion-coloured mill that towered over the town.

Here, Gary leant against the decaying brick wall and lit his untipped cigarette, puffing out great billows of dark grey smoke in between bouts of harsh coughing. Neil kicked around in the bushes to find stones to throw into the infants' playground that backed onto the main road. His little Brother Sam was in the first class and it was Neil's ambition to hit him at least once with a well-aimed stone: preferably without getting into trouble with the teachers, Mrs Mulroy, the dinner lady, or his Mother, when he got home.

I explored the dank old toilets, sometimes coming across great treasures, but mostly only discovering empty toilet roll middles and soggy fag ends.

Some days I found treasures more precious than I could ever imagine.

My collection of finds was a constant wonder: A signed photograph of Gregory Peck from *Film Star* magazine,

A string of simulated and paint-flaking pearls,

A half-used pack of pickling spices.

I gave the pearls away to my new friend Rachel. She was the most beautiful girl I'd ever seen, though this was a fact I decided to keep to myself for fear of the further ridicule I'd weather from Neil. He'd sussed out my interest in Miss Clumber, laughed scornfully and called me a 'queer'. I didn't understand what it meant but knew it was offensive. From then on I vowed to say nothing in the hope no one would discover I was different.

Gregory Peck I handed over dutifully to my Brother in his playtime visit. He seemed genuinely pleased with it, giving me a whole fifty pence coin; I smiled gratefully and shoved it in my coat pocket.

The packet of spices I kept for myself because I'd read in my *School Atlas of Discovery* how valuable they were. I dreamed of being the Queen of Sheba in her heavy azure silk robes, carrying voluminous bags of cloves, nutmegs and peppercorns that grew on the wild vines of the Indian monsoon forests, and cinnamon from Sri Lanka, once thought more valuable than gold.

In school I read of adventurers and explorers: Ferdinand Magellan and Sir Francis Drake, plotting their routes around the world to Tjilatjap and Rio De Janeiro on rough drawing paper. I used coloured pencils to shade the areas they'd visited: brown for Drake and black for Magellan. Soon the map I'd spent so long on and traced so neatly had turned the colour of a rather nasty bruise. Disappointed by quarter-past-three, I threw down my pencils, got out my bus fare and put on my coat ready for home.

On the triangle of paved ground where I stood for the bus each evening after school – apart from Friday's shopping expedition – I lingered, waiting for the girls from the convent school further up the road to arrive. They wore brown tunics with yellow and brown ties and, in the summer, sand-coloured straw boaters. Sometimes the nuns that taught them would accompany the smaller children to the stop, making sure they got on the right bus. Mostly, though, the older girls were there and the nuns would only walk to the zebra crossing, seeing them safely across before hurrying back up the road like old moles in long black capes. Once they were out of sight the convent girls and I would play fast games of British Bulldog and Off-Ground-Tick. Some days I was catcher and other days I was first to be caught; once or twice we missed the bus and I had to walk home, much to the consternation of my Mother.

The day I returned home with the bag of spices that made my pocket smell like pickled onions, and the fifty pence piece to put in my penguin moneybox, I'd been the bulldog catcher. I caught six convent girls, my beautiful schoolmate Rachel, and my foot under a loose paving stone.

As I fell, my nose hit the concrete and burst into a pool of dark red blood. It dripped down the front of my school shirt but I stood with valour, wiping it away with the arm of my blazer. I tried to laugh, but the blood poured more and more until a kind woman with long brown permed hair came across to the bus queue and gave me her clean white handkerchief.

I mopped away the mess and tried to give back the now bloody piece of cloth, but the woman looked aghast and told me to keep it. Stuffing it into my pocket, I got on the bus, nose throbbing and eyes watering.

Accidents, no matter how accidental, were a point of conflict with Mother. Even when the explanations were plausible, she didn't believe them. Once, after twisting my ankle, she all but flew up to the school, telling the teacher I'd been forcibly pushed and my blue and purple ankle was a direct result. I'd told her at least ten times I'd merely slipped on some wet steps but she still thought I was lying. Only after Rachel corroborated my story did she drop the subject.

My nosebleed was going to be harder to explain away.

As I got off the bus and reached into my pocket for the door key, I heard the music drifting from our house. As I neared the door the sounds became clearer: 'Country and Western'.

'Rose Marie, I love you, I'm always thinking of you…my Rose, my Rose Marie.'

My stepfather was at home.

This was his last week working in the graveyard. He said he was getting too old for digging and mowing and so, with the help of my Mother, he'd got a job at the factory across the road. He was to become a plastic extruder; it didn't sound very interesting, but at least when I had to tell people what he did for a living, I would no longer have the constant embarrassment of admitting he buried people. Neither would I have to lie about him being a salesman or working in an office like my friend's Dad's did.

I had told the religious education teacher, Mrs Rawlings, that he was a coffin salesman; not too far from the truth, so I didn't feel too guilty. Besides, Mrs Rawlings looked like a jackdaw, all black-haired and sharp-beaked and I didn't like her anyway.

Inside the house he'd put the potatoes on for tea. Potatoes, I once mistakenly told him, took twenty minutes to boil; Mrs Barnford had told us in the previous week's cookery lesson. I got a swift clip round the head for my trouble. It was still three quarters of an hour until Mother came home. I didn't say anything; it would have to be mash for tea again. I usually cooked the dinner and managed to watch a bit of telly before she got back; I had my routine.

As usual, he looked miserable. He never smiled, at least not at me. I decided to tell him about my nosebleed as I couldn't hide it and would have to soak my shirt in the sink with some salt to get the stains out. I pulled out the hanky to show him how much it had bled.

The packet of spices and new fifty pence piece fell out of my pocket. He picked them both up, slamming them on the table.

'Where did you get these from?' he questioned.

I told him I'd found them, again not really a lie; I had indeed found the spices.

'I hope you haven't been taking money from strangers,' he bellowed.

I replied, no: I'd found the spices and someone had given me the money, but it wasn't a stranger. This was a mistake, as I later found out; I'd been seen talking to my Brother by Miss Banks from across the road. She was Belford's very own secret information network.

On afternoons when the sun was noticeably bright, the windows of the houses directly across the road shimmered as if they were made of gold. Sometimes the noise of the traffic which continually went past our cottage was dulled by the sound of the brass band concert from the park in the nearby town and I'd sit on my bedroom window sill listening, keeping an eye on Miss Bank's bungalow.

I'd been told she had a telescope trained on the houses on our road; this was so she never missed out on any gossip. No one told her anything. She had to find out things where she could. She always knew all there was to know; often, it was rumoured, before it happened.

I watched for any signs. Sometimes I swear I saw the glint of glass through her thick net curtains. More often than not, I fell asleep in the warmth of the window, dreaming of different lives and different people.

Now, due to Miss Banks, I ended up in the spotlight and my prized pickling spices ended up in the dustbin with the Saturday morning clearout of the kitchen drawers.

'There's nothing you can do with those spices, they've gone off,' said Mother gruffly, while tipping the contents out of the window and throwing the empty packet into a brandished bin liner. 'And that money John gave you has gone the same way. If he can't be bothered to come and visit us all then he's not going to see any of us. Loitering around the gates like some pervert, I won't have it. Nothing but trouble that school's been: costumes for the play, money for this, money for that. It'll be the death of me.'

My nosebleed had been forgotten.

Like Jack's magic beans my cherished spices had been cast out.

Irradiated spices, though, do not grow like fairytale green beans, especially in England. The seeds blew in the wind onto

225

the damp soil of the back garden, embedding themselves under the dark foliage of a Mulberry bush. But no beanstalk sprung up. There may have been no ladder to the sky, though my desire for freedom and the need for something that was unfamiliar still grew.

Chapter 37

The next two years passed very much as the previous five: all innocent playtime games, cemetery rambles, imaginative stories and the odd day-trip to Blackpool. I'd grown a couple of inches taller, my hair was now a waist-length, unruly straggle and the advance towards a new school manifested itself on the steady horizon I'd been accustomed to. High school was an alarming prospect to our class; for one year we'd been the crème de la crème of the little school.

We were the lunchtime meal monitors, the servers who collected the offerings from the kitchen hatch, and the ones that decreed who ate their parsnips and who didn't.

It wasn't so much that the little children saluted in the playground as we passed or gave us their daily quota of sweets, more the fact that we were at the pinnacle of our lower school career and the rest of the institution knew it. They watched us sneakily from the corners of their eyes with the full and resounding knowledge that at the end of the year we would be deposed and this privileged position would be theirs.

However, the authority of those last few weeks was solely ours.

At dinnertime we settled on our serving partner and went to pick up the steaming metal containers of food from the dinner ladies. Mrs Sanders dished out the vegetables, Mrs Peters the meat and Mrs Jefferies, who doubled as the lollipop woman outside the school gates, gave us our share of puddings.

Queen of puddings ~ *stewed apple with a sponge topping, coated with sugar. Bake in a heated oven for twenty minutes on gas mark 5.*

Manchester Tart ~ *pastry base with strawberry blancmange, strawberry jam and a coating of toasted coconut. Bake the pastry blind in the oven for ten minutes, chill and fill with toppings. Serve refrigerated.*

Cornflake concrete Pudding *pastry base filled with cornflakes and covered with treacle. Bake in a hot oven for ten minutes. Allow to set and serve cold with custard.*

Some days dinners were as delectable a dish as any television chef could wish for. Other days, when Brussels sprouts and chicken crumble were on the menu, it seemed like we'd been taken over by Wormwood Scrubs kitchen staff and a master poisoner had made his home in our school canteen.

It was with these meals that the servers came into their element.

The dinner hall had a nauseating aroma, an intoxicating combination of floor polish, boiling vegetables and sweat from the P.E. classes that used the wall bars and long tied-up rope for their weekly torture sessions. Each day, at precisely twelve o'clock, we waited for the sign that meant it was time to fetch the younger children to the table. As the Venetian blinded hatches began to open upon the new day's lunchtime rush, we marched out into the playground to round up our assigned groups and shepherd them to their respective tables. Like Moses and the people of Israel, each little tribe was slowly settled into place. After a race through 'for what we are about to receive, may the Lord make us truly thankful', it was the moment we had all waited for... drum roll... the lifting of the metal lids to reveal what lay inside.

Tradition, as in most schools, played its part. At ours, dinner was endured in muttered complaining; one hundred suffering voices each sitting, uttering the long-hallowed, if whispered words; 'but these aren't chips, they're roasted parsnips and I'm not eating them!'

In some crafty and undercover way, as if to prepare us for parenthood, our free choice of serving partner was curtailed to the opposite sex: twenty-five newly formed families to be divorced as quickly as dinner was over and the plates cleaned away.

I chose my partners well, from unfortunate past experience, alternating between Gary and Neil for the safest option.

Once, swayed by the promise of sweets and a go on his 'Simon' electronic toy, I'd suffered humiliation at the hands of Patrick Simms, who inadvertently managed to drop a whole tray's worth of pudding on the floor while attempting an impression of the waiter he'd seen with his parents at the local French restaurant. Later that day, after being refused both the sweets and a chance to follow the light sequence on the game, I came to the conclusion it was best to play safe and stick with what I knew.

Occasionally, during the bedlam of pudding, when everyone seemed happy, I glanced across at the opposite table and agonised over Rachel and her newly made dinnertime family.

It was about this time I began to appreciate that perhaps things didn't always happen in the traditional manner implied by my Mother's 'Mills and Boon' romances.

In the top playground the elder boys discussed their five-a-side football tactics and leaned on the creaking wooden fence in an exaggerated effort to look like the latest television heartthrob. The girls were oblivious, standing huddled in distinct gabbling clumps, apart from when they stole the odd admiring glance across as a loud noise erupted from the boys' direction.

Neil, with his grey school shirt open at the neck, wore his '*Blake's 7*' pencil case around his wrist on a piece of string as a badge of his estate. Gary lurked around the edges of the fence, occasionally shooting at shadowy spies from the Eastern block, China or Russia. It little mattered where they came from; they all died the same. Usually with much screaming.

That day in Mr Parkin's maths class, we'd been given a letter. This in itself was not unusual; school trips abounded during these last summer weeks. We expected Twycross Park and Zoo, or at least a day out on Stanton Moor exploring burial mounds and filling in worksheets about druids and the Celtic religion. For the past two years we'd managed to convince Mr Eldridge, the English History teacher, that it was useful for us to view the way in which human sacrifice would have been offered to the ancient gods of the forest. Each year, Eleanor 'druid' Davies had been laid screaming onto the flat sacrificial rock we'd named in her honour.

This year, however, the much-hoped for school trip was not quite as far afield as we'd imagined. Our hallowed letters were stapled shut.

Doors, no matter how tightly secured, were no match for a crack team of girl snoopers. Locks were there to be opened, with or without keys, and secrets were only secret until one or another found out. Staples therefore, were not exactly a challenge.

Together we knew all there was to know. If it didn't impact on our collective consciousness it was not an issue, nothing worth our time and attention. Stapled letters, though, were most definitely an issue.

The month before we moved on to the higher school, year seven, with written permission from parents, we were to be taught the rudiments of sex education.

Each Wednesday, for the last four weeks of term, we suffered inexplicable torture and embarrassment at the hands of the biology teacher, the local authority projectionist and the sanitary nurse from a rather famous tampon company. She informed us that during the menstruation cycle we girls would lose the equivalent of one eggcup-full of blood per month. Mary Bilby, who bragged she was forward for her age, confided later that this little snippet of information was not necessarily true. Most of us found this out anyway in the years to come, much to our dismay.

The boys did not attend Sandra the sanitary nurse's lectures; they went to a separate talk given by the R.E. teacher. We weren't privy to what he imparted, but later on in the playground they sidled further away from us and sniggered quietly to themselves, happy with their newfound knowledge.

The break-time bullring games were forgotten and it was time to put away my Spanish dress forever; my dancing days were over; ahead lay only sex.

Chapter 38

With the new enlightenment of our biological future stored safely in the backs of our minds, rumour again became the fixed interest of our group. In those last remaining days we were 'assigned our targets'. Mine was Mrs Eldridge, wife of the English History tutor, who herself filled in as a supply teacher in any subject that was needed.

Mrs Eldridge was a small, colourless, grey-haired woman of about fifty. She was married, had one son and went to church each and every Sunday. I'd seen her outside the gates as I passed by on the way to the newsagent's to collect my Sunday 'paper round'. I delivered, as a favour, three papers to the neighbours: two were the *News of the World* and the other the *Sunday People*. They gave me sweets for my services. I didn't mind the effort. I read the problem pages and soaked up the scandals that had come to light during the week; they entertained me during the mile and a half walk home. I was grown up and educated now, almost knowing what the words meant.

Mrs Eldridge was a mystery to no one. I'd wanted someone more exciting, Miss Clumber for example, but was beaten to it. Instead, I had to report my rather dreary findings to the rest of the group and wait with torment to find out more about the woman who'd filled my mind with strange thoughts for three years.

Miss Clumber, as I already knew, was not married. She was almost thirty according to Victoria Gilbert's calculations and each evening whilst her car was waiting to be mended at the local garage she was picked up from the school gates by a woman in a black hatchback.

'They live together,' Victoria stated. 'Her name's Jenny.'

We didn't ask where she got her information; to us rumour and speculation were equally as good as truth.

Later that day Victoria informed us she'd seen them kiss as Miss Clumber got into the car. With this fearless exposé she reclaimed the limelight and for the rest of the afternoon was the star of the snooping squad.

True or not, news of the kiss was a revelation. It fuelled my waking moments and crept into my dreams; at least until someone else took my attention, filling the six-week holiday that fell immediately before my move to the high school.

Rachel was as much a mystery to me as my feelings for Miss Clumber. Living at opposite ends of town and being taught in different classes meant that apart from break-times and home time she remained pretty much an enigma. Watching her serve out potatoes to her makeshift family was more than irksome; I had no power over the situation, could not even be part of her clan for this half-hour session. All I was able to do was sit and watch enviously.

The last day of term in assembly, where the rest of the school said goodbye to the top year – no doubt secretly glad we were going – I managed to position myself in a seat behind her class, directly behind Rachel's chair. Her long blonde curly ponytail draped over her shoulder exposing the soft nape of her neck. For almost half an hour I watched with relish the hairs on her silky brown arms glistening in the sunlight that glared through the hall windows, wanting to be able touch them, stroke them; most of all yearning to say something to her, something to fill the emptiness of the silence I felt inside.

The last strains of 'Morning Has Broken' petered out into a dirge of coughing and we all turned to file out for the last time. I timidly filled my lungs with the stale air, breaths of so many children, some of them hers, and quickly stammered out.

'Will you come and see me next week? We could go for a walk or something?'

As I anxiously looked up at her, she grinned and nodded that she would. Two little gestures and I wandered blissfully into my last day at little school.

Lessons finished, I packed up the rubbish collected in my desk and stuffed it into my bag, topping the pile with the autograph book I'd filled with funny sayings and sentiments from children I'd see just a few short few weeks later. At that moment they seemed important to keep.

Holidays started for most children but not for me, I was still expected to tidy the house, push the Hoover round and do the washing. If I was lucky, I had free afternoons to watch the telly, trying to find black and white films to escape into before cooking the tea and dishing it up. Actually all films in our house were black and white. Mother wouldn't have a colour TV, said it gave her a headache. She and my stepfather returned home from work and ate what I'd made without a thank you, then I washed up. It seemed unfair to me that my contemporaries enjoyed six weeks of youth clubs, family holidays and mucking around while I was cooped up like Cinderella with a mop for a friend.

The day of Rachel's visit got closer and I started to panic more and more about the mess we lived in and called a home. I had to try and make it look inviting, like the pictures of houses in the magazines at the dentist. It was a complete non-starter. No matter how I arranged the cushions or plumped them, they didn't look ethnic or trendy, the carpet looked threadbare and dull and the wallpaper around the fireplace was peeling. I would keep her cocooned in the kitchen or she could go in my bedroom; they were acceptable, at least as far as I could see. I cleaned from top to bottom, sprayed and polished, brushed and mopped; soon it was ready, smelling of Pledge and lavender air freshener: not exactly a show home but the best it would ever be.

Mother was suspicious about the amount of cleaning and sprucing I'd done in the house, questioning sarcastically, 'what's the funny bloody pong in here? Smells like an old woman's bedroom it does.'

She didn't know I was having a visitor; I couldn't tell her. She didn't like me to have friends; it was easier not to have strangers in the house.

The last time I had a friend over my stepfather ranted after we'd tramped mud into the front room on our shoes. He sent her packing with a verbal flea in her ear. Never one to sugar-coat his words, she caught the harsh side of his tongue and fled in tears. She never heard it again because she never came back. For many years no one else came either. Presumably forewarned about his foul temper they'd been advised to steer clear.

Rachel was going to be different; I was determined. They wouldn't know she was coming or that she had ever been. This was to be my secret, at least for as long as it took for her to like me in the way I liked her, though I wasn't sure how I would know or what that really meant.

Next morning was the day of her arrival. I ran the Hoover around the room three times with sheer nervous energy, bleached the sink, filled and refilled the kettle and cut up a cake, arranging it on our best serving platter. The plate was strategically placed to cover the fag burn in the tablecloth. I sat apprehensively fidgeting before noticing Rachel standing outside the back door with her cheeky face pushed up against the glass, grinning in at me.

'Hello. You were miles away weren't you?' she teased as I opened the door.

I laughed and nodded, giving her a fleeting hug. She felt warm and smelt of her Mother's expensive perfume. I poured the hot water from the kettle into the chipped old brown teapot trying not to show how uneasy I felt being watched by those wonderful blue eyes; frightened I would spill the tea as I tipped it into the cups and she would see how inept I was. Rachel slouched back in the kitchen chair, clearly at home in a new situation, making it easy to chatter on about what she'd been doing since school ended, who she'd seen and spoken to. I avoided reporting what I'd been doing; it was mundane and boring by comparison.

After scoffing cake, it was time for the tour. It wouldn't take long: the house was tiny, a little limestone cottage, much like all the others in the dales where I grew up. Nothing grand, that was for sure. She seemed to like it though and was most impressed by the view out of the landing window which gave a picture postcard scene of the hills in the distance and this year's half-grown lambs in the foreground. I couldn't quite see what was so fascinating, especially when my prized collection of Abba posters was only feet away behind the closed door to my bedroom. It was only the view I'd seen and been part of all my life.

On the nights when I couldn't sleep I would leave the curtains open so the light from the streetlamp would filter into my room, allowing me to read undetected or gaze up at the posters of my favourite band, dreaming I would meet them. Mostly I wanted to walk in the snow with Frida, holding her hand as she sang to me softly in Swedish. It was a nice gentle dream and I fell contentedly to sleep on many nights.

I was incredibly proud of those posters and my membership of the Abba fan club. I had all the newsletters displayed on the wardrobe door and my large fan club badge attached to the big old brown bear I'd had for as long as I could remember; apparently a present from my Dad the day I was born. I called him Bear. As good a name as any.

Rachel looked around the tiny room making the right kind of admiring noises about my posters. She perched on the end of my single bed to leaf through old copies of *Look-In* and sing lines of the latest tunes with a warbling voice and a slight giggle. Each time she laughed I became aware of a strange feeling of flux in my chest, almost like the rhythm in my heart changed, like it missed a stroke or had more than one beat. I worried in case I was ill. I watched too many hospital dramas and for a long time had been involved in a future dream career as Nurse Clarke, blue-uniformed angel, striding the corridors of the large brick hospitals, saving lives and bringing light and brightness into the last days of the dying. I really started to believe I was poorly when she tapped me, drawing attention to the picture of The Specials, her favourite band of the moment. Her fingertips touched the top of my hand and quickly moved towards the magazine to point at the picture of Terry Hall; I looked towards the page but couldn't even half-concentrate on the image with my stomach doing somersaults and turning itself inside-out. It was a bizarre sensation, but after it subsided, I missed it and wanted it to start again. I felt excited and vibrant; the blood in my cheeks flooded to the surface making me glow like a beacon in the dingy room. I hoped she'd touch me again to see if it happened twice. Was the strange feeling a reaction to her fingers or, if not, did I need a Doctor?

Time seemed to slow in the bedroom that day; I catalogued every minute detail, savouring those moments just in case I never experienced that gut-wrenching excitement again. In fact, time had passed only too quickly and Rachel had to leave. We happily gabbled our way through the village and down the road which led eventually to her front door and hopefully a lift home before my Mother and stepfather discovered me missing. I was invited in, something I'd not anticipated. Stepping over the threshold was like entering another world; everything had its own pristine, gleaming place. Wall-to-wall shag pile covered the floor in every room. As I stepped into the lounge – as Rachel called it – I seemed to sink into the carpet. The room was large and airy with a low table in the middle covered with artistically placed books and magazines. A 'coffee table', apparently. In our front room there wasn't space for one of those and no one drank coffee anyway. I'd never been in a house like it; a tinkling ring from the hall further underlined our different lifestyles. They even had their own telephone. Fairy cakes were offered on a cut glass stand and ice cream was served up in proper sundae glasses with sauce and chopped nuts. Suddenly I felt very rustic. I quickly gobbled down the delicacies with as much politeness as I could muster, now extremely conscious of the need to get home and put the tea on. Before I left I hurriedly asked Rachel if she fancied a walk the next week. I wanted her to know the real me, not the one from the school playground, and I longed to show her round the cemetery, inviting her into my fantasies and secrets.

Tuesday week we were back in my kitchen putting together a picnic: butties, fruit, a couple of bags of salt-and-vinegar crisps and a bottle of orange squash. To me it was a scene of domestic perfection, one unfortunately interrupted by the chore of preparing the evening meal. While Rachel cut the cheese sandwiches into triangles and packed them in bags, I adeptly peeled a pan of King Edwards, putting them in water on the stove ready for their tea.

'Do you always cook their dinner?' Rachel asked, in awe that I could manage a whole meal like this by myself.

'Yes, every night, more's the pity,' I replied, almost ashamed. 'I'd be in trouble if it wasn't on the table when they walked in,' I said laughing, trying to cover my discomfort and keep the secret of my skivvying existence hidden. I'd become a good little actress when I needed to be, or at least I thought so.

We left the house, walking quickly out onto the road and passing the end of the lane at rocket pace. Mother would be none too pleased if she glanced out the factory window and clocked two young girls making off with the contents of her larder. After this point I slowed to a meander, hoping Rachel hadn't noticed the burst of speed.

We picked our way though the graveyard, gazing at the crumbling headstones, me explaining the history of the vaults I knew about and making up the rest to amuse and scare her. The woods got thicker as we moved upwards along the cemetery path that wound from the valley to the skyline. Once our lungs had recovered at the top, the mile of steep labouring climb was worth every panted breath as we turned and wondered at the view. The mighty panorama of the valley, with its river snaking through the scenery like a huge grey-green serpent, was dazzling. Occasionally a blackbird or the odd squirrel would scuttle across in front of us and disappear into the trees; the undergrowth grew increasingly dense, casting shadows across the way forward.

As we turned the corner I laughed out loud at Rachel's sudden start and sharp intake of breath. We'd come across the huge alabaster angel, its outstretched wings looming over the last corner of the cemetery – the piece of ground kept specifically for Catholics.

Mother told me they bred like rabbits. I'd misheard her and for a few years thought she'd said Catholics bred rabbits. My interest in the notice board outside the local Church obviously worried her and she commented on the amount of time I spent reading the flyers, asking impatiently: 'What the 'eck are you studying now? Why is it we have to stop here day in, day out,

237

so you can read that bloody board, eh? No matter what weather: rain, hail, snow... anyone'd think you wanted to join 'em.'

When I cottoned on she was annoyed, I looked at her in bewilderment, replying quite innocently that I was only looking for adverts about baby rabbits that needed a good home. Obvious, I thought.

'You want to look in the post office for that sort of thing, but I wouldn't bother if I was you. You never looked after that fish you wanted from the fair. It's me that has to clean it out and wash its bowl and feed it every day. Poor thing'd be dead if it was left up to you,' she chided.

I resisted the temptation to tell her I'd never wanted the fish in the first place, but thought better of it. In her present mood Moby would end up swimming for his life down the toilet pan.

As Rachel jumped, her reaction was to grab my hand, squeezing my fingers tightly. She didn't let go once she'd calmed down and I, enjoying the feeling of holding this little slender hand in my own, didn't try to shake her off. We walked on, she seeming oblivious to the unfamiliarity of the situation and me in petrified delight at the startling pleasure of holding a hand which was freely given.

We sat to eat our sandwiches in the overgrown meadow next to the cemetery where the long grass sheltered us from the occasional dog-walker's prying eyes. My appetite had vanished and salt-and-vinegar crisps had lost their appeal. My mouth went dry as I tried to summon up the courage to tell her about my feelings, spending agonising minutes quietly threading strands of grass together into a haphazard pattern. I was deep in thought, when she prodded me playfully in the ribs, asking, 'What's up chuck?'

'Oh, nothing,' I lied. 'Just thinking about something.'

'About what? You've been quiet for ages.'

I suppose I must have then let out a long sigh because she looked at me quizzically and tugged my fingers. I glanced back at her, blinking away the tears that had started to prickle in my eyes.

'I don't know how to say this... but... I like you,' I stumbled.

'I like you too,' she laughed. 'That's not something to cry about is it?'

'No... but I mean, I really like you... think about you all the while... I don't know what it means... I want to touch you... I'm sorry.' I turned away, waiting for her to react, thinking she would shout or hit me or leave me there. I had gone through the scenarios in my head hundreds of times over, all different, but all equally disastrous. They flashed through my mind in the seconds that passed before she spoke.

'I think I knew that,' she blushed.

She was quiet for a minute, then reached over and grabbed my hand, gripping my fingers as tightly as before when she'd been scared. Smiling weakly, I raised my eyes and they met hers. She grinned at me, leaned forward and gave me the quickest, softest kiss; more of a peck, but nevertheless a kiss. My first kiss.

Chapter 39

For weeks I rebounded between a cloud of absolute terror, petrified of being found out, and a mist of total bliss: happy, bewildered and scared at the same time. I blundered through my days, the weeks of the holiday slowly trickling past, each one the same. The only highlights were visits from Rachel. The days before them I was on tenterhooks, willing her to come quicker. The days after I felt bereft and didn't understand why. I had to be my usual self or my Mother and stepfather would find out. If they discovered the nature of our relationship he would stop me seeing Rachel altogether. Therefore I had to pretend everything was ordinary and everyday. I did my best to behave as before, trying so hard to appear normal that I seemed abnormal to myself. It took a huge effort to be humdrum. I wasted days folding washing and ironing tea towels, cooking chops and boiling potatoes, mowing lawns and pulling weeds. I only ever wanted to be in the vicinity of Rachel, feel her close by, have her hands on my skin and be tantalised by the tiny hairs on her neck, the ones that stood up when they felt breath or a sudden change of temperature.

Eventually an idea came to me and I decided to visit the library. I sat in the adult reference section tucked away in the corner and looked through the encyclopaedias, trying to find something that would explain what was wrong with me. Why did I feel so confused and stirred up? Why couldn't I stand seeing Rachel leave? Why did it hurt so much? I tried to stay out of the librarian's glare; she was keeping a distinct weather eye on me, not understanding why a young girl would be sitting so quietly in the reference section in the middle of the school holidays.

I read sections of books that described symptoms of madness. None of them fitted and yet they all fitted perfectly. But I didn't feel mad when she was close: I felt alive, could sense the blood in my veins and the breath in my chest. I was scared of things that I'd never experienced before, things I yearned for, like the sensation of her skin under my fingers. Books had been my friends for as long as I could remember. In some way they always helped me understand or find another place to exist, even if it was only in my head. These books weren't helping me now, though; there were no magical solutions in *The Famous Five*, at least not that I could think of. Julian, Dick, Anne, George and Timmy only ever dealt with ginger beer and cases of missing uncles, not intense emotional heartache.

Idly I sat there, flicking through the pages of the closest book to hand, the big leather bound dictionary; the type with finger holes cut in the side allowing easy access to the alphabetical sections. Words fascinated me and it was comforting to know what they meant and how they could be used. I slowly inched my way through the alphabet, skimming the main bold text until, after reading lots of entries that didn't fit, I remembered my forays into the Sunday tabloids and that there was a word I needed to look up:

Lesbian ~ homosexual woman: a woman who is sexually attracted to other women.

There it was in black and white. Me, described on a page. Well, I thought it was me, I didn't fully understand all the words but got the gist of being attracted to another girl. The cold print on the page didn't give me any clues about what was supposed to happen next and Sandra's menstruation and no-sex education lessons hadn't touched on anything; it was all still a mystery.

I quickly shut the book with a thump when I spotted Mother's workmate waddling towards me. Doreen Stott worked in the canteen; she had been on the shop floor until nearly getting her hand stuck in the back-winder and deciding it was one brush with certain death too far.

Doreen was known for her long one-sided conversations where the other party could never get a word in because she

241

didn't stop for long enough. People said her lung capacity meant she could dive for pearls off the coast of a Pacific island without an oxygen tank. She talked from the start of work until clocking-out time and was known to be still gossiping as the bus doors closed on her conversation at five o'clock. Doreen loved to talk; no one had any choice but to listen.

It was her constant chatting which broke the concentration of the maintenance man, Harry. Not one to appear rude, he'd stood and listened to the long and in-depth didactic about the declining popularity of pickled beetroot. He'd been adding new bolts to the back-winding machine; replacing old worn fitments which made it liable to break down at inopportune moments. Harry hadn't got the guard back on when Doreen, still in full flow about vinegar and whether white was better than malt, reached over to pick up an end for the clothes line bag. Her overall sleeve got caught in the winding mechanism and she started to feel her arm being pulled into the side of the machine. Luckily Harry saw what was happening just as Doreen detected something was amiss. The colour drained from her face; for the first time in her life she was struck dumb, standing transfixed as first her sleeve then her whole arm was yanked towards the locking teeth of the machine. Harry pushed the emergency stop button on the wall. Everything went dead, the electricity supply was interrupted, radios ceased their babbling, workers stopped and machines ground to a halt as the smell of burning material hung in the air. Doreen was left in an eerie silence, missing half a sleeve. From then on she was adamant that the factory floor was much too dangerous and asked for a transfer downstairs. She seemed much happier with her part-time hours: calmer, less prone to dropping pan scrub boxes and crying over spilt 'Percy Thrower' plant rings.

'Hello Pet,' Doreen blurted out loudly into the quiet space. 'What you doing in here on this lovely day? You should be out in the fresh air, not stuck in here with all these dusty books... your Mother says the same. You'd be better off taking up a hobby, going to a club, seeing other girls of your own age. That's the ticket, better than sitting in and reading all them novels you take out of here... A young girl like you, plenty of time for reading when you get to my age. You'll be glad of a book then. Mark my words, you make the most of the time you have while you're young. Go out with your friends. What about that lovely friend of yours, Rachel, eh? Where's she?'

The mention of Rachel's name sent me as red as a post box and I stuttered out something about doing homework for the next term. Doreen didn't need to know there wasn't any before moving to a new school. It answered her question and I hoped she'd go away as quickly as she'd arrived. Her mouth opened and another endless stream of conversation was on its way when the librarian saved me with a loud. 'Shhh! This is the library, madam.'

Doreen got the message and gave me a cheeky wink. Demented sign language told me she was going to the romance section and please would I get out of here into the fresh air. I smiled and nodded, deciding to make my exit, bemoaning the fact that I couldn't even read the dictionary in peace these days. I felt trapped and hemmed in. Someone was always looking over my shoulder.

Still, Doreen had spoken some sense amongst the misplaced concerns for my well-being; I did need to take up a hobby.

Each remaining week of the holiday I got to see Rachel for a few hours on my own. They were grabbed in an afternoon or over lunchtime, usually with a white lie to say I was going to see someone about homework or taking books back to the library. The summer of 1978 was over in a flash. Once we'd embarked on our high school career and lessons began in earnest our time was no longer our own. She was not in any of my classes and what with homework and domestic chores I'd have to hatch an ingenious plan to see her at all. I decided to go for a couple of hours every week to the St John's Ambulance brigade headquarters where I could see her legitimately. Not only could I be trained for a future as angel nurse Clarke, I would also gain a few precious moments near her. Two birds, one stone.

My new hobby.

A hobby that was, for once, not frowned upon by my stepfather, even though it cost fifty pence a week for attendance and subs. I think he thought it was a fair price to get rid of me on a Tuesday evening.

Rachel had been a nursing cadet, as they were called, for about two years and was very skilled at teaching the novices the rudiments of first aid: splinting a leg and how to make a tourniquet with a triangular bandage, protecting a broken bone which was penetrating the outer skin. Rachel stood at the front of our little group in her elephant-grey A-line uniform, black tights and sensible flat black shoes explaining how to construct perfect hospital corners when bed making, elevating a leg using what was available and putting a casualty into the recovery position. I marvelled at the capacity she had to remember all these techniques and wondered if I would ever be that good. I tried not to marvel too much for fear someone would notice my dewy-eyed expression.

After our little band of new nurses had been to the training sessions for three weeks, we had to meet with Ada, the nursing leader of the local branch, to see if we all wanted to enrol properly into the corps. It was not a certainty that each of us would be invited into the inner sanctum of the unit. Ada was very protective of her cadets, wanting them to be the best first aiders they could be, intending for them to win competitions and cups and go on to become professional nurses, maybe even doctors. When she spoke at training sessions and events it was easy to hear the pride in her voice and feel the strength in her conviction that her company were the best in the county.

We had to be potential Florence Nightingales to be invited into Ada's corps. It was a worrying time; futures depended on the correct positioning of a safety pin.

Ada sat at the front of the hall, a little woman, no more than four feet eleven. I already towered over her, but her height was no indicator of her stature in the local community. When she walked down the main street on a Friday teatime to do her weekly shopping, people smiled and said hello, elderly men tipped their hats, doors were opened and bus drivers pipped their horns. She was something of a local celebrity.

One evening when Mother came to meet me from the Memorial Hall I asked why Ada was so well loved in the town.

'Well, she is sort of famous round here. She saved a kiddy's life a good few years before you were born. He fell in the canal down by the mill cut and couldn't get out again. Poor little sod wasn't a good swimmer, kept going under. I was surprised he didn't die from the water he swallowed, it was filthy down there. They've cleaned it up a lot since. Anyhow, she were coming home from work at the sweet factory, worked on the toffee line. She always walked down the towpath home, short cut you see. She heard the splashes and saw the lad disappear under the water, only he didn't come up again. Anyway, bless that woman, she jumped in and dragged that little lad out. She was no swimmer either, but she was determined. He'd stopped breathing and was going blue. She gave him the kiss of life for ages and eventually he coughed up this great lungful of dirty water and came to again. Poor woman was soaked through, but she wouldn't leave that lad 'til he was in a hospital bed and his Mum was there with him. She came home on the bus and thought no more of it 'til the Belper News came out the next teatime and her photo was plastered all over t'front page. She was suddenly famous, no one has ever forgotten, that's why.'

I was suddenly in awe and desperately wanted to be chosen to join the corps, and now not just to be near Rachel. A few weeks later we were tested on the skills we'd learned. At the front of the hall, Ada sat watching as her potential new cadets were put through their paces. We moved around in a circle, eight tests in turn:

1. Bed making and hospital corners.
2. Supportive arm slings.
3. Tourniquet to hold a piece of glass in place in a cut on the arm.
4. Splinting a broken leg.
5. Bandaging a twisted ankle.
6. Recovery position performed on the rubber mannequin called Annie.

7. Bandaging a broken collarbone.
8. Effective treatment of a burn or scald.

It was extremely nerve-wracking. At each move and first aid test we were scored out of ten, though weren't privy to our marks; on each station I became a little bit more stressed. By the time I got to bandage a twisted ankle I'd inwardly convinced myself I was doomed to failure. Luckily, the twisted ankle I had to bandage was none other than Rachel's.

'How do you think you're doing chuck?' she whispered with concern.

I fiddled with the end of the bandage, nervously pulling off the stray threads.

'I don't think I'm doing very well really. My corners were OK but my sling was a bit loose,' I mumbled dejectedly in reply.

'Look, don't give up. You only have to pass six out of eight to be in. I'm sure you'll get that. I'd pass you. Now get on and bandage my ankle girl!'

By the end of the eight tests I was exhausted with the tension and concentration, just wanting to know how I'd done. There were twenty of us up for selection but only fifteen uniforms hanging like trophies at the front of the hall. None of them looked like they would fit me. I was convinced I was out of the corps, would have to give up my stethoscope before I'd even examined my first patient. It was only a matter of time before my fate was announced for all and sundry to hear.

The would-be lifesavers sat in the double row of chairs that had been put out like church pews. I plonked myself at the back and slouched in my seat as Ada cleared her throat and started her speech.

'Well, you've all worked really hard over the last few weeks. I know it's not been easy, there's a lot to learn, and even I learn something new each time I go on a training course. Learning is good for all of us. Sometimes, though, we aren't suited to all we try and that's why we have to be tested, to see if we have aptitudes for the things we want to do. I'm pleased to tell you that there are fifteen of you that I'm going to invite to join the corps. The five which aren't selected this time I would like to invite to try again. We should all remember there is no shame in failing.'

I wasn't sure I agreed; I didn't want to crawl home and tell Mother that I hadn't got in. Not that she would have thought anything bad of me, but my stepfather would have loved it. Whilst I was lost in thoughts of my impending disappointment, Ada continued with her talk.

'Look at Karen here; she's going to Derby Hospital to train as a registered nurse. Karen failed her initial testing with the corps but she didn't give up. She kept trying 'til she got in and rose through the ranks. She had a belief that she could be a nurse so she kept going. Those of you that don't get in tonight think of Karen and try again. Now, the all-important names of those I would like to invite into the corps.'

Everyone else sat up a bit straighter in their chairs, though I still hid behind the girl in front, not wanting to draw attention to myself when my name wasn't called.

'Congratulations to Helen Broad, Elizabeth Carpenter, Abigail and Bethany Jones, Jane Nicholls, Deborah Harvey, Myra Slack, Jenny Stevens, Robert Smith, Caroline Clarke, Samantha James, Jane Knutton, Robert Bird, Louise Bell and, finally, Michael Fern. Well done all of you, your uniforms are behind you. If they don't fit, don't worry, we'll measure you up for a new one and order them in. The remaining five of you please don't think badly of yourselves, not one of you scored too low in any of the tests and I hope you will try again.'

I'd slumped further in my chair. I'd stopped listening to the names when I hadn't heard my own in the first three, assuming Ada was doing the list alphabetically. When my name hadn't been read out I resigned myself to my fate. The rest of the corps clapped and I joined in out of politeness but was already thinking about getting my coat, skulking out and starting the long walk home. Rachel dug her finger in my back and I turned. She was beaming at me.

'Said you'd pass didn't I? Go on, you'd better go and get measured for your uniform and then I'll walk you home. Might even buy you a bag of chips if you're lucky!'

Chapter 40

It was difficult to see Rachel at all. On school days any clandestine encounters were limited to snatched moments at break-times where there was always someone else getting in the way. At weekends it was impossible for either of us to get away from our respective families. My Mother had a routine. Friday nights we went shopping and I carried the bags; she piled them on me one after another like a pack animal until the plastic handles sliced into my fingers, cutting off the blood supply. It took hours for them to return to their former shape. She wasn't allowed to carry anything heavy after she'd had a hysterectomy when I was nine. The Doctor told her she'd have to take it easy for three to four months; she would spin it out for three to four years. She was clever in her own way.

Saturday and Sunday were quiet days: we cleaned, she ironed, she baked, and I washed up.

My stepfather cleaned out his new passion, racing pigeons. He stood in the garden proudly watching them swoop and wheel round the house; it was like being in a poor man's Hitchcock film. Sunday mornings were worse. He was out there at eight o'clock rattling pigeon peas in the biscuit barrel he'd taken from the kitchen cupboard. It once held flour; he'd dumped it in a bowl assuring us he'd make a cake with it later. The promised sponge never materialised.

Through the bedroom curtains I could see the dark shapes of birds flying past the window, the swooping and cooing and shaking of the tin irritated me more than I could safely express.

By the time I got up Mother was usually beside herself; the infernal pigeons drove her mad too. She started on her weekly rant; a similar theme every Sunday, slightly different wording each time but always the same end point: my stepfather and his selfishness. It wasn't that she thought he was generally selfish, only when it came to his hobbies.

'If he isn't out there with them bloody birds then he's running down to Belper to put money on horses that never win. Then he's stuck in front of the telly watching the bloody things run. The newspaper's always on the racing page, I can never get to the crossword. He's enough to drive a woman to drink and I would if I didn't have dinner to cook and a bathroom to clean.'

I helped her peel potatoes and place them round the beef joint. She skinned little onions and they went in with the spuds. Lastly, in went the parsnips. He didn't like parsnips, but on Sunday mornings she didn't care, even gave him extra. I wasn't that fond of them either but suffered in silence. The knowledge that he struggled to clear his plate was sweet revenge for his feathered friends.

The dinner went on at half past ten. She made three mugs of Camp coffee with full cream milk and we sat down to drink it; us in the kitchen, him out on the steps of the pigeon loft. I watched him through the back door window, sipping at the steaming mug and keeping his beady eyes on the sky around the house. Occasionally he called to the birds and some of them would land and scuttle up to his feet looking for bits of food. Sometimes I thought he must have a kind streak under that thin, harsh exterior. Usually someone who displayed a tiny amount of compassion for a small creature would be seen as benevolent, but in his case it was all about control. He decided what they ate, how much, and when. Benevolence didn't come into it.

After the coffee I had an hour to spare. Mother curled up in the front room and dipped into her latest Mills and Boon and I went upstairs and wrote letters to Rachel.

Proper writing paper was a no-no in our house; my messages were scribbled on blank flysheets torn from library hard-back novels and dispatched in homemade envelopes. Initially notes were timid, more like something you would send to a pen friend in New York, stilted and routine, ending at the bottom of the page with a kiss mark. They were short letters then, a single sheet of what I'd been doing in the time I hadn't seen her, usually just about washing, the shopping we'd brought in Fine Fare or what I'd watched on the television. After we saw *Abba The Movie* the tone of the letters started to change.

Mother and I went to the pictures every Friday, money permitting, to see the release of the fortnight. New films at our local cinema were shown about three weeks behind the national release date. I read previews of what would be coming, how it'd been received by the cinema-going public of London, then we had to wait for it to get to our little Derbyshire town. It was almost as if the film distributors couldn't find us on a map. We had one new film every two weeks. The cinema had two screens, one showing the 'new' films, one running old classics, kids specials in the holidays and re-releases. Each ran for fourteen days, apart from when *The Sound of Music* came to Belper, before I was born, and it ran for eight weeks solid according to my Mother. She saw it four times; she had to, it was so popular it was the only thing on and the other projector had broken down. She couldn't stand Julie Andrews, lederhosen, or nuns and would never admit to being a closet *Sound of Music* fan, loving the music or knowing all the words.

Along with romance novels, cinema was her escape when things got difficult with my stepfather. She waited for Fridays, when enough money was scraped together for two cinema tickets and a bag of chips each, then she could desert the house, at least for the length of an epic.

One Thursday morning in October I spotted excitedly that *Abba The Movie*, was to be re-shown the following month as part of a double bill. It had originally been released much earlier in the year but I was banned from leaving the house with a bad case of chicken pox, and no amount of moaning or sobbing into my pillow would make the spots go away. I was inconsolable. The chance to see my beloved Frida on the big screen had been ruined by a viral infection. I couldn't believe I had another chance, even if it was after everyone else had seen it. *Abba The Movie* was supposed to be the supplemental film, just to add extra value and entertainment to the main billing. I thought it was a way of getting people to spend their money in the interval on sweets and ice cream. My Mother didn't do this though; if a double bill was on she took a flask and packed up a sandwich to tide us on until it was time for our chip supper.

I liked it when the feature presentations were combined with an offering from the Children's Film Foundation; they were often gritty northern dramas about pit ponies finding freedom from the mines in the fields around Sheffield and were tacked on to blockbuster films such as *Saturday Night Fever* or *Grease*.

Strangely though, these little low-budget flicks were the ones I remembered more vividly than any of the big releases. A half-blind pit pony emerging into a new world which filled it with a resounding optimism for the future touched me with its message of hope, and an orphan who took his place in a Scottish border community when his dog won a sheepdog trial hinted that anything was possible, even if you'd had the worst start in life.

By the age of nearly twelve I couldn't bear the sensation of letting someone down; it must have been hereditary. When Mother was needed by an old man, she'd stepped in, marrying to make everything above board, silencing the gossips and caring for him in the few years before he died. When the Jehovah's Witnesses called, Mother took their copies of the *Watch Tower* – not that she wanted them – and when they asked her to read them, she promised to do so, even if it was laboriously done, with much accompanying swearing. She often thought back to a night which haunted her; the one when she should've gone out with her old friend Mary, but instead had gone to meet a man; the man who ended up being her first husband, the man who was violent and made her life a living hell. If she had stayed true to her commitment and hadn't let Mary down that night, the marriage would probably not have happened and her life would have played out very differently. She vowed never to do that to anyone else, no matter what the circumstances.

It was an extreme occasion if she had to disappoint someone or go back on a promise, and she was a woman of extremes.

I found out as the years went by that I was indeed my Mother's daughter.

Abba The Movie was a quandary for me. I should go with Mother, I always went to the pictures with her, but I so desperately wanted to go with Rachel. There was no way I could go twice. We couldn't afford it and apart from the odd coppers in my piggy bank I didn't have any money of my own. My Mother didn't agree with the idea of pocket money, it was an alien concept to her; children running around wasting money on Dolly Mixtures and comics was ridiculous. If I wanted something specific I'd been told to ask and she would get it for me. Though in her contradictory fashion I'd also been taught from an early age not to ask for things in case she couldn't afford it, avoiding embarrassment for her and upset for me. I weighed up the two options and concluded it was easier not to ask for anything at all.

It left me not knowing what to do.

I had to pluck up courage to ask Mother if Rachel could come with us. It took days of torment and felt as if I was trying to raise the confidence to ask for her hand in marriage, not whether she could simply come to the cinema. I agonised over broaching the subject and how to react if she said no. I'd read books on etiquette in the library, chapters on how to behave like a lady in difficult situations, but knowing where to place a soup spoon was not much help with my predicament. These books were in the reference section; I'd given up looking for information about how I felt inside. There seemed to be nothing in any book in Belper apart from the dictionary definition and a really thin volume by a woman called Sappho who lived in Greece and wrote poetry that I didn't understand. Interesting as it was to think of myself living on an island in the sun waiting for my muse to strike me, I lost interest in Sappho rapidly. Her life bore no similarity to mine, especially as the closest I'd actually been to a Greek island was a cheap week in an Isle of Wight guesthouse and the occasional day trip to Skegness.

I thought that etiquette might have given me a way to ask Mother about the cinema but it didn't help at all. I moved on to other books to fill my time in the library, quenching the need I had for knowledge, no matter how useless.

A few years before, I found out a little knowledge was a dangerous thing.

I saw programmes in the mornings during holidays, when the telly was still showing schools educational programmes, though who was actually going to be in school to watch them was beyond me. I knew that Mr Grayson, the head caretaker, stayed at work when the kids and teachers were off, giving me a mental picture of him sat there in his khaki overall, mug of tea and custard cream packet to hand, watching documentaries about how molecules were formed and what the meaning of philosophy was for Jung and Freud.

I watched a programme called 'Knowledge is Power' that talked about learning. It was a bit dull but I sat it out just in case it told me anything valuable and useful for the future. It didn't. However, it gave me a sense that it was important to know things and understand them. I learned a lot from schools television and could never really understand why we didn't watch it in school itself; perhaps it was a Union conspiracy to keep teachers in employment.

I learned about the Victorians and how they used to live, I learned about the emergence of footwear and how shoes became the practical and impractical essentials of our everyday lives. I learned about the industrial revolution, which meant I could discuss with Mother her love of the canal system, she explaining how the locks and levels of water made boats rise and fall and me talking about the 'Spinning Jenny' and 'Compton's Mule'. It's funny, I went through the whole of school knowing about the rudiments of canals and industrial techniques and not knowing how to tie my own shoelaces. Some things weren't important enough for my Mother to teach me.

And I learned about revolution in a different way. I watched programmes about the Bolshevik uprising, wars in countries I'd never heard of and revolts that started over the price of a loaf of bread. I watched modern riots where the combatants used petrol bombs to strike. In my spare moments I considered how useful it would be to know how to fabricate such things just in case the revolution started in Derbyshire and I had the calling to take up homemade weapons for a rightful cause.

At nearly nine years old I had been incredibly impressionable.

I mixed up practice batches of petrol bombs using milk bottles pinched from the crate outside the front door and petrol siphoned from my stepfather's motor mower. I couldn't drain off a great deal from the tank because even though it was getting towards the end of mowing season, he would have known if too much petrol was missing. I had to be canny. I added various solutions to my three milk bottles in order to bulk them out.

A little water in the first one, but when it came to lighting the rag stuffed in the neck of the bottle it wouldn't burn properly and I had to tip it away. To the second I added washing powder. It turned the petrol a funny shade of yellow and smouldered when it was lit, but nothing more. It too, was washed down the drain. The third was much more of a triumph. With an old ripped piece of pillowcase rammed into the bottle, it was a mixture of a tiny amount of petrol with white spirit. I lit it and threw the bottle into the side of the overgrown coalhouse; it hit the target and smashed, illuminating the walls with a sudden burst of blue and yellow flames. It was brilliant to see: my first success. In fact, my only success; the flames caught hold of the Virginia Creeper which was growing through the rickety roof and down the inside of the wall. I watched with absolute blinding terror as the fire climbed the vine's tendrils, scorching the leaves and tiny hairy suckers that clung to the bricks. By this time I was standing in the doorway to a smoke-filled chamber. It was nearly dinnertime, I was aware Mother would be at her vantage point, on look-out duty from the factory window, making sure nothing untoward was happening at home. She had threatened me the first time I was left alone in the school holidays. At eight years old I'd been passed from pillar to post, anyone who had a few hours spare ended up looking after me. Now, when a sentinel wasn't available, I had to be trusted on my own in the house. Mother announced she stood guard every day; it was her way of letting me know I couldn't get away with anything.

'I'll be watching you my girl; I can see the house from the factory windows. I can see everything. We'll all be keeping an eye out to see what you're up to, so make sure you don't put a foot wrong.'

And here I was, barely a year after her warning, looking on in horror at the inferno engulfing the coalhouse. Slightly more than having put a foot wrong, even a whole leg wouldn't cover it. She would kill me.

Within a few minutes my executioner was across the road, overall blowing in the breeze like a billowing cape. Granville came rushing down the yard after her with a fire extinguisher, pointing it into the coalhouse and spraying until the blaze was out. I stood there, praying my death would be quick.

She was beyond furious.

'What the hell have you been doing? Look at this mess! Wait 'til your Dad gets back from work. You'd better get it cleaned up as best as you can, then get yourself inside and let's hope he doesn't notice. There will be all hell to pay when he gets home.'

Notice? How could anyone not notice?

Granville smiled at me as my Mother stormed across the yard, back to work. He knew I'd be for it come finishing time; the smile was one of abject sympathy. It was hardly my finest hour. Left standing alone to survey the scene of my crime I became aware I was shivering, freezing in spite of the warmth from the embers.

I shovelled all afternoon, clearing the burned leaves and scrubbing at the smoke-encrusted walls. No amount of scouring and cleaning would hide what I'd done, my fingers were bleeding, both palms were blistered and I couldn't control the tears. I realised what little I could do to change what was in front of me. The Derbyshire Revolutionary Front would have to find another arsonist. The only option left was waiting until he returned home and holding my bandaged hands up to my latest felony.

The closer it got to his arrival home, the more the feeling of sickness grew in my stomach. As soon as the door flew open and he slung his knapsack down heavily on the bottom of the stairs I knew my head was on the block. I never even had the chance to justify what had happened, not that it really would have made any difference; learning to make petrol bombs was hardly an acceptable explanation. He was purple with anger, apart from his fingers, clenched so hard into a fist they'd turned white. I noticed them as they slammed into the bridge of my nose, bloodless knuckles that brought instant darkness. By the time Mother got in I'd already cried myself to sleep, wrapped in my bed covers and out of harm's way. The next morning I deliberately got up after she'd left so the damage wasn't seen until teatime. I lied, telling her I'd tripped and fallen, smacking my nose on a wall; there was no point in telling the truth. She wouldn't have dreamed him capable of such levels of brutality.

Chapter 41

I was never the same after that day and neither was the coal shed. On one side the roof beams were completely destroyed; the ones on the other side had only been licked by the flames. Smashed slates littered the floor, the door had burned away leaving the massive rusted hinges as a reminder, and only three walls were left standing. From then on it was used as a dumping ground for pulled-up weeds, old junk, a broken fridge and the clapped-out copper Mother had used for boiling water before we attained the dizzy heights of a twin-tub washing machine. In a way, I'd done him a favour; it meant he had somewhere to store his rubbish and throw fag ends without having to go around clearing them up. My stepfather took the remaining roof timbers off and stacked them in the garden ready for bonfire night, when the rubbish and detritus of the previous few months was burned and easily got rid of. There were never fireworks to be had with bonfires; he thought them a waste of time and money. A celebration for Guy Fawkes wouldn't be allowed this year either; I'd already had mine in August.

'Sit up in the bedroom window and watch the ones at the pub if you must. Bloody waste of time and hard-earned money, if you ask me. People would be better keeping their hands in their pockets. I've got better things to be spending my wages on.'

Peering across at the 'Fisherman's Rest' car park reminded me of the day I burned down the shed. As I watched their contained bonfire dance, I imagined the illuminated silhouettes of those stood around its base, waving sparklers and munching on toffee apples. It seemed as if everybody was out enjoying the crisp November evening and I was separated from the world by a cold sheet of glass. I wondered where my Brother was; it was his birthday after all. Was he as unconnected from humanity as I was?

Two years on I had been forgiven enough to stand in the back garden and watch our own paltry bonfire burn. Mother was in the front room lost in *Emmerdale Farm*, not wanting to 'go out there muffled up to the bloody ear'oles in the freezing cold.' He was fussing over his birds, making sure the precious pigeons didn't choke. Three people within forty feet of each other and yet still separated. Rachel's family ties were stronger; they were all going to watch the professional display at the sports centre. She would be scoffing candyfloss and hotdogs, laughing, standing in the smell of sulphur and smoke which would taint her hair and skin. The skin I dreamed about touching. I wanted to see her so much and be close all the time. It was painful being apart from her. Half term was now over and we were divided by Maths lessons and French homework again. Somehow I had to try and see more of Rachel.

Abba The Movie. Nothing I'd read in the library or seen on the television gave me any idea how to broach the subject of the cinema with my Mother. I pondered it until two days before the film was scheduled, then there was nothing to do but spill out my request. I dithered for as long as I could, trying to catch her in a good mood.

'Mother, when we go to the pictures can someone come with us? If that's all right with you? It's Rachel. She really likes Abba and she hasn't got anyone to take her.' I tried not to sound desperate or mention she'd seen it the first time round.

She ignored me for a minute, then looked up from the table where she was busy making a cake, folding currants into the soft white mixture rather aggressively.

'Well, it's all right as long as it doesn't happen every week. I can't afford to be paying for three of us all the time. Once in a while on a special occasion, that's fine. She's a nice enough lass, mind.'

'Oh, no, I don't think she expects you to pay for her,' I protested.

'Well, if she's coming with us then I am paying for her and that's all there is to it. I won't have her Mam and Dad thinking I can't afford to take her to the pictures. I've got a bit extra in my purse this week; we'll have enough.'

The small ticket price was nothing for Rachel's family yet was a huge outlay to my Mother. Her insistence on paying lay in the principle that her money would always be as good as the next person's in this life; she would pay her way as everyone else did.

'Just don't tell your Dad; he won't like it,' she added.

So I didn't tell him, not that I would have told him anything anyway. But I did wonder why I'd been scanning library books and watching strange programmes for three weeks looking for a solution to an incredibly difficult problem that was solved so simply in sixty seconds. I paced up and down my bedroom with pent-up excitement until the next morning when I had the chance to tell Rachel that the cinema trip was definitely going to happen.

We met on the Friday evening as Mother and I turned the corner opposite the cinema, there stood Rachel with her father, who'd clearly come straight from work; he was still in his business suit and smart company tie. I thought about how my Mother and stepfather came home from work, filthy dirty and more often than not covered in oil or dirt from the machinery. Rachel's Father was clean and almost serene looking; he didn't even look tired. I'd once asked her what he did at work and found out he was actually the manager of a large department in the local council, commuting back and forth to Matlock daily. It confirmed the opinion I'd formed at her house: although we shared so many similarities there were huge gaps between Rachel and me, mostly down to money.

Mother was very formal with Rachel's Dad. She politely shook his hand, saying how pleasant it was to meet him, all the time keeping an eye on his manner in case he was judging her. I'd seen her turn on people when she felt looked down on; I sincerely hoped tonight wasn't going to be one of those times. Luckily she seemed to feel quite at ease with him and the exchange of Rachel from one guardian to another went off smoothly and without hitch.

Inside the auditorium I couldn't work out if the excitement I felt rising in my belly was because she was sitting beside me in a darkened room or due to the anticipation of seeing the film at last. It little mattered which was the case as I found it almost impossible to sit still and relax or take the beaming grin off my face.

She made my stomach turn over. I'd read that expression in one of Mother's Mills and Boon novels; it was the only thing to read one day when it was chucking it down with rain and I'd finished all my library books. My stepfather didn't agree with buying books to read, not when there was a perfectly respectable library just down the road. Years later, when I received any money for birthdays or Christmas, I invested it wisely in the printed word; it was a further point of dispute between us.

'Why can't she be like her cousin Dawn, eh? I ask you? All she does is bloody read. Our Dawn, she likes her clothes and fashion, not being stuck in her room all the time. She'll read her life away that one. Still, there's no telling her I suppose. Kids these days, they all think they know best and you do nothing to dissuade her from all these books do you?' He would rant at my Mother in the large book store in Derby as she waited for me near the Penguin classic novels with their black and red spines.

I heard Mother's muttered reply and smiled. 'Well at least she won't grow up stupid like some folk are, a bit like your bloody special Dawn.' She spoke quietly so that he wouldn't fully hear. He was going deaf in one ear and it gave her an opportunity to answer him back. It was another tiny bit of revenge.

There were no words adequate enough to explain how I felt that night. At least then there weren't. I didn't have the vocabulary. I sat next to Rachel and the hairs on my arms stood on end as if there was a sudden icy wind blowing across my skin; at the same time my temperature rose, my cheeks flushed and I could sense a film of sweat building on my brow. Luckily it was warm in the cinema, the extraction fans having long broken down.

She placed her hand on her thigh and I watched it settle close to my own leg. I wanted her fingers to move closer but they stayed exactly where they'd been placed. It was the most intense feeling of need I'd ever experienced.

The film ended and the strains of ABBA petered out as the lights penetrated the room. Mother had been asleep and woke with a start, momentarily seeming a little confused as to where she was. I sat in a world of wonder, humming 'Dancing Queen' and smiling to myself.

Whilst Mother went into the chip shop on the corner of Mill Lane, we squabbled playfully about which song was the best, which costume we'd most like to wear to the school Christmas party and whether Agnetha or Frida was prettier. We would never agree on some things. Rachel suddenly grasped the fact Mother would be back any minute.

'Shut up and give us a kiss before your Mum comes out the chippie.' I was only too happy to oblige.

From then on my letters changed. I sent her poetry copied out of books, mostly old works from Byron and Shelley and once a whole section of Christina Rossetti's *Goblin Market*, which I ripped impatiently from an anthology and then bitterly regretted not taking the time to write it out. I read any poem I could get my hands on; in relative terms very few. I relied upon *Palgraves Golden Treasury*, given to me by Uncle Jack, and the little snippets found in Mother's *People's Friend* magazines. I tried my hand at writing my own but they were ragged and disjointed. I didn't fully understand the mysteries of rhyming couplets or alliteration, but I tried, and my heartfelt outpourings were bundled up with the letters and sent to Rachel too.

I expressed the true nature of my feelings, what they meant, how they confused me and the overwhelming desire to be near her whenever I could.

She replied to each letter in similar language and I hid them safely away in places around my bedroom where I thought the prying eyes of my Mother wouldn't go. She never admitted it but I knew she looked around my room. So I set traps, pieces of cotton strung across the bottom of the doorway and cunningly placed objects that if moved would be instantly noticed.

Chapter 42

For the first week of the Christmas holiday me and Rachel spent most days together; Mother and my stepfather were still at work and Rachel's Mum was much more liberal in the way she brought up her daughter. As long as she came home at the allotted time then Rachel more or less had free range to roam at her leisure.

There was a sense of excitement in the air as we meandered around the main street of Belper. The shops were decorated for the festivities ahead; even the butcher had cotton wool snow edging his window. If you looked carefully enough there were spots of blood from the close proximity of the liver and chops. Roystone's Butchers had been established as a family firm in town for over a hundred years and behind the counter, underneath the fly zapper, there were curling sepia photographs of men in striped, blood-splattered aprons. It was 'a proud heritage', so the sign over the door told customers as they walked in, the doorbell announcing their entrance into a shop where the smell of hanging carcasses and death immediately hit your nostrils. 'Old Man Roystone', as Mother called him even though he was no more than fifty, had an interesting sense of humour. He liked to celebrate the changing seasons with his window decorations, really going over the top at religious festivals such as Easter and Christmas. He wasn't a fluffy animal kind of man; Mother said a butcher couldn't afford to be. This year he'd excelled himself with the turkeys. They hung from window hooks with frilly white paper bands around their feet, sporting festive red and green tinsel collars on their necks. We couldn't help but laugh at his macabre example of seasonal cheer as we stood out in the icy wind gusting down King Street as if it was straight from the North Pole. My Mother had tried so many times over the last year to get me to change my mind about turning vegetarian. Christmas was no different; she still attempted to call me back to the carnivorous fold: 'Come on now our Caroline, a bit of Turkey won't hurt you, will it? How can you have Christmas dinner with them funny bloody Tofu things you eat?'

It hadn't worked so far and Roystone's window decorations didn't tempt me back either; I was proud to be a veggie. My stepfather thought it was a passing phase and I'd eventually grow out of it. He liked to tell Mother about his Sister Valerie and how accomplished she was in all areas, particularly the kitchen.

'You take her daughter Dawn. She went all new-fangled and vegetarian nearly two years past. Too much listening to *Mull of Kintyre*. That bloody Linda McCartney has a lot to answer for if you ask me. She was that strict with it mind you. Crikey, our Valerie had a job to get her to eat a sausage sandwich of a morning never mind a Sunday roast and you know how folk queue up to eat her dinners. She'd knock your cooking into a cocked hat. Still, Dawn soon came round and saw sense and that silly sod of a daughter of yours will follow suit, just you mark my words.'

The rest of Belper's decorations were as you'd expect for a Derbyshire market town; sparse in the streets and left to the shop owners to make the best of a bad job. People groaned every year when the council van rolled into town with its extending crane to mount the lights and wrap tinsel on the lamp posts.

It seemed that the arrival of the twinkling sign which said 'Merry Christmas Belp' – the last two letters stopped lighting when a pigeon flew into them eight years ago – brought out the worst whinging streak in anyone over the age of twenty-five. The same conversation could be heard all the way down the road if you listened hard enough, repeated in more or less the same tone. Mother said they reminded her of stuck records but was nevertheless given to join in the chant herself from time to time.

'We pay our rates year in, year out and look at what we get for them, eh? One string of lights, a bit of old ratty tinsel and the dustbins emptied. I despair I do…'

We'd done our Christmas shopping already; Mother had been ordering gifts from her many catalogues as far back as January. When she saw something on offer she ordered it there and then and it arrived in grey plastic packaging a few days later, being hurriedly squirrelled away before my stepfather could see it. On my behalf, she ordered the odd things I'd seen for relatives and school friends. By mid-September we had everything wrapped and labelled for delivery. All my gifts were organised apart from the one for Rachel. It was with this in mind that I followed her round the shops, taking note of what she looked at so if something was in my modest price range I could nip back later. My spending power was limited. I hadn't managed to save that much over the year but luckily I'd been given a crisp new five pound note for my birthday a couple of weeks previously. It'd been tucked inside a card from Auntie Joan and I'd secreted it into my pocket without Mother noticing. After covertly thanking my Aunt in person, I earmarked it for Rachel's present.

In Woolworth's she flicked through the L.P.s, spending a long time reading the inside sleeve of Kate Bush's 'Kick Inside' album. It had a gatefold cover print of Kate, and Rachel enthused about it making a brilliant poster for her bedroom wall.

'Maybe someone will get it for Christmas for you?' I questioned surreptitiously, hoping she would say it was unlikely or she was saving for it herself. Later that day, after I'd walked her home, I raced back to the record department, parted with my £4.99 and returned to Belford, belting down the road and wrapping the disc without Mother knowing. I would've liked the record myself and thought about taping it before giving it to Rachel but decided she deserved to have the first play as it was her present. There would be plenty of time to ask her to copy it in the future.

The day before Christmas Eve was filled with animated walking and talking, and when the lanes were deserted, holding hands. Mostly we rambled in the hills guarding the town. There was an old Roman road that ran down to Milford and I entertained her with renditions of 'Friends, Romans,

Countrymen, lend me your ears'. It was the only line of the monologue I knew and I deliberately overacted Caesar's death scene, falling behind a craggy wall for comedic value. I could hear the effect it had: she was laughing so hard I imagined her doubled over waiting for me to reappear. However, in my attempt at slapstick, I'd tripped, landing in a heap against a fence. I couldn't disentangle myself from the jagged wire netting originally erected to stop brainless sheep with no road sense from wandering out into the traffic. After fighting to get her laughter under control, she unsnagged me and we sat huddled up against the wall, away from view and gazing out across the valley. It was bitterly cold there, sitting with my coat laid across us as a blanket, but neither of us wanted to move or break the comfortable feeling of complete peace. She laid her head on my shoulder and I kissed her hair, smelling the intoxicating scent of shampoo mingled with the smell of her own skin. Eventually the cold took its toll, seeping into our bones, so we decamped back to Belper and treated ourselves to two large frothy coffees in Claude's Café, defrosting our hands on the hot beakers.

I'd carried her Christmas present with me all day. She must have guessed it was for her but had graciously not commented on the hastily wrapped square item in the Woolworth's carrier bag. I could see the delight in her eyes as I passed it over and wished her 'Merry Christmas'. After delving around in her own bag she produced a beautifully packaged gift with a glittery bow and card stuck on the front.

'I hope you like it,' she said brightly. Hesitantly looking round the café to make sure no one was watching, she leaned across the table and gave me a very quick kiss on the lips. 'A kiss for Christmas'. I didn't need her wrapped offering, it was the best present I'd ever had.

She walked me home to Belford then called her Mum from the phone box, asking to be picked up. Their family, including Grandma, were all going to York for Christmas, leaving at teatime and not coming back until the day before New Year. As the car drove out of sight I was suddenly bereft, the thoughts of spending a week without seeing her was like purgatory. My only consolation was that it was Christmas the next day, a time for families. Some consolation.

Despite not believing in Santa Claus, Mother still insisted in sneaking across the landing with a pillowcase full of presents for me, leaving them outside my bedroom door with a thump as it hit the frame, somewhat giving the game away. I didn't bother to get up and excitedly rip the paper off as I used to when I believed. Instead, I left them until the morning. There would still be talcum powder and socks, the same as the previous year and no doubt the same as the next. How much talc did a twelve year old need? I would be caked in a three-inch layer like the abominable snowchild if I used it all. I did though, tear into the present Rachel had given me. She'd obviously taken a long time over the wrapping: it was neatly folded and the corners were as good as any hospital bed sheets I'd ever seen. Inside lay a satin-lined box of expensive monogrammed writing paper and envelopes, a sheet of six first class stamps and a beautiful fountain pen with a pack of black ink cartridges. It had a note attached.

No more tearing up books now! Write to me xx

The Christmas card had two polar bears on the front with mistletoe over their heads. Inside she'd written just her name with several kisses. It was simple and plainly done but meant the world to me.

Christmas day rolled past with a diet of soggy vegetables, as usual disintegrating on the plate into a soup, and a portion of extremely stodgy, Brandy-filled Christmas pudding.

'That'll put hairs on your chest and keep you going 'til teatime won't it,' Mother remarked heartily.

I knew from previous experience that Christmas tea would be laid out on the table virtually as soon as the dinner plates were cleared: sandwiches, pickles, pork pies, crisps, iced fruit cake and the largest trifle anyone could make. It would be there waiting for Grandma's arrival, along with the obligatory sherry bottle, bought especially for her. By eight o'clock Grandma would be on the brink of drunkenness and raring for an argument with anyone willing to provide it. It usually stemmed from a game of whist where she would swear someone was cheating her and had to be placated with a mince pie and a cup of tea. Mother groaned when the cards came out, knowing what the outcome would be before the deck was shuffled. This year my stepfather was the swindler at the table.

'Eh you, you cheating Arab. I know you've got a card up your sleeve. I've been waiting for that two of clubs for the last six goes. I know your sort. Don't you be denying it...'

Soon after, she would be guided upstairs to my room. I slept on the floor while she lay in my bed snoring the night away, oblivious to the offence she'd caused or the ill-feeling he'd still harbour for her next morning.

After a hungover Grandma had been picked up and hauled off to Auntie Joan's, Boxing Day was a silent affair for us. The horse racing would be on all afternoon, no matter what epic film or musical was on the other side. It was business as usual. All festivities were suspended; decorations in the front room were already down and stuffed back in a box in the loft. It was as if Christmas hadn't even happened. 'Another bloody racket if you ask me, just like New Year is,' my stepfather moaned.

A week later we waited for midnight to chime, Mother glued to the Scottish Hogmanay on the telly and me full of hope for the following months, excited at Rachel's impending homecoming and being able to see her again. He'd already gone to bed.

After the piper had played his last tune we went up ourselves, but I hardly slept at all, knowing that tomorrow Rachel would be in Belper, then the next day I would be meeting up with her again.

Chapter 43

The first domino at the head of the line started to wobble on the table when Rachel's little Sister Jenny walked into the bedroom one evening. We were watching her television. I couldn't believe she was allowed to have her own; the luxury of choosing what to view was incredible. It was on louder than normal, 'Top of the Pops' was blaring and we were singing along.

Jenny wanted to come in and join us. She didn't knock, she never did. It annoyed Rachel something chronic and Jenny had been banned from her room several times. This time she nearly killed her.

Sat on the bed next to each other, my hand had played its way up her thigh and was happily nestled. All was well with the world until Jenny barged in without warning.

Singing to Blondie, we didn't hear the door swing open or even notice anyone was there until she stood overlooking the both of us, opened mouthed.

I whipped my hand away sharply and Rachel sprung up off the bed.

'What the hell do you think you're doing in here?' she screamed.

Jenny stuttered and went red in the face.

'I wanted to watch telly with you. It sounded fun.'

'Well, just get out. You aren't welcome in here and 'til you can learn how to knock you won't ever be!' bellowed Rachel.

Jenny rushed out in tears, running down the landing and banging her bedroom door.

Downstairs, Rachel's Mum heard the commotion and called up from the living room. 'Girls, whatever are you doing? I hope you're not arguing again. Never a day goes by when I don't have to break up some kind of row between you two. It's got to stop.'

It all went quiet, the living room door closed again and the argument was apparently over. It was silent in Rachel's bedroom now; she looked white and clearly shaken. I tried to put a sticking plaster over what had happened.

'Look, Jenny didn't really see anything. It could've been a lot worse. Let's just pretend nothing's happened. Just be normal with her and she'll forget she saw anything at all. If she does crack on to your Mum, just deny it.'

Rachel nodded blankly, but I could tell my words hadn't given any comfort.

'Shall I go home now, let things calm down?' As I spoke Rachel grabbed my hand, appearing to shrink before me. This was the first time I'd known her look fearful.

'I don't want you to go. Not now, not ever. I need you,' she cried.

So I didn't go. I sat back down gently. After a few wordless minutes her sobs lessened and she dried her eyes; I put my hand out to her. She grasped at it urgently and squeezed my fingers. I gave her the biggest grin I could possibly muster and she managed a weak smile back.

'It'll be all right flower. You'll see,' I said. At that time I believed it.

She stroked my face, leaned forward and kissed me softly. My heart fluttered and I could taste the salt from her tears before she pulled away slowly.

'I suppose you'd better go home really. I'll go and sort it with Jenny. I'll still see you tomorrow won't I?'

'Of course you will. I'll meet you in the library at two, near the reference section. I'll be the one reading the dictionary!' I tried to lighten the atmosphere and she squeezed my hand again.

I trudged down the stairs under Rachel's watchful eyes. At the bottom I turned and waved. She looked small and defeated. I shouted goodbye to her Mum and left, closing the door behind me.

The next afternoon I settled myself in the reference section as promised, picking up a book of poems written during the world wars. After twenty pages I looked at my watch. After another twenty pages I checked again. She hadn't shown up and I was starting to worry. At page nineteen of my next twenty, none of which I'd taken in, I decided to give her another ten pages then go up to her house and find her. Four pages later she fell into the seat next to me, out of breath and harassed.

'I'm really sorry I'm late. I've been having problems with Jenny, she won't leave me alone. Whenever I've turned round she's been there. I've spent all morning playing board games just to keep her quiet. We've played three rounds of 'Game of Life', one game of 'Cluedo' and then to top it all I had to help her put her 'Girl's World' head in curlers. What a morning! And she's loved every minute of it! I only got away half an hour ago because Gran came round and took her off to Derby to see 'Alice in Wonderland'. Thank God for Grans and Walt Disney. She wanted me to go with them but I told her I had homework so we have a good three hours before she gets back. I'm not supposed to be out of the house so we'll have to be careful I'm not back late. Let's make the most of it, eh?' She spewed all this out then flopped back in her chair grinning at me. Her eyes were alight and I pulled on my coat, putting the barely looked at book back where I'd found it.

We walked; we had to do a lot of that. There wasn't anything much else to do in our little town, not until you turned eighteen; then a new life of pubs and alcohol beckoned. Belper was renowned for its volume of pubs. The whole town seemed to run in little circuits: pub, hairdresser, estate agent; it was a pattern that repeated. The main street itself had five public houses; within a radius of a mile and a half there were twenty more. But for young, almost teenage girls, beer, blue rinses and houses for sale were of no real interest. The cinema was closing to become a bingo hall and the little bookshop at the top of the street was being taken over by a Christian Fellowship bookseller. I had no interest in biblical falsehoods like the story of Sampson and Delilah. How could someone lose their strength because of a hair cut? I'd had mine chopped into a bob four months ago but it hadn't stopped me from carrying the shopping home. So we walked. At least we were together.

We strolled through the boggy fields by the River Derwent, keeping to the well-trodden paths to avoid being stranded. Mother had tales about cows that had sunk in the mud near the edge of the river, never to be seen again, though she did admit most of them were pulled out by farmers' tractors and lived to wander down to the riverbank and get stuck once more. Cows, she lamented, were daft like that. Before the boggiest patch, where a stream joined the river, we crossed the meadow, emerging onto the road and climbing over the wall into the donkey field.

No one really knew why it was called the donkey field; I'd certainly never seen such a creature in it. Near the bottom where it met the roadside, just behind the hedge, there was a slope leading down into the earth, almost like the driveway to a strange subterranean house. Though the pathway was overgrown and full of blackberry brambles, it did indeed lead to a stone-built underground room.

I'd found this place, well, more my Mother had, a couple of years previously when we were picking blackberries. She'd stepped backwards to reach a briar full of beautiful juicy fruits and had fallen down the steep pathway, disappearing completely, landing at the bottom of the path on her backside. The air was blue when she finally struggled back through the brambles and up the path.

'Who the bloody hell builds a room under the ground and doesn't mark the spot? Nearly broke my bloody neck,' she shouted, then burst into laughter at the sight of herself covered in blackberry pips and juice.

Still, the discovery was a good one and the underground room became my own private hideout. It was exciting to hear people walk by, deep in their own conversation, not knowing I was twelve feet below listening in like a secret agent. The room was definitely peculiar. There seemed to be no reason for it to be there. It was perfectly square and built with blocks of limestone, much like the walls of the cottage I grew up in. There was no door, but there were the iron hanging brackets where a door had either once stood or was supposed to have been, and there was a hole for a window. No glass, but it had a sill and a groove where a pane was supposed to go. The view looked up the steep pathway.

It wasn't the most sanitary of dwelling places but with a sweep out and a cloth put over the windowsill it looked better. Over the times I visited I took little trinkets that Mother had cast out for one reason or another.

A little red vase with a chip at the rim. Flowers never lasted more than a few hours down here before they wilted, but for a time they filled the room with a fresh fragrance and a happy feeling.

Then there was a stool that had lost a leg. Mother had thrown it on the fire heap to be burned the next time my stepfather lit the bonfire. I salvaged it, wedging the leg back in until it stood fairly straight again, the woven top looking nice in the sunlight that filtered down at the height of the day.

Lastly, there was an old gilt candlestick, chipped and tarnished beyond repair. It had sat in the cubbyhole under the stairs in the kitchen before the extension was built. I'd never seen the candlestick used and despite Mother's hoarding instincts, she'd decided to throw it out. With a couple of cheap household candles purloined from under the sink, it lit the underground room fairly well. The flickering light cast eerie shadows, especially when it rained and stone-filtered water ran down the back wall, adding to the damp. I thought it was romantic in a dank sort of way.

This was the one and only time I would entertain Rachel in my own private space. We walked down the pathway. I held my hands over her eyes to surprise her. She knew about the donkey field and the room, but had never been there. At the bottom of the slope I took my hands away and she exclaimed appreciatively, 'look at this place! If we had heating and a door we could live here! It's really cosy, if a bit cold!'

We sat on the ground, using an old sack advertising horse feed from 'Harvey's Feed Merchants' as a carpet; I'd found it in the top field, dried it out and shaken the mud off. The candles were lit, burning with a pale glow which cut through the gloom. It was always cold down here; I'd made a circle of stones where I intended to light a fire but the inaugural attempt with twigs collected from the hedgerow just ended up smoking the place out. My eyes watered so much I couldn't see and it wasn't something I wished to subject Rachel to; instead we cuddled up for warmth and I rested my head on her shoulder. We sat in silence and it was comfortable. She felt like a blanket around me, safe.

She turned her head and looked at me with a smile – that familiar warm-eyed smile. I beamed back and sighed contentedly.

'I wish we could stay here all the time girl,' she said wistfully.

'So do I, but I reckon we could do with a bit of furniture,' I replied.

She looked downcast as she continued, 'I'll have to go soon. I don't want to but Gran will be home with Jenny and I can't go through all that questioning again. She's like MI5 when she gets going.'

I laughed even though she wasn't being funny. 'So has Jenny been going on at you?' I asked.

'Mmm, she's just been questioning me all the time. She went through my box with your letters in. It's lucky she can't read your writing; spider scrawl is useful sometimes, eh? Then she was asking why I had letters from you when I saw you at school anyway. I tried to gloss over it but she won't leave it alone. It's getting on my wick.'

I gave her a hug and she giggled.

'Oh well, I guess I'll just have to bite my tongue and put up with it. She's bound to forget about it sooner or later.'

I hoped she was right but had a niggling suspicion in the back of my mind that a countdown had begun; Jenny was a time-bomb waiting to go off.

We walked quietly back through the donkey field and out onto the cemetery road. At the brow of the hill we separated, but I didn't leave immediately. Something I didn't understand rooted me to the spot; I watched her walk away, getting smaller and smaller in the distance until she was gone. Forever.

We'd made a date to meet in the library the next day.

Chapter 44

The next afternoon came but Rachel didn't. I waited an hour and a half before I gave up, lumbering home with a sense of doom.

I waited the next day, and the day after that, but still nothing.

On the fourth day I waited in vain again. What was going on? Then, through a blur of tears, I gathered my things together and headed home. When I rounded the corner I wished I hadn't.

Rachel's father was just pulling away. As he swung round in the road, incensed eyes met mine, his face full of utter contempt. The window wound down and he shouted his disgust and revulsion for all the world to hear.

'You won't be seeing my daughter again, young lady, never again. I've bought your sickening letters back, I was going to burn them. I don't want that filth in my house, but then I changed my mind. They make interesting reading so I left them with your poor Mother.' With that he speeded the car up and disappeared down the road.

An overwhelming tidal wave of emotions hit me all at once. Anger, sorrow, fear, grief and loss all swirling around in my head making me dizzy. Nothing made sense.

I stood outside. Frozen. Paralysed. I stood there for ten minutes. Longer. It took everything I had to summon the courage to walk down the yard and into the kitchen. He was at his Sister's, Mother was in the front room. It was deathly quiet; even though I was obviously in the house she didn't come out. The silence was suffocating. I took my coat off, hands trembling so violently I could barely undo the zip. Stepping into the front room I shook like a convict going to the gallows. My executioner was sitting on the sofa with a pile of letters on her knee. I steeled myself for the fury that never came; Mother simply raised her head despondently, face blank, unreadable, and she didn't speak, just shook her head and looked away.

'Can I have them back please?' I asked hesitantly to break the thickening silence.

She looked up again. 'I think you'd better put them away before your Dad sees them. He won't be too impressed I'll tell you lady. I knew there was something not right between you and that girl. I knew it. Then having her bloody father in here laying down the law. Well you won't be seeing her again. He's shifting her to that Catholic school in Derby so you wont be tempted anymore.' The significance of her last sentence was lost on me; I was so confused by her calm, almost robot-like manner.

She handed me the pile of letters. I took them gingerly and turned to creep away, but she started to speak again.

'Is it my fault? That's what I ask myself. First your Brother and now you. Did I let you both have too much of your own way, is that it? I don't know what to say, I really don't. But I will have to say something to your Dad. I won't tell him about all the trouble, but I can't keep it all between us, he'll find out anyway. It would be better if I said something now rather than leaving it.'

Heat rose in my chest, I started to feel faint. I was frightened of what he would do. I begged her not to, pleaded, but she told me not to be stupid; he would understand. He wouldn't do anything to me; he'd only be as shocked as she was.

She believed everything she said.

I took my letters and fled upstairs. Behind the closed door I slumped down on the bed, clutching the pages, not wanting to let them go. The previous hour flashed through my thoughts: Rachel's Dad shouting, the serenity with which Mother had delivered her verdict, and then it finally started to seep in. Rachel was gone.

The most important person in my life, the only thing that made it worth living, had been taken away. Snatched up and banished, exiled simply for being in love. I never even had the chance to say goodbye.

The back door opened and I heard his gruff voice filter through the downstairs rooms. Grief and regret temporarily replaced by a sudden blinding fear. Mother was speaking calmly still. I tried to hear what was being discussed but the strains of 'East Midlands Today' mingling with the clatter of pots and pans from the kitchen made it impossible to decipher anything properly.

There was no shouting. I didn't know if this was a good thing or not.

I sat rigid, unable to move a muscle, until Mother shouted to me for tea. I tiptoed down the stairs in absolute terror. Dinner was eaten in an oppressive atmosphere. I felt sick. He had a face like thunder and only Mother seemed to be carrying on as if nothing had happened. I picked at my quiche and chased a pea around the plate without really trying to catch it. Mother guessed I couldn't face the food and whipped my plate away swiftly when he wasn't looking. I wanted the whole dreadful evening to be over, for it be time to go to bed, longing to hide my head under the covers and hope I wouldn't wake up in the morning.

An uneaten apple crumble later, I made the escape up to my sanctuary and closed the door. As awful as it was, it was far too calm. I was sure all hell would break loose in the morning and things would get a hundred times worse. He was biding his time like a spider in its web. For hours I lay waiting for the darkness to enfold me, for my eyes to close. I don't know whether sleep came or not but eventually the light in the room changed and a new morning had arrived.

It was bright outside and extremely quiet in the house, as if there was no one in. I lay straining to listen for ages but all I could hear was the wall clock on the landing ticking the time away. Convinced I was on my own, I got up, dressed, and made my way uneasily downstairs. In the kitchen I put the kettle on and got some bread out to put under the grill, but as I turned I was aware of an ominous presence. There was someone watching me.

My stepfather stood between the kitchen and the front room; he was white with anger and his lips, thin at the best of times, looked even thinner and more brutal than ever. The brooding anger in him permeated the air, only just contained; it wouldn't take much for it to be unleashed. I'd felt this threat of evil before and couldn't decide whether to bolt for the door or stay and placate him.

I went for the second option when I should have gone for the first; run out the door and not stop until I was so far away I was never able to come back.

'Do you want a cup of tea?' was all I managed before feeling the agonising weight of his fist in my back. I stumbled forward into the cooker front. The force of the blow and fall onto the hard surface took the wind out of me completely and I crumpled over. I could hear him behind me cursing and shouting but his words were wasted. I was trying so hard to catch my breath and clear my head I couldn't take them in. Managing to stand up straight, I propped myself against the sink unit, fighting the mounting pain and desire to be sick.

He had the capacity to be violent. The coalhouse episode had been a patent demonstration of how vicious he could be. But even without that incident I'd witnessed it regularly. I'd seen the cruelty in his face and felt it in the slaps of chastisement he meted out when I apparently stepped out of line.

He was directly behind me now; the force of his breath scalding as he yelled at the back of my head. I was too scared to turn around, afraid of meeting those hate-filled eyes and seeing the malicious intent on his face. His hand was gripping my shoulder, nails biting into my skin, fingers grabbing at the cloth of my T-shirt and yanking me round to face him. Narrow eyes filled with fury seared into mine.

'You are filthy, sickening. There isn't one ounce of decency in you, is there? Your poor Mother has done her best to bring you up right and this is how you repay her. Well, is it?' One hand held my jaw in a vice-grip, painfully preventing any turning away; with the other he continuously rammed his finger into my shoulder blade, each of the jabs emphasising his words, stabbing like a blunt knife. 'No daughter of mine is going to be a filthy pervert. You had better change your ideas lady before I have to start changing them for you, do you hear me?' With that he shoved me away in disgust.

I collapsed into a fit of sobbing, not only down to the absolute fear he'd instilled or an intensifying pain my back, but because I suddenly thought about Rachel. The notion that she might be physically and emotionally suffering a similar fate hurt more than anything he could ever do.

'And you can stop that bloody crying before you start. You have to learn lady. You make your bed and you have to lay in it in this life. Your sins will find you out and it's a good job you have me to put you back on the straight and narrow. I will not have you messing about with girls. It's not right. There's nothing in the bloody Bible about women being together. What will people think of your Mother? Well, I tell you, they won't think much because this is where it stops, once and for all.'

And with that distorted reasoning he raised his hand, slapping me so hard I stumbled backwards and hit my head on the sink. I woke up on the cold kitchen floor, dazed, unsure if minutes or hours had gone by. He was sat malevolently on the stairs, hovering like a bird of prey. His quarry was trapped. I rose unsteadily and he swooped in for the kill.

'Well, that's what happens if you cross me. Happen you will remember that next time and think better of it. No daughter of mine is going to be a dirty lesbian. I'll cure you of that one.'

What did he mean by 'cure'? My head was swimming; I put my hand up to the developing swelling on the back of my head and winced. I felt sick; black spots were appearing in front of my eyes, so I turned, steadying myself on the sink unit, and poured some icy water from the tap, gulping it down.

'And you hadn't better tell your Mother about what's happened here today. If you do then it'll only be worse for you. It's better she doesn't know. Let her think everything in the garden's rosy. I don't want to have to raise my hand to both of you, now do I?'

And that's how it was from then on. He didn't raise his fist to my Mother, I made sure of it, never uttering a single word about what had happened that day. Over the years I became

278

hardened to his violence. He thrived on my tears, so I stopped crying when he hit me, trying to show him I wasn't totally defeated and therefore he would never completely win. On some small scale it made me believe I had a shred of dignity left.

There were many times I thought of telling Mother about what he was doing. She had a right to know what a cruel, sadistic man she'd married. As his abuse escalated, my fear of not being believed grew alongside the indoctrinated view that if I indeed spoke out he would turn his attention to her. Acquiescence was the only option.

Chapter 45

Returning to school after the Christmas break was distressing, yet a relief at the same time. There was nothing to look forward to any more, the void Rachel had left seemed even more apparent there. Each turn of a corner made my heart leap in anticipation, then free-fall when I remembered she wasn't there, would never be again. Each break-time dragged on eternally. I spent them with friends from my classes but none of them was her. Nobody ever would be. School seemed pointless now. Patrick Simms and Martin Falconbridge told the truant officer there was no need for them to be in lessons, there were much better things they could be doing with their time. That's why they bunked off and hung around street corners pestering old ladies. I had the opposite view: pointless it may well have been, but even though I was miserable and lonely I stuck at it. At least I wasn't at home with him.

The 'cure' began in earnest around the same time. It started one afternoon whilst Mother was at work and he was home early. I came back from school with my cookery basket, having lovingly prepared a spicy sausage plait.

I'd followed the recipe to the letter. It looked the part, the plait was exactly like the picture and it smelt nice as well. I was very proud of my efforts even though it wasn't ever going to get eaten in our house. Mother didn't hold with doctoring food. She liked her meals simple and plain, one 'foreign' ingredient was bad enough, but garlic, chilli, mixed herbs and cumin would finish her off. I argued with her from time to time but never managed to win. Once, I cleverly thought I'd caught her out by informing her that sage and onion stuffing was, in fact, derived from herbs. She wouldn't have any of it.

'It comes out of a packet. There's nothing in there I wouldn't eat. Good honest food is sage and onion stuffing, none of this mucking about sprinkling this here and that there.

You know where you are with stuffing.' Adamant to the end, there was no changing her mind or refuting that kind of logic.

I laid the pastry plait down on the table and chucked the basket under the stairs along with everything else that didn't really have a proper home. There it teetered on top of read library books, dirty washing and a crate of baked beans. My creation sat covered with a tea towel until Mother came home. She might not eat it, but it wouldn't stop her admiring the hard work I'd put in.

Concentrating on peeling potatoes and carrots for tea, I was lost in my own thoughts and didn't notice my stepfather sneaking into the room. Suddenly he was there. I could hear him breathing, which meant he was closer than I wanted him to be. I liked to make sure he was where I could keep an eye on him. Advanced warning was everything; the carving knife always needed to be close at hand just in case, the sight of the long steel blade made me feel safe even though I was deluding myself about ever using it. This time I was caught off-guard. Before I could move he was directly behind me, pushing his bony body against my back. Ribs dug in, every breath in and out increased the pressure, and I stood petrified, expecting the pain from his fists to begin.

'There, that's nice isn't it? You see, I don't always have to punish you, do I? I can be nice too, and I think you should be nice back, don't you?'

His hand was around the front of my school skirt, pushing under the waistband. I tried to struggle away but couldn't fight him off. His fingers edged lower: into my knickers. Inside me. Moving. Pain. I stood paralysed, blank, staring out of the window, completely motionless, waiting, desperate for it to stop.

That was the start of a completely new phase of his tyranny against me. It never happened when Mother was at home so I constantly tried to stay out of the house when she wasn't there. There were only so many reasons not to be indoors. I couldn't always avoid him. The pain, torment and shame that went with the ordeal never seemed to lessen no matter how many times it happened. Repetition did not mean I would ever get used to it. I was an automaton. My mind would shut down; there was no feeling, no care or love involved. It wasn't tender, like the short time I'd spent with Rachel. I knew the difference. What my stepfather did wasn't right.

Mother wasn't one for discussing anything that mattered, such as emotions or problems that concerned a young mind. It wasn't that she couldn't talk about them; more that she wouldn't. Everything that was important about my physical self or feelings and experiences, I picked up first from Grandma, then, after she'd died, I learned myself, usually the hard way. It wasn't that I hadn't tried with Mother, more that I had tried and been ignored so many times I'd given up. To me, she seemed to have grown barren of emotion or was certainly unaware that I had any worth taking note of. The last two occasions I'd tried to talk to her were difficult because of the subject matter, but her reactions were not what I would have expected from a concerned parent.

I knew about monthly cycles. The Dr White's nurse had told us all about them at little school, a time which now seemed an age ago. Most of the girls I knew were already old hands at this topic, readily talking about their periods and being looked at with reverence when they were allowed to sit out swimming due to blood flow. Deborah Hardy had so many periods during the swimming season I only remember her going in the water once in three months. The teacher never seemed to notice; I often thought that perhaps she was more trouble in the swimming pool than she ever was out of it and Miss King was probably secretly pleased to let her off.

I suppose I was a late developer, at least in comparison to my classmates. One Saturday morning, after feeling uncomfortable for a couple of days and worrying that my stepfather had hurt my insides, I got up to find I was bleeding. Not profusely, but, nevertheless, it was there.

Of course I didn't have any 'sanitary protection' as the Dr White's nurse had called it, but I'd kept the booklet about what provisions were needed and rooted it out from the bottom of my set of drawers. At least I knew what I had to go and buy. After clumsily fashioning a pad out of toilet roll, I dressed and ventured downstairs to broach the subject with Mother, who was getting ready to put a Madeira cake in the oven, tipping the mixture from the bowl into the tin. She wasn't in the best frame of mind. I could tell from the belligerent way she banged the mixing bowl and wooden spoon down on the table.

'Kettle's boiled if you want a drink; make me one while you're at it. I've had just about enough this morning, bloody pigeon racing. Them birds will be the death of me, they will. All I hear about morning, noon and night, bloody things.'

The pigeons were a battle she was never going to win so she just moaned about them. Only to me: we all knew better than to say anything to my stepfather.

I'd cobbled together something to say and began tentatively: 'Mum… I've started to bleed… what do I do?' I thought that maybe she would sit me down and talk through what it meant over a cup of tea and a digestive biscuit. Sandra the sanitary nurse, said this was what would happen – mothers and daughters together discussing a girl's transition to womanhood. Sandra had obviously never met my Mother.

Mother looked at me dismissively for a second then turned her back, opened the kitchen drawer, and took two pound notes from her purse. She wheeled round to face me again and pressed the money into my hand.

'Go to Belper,' she said.

And that was her Motherly advice on the subject of menstruation. Thank goodness for the Dr White's nurse and her leaflet. Without it I wouldn't have known what I was going to Belper for and might have come back with a bag of Pic 'n'ix and a magazine. Perturbed, I walked off down the road some twenty minutes later with a list of necessities to bring back from the shops for her, wondering how self-raising flour and Fairy Liquid could be more important than me becoming a woman.

Then there was my second and final attempt to talk to her. I waited until my stepfather had left the house; he'd gone down to the pigeon club with a basket-load of birds to be sent to the race from Berwick the next morning. Saturdays in the pigeon-racing season were worse than normal Saturdays; the tension of waiting for the birds to come home was unbearable, so I usually tried to get out as much as possible. I'd taken an unpaid job in Oxfam to lessen the time spent at home, but one Saturday out of the month the shop closed for a general clearout of the work rooms. According to Rita the supervisor the amount of clothes with holes in and odd socks lying around would become a health and safety hazard without the once-a-month shut down.

'Folk don't realise the problems they cause donating worn-out shoes and things with rips in them. They think they're being kind and helping starving kiddies in Africa, but all they're really doing is giving us a fire hazard meaning we have to get the clothes recyclers to come and pick up more often, and you should hear them moan on,' she said, moaning on.

I volunteered to help with the clean but Rita was protective about her back rooms, insisting she was better off on her own. On those Saturdays I had to stay at home.

I'd been trying my hardest to bring up the subject of my stepfather for weeks, feeling sure that if I could get Mother on her own and find the courage to spit the words out then she would help me and make it stop.

I'd read about Mother and daughter relationships and how they were supposed to be close, sharing important things. There were always stories about devoted family relationships in the *People's Friends* that she brought home from work. They had dog-eared pages full of loving stories and I'd seen those bonds in action with Auntie Joan and my cousin Marie. They could talk about all kinds of things; Marie seemed to have no problem asking her Mother about anything, from make-up techniques and clothes to boyfriends and sex.

I wanted us to be like them and hoped this would be as good a time as any to start breaking down the barriers.

It was a crucial day for me; for the past week I'd gone over the scenario, spending hours rehearsing what to say when the chance presented itself. It was worked out like a play in my head. The cast of two would talk through the issue, shed a few tears, embrace affectionately and it would be over. The end. Final curtain. Yet still I was apprehensive, worried I would forget my lines, and knowing Mother hadn't read the script. He would be out the whole morning, rehearsals were over; the moment had arrived. Unlike a stage production there was only going to be one opportunity to do this properly, no second night. I had to get it right first time. Now or never.

She wasn't in the best of moods. It was easy to tell, and not just because she banged things about more than necessary and swore under her breath; she was also adding superfluous words into her sentences, something only done in times of utter frustration. Word of choice was 'so', it was a clear indication she was best left alone. Anxious not to let my moment pass, I didn't heed the warning.

'Do you want me to help with that baking Mother?' I asked, smiling, thinking that a shared task would make it easier to strike up a conversation.

'You can if you want. So, it's up to you, please yourself,' she replied without looking up.

'All right then. Shall I grease the tins?' I said, picking up a piece of paper and rubbing margarine around the pan.

She didn't answer. There was a lot more than coconut sponge and boiled fruit cake on her mind. A few tense minutes followed then she launched into a tirade, one of the sort that doesn't involve stopping to draw breath.

'I am fed up to the back teeth with your Dad. He does nothing in this house and I seem to do bloody everything. So, if it weren't for you I'd drown under all this bloody work. It's not right. He just takes me for granted, swanning off to Belper putting his bloody bets on at the bookies. Good money after bad that's what it is, and if it's not bloody horses then it's them sodding pigeons. So. Anyhow, I've told him he's got to start mending his ways. He reckons he does enough round here, yet it's always me that seems to end up doing bloody everything. I'm surprised he doesn't expect me to clean them bloody birds out as well, filthy things. Well, I tell you I'm not.'

She was certainly angry with my stepfather that morning, jumping from one rant to another, the thread running through them the same every time. I never did find out what exactly had set her off.

I should've known not to say anything; these moods were not exactly conducive to a heart-to-heart. But I'd waited a long time and came down the stairs that morning full of hope, ready to try and tell her what had been going on, desperate for our new beginning. I mistakenly told myself that if he'd already upset her it would be much easier for her to believe he could be spiteful to me too.

'Mother… you know when you're at work…' I started cautiously, '…and he's at home…' I stopped and drew in breath, '…well, he touches me… you know… where he shouldn't.' I didn't know what else to say. It was too hard to find the right words. How do you describe something which you've spent the greater majority of your time trying to avoid thinking about?

She was quiet for a long time, seeming to hunch over and get smaller. The cake was starting to cook: a waft of coconut emanated from the oven and drifted across the kitchen. She started to bang the pots and pans about in the sink with her back to me and wouldn't turn around. I wasn't sure what to do. Nothing was going to plan, I thought I'd better try and attract her attention.

'Mother… did you hear what I said?' I asked timidly.

All of a sudden she swung round, looking intently at me. The look was one of complete disbelief and I knew instantly all hope was gone. There would be no words of comfort, no understanding and no saving me from the relentless persecution.

'Don't say things like that to me. I know I complain about him but I also know he'd never do anything like that. You'll end up in that children's home on Chesterfield road talking like that you will, so think on and look sharp. Believe me, this isn't the first time I've thought about putting you in there. You've been nothing but trouble the last couple of years: bloody shed and buggering about with that girl. I won't have you say things like that about your Dad, I won't. And you'd best not let him hear you talk like that. You'll break his heart.

You know he dotes on you. Say anything else like that and you'll feel the back of my hand, so just think on, lady.'

The play I'd spent all week writing in my head had not gone according to the script at all. There was no conversation, no conciliatory hug, nothing was over and the only tears shed were mine.

It was pointless to try and make her see. She wasn't going to listen. At first I thought that maybe she didn't love me. If she did she would've taken my side and stopped it all. After a couple of weeks I started to think she'd been brainwashed and didn't know any better, they were married after all. I'd read the marriage vows in the library and they said you had to stick with someone through thick and thin – not exactly those words, but I got the gist. Vows told you how to deal with a husband but had no mention of children; perhaps she didn't know how to cope with them.

Even if she couldn't cope with me how could she not see the menace in front of her eyes? For a while I clung to the faint hope she would see the truth and save me. That hope diminished over time, I came to realise there was no choice: I had to save myself.

The assaults continued; his attacks on me became more insistent and regular. I tried anything to stop him from coming near me; I put a lock on my bedroom door. He broke it, forcing his way in; I tried to use the wardrobe as a barricade. He punished me for making too much noise and marking the carpet. Finally I hit upon the solution. If I made myself horrible, surely he wouldn't want to come near me.

It would take a concerted effort.

It seemed like a good idea to put on weight. I read about it in the Sunday papers: the problem pages were full of sad stories of misery; husbands that had gone off their fat wives, boyfriends that had affairs because their girlfriends were too fat, and even a vicar that had been sleeping with three women from his parish at one time. He'd only been found out when he'd spurned the advances of an overweight woman who told the bishop all about his shenanigans as a way of getting her own back.

All these women had been sidelined because of their weight; if I didn't want his attention and therefore piled on the pounds then maybe it would have the same effect.

One day I'd heard him comment snidely about a woman who got on the bus: she was a large cheerful lady with a beautiful smile and friendly manner.

'Ugly bitch. She'll never find a man. Not with all that weight.'

I had something to aspire to.

I upped my calories, reading the calorie-controlled diets in Mother's second-hand magazines brought back from the factory. I examined the before and after food intakes of women wanting to lose weight, but instead of taking the low-fat option, I went for the menus they'd eaten in the first place.

Monday through to Friday I went to school, using the bus fares I'd been formerly saving for my rainy day fund on buying chocolate from the shops on the way home. I had just enough money for two full-sized bars and a bag of crisps each day. At school I had a full dinner, whatever it was came with chips. My choice, the more fat and calories the better. Slowly but surely the pounds began to stack up, my clothes started to get tighter and when I found I could no longer fit into my P.E. top. I congratulated myself for achieving the first rung on the ladder to success.

My Mother noticed, so did Grandma; they both warned I should try and cut back. I didn't cut back. The plan was taking shape; I added more weight instead.

I ate crisps and chocolate washed down with full cream milk. I ate family packs of digestives and six Club biscuits in one sitting. I ate chips and fried bread garnished with brown sauce and scoffed full boxes of Liquorice Allsorts, though I threw the bobbly pink ones away. Even in dire circumstances there were lines I wouldn't cross. I dunked my way through packets of ginger nuts, rich teas, shortbread biscuits, Scottish shortbread fans, petit fours, chocolate fingers, garibaldi slices, fruit shortcakes, custard creams, bourbons and pink wafers by the pile.

I munched my way through Eccles cakes, Madeira cake, sponge fingers meant for trifles, cherry cake, Genoa cake, ginger sponge and chocolate cake bars.

Then fruit pies, apple tarts, strawberry trifles, raspberry splits, egg custards, chocolate shortcakes, cream horns, choux buns and jam tarts.

Finally, I chewed through pear drops, toffees, chocolate misshapes, cream eggs, plain chocolate, milk chocolate and white chocolate. I even tried dog chocolate, but it stuck to the roof of my mouth and was so dry I could hardly swallow it.

Some days I felt so sick by the time I went to bed I worried I would throw up everything I'd forced down my throat. But I didn't. Slowly but surely it worked; first it was a couple of pounds here and there, then a couple of stone, then a couple turned into ten. I achieved so much in a relatively short time. It was amazing what you could do if you tried.

I went from a size twelve to a twenty-four in less than six months. I was only thirteen years old.

Surely now he wouldn't want to come near me, wouldn't fancy me? Now I was so much bigger, the way people sneered at me when I waddled down the street would put him off. I would be free of him.

It didn't work.

The only thing it did do was upset Mother. The shopping budget was five times more than it had been and every fortnight I needed new clothes.

Nothing changed with him; he carried on in exactly the same way. He hurt me and carried on hurting me and nothing I could physically do stopped him. I had gone from average-size to outsize for nothing.

I realised years later that it wasn't about him finding me attractive; it was about having power.

The powerful and the powerless. I was in the latter category.

By fourteen or thereabouts, he was using other, more masculine parts of his body as well as his fists to hurt me. But never anywhere a blemish could be easily seen. From the neck up every inch looked fine and well whilst below my jumper the bruises bloomed. A few new ones each week, sometimes each day, purple ones blossoming over the old yellowing marks of previous mementos. No one knew, I had no one to tell. There was no one to believe me, no one to save me.

'Tell your Mother and she won't believe you,' he sneered. 'Tell your Mother and she'll believe me. Tell your Mother and you'll end up in a children's home. Tell your Mother and your Mother's next.'

So I told no one.

Extra pounds, extra skin, extra room for extra bruises; perfect in its own imperfect way.

If I displeased him by struggling when he pushed himself inside me he would hit out, punch me. Though not until afterwards, the challenge excited him more. After he'd finished his eyes glistened with hate, almost as if I'd made him do those things and needed to be punished. He would hold me down or push me against a wall, pull back his fist and let fly. I never cried; it made the beatings far worse. I wouldn't let out a single tear in front of him; I saved that until I was on my own.

Eventually I had no choice but to become accustomed to the bruises and wincing when I turned my body in a certain way; I hid things well. I learned.

Taking refuge in my bedroom, I spent time with my books, hiding away with Jane Austin and the Brontës, imagining myself in another place and time. Occasionally, when I felt strong enough, I took out Rachel's letters and read them again.

I missed her.

I couldn't talk her to or be close, she was completely off limits and I felt the loneliest I had ever been in my short life. I'd lost the one person that had really mattered; at least I still had Grandma to make me feel worthy of something. I read books and saw Rachel's name in every page and her face in every character, I searched for her in the street and hung around near her road in case she walked past and I could speak to her, but it never happened. I wrote her letters in the beginning, disguising my handwriting and posting them in Derby or Wirksworth so the postmarks wouldn't be immediately recognisable to her Mother and Father, but I never heard back. Eventually I gave up. She had been packed off to another life in another school, a Catholic high school in Darley Abbey, a high-class establishment where the nuns taught proper behaviour and the pupils got decent grades. A place where she could be watched and put back on the right track to becoming a 'good girl' again. I, apparently, was the wrong track and was never allowed to forget it.

Every female friend I made at high school was frowned upon at home in case she happened to become another Rachel. I could see how Mother scrutinised the girls I talked to in the street, asking me how I knew them and whether or not they were 'courting', as she put it. Unattached boyfriendless girls were dangerous temptresses in her eyes and were to be avoided at all costs. Her feelings on the suitability of any possible friends were made all too apparent.

'Your Dad wouldn't like her. I think it'd be better if you steered clear...' It was amazing how many 'dangerous' girls there were in such a small town.

No one matched up to Rachel and at that point I thought no one ever would again. But even if I had found someone at school, I could've done little about it as I'd become so reticent with people I was now classed as being painfully shy. Though I tried to join in and enjoy the time away from home, I was wary of letting anyone get close in case they found out what life was like for me. Also, I was fat now. I'd made myself as ugly as possible, people shied away. The only person it didn't put off was my stepfather.

Chapter 46

I lived in a parallel universe from my Mother. She still moaned about my stepfather, that he was tight fisted, that he spent more money on his hobbies than he ever did on her or the house, that she was left to pay all the bills and that he was selfish. Ultimately, though, she loved him. When he came up on the horses, rare occasions that these were, he would buy her a bunch of freesias and a quarter of sugared almonds. Occasionally he would take her out for a drink in the local pub and they would have a bar meal. He grew her favourite flowers in the garden and brought her the first potato from the new crop as if it were a rare jewel to be presented to a queen. He charmed her; she didn't really know what he was like. Then they would go upstairs together on a Sunday afternoon, leaving me to endure the grunting noises and creaking floorboards; I learned to turn the sound up on the television and drown it out.

'I know I moan about him,' Mother said reflectively one afternoon, 'but he's a good man really for all his faults.'

I couldn't compete with that concrete belief. She never saw the marks on my skin; they were well hidden. Never saw him lay into me with his fists for not setting the table properly, or for speaking out of turn, or, in fact, for not speaking at all. Never saw the retribution meted out for my supposed crimes and misdemeanours. She never saw any of it.

Grandma suspected though. She watched the vibrant child she'd half brought up change into a shy, weighty, sullen teenager before her eyes: a child who stayed locked away upstairs more than anywhere else, barely seen, barely heard. Mother told her I'd become a book worm, that I was at an awkward age, that I was moody, that I would grow out of it and that I didn't know when I was well off. Grandma listened but didn't take much notice; she supposed there might be more to it than that.

The autumn before my fifteenth birthday I was sent to stay with Grandma for the week of half term. Mother was going into the women's hospital in Derby for a gall bladder operation and thought it was best I stay with Grandma, as my stepfather would have enough to worry about without having to bother with me. I gladly went. A week staying at home with him on my own was more than I could face.

We baked and cleaned in the mornings; after dinner we ventured out and walked the dog over the quarry tops. Sandy was full of energy, a Labrador cross something huge which Granddad had brought back from the RSPCA kennels. She was a lovely mountain of a dog, full of mischief, but loyal to her bones. Never far from Grandma's heels, she'd been mistreated and wasn't keen on men, particularly the paper man whom she disliked on sight. He got pinned against the gatepost on more than one occasion. It was something to do with the way he rolled the newspaper up and walked down the yard beating out a rhythm in his hands. Sandy tolerated Granddad when he was alive but was totally devoted to Grandma, a devotion which was transferred to me after she died. This particular day Sandy ran around bringing sticks and bits of limestone for us to throw. Grandma was careful not to toss them too close to the edge of the quarry tops in case the dog fell over and we had to mount some kind of mountain rescue.

We walked and talked about the things we saw. She told me the names of flowers, showing me how to pick out the various types of grasses and their seed heads. The one I liked most was the greyish-silver stem with thick wispy fronds of seeds; if you held it up to your ear and the wind caught it, it sounded as if it was talking, well, more murmuring. 'Whispering grass', that's what Grandma called it. Several years later I read it had become a rarity in the English countryside, yet I can remember it growing in abundant clumps all along the edges of the limestone walls. Perhaps my picking it then led in some way to the depletion of the national stock.

While we strolled she gave me in-depth information about the nature we came across, but also brought up other subjects for discussion, some of which I didn't want to think about.

'That stepfather of yours,' was one of her opening gambits. 'Is he as good hearted as your Mother makes him out to be?'

I struggled with the answer, so replied with the first complete sentence that came into my mind.

'Well, he buys me Pick and Mix when he comes up on the horses.'

'That's not very often then is it? No, I meant is he as kind as your Mother says? I remember that first rogue she married and what he put her through, so she's no great judge of characters. I know that. Maybe I'm wrong about your stepdad. She never tells me anything 'til it's too late, so I'm relying on you to tell me if there's something I need to know about.' She let the statement hang in the air like a question waiting for an answer; but I didn't have one.

She filled in the gaps again whilst I tried my hardest to think of something.

'Well, all I want to know is that you're all right. I've heard from your Brother that all that time he lived under the same roof your stepfather was a nasty bugger. That's why your Brother left home when he did. I've never told your Mam that; she had enough heartache with him leaving in the first off without being told the real reason why he'd gone. But, as I say, I just want to make sure you're all right and he isn't the same with you.'

It would've been so easy to have acknowledged there and then that in fact he was far from being good natured, had hurt me in ways that I couldn't describe, but before I could open my mouth the dog deposited a half-dead baby rabbit on the floor at Grandma's feet and the conversation was forgotten. The rabbit died in her arms as we walked home. I cried as we buried it, tears not only for the poor little mite but also for myself: a chance for salvation might never come again.

I tried to forget what was happening at home whilst I was staying with Grandma; with her I was safe and secure and could just be. At home I was on edge and frightened most of the time, even when I'd fortified my bedroom by pushing all the furniture up against the door. A leaning wardrobe and a battered chest of drawers didn't provide a guarantee he wouldn't force his way in.

Grandma was getting on in years. It showed in her demeanour and the way her eyes looked dimmer, the twinkle once in them slowly fading. Mother was worried about her. Every now and then she'd try and help her out in the kitchen or with shopping but Grandma was stubbornly independent and wouldn't let her. It was one of the obstinate traits which ran through the maternal line of our family.

'Eh, your Grandmother, she's such a bugger. I try and go up there and help but will she let me? No, she won't. I went up there today to do her washing and she'd only stood and done it all yesterday. I had a go at her but she just said she didn't want to put me to any bother. Honest, there is no helping that woman.'

She was right. At weekends I tried my hardest to help with the daily chores. But, again, either she'd done all the cleaning and polishing before I arrived or sneakily got the cloths out after I'd gone. Grandma was far too proud ever to admit she couldn't manage. Her main priority in life had always been making sure everyone else was all right, that wasn't going to change because of two petty swollen ankles and a few crumbling old bones. In her mind she was doing the best thing all round by refusing help; didn't want to be a burden, especially when her children had so much on their plates already. Eventually her bloody-mindedness was her undoing; at least that's what Mother thought.

She was just past her seventy-sixth birthday when a rapid decline was noticed. Granddad had been dead for ten years by then. Every week she laboured up the hill to lay fresh flowers on his grave, wiping over the smooth marble headstone and raking the green chippings that covered the earth he was laid within. The grave was immaculate: she was dedicated to keeping his final resting place neat and tidy, telling anyone who asked that his sheets were always clean and pressed when he was alive, he wasn't going to sleep in an untidy bed now. The surrounding plots had a wild unkempt charm to them, but not my Granddad's: it was pristine, not a single blade of grass out of place. She tutted when the man who mowed sprayed cuttings over the edge of the grave and woe betide anyone who didn't take out the dead flowers when they went to visit.

She was found one afternoon by the Verger, slumped over the grave, having an asthma attack and almost unable to breathe. Her face was grey and by the time the ambulance sped to the cemetery she'd gone cold and clammy. The Verger put his coat around her shoulders and insisted she keep it on as she went to the hospital. The coat came top on the list of articles for collection once her body had been taken to the morgue, but no one knew where it came from or whom it belonged to. After a few weeks sitting over the edge of the stair rail it was consigned to the bin. The Verger never did get his coat back or receive any gratitude for his kindness.

She was taken to the local cottage hospital. During the war it had served a dual purpose. It was a maternity hospital where mothers-to-be would go to have their babies in relative safety, not being the obvious target that big Victorian red brick hospitals were to the German bombers. The next generation of young English men and women would be safeguarded to fight the enemy in the future. It also served as an isolation unit. Grandma once told me about old Enid Belfield who'd been taken into the segregated wards when they found she'd contracted a contagious chest infection that was spreading through the Derbyshire villages at wildfire pace. She'd died in there, all the windows and doors wide open in the midst of winter with snow lying thick on the ground outside. Standard practice for that kind of ailment. Enid had died there and so did Grandma. The only difference being Enid passed away in pain on her own and Grandma died peacefully in a warm bed with all her family around her.

She'd waited for all her sons, daughters and grandchildren to arrive before she went. I sat at her bedside miserably as she fought for breath and rattled out cough after cough, each sounding weaker than the last. She held my hand, her bony fingers wrapped around my own chubbier, meatier digits. It was as if I could feel the life draining out of her as I sat. Mother was the last to get there. As usual, she'd left early enough, but she'd had to get out of work and catch the bus over to the hospital: no easy journey at the best of times, let alone when aware her Mother was only hanging onto life by

296

the thinnest of threads. The bus had travelled through every village in Derbyshire, stopping twice to let old Mrs Wilcox gather up the tins of mushy peas that kept making a bid for freedom from the top of her shopping trolley and rolling down the aisle.

She arrived just in time. Grandma had opened her eyes and was moving them carefully from each one of her children to the next, seeming to be weighing them up and at the same time trying to keep an image of their faces in her mind to take with her on her journey. Mother perched herself on the corner of her Sister's chair and smiled at Grandma.

'Sorry it took so long Mam. Them bloody buses, they always end up going round the villages when you least need them to.'

Grandma lifted her head, looking straight at my Mother as if in weary amusement. She said something to her; the rest of the family didn't catch the words though I heard clearly and smiled.

'What did she say?' Mother asked in a panicky voice, aware that her own Mother was slipping away before her eyes.

My face coloured up. 'She said it's about bloody time!'

Grandma coughed loudly. I swear it was to hide a laugh. The cough turned into a choking rattle which petered out into rapid, light breaths, then before I knew what had happened they'd stopped altogether. She was gone.

I continued to hold her hand and felt the warmth slowly ebbing from the surface of her skin. Her face relaxed and suddenly she appeared to lose the years of hardship and struggle, looking at least ten years younger.

Ten days later she was buried in the same grave as my Granddad in Middleton cemetery. She wouldn't have liked the mess they'd made opening it up again. I stood forlornly at the back of the group of mourners and thought about what it meant to be dead, where you went, if anywhere, and whether or not it would be better than where I was now. Rachel was exiled. She was as good as dead, and now my Grandma was gone. The last person I hoped would save me really was dead.

I stood and stared morosely around the graveyard, thinking about all those people who'd once lived, thrived and laughed, getting on with it as best they could and now were all gone.

Behind the last row of graves was the tiny chapel of rest, only big enough for one coffin lying on the granite slab behind its cool white-washed walls. When I was younger, Grandma had relished in telling me ghost stories about the people that had lain in that tiny place and the huge, black dog that prowled the graveyard, sleeping in the chapel, guarding the dead. She'd never seen the dog herself, but had heard it howling balefully in the night. I was never sure whether the tale was real or fiction but it didn't matter. Staring across at the stone wall of the chapel I could have sworn I saw a huge, great dog flash by, racing across the newly filled-in graves near the perimeter fence. It probably hadn't been there but it made me smile nevertheless. It was like a sign that all was okay on the other side.

The vicar was passing the box of soil around and mourners paid their last respects before wandering away. I was on my own now, in more ways than one.

Grandma's house was sold two months later. The family vultures picked through the remnants of her life and there was nowhere left to escape on weekends or during school holiday anymore. I still had years at the hands of my stepfather ahead of me. Life lurched from one horror to the next interspersed with high calorie foodstuffs and larger-sized clothes.

I planned my getaway so many times, but something always cropped up to wreck my chances of success.

There seemed to be three options:

**To do nothing and let life carry on in the way
it had been going. An intolerable thought.**

**To wait for someone to come and save me. An unlikely
thought.**

To try and save myself. The most plausible thought.

I tried them all again and again.

Chapter 47

Plan One: Say nothing and keep quiet about what was happening.

Pretend that my family was the same as everyone else's; that I was fine; then maybe he would give up and stop hurting me. I'd read a book in the library's self-help section about abuse and power. It made sense that if the power in a situation was taken away maybe the reason to undertake such acts would stop with it. I decided that if I could be cheerful and not let him see he affected me as he did, then he would give up. It didn't work. Each time he raised his hand I tried to smile. It made him worse and he hit me harder. When he forced his way into my room I tried not to show I was bothered, but he knew how to make the experience even worse, forcing his face into mine and kissing me. It turned my stomach. After he'd left I was often violently sick.

Chapter 48

Plan Two: Find someone to save me.

I had a fantasy woman who was going to come and sweep me off my feet, out of the nightmare I lived with day in, day out. I saw her wherever I went, in every woman: younger, older, blonde, brunette, short or tall. She didn't have a particular look or a specific name but she was going to come along, pick me out of the crowd to be her mate for life and whisk me away. I think I must have watched too many black-and-white films on a Sunday afternoon, filling my head with 1950s Ealing comedy sensibilities. Unfortunately, they didn't fit with what was happening thirty years later.

I watched and waited and didn't give up hope, at least not totally. Hope was a tiny, battered commodity in the end, but it was never fully extinguished. And, though she didn't come along for a long time and didn't actually save me from anything, I never gave up looking.

There were opportunities and there were threats through the years I stayed confined at home with my Mother and stepfather. And there were distractions. Some of them came close, at least for a little while, to helping me forget how hard life in that cottage was.

Mainly there had been Sophie; she'd come along out of the blue. I'd found her in the advertisements of a weekly music paper; she was looking for a pen-friend. I wrote a letter and she replied. Eventually we met after the postman had lugged several hundredweight of paper through the postal system. I knew what she looked like from pictures: long white-blonde hair, bright blue eyes and a way of wearing a shirt that made me anticipate what was beneath. In the flesh she was beguiling. Her way of speaking in a pronounced cockney accent, with a slight lisp, and the fact she'd never been out of London before made me feel excited and proud, amazed that this fascinating creature wanted to leave the city to walk next to me.

I pretended she was just a pen-friend, made out I wasn't bothered whether I saw her or not. Though I desperately wanted to have her near me I couldn't let Mother, and certainly not my stepfather, see any sign for fear of the havoc it would cause.

'Mother, can I have my pen-friend Sophie to stay for a few days? She could come down on a Thursday and go back on Sunday?' I asked nonchalantly one morning, trying not to sound too eager. 'It doesn't matter if you don't want to have her here. I know you don't like entertaining people you don't know.'

She was quiet for a minute, obviously considering my request.

'Well, I'll have to ask your Dad. It's him that doesn't like people in the house. It doesn't bother me one way or the other. He doesn't like having to mind his 'p's and 'q's. And you know he doesn't like eating in front of people, what with him chewing so slowly. We know what he's like, but other folk don't, do they?'

So I thought that was it, scuppered, there was no way he would agree. Mother told me to wait a couple of days then she'd let me know. She'd pick a good time and hope for the best, but I'd already resigned myself to it not happening.

Four days later, just as I'd decided to put pen to paper and tell Sophie she couldn't come, Mother arrived home and stunned me with the news that he'd agreed to her visit. I couldn't believe it; it was out of character, making me suspicious he had an ulterior motive.

I met her at the coach station one sun-drenched day in July and carried her bags home, worrying all the time she'd think I was a country yokel and wasn't sophisticated enough for someone who'd been brought up in the bright lights of London. She was lovelier than I'd imagined, all long legs swathed in black sheer tights, semi-hidden beneath a short skirt edged with tassels that bounced off her thighs as she walked. She smelt of a heavy scent, a combination of incense and perfume that lingered in my room and on my clothes long after she'd gone. All of a sudden a whirlwind of sound and laughter had tumbled into my life, turning the stillness into commotion and silence into happy hilarity. It was as if everything had turned on its head. We sat in my bedroom, sipping tea, chatting about literature and the colourful places she'd visited. I was surprised someone as exotic as her showed any interest in me at all; she was quirky, unusual and well-travelled as well as being pretty, and here was I, overweight, quirkless, been nowhere, with no dress sense whatsoever. The hot-blooded kiss bestowed on me in the confines of my room was just one of the ways she showed the attraction was mutual.

I couldn't offer her Arabian souks or glamorous skyscrapers, so we wandered around looking at the Derbyshire countryside with her 'oohing' and 'ahhing' at the local animal population. The fact she'd never actually seen a lamb in the flesh before made me smile. The sheep bleated, the cows lowed and the country life seemed less grey than it had. For that weekend I was elated and proud, as if the world was at my feet. I hadn't felt like this since the last time I'd been alone with Rachel. Even though Sophie could never be her, it was still a vibrant, exhilarating feeling.

Sophie was daring, a lure for danger. If there was an obvious line she liked to cross it. Curfews were there to be broken, rules to be breached and conventions ignored. Saturday night we ventured out to Belper at seven o'clock with strict instructions to be back by half past ten, but it was nearly one in the morning by the time we crept into bed, the hours in between full of new experiences for me. Sophie was a steep learning curve. I'd never been in a pub on my own; hadn't been in with my family either more than a couple of times, so walking into the Queens Head on the Market Place was thrilling as well as slightly unnerving. Convinced we'd never get a drink, I hid in the corner and let her go to the bar alone; she came back five minutes later with two pints of cider. I watched with complete admiration for her brazenness, provocatively half-sitting on the edge of a bar stool waiting for the drinks to be poured; the barman, clearly with an eye for the ladies, was suitably attentive. She giggled as she nestled close to me in the booth at the far end, telling me proudly she'd got two pints for the price of one. Mother would have called her jailbait if she'd seen this sort of behaviour, my stepfather would have called her a slut. I just thought she was confident, outrageous and perfect. The warm feelings growing in my chest, as well as other places, snowballed after the second pint.

At throwing-out time we meandered through the tiny, narrow roads, street lamps shining on the pavements in pools like spotlights. Each one she stepped into revealed something else magical about her, the curve of her breasts under her flimsy shirt, the goose bumps that formed on her arms before I offered my jacket, and the mischievous glint in her eye when she looked at me.

Sophie wasn't one for short cuts: the longer the route home the better; when we reached the lane that ran down to Belford she decided we'd take a different road. My watch already warned we were nearly an hour late and I thought of Mother impatiently waiting for us, cursing through her bedroom window. Sophie's hand in mine, her naughty expression, the balmy air and two pints of cider made me forget any responsibilities I had.

We walked slowly through the private grounds of the convent school, across the massive field used as a nature garden by the resident nuns. Lights from the building in the distance were burning through the darkness. Sitting down amongst the long grass at almost midnight on a Saturday evening seemed to be the most natural thing to do, as did the kissing, which began in earnest almost as soon as we'd touched the ground. Sophie was much more experienced than me: it was obvious from the way she undid my shirt buttons and slipped her fingers inside my bra cup without taking her lips away from mine. One thing led to another, though I fumbled my way through the whole experience, taking lessons from her hands and movements and applying them to her body. I felt amazing, and as she shuddered underneath my hand, I knew she did too.

My first sexual experience of my own making. At least the darkness hid his prints on my skin. The walk back towards the cottage was slightly breathless and full of absolute wonder; I

303

was amazed that someone could make me feel completely relaxed and yet totally wired with intensity at the same time. It was like an unstoppable hand had switched on all the lights in the world and I could see more than I'd ever thought possible. My elation didn't come without a tinge of trepidation, however, I was terrified they would still be up at home, that we would stray into a war zone and be ambushed. It was worrying that someone who knew Mother might have seen us drinking, and there was the slight concern the nuns at late-night devotions might have seen what had happened in their butterfly garden.

No one seemed to have noticed anything.

Sunday afternoon came around and Sophie left as she'd arrived: city glamour and allure on a National Express coach.

The next day I woke with an empty feeling in my stomach and a sense I was missing out on life again. For the second time I'd seen that there was more to life than sitting in my bedroom and being scared for my sanity. It was as if a little window had opened and the light had been bright, but now the portal was closed, intensity was fading away, and quickly.

Over the weekend my stepfather had been watching me and Sophie together; not that there had been anything for him to see. Dreading him being home from work, I returned from the library, bag laden down with books as usual, to find him sitting in the kitchen smoking yet another cigarette and flicking the ash into the yucca plant at the bottom of the stairs. He said nothing, just stared malevolently. His eyes were on me wherever I moved. I really wanted to flee upstairs, get away, but this involved having to walk past him. I summoned the courage, picked up my bag and edged towards the stairs. He stood up calmly, looking as if he was going to let me pass, but instead stepped ominously across my path, like a huge threatening shadow.

'I told you before about messing with girls, didn't I? Well you're going to have to take notice of me soon my girl or I will bloody well knock you into this side of next week. Just you see if I don't. You won't be having anyone else to stop in this house until you mend your ways. I thought you'd have learned the right way by now. Well I'll teach you if it's the last thing I bloody do.'

As his words reverberated round the room he raised his fist and punched out. Sensing what was coming, I swiftly dodged sideways and avoided his furious lunge. His anger rose; the next punch wouldn't miss.

I wasn't allowed to see or write to Sophie again. Any letters I didn't get to first were scrutinised for a London postmark, suspiciously franked envelopes were promptly ripped up and thrown away. After I'd lost a number of letters to the dustbin and bonfire, we managed to communicate via another address but long-distance correspondence wasn't enough in the end. She moved on to another woman who lived closer to home.

Sophie was not the saving type.

Chapter 49

Plan Three: Save myself.

The opportunity to set the third option in motion didn't come along for two years until I found myself in the last few weeks of my second year of sixth form. Along with everyone else, I'd applied for universities, being accepted at Manchester Polytechnic. The end of my time at home was drawing close. I just had to get through these last few weeks, sit the 'A' level exams and pass them; then I could make my getaway and spend the next three years sitting in a library reading classic literature.

Working in Oxfam on Saturdays was useful. I started to save up for my 'bottom drawer', as Mother put it. This was something usually meant for girls planning to marry, but in this case they were my escape provisions, and as long as she didn't try and stop me, I didn't care what she called it. I was given an old stereo system; the shop couldn't sell electrical items because a customer might end up electrocuted by possible dodgy wiring, so I ended up with any donation that could be plugged in. The stereo was one of those long flat 1970s models but had been well looked after and was in perfect working order, more than could be said for the toaster which grabbed each slice of bread with a crab-like grip and wouldn't let go until it was pried out with a knife.

I was given curtains, nets and bedclothes, tea cloths, towels and dusters. I had planks of wood to make bookshelves and a huge bag of kitchen cutlery, servers and sieves; the list went on. Packing boxes, I tried not to look at Mother. Each time I did I could see the pleading expression in her eyes, silently begging me not to go and leave her.

The 'A' levels came and went. I did the best I could, coming out of the exam room each time with my hand aching from the pressure of writing so much so quickly. Failure was not an option; my future and sanity depended on it.

The day the results envelope came the house was silent. It was chucking it down with rain outside and I peered hopefully through the slate-grey morning in search of the postman, a little man who would bring my big future in his mailbag. My Mother and stepfather had gone to work early. There was no 'good luck' note and I don't think they'd even remembered what an important day it was. A feeling of loneliness descended on me as I thought of young expectant teenagers all across the country waiting with their loving parents and families for the brown envelopes to drop through the door. I sat, sipped a cup of tea, and waited. Apprehension. Then I had another cup and waited again. More apprehension. Eventually the postman arrived. I weeded the source of my anxiety from the pile of bills, catalogue statements and junk that had come with it. My mouth went dry; I stared blankly at the type for a number of minutes, then ripped open the top and pulled out the white printed sheet inside.

> English History: Grade B
> Design and Technology: Grade C
> Sociology: Grade C

My grades were high enough to go to Manchester, so I could continue packing the rest of my belongings with a sense that life was going to change, and surely it had to be for the better. The rest of the day was spent putting my letters and photographs safely together in a strong cardboard box. There was a set of pictures of Grandma and Granddad, Mother and me as a child, and a couple of snapshots of my friends which I'd taken at school. Rachel appeared in one of them so I sat looking at the photograph, regretting the time we'd lost. Seven years would have changed her face considerably. Would she still be recognisable if I passed her in the street? Would the girl I'd given my heart to, the one who still owned the best part of it, remember me? These thoughts troubled me for a while before I shook myself back into motion and stacked her letters together with the photo, tying them into a neat pile with a shoelace. Keepsakes I'd collected were split into two piles: one for saving and one designated for the dustbin. The latter grew much faster than the former, making me question why I had kept some of the items. Why did I need a piece of a red brick, or a five pence coin that had been squashed in a pressing machine and overprinted with a picture of an owl? What was the significance of the tiny seashell that lived in the matchbox along with a long dead dragonfly? The bright azure blue of its tail had been conserved in the darkness of the Bryant and May box for as long as I remembered. At some long-forgotten point they'd meant something, held a significance which made me hang onto them, filling bags and drawers. There was a lot to throw out. The whole afternoon of sorting and sieving left a black bin-bag of rubbish, a small pile of things to pack and three empty drawers in the wardrobe. Traveling back through memories had been pleasurable but time-consuming, and before I knew it dinner needed to be put on the table. The prized envelope sat on top of the Welsh dresser in plain sight; no one could miss it, I would get it down once Mother had noticed and broached the subject.

At about quarter past five Mother busied in, closely followed by my stepfather, both stripping off their overalls and flinging them over the bottom rung of the stair rail. Mother was midway through a lengthy tale and continued the saga as she sat at the table.

'And so I said if she felt like that then she should go and sort it with the person she has the problem with. That's what we all do isn't it, not just ignore things, that's no way to carry on is it, eh?'

My stepfather didn't answer, not that it made any difference; she knew he never listened to anything she said anyway. She looked to me to corroborate her shrewd assessment but I didn't want to reply either. People ignoring things? I wondered if she could see the irony in her 'wise' words.

If she could, there was no glimmer of it showing on her face, so I served up the tea and carried on as normal. My stepfather was the same as usual too: gruffly silent as he stabbed at his lamb chop. Mother, on the other hand, was twitchy, wanting to fill the house with language as if glossing over a subject that needed discussing. She rambled on about the pigeons and where they'd be racing from this coming Saturday; grumbled about the smell from the dustbins and wittered about the gas bill and who was going to the post office to pay it. Bills were an ever-ready topic of conversation and this finally pushed my stepfather into finding his voice.

'Never-ending bills, that's all we seem to get in this house. I'll be glad when she starts bringing a few quid in, that'll make a big difference. Mind you, if you didn't have so much from them club books we'd manage a whole lot better.' He stared coldly at me whilst moaning at Mother, looking me up and down, narrowing his beady eyes.

I knew what that look meant, I saw it frequently: a precursor to what would happen once I was alone in the house with him.

They ate their tea and still didn't ask about my results. I thought I'd seen her eyes flit to the envelope once or twice. Why hadn't she mentioned it? I knew he wasn't remotely interested in how I'd done, didn't see the point of an education when factory work was plentiful in the surrounding towns. He'd rammed his point home so many times I had no doubt my results wouldn't change his mind.

'You don't have to be clever to work in the cotton factory, you just have to work hard: something these folk who go to them universities don't know owt about. Too frightened to get their hands dirty. There's plenty of work out there for them that's not too idle to do it.'

It was apparent no one was going to ask so I decided to bring up the subject myself. There was just over three weeks left to confirm my place at the polytechnic; then I'd have to start searching for somewhere to live.

They were both still sat at the table, he slowly ruminating on the crumble I'd bought from the Co-op the day before and passed off as my own, she scrubbing at a stain on the front of her work T-shirt. It looked like oil; the more she scrubbed the more it spread. I could hear her annoyance under her breath.

There was never going to be a good moment to get the envelope out, so I braced myself and reached for the dresser.

'I got my results today,' I said quickly, pulling the printed piece of paper from the envelope and thrusting it at Mother with a hopeful smile and hands shaking nervously.

'I haven't got my glasses on. You'll have to read it out for me,' she said hesitantly.

I blurted the list out before I lost any momentum, then looked expectantly at her, waiting for approval.

She scowled at my stepfather, then turned her attention back to me before speaking.

'That's good isn't it, love. You've done well. Where does that leave you now?' she asked, almost without wanting to know the answer.

I gabbled out that I'd been offered a degree course at Manchester and had to ring them up and accept the place formally, meaning I only had weeks to find somewhere to live. She nodded blankly as I carried on excitedly, asking if she'd help with my packing and search for digs.

She was non-committal and the conversation ended there. I took this as a show of upset because I was leaving home. It took until the next morning to find out the real reason behind her lack of enthusiasm and nervy behaviour.

I'd lain awake reinvigorated with visions of my future, planning a new life, how it would be in Manchester and the way I'd reinvent myself. I wanted to prove that an ordinary girl from a Derbyshire mill town could go beyond apathy, marriage, children and a 'career' in the local knicker factory, envisioning myself thin, trendy, teaching English and, most of all, happy. Happy and a long way from here.

Mother crept into my bedroom soon after I'd sprung energetically out of bed.

'You'd better come down sharp like. He's on the warpath again. Says you're lazy lying in bed when the rest of us are up working, you've got to change your ways, bring some money in and stop expecting us to keep you. You've been at school long enough already without spending another three years in a different one. You've got to go up to Blount's on Monday; they're hiring new machinists. You'd better go. He says you're

to ask for Dolly: she'll put you through your paces.' The full impact of her words didn't even begin to sink in.

'But I'm off to Poly in September. There's not much use in me going to do the training for that short a time is there?' I pointed out.

'No, you aren't going anywhere; he won't let you. Reckons that if you try to go he'll come and bring you back, kicking and screaming if need be. You know he will. He isn't having any of it, says you're going to work to pay us back for all the years we've supported you. I'm sorry, but there's nothing I can say. You know what he's like once he's set his mind to something,' she replied again in a straight mouthful, and this time the penny started to drop.

So there it was: any ambition this ordinary Derbyshire girl might have had was to be cruelly stamped out, crushed before I'd even walked out the front door. Mother didn't agree with him. She didn't say, but I could tell. My stepfather's commandments were law and that was that. I felt dead inside, like the world I'd started to imagine, the one where I had independence and a self-belief, was gone. He'd put his fist through my dreams, taking them as easily as he had everything else.

Anger and frustration were building up, the feeling of being about to explode was growing stronger with each moment I failed to fight my own corner. For months, since my eighteenth birthday, I'd berated myself with the belief I was weak and couldn't stand up for myself. Why not? Mother had eventually found an inner strength when married to the bus driver and Grandma showed huge courage in looking after Granddad when he was wasting away before her eyes. She'd never baulked or shied away no matter how hard it became to watch the man she'd loved all her adult life dying before her. I remembered the stories Grandma had told about our distant relatives, their bravery and determination; yet here I was, young and strong, but frightened of my own shadow. They would be ashamed of me.

These thoughts had been building since the day of my coming of age when I had gone on a trip with Ellen, a friend from school. Mother lied to my stepfather, telling him I was going shopping in London as a birthday treat; my actual whereabouts would've been met with snarls of misunderstanding and hatred.

My eighteenth birthday was spent sliding about in ankle-deep mud outside the perimeter fence at Greenham Common along with a cornucopia of women of all shapes, sizes, ages, skin colours and accents. The air was filled with sounds of resistance: whistles, drums and strength. I saw huge lengths of concrete-enforced wire fall and women get dragged away by military police who were circling the barrier like sharks homing in on a shoal of fish. I'd never seen such an array of women together in one place, with one purpose, and it planted the seed that anything could be done if only I put my mind to it.

The only stumbling block was my stepfather. One man. Surely he couldn't be that hard to stop, to push out of the way and put behind me. The thought stayed with me: from now on every time he hurt and humiliated me the sense that I wasn't standing up for myself grew stronger and my indignation grew with it.

I got home covered in thick mud, my blue pixie boots now brown from toe to turn up, and my long heavy military coat reeking of the smoke from many defiant bonfires. Mother ushered me surreptitiously upstairs to change my clothes, thrusting a carrier bag in my direction and telling me to bring it down when I'd erased all evidence of my secret day out.

'There's a few bits in that bag that you've bought today. Bring them in and show them to me. There's a bar of chocolate for your Dad. It's the one he really likes, should keep him sweet. He doesn't know where you've been,' she whispered.

I rushed upstairs, changed quickly, then appeared down in the front room, seeming innocently back from a day's shopping, duly displaying the items Mother had given me. He was watching the Saturday evening news but managed to mutter a begrudging thank you for his chocolate, ripping it open and biting into it immediately, his mind briefly taken off the TV screen. The news turned to matters at home and its leading story was the protests at Greenham airbase. I could see Mother's face turning deathly white. She started to twitter nervously about what she'd done through the day; how Auntie Joan and my cousins had been down to see her, how Marie's new perm looked akin to a used pan scrub, deliberately talking loudly all the way through the article and trying to deflect his attention. Luckily the film cameras hadn't captured me and I was safe from his wrath.

I wouldn't unpack the boxes I'd put together for my escape, couldn't bring myself finally to give up the little dying hope I had left. They were stacked in a corner, collecting dust and the occasional cobweb as the weeks trickled past.

Chapter 50

Every fortnight I made the trip down to Belper to sign on at the job centre, then three days later I'd make the same journey back to town to cash the giro cheque that came through the post. I gave most of the money to my Mother, keeping back a few pounds for myself, trying not to spend what little was left in an attempt to save enough to get away. It was going to take years to manage it, a daunting thought.

I tried to get work. I didn't want to end up in a factory for the rest of my life but was willing to do a few months of anything in order to raise a bit of money.

I went for the trial at Blount's, the cotton factory up on the top road out of Belper. They made underwear, men's and women's, fancy and plain. My stepfather said I was bound to get the job as Dolly from up the hill was going to be assessing my suitability.

'She'll sail through them tests. Dolly'll make sure of it. There's only three other girls going for the job and Dolly's certain she can swing it as long as that daughter of yours doesn't make a mess. Well, she better hadn't, anyhow'

And so I set off, trudging slowly as if I was going to my doom. The great, green iron gates swung open with a creak: the hinges had slipped and the metal grated along gouges in the concrete. Unless I was careful, I would end up here for the rest of my days, like those women I saw walking home at the end of their shifts with bits of cotton thread hanging from their clothes and fluff in their hair, as if they were part person, part cotton plant, devoid of any ambition, just accepting their daily grind.

The skills learned in my needlework classes at school had given me nothing useful to show once I was sat in front of the industrial sewing machine. The first thing I'd made in Mrs Horn's class was a grey felt elephant; I ended up making too many as I cut the same piece out three times and she was a stickler for not wasting fabric. They were stuffed in the back of one of my cupboards, slowly going damp. One had a wonky trunk, one had a back leg which faced the wrong way, and the last was almost perfect apart from the embroidery on its eyes which made it look demonic. Dolly gave me the cotton and demonstrated how to thread up the machine then pushed a pile of plain white towelling parts for me to sew into high leg knickers. I had an hour to do as many as possible.

The needle snapped in the hem of the first piece, snarling up the thread, so it ended up looking like a terry towelling spider web. I unravelled the mess, asked the woman on the next machine for another needle, put it back in and started again. I managed the side seam of the left leg perfectly before realising I'd actually sewn it to the wrong side. It was the elephant all over again.

I started another pair. By the time, Dolly reappeared to check my work I'd managed to put together two and a half pairs of knickers and a small pile of ruined fabric. She was none too impressed, tutting at the waste I'd produced.

'Hen, you'll no be the best worker I've ever had.' Dolly was a thick-accented Scottish woman who cut no bones when she had to tell people they were useless at their jobs. 'I think you'll be needing a long time to get the hang of it and I dunna think we can spare the hours to train you, so I'm sorry Hen, this job is nae for you.'

I didn't know whether to be relieved or petrified. Relieved I didn't have to set foot in there again or petrified of going home and telling my stepfather I'd failed.

I walked home the long way. The really long way. Whenever I came to a road which was more direct I took another until I got to the point where there was nowhere else to go but home. Walking in the crisp air had given me time to think. He was sat at the kitchen table studying the racing form, writing out his bets for the next day.

'I didn't get the job. There were five other women going for it and the one that got it has worked for Blount's before, I didn't stand a chance. I did my best and that's all I could do.' I lied through my teeth and hoped Dolly wouldn't drop me in it the next time she saw him.

He didn't respond immediately; I could see him mulling over the excuse I'd given.

'Well, you tried I suppose. There's other places you can go. You'll have to start looking again tomorrow, eh'. It wasn't said with compassion, more with malice and warning and I knew that if I failed again his response would be a lot more explosive than it was this time.

I went down to Thornton's factory. It was Thursday and the smell of burning toffee was hanging over the town like a great sticky cloud. The woman at the reception desk wore a blue business-like suit with the traditional hair net sported in the factory. She said there weren't any jobs at the moment, they'd just taken on ten trainee fudge workers and wouldn't need any more until the new factory was built in Somercotes.

She stood up, pulled open the drawer of her filing cabinet, rummaged for a minute then turned around with a form in her hand and passed it to me.

'If you fill this in and drop it back in the next couple of weeks then we'll put you on the list for the new jobs if you'd like. When you bring the form back you'll have to supply us with a stool sample so we can give you a test to make sure there aren't any germs in your body that could be transferred to the chocolate. It's standard procedure. That's not a problem is it?'

I stuttered out it wasn't, grabbed the form, bidded her a hurried goodbye, then rushed out of the factory office. I couldn't give a stool sample; since I'd been overeating, piling on pound after pound, I'd developed really terrible stomach upsets. The doctor called it 'irritable bowel' and advised trying to cut out fat, bread and other wheat-based products from my diet.

'Try and eat more healthily,' she'd said, peering over the top of her half-sized glasses. 'Try having more fruit and yoghurt. It'll help settle down your digestion and you'll also lose weight. That's two birds with one stone isn't it?' she smiled piously at me.

She had a point and made me feel ashamed to be the size I was, but I couldn't even contemplate starting to lose the weight. I'd worked hard to get to this position and, though it hadn't changed what was happening with my stepfather, I assumed that if I ended up thinner things would only get worse.

So that cut out Thornton's.

That same day I called into the job centre to see if there was anything new on the display stands. There wasn't usually, just the same jobs, none of which I would stand a remote chance of getting. I scanned over the boards of neatly typed cards advertising the need for plumbers, machine technicians and mechanical engineering jobs. There was nothing new, nothing that stuck out, and even if there was I didn't have the qualifications. Wandering around aimlessly for another couple of minutes, I became aware that the woman on the desk was watching me. I smiled hesitantly and went over to where she was moving a pile of papers about, shuffling them from one side to the other with no apparent reason.

'Can you tell me if you have any new jobs in this morning? I've looked at all the boards but there isn't anything I could apply for. Could you just have a look for me?'

She shuffled the papers further, putting them down in a neat pile in front of her, then picked up two small white cards from the top of the blue plastic tray marked 'In'.

'Well, there's only two today. It's been a bit quiet on the work front over the last couple of weeks. Let me see, there's a part-time job in Fine Fayre, afternoons, or a twilight shift at Springer's. Either of them be any good to you?'

I didn't think Fine Fayre would be the best bet for me. I'd somewhat blotted my copy book when on work experience there, ruining a whole consignment of custard powder by opening the cardboard packaging with a knife. Mother only had drums of custard powder: metal containers with lever-off lids that you pushed the end of a teaspoon under before being able to break the paper seal and get at the contents. How was I to know that custard powder came in packets as well? I was not the best work experience girl they'd ever had; they wouldn't exactly welcome me back with open arms. So that left Springers.

The job centre clerk rang through to their office and I was dispatched straight away. It was a short distance. I walked at my slowest pace but still didn't have time to think about what questions would make me look interested or what to say when they asked why I wanted the job. The truth was probably not an option to bring out at a first meeting.

Getting to the office meant walking through the loading yard where huge cases of cotton and wool thread on spindles were driven on forklift trucks through roll-up doors. I'd developed an innate fear of forklifts since the times Grandma took me to visit her Aunt in Ambergate when I was a little girl. The Aunt lived up in the houses that had been built to nestle in the green canopy of trees on the other side of the Derwent River. It had been an idyllic settlement with its own tiny gravel road that crossed the river via a small stone bridge only wide enough for one car to cross. A few years later, though, the peace had been somewhat shattered when a huge sheet metal factory was constructed just across the river, sharing the road to the houses, employing over a hundred men and being seen as a great addition to the prosperity of the local community. The access road to Grandma's Aunt's house was then surrounded by factory yard on either side. With the sparks from the welding sheds, the smell of burning and the forklifts whirring about with huge armfuls of rusting metal sheets, I crossed the road in fear of my life. At Springer's I gave the forklifts a wide berth, stopping to let them pass safely and waiting to make sure they were well out of the way before starting forward again.

I walked through the edge of the knitting room, hearing the machinery clanking and seeing huge bobbins of coloured threads turning slowly on metal spindles. Beyond this the sound of voices and occasional laughter from the workers was almost stifled by the sheer volume of noise. At the office door I stopped and took a deep breath before knocking.

Inside, I sat down across the desk from the works manager Mr Jenks, wondering how on earth he managed to do any work with the noise of the factory continually droning on in the background.

Mr Jenks turned out to be rather deaf in both ears. When he asked about my previous experience in knitwear I had to repeat myself in louder and louder tones until I was virtually shouting my replies at him. At least I could now understand how he managed to work through such a racket – he simply didn't hear it.

'Do you think you have the right qualities to work in the finishing department? I've been looking at your fingers. They are, if you don't mind me saying, rather fat... Do you think you'll be able to work with yarn? It's a fiddly job,' Mr Jenks asked, looking directly at my hands.

I moved them off the table, hiding them below the surface of the desk because his staring was making me distinctly uncomfortable. I looked down at my fingers, trying to gauge whether they were any fatter than those of anyone else I knew. I wasn't sure. In proportion to the rest of me they weren't.

'I've never had problems managing fiddly jobs before, Mr Jenks. I use a sewing machine and knit and sew by hand. I don't think using your machines would be a problem,' I shouted across at him. It was lucky the factory was so noisy or the whole world would have heard.

He looked at me again over the rim of his glasses, seeming to be scrutinising my appearance further. Apparently satisfied, he stood up, walked around the side of the desk and held out his palm towards me. I took his hand and shook it tentatively.

'So will you be available to begin on the evening shift starting Monday next? I'll walk you through to the factory and introduce you to Joan. She'll train you on the two machines you'll be using,' invited Mr Jenks.

I nodded I would start the job and began to experience a strange feeling of nervousness as I followed him out of the office and through the maze of machines and women pressing pedals and buttons. The air was full of cotton thread residue which settled on the machine tops and window ledges, and on people if they stood still for long enough. The factory had the appearance of not having been cleaned for a long time. There was a distinct smell of oil in the next room and the heat from the machines was noticeable as we came to a halt against a large green one which seemed to be sucking in long strings of socks and forcing them out the other side. Joan stood next to it with her back to us; oblivious to the fact we were there because of the clamour from the room.

She was a woman of about fifty years with greying curly hair and wearing a blue checked overall; the type that slipped over your head and tied at the sides. It was about two sizes too big and drowned her small frame.

Mr Jenks tapped her on the shoulder and she turned with a start before raising a huge welcoming smile.

'Is this our new young 'un then?' Mr Jenks opened his mouth to reply but before he got a word out Joan carried on. 'Well, don't you worry yourself girl; we'll soon whip you into shape and get you up to speed on these two machines. It's not a hard job as long as you keep your mind on it. I've been at it for the past seventeen years and have loved every minute of it.'

Seventeen years? That was almost as long as I'd been alive. How could anyone spend that long standing in the same position, staring at the same view and working the same machine? To fill eight hours of each twenty-four with such mindless boredom was a hideous prospect.

As the weeks went on I grew accustomed to winding the long strings of socks through the extruding pipes, turning them inside-out. The inside-out streams were then fed into the cutter which produced individually cut socks that only needed to be finished. Thousands of argyle, striped and plain socks passed through my hands every evening and after a couple of weeks I became convinced that Joan must either be quite mad to have done the same job for all those years or she had an extremely high boredom threshold. The only saving grace was the genuinely good-hearted, kind people I had to work with. They always had a comic story or bit of gossip to pass on and made me feel part of the team. I couldn't see myself being able to stick the amount of tedium for another year, never mind seventeen no matter how jovial the workforce was. Luckily I had developed a plan.

Chapter 51

Unbeknown to my Mother and stepfather I'd been up to the community school on the hill as I'd seen a poster in the job centre encouraging older people back into learning. It seemed like a good idea and, after speaking with the school about how the courses worked, I went and signed up to do another two 'A' levels in a year in order to apply for university again.

I chose English Literature and Social History and began the double workload without finding it a problem. Having the break from studying had made concentration easier. It was a means to an end and a way of sharpening my wits in order to ensure I could finally escape the nest. I had no choice; I simply had to do well. It did help that the English course was taught by a vision of a woman who turned my head from the minute I saw her.

Suzanne Jacobs was getting on for forty with the blackest hair I'd ever seen and a smile that could light a room. When she was angry with the class for not paying attention or something similar, her eyes would flash with a fire-like quality, almost as if they were giving a warning of what could happen if things didn't improve. She was fascinating and, together with the encouragement she gave, I started to excel in her classes. It was wonderful how a little support along with compliments on my skills pushed me to higher grades and a better understanding of what I was reading and writing about.

I didn't have to pay towards my course as the county council believed that people over school leaving age added to the vibrancy of the place and acted as role models for the younger students. I seriously doubted I was qualified to be a role model for anybody but was very glad I didn't have to contribute any money, otherwise my stepfather would have cottoned on to my wages not being as full as they should be.

I developed stealth when it came to money. The evening shift was on a piecework rate so the harder I worked the more money I took home. I never told Mother what I really earned, instead gave her fifty pounds each week for my keep and pretended that I kept only twenty pounds for myself. True, but on a good week I could treble that with working quicker and cutting short my tea breaks. I figured out that if I carried on at this pace by the time university started I would have a good few hundred pounds to help me along with moving and setting up home somewhere else.

When my Mother and stepfather went to work I was in the house where I was supposed to be. Then I spent an hour rushing around cleaning manically and making it look like I'd taken a long time over what I'd done. I hurried up to the school to undertake my lessons, books and notes hidden in a carrier bag so it wouldn't be suspected. Essay writing was harder to keep undercover, though the long periods hidden in my bedroom weren't thought to be out of the ordinary. As my work started to roll back in with high grades and good comments, the certainty I could do well and get another university place grew in my mind; hope was a precious commodity. Working in the evening and being out a lot meant that on the whole I managed to evade the advances of my stepfather. He still made every attempt he could to terrorise me sexually and emotionally, but being bored beyond belief on a sock-extruding machine had some distinct advantages.

Chapter 52

The months at the factory passed uneventfully. Every day I was cooped up in there felt like a lifetime. I spent the weekends mooching around the lanes and sitting in the cemetery with the dog for company, watching people go by, couples together walking, exuding warmth and life. Things far removed from my own existence.

I clung to my escape strategy and started adding to the boxes stored in my bedroom. I'd decided not to say a word about moving out until I had a definite university place and some idea of where I was going to live.

Spring began in earnest, the budding trees suddenly bursting into life with the mild warmth of the early sunshine, leaves the most vibrant green appearing swiftly to cloak the hills and revitalise the landscape. Mother, in her usual style, started to get twitchy about spring-cleaning, making a list of the things she wanted to do, mostly painting and washing pots and ornaments, no mean feat in our house. Mother was a hoarder, she called it 'collecting'. Her collections were varied and usually started out by having two of something. Two grew into a dozen and a collection was born.

The old part of the cottage had a beamed ceiling; the beams were oak but had long been painted black and made to contrast with the white plaster as a feature. Mother's first collection was displayed on these beams. Every six inches she'd inserted a cup hook and dutifully hung a mug gathered from every place visited on trips out. Soon other people started to bring them back from their own holidays until the whole ceiling resembled something from *The Old Curiosity Shop*.

Along with mugs she also collected decorative plates, mounted on sprung hangers nailed into the walls of the front room. They covered three sides, so when it came to spring cleaning the washing of the china took hours in itself. We had to put aside a whole day to take on the task. By the end of it, two pairs of hands were wrinkled from being constantly wet and all the tea cloths in the house were lined up in front of the coal fire steaming dry. Every year when the washing extravaganza was finished she'd stand wistfully with the last clean mug in her hand and announce, 'one day when I'm gone our Caroline, these will all be yours. You'll never be short of a mug again!'

And then she'd laugh teasingly, as if knowing the thought of this odd bequest bought out a real sense of horror in me.

I not only dreaded the inheritance that was coming my way at some point in the future, but also the beginning of the cleaning season. I wouldn't be able to stop either.

I walked home one Saturday from my stint in the Oxfam shop – other people's cast-out, unwanted things were preferable to my Mother's – and was confronted by the smell of a bonfire which grew stronger the closer I got to the cottage. As I rounded the corner the flames were clearly visible licking around the boxes and pieces of wood piled up high at the edge of the garden. The smoke was floating across the road in swathes.

Inside the house, piles of boxes, overflowing bin bags of papers and old kitchen utensils surrounded my Mother who was struggling to force a potato masher into the top of a sack with great gusto.

'Bloomin' heck Mother, you've been busy haven't you? Have we got anything left in the house?' I laughed knowing full well that the work she'd put in would have only made a small dent in the bits and pieces she had stuffed in the drawers and cupboards.

She obviously wasn't in the mood for chatting so I decided my best tactic would be trying to help, telling her about my day until she'd thawed out enough to let me know why she was so angry.

I took the bin bag and squashed down the paper inside, then tied up the top.

'Shall I take this to the dustbin or do you want me to put it with all the rest he's burning outside?'

She didn't answer, so I picked up the sack and carried it round to the bonfire heap. He wasn't there but the smell of cigarette smoke hung in the air, so I guessed he was sat in the outside toilet and was relieved I didn't have to get into a conversation.

Back inside the kitchen Mother was stood on tiptoes on the seat of a chair pulling down boxes from the top of the kitchen cupboards.

She still wasn't speaking and I couldn't see any other way of making myself useful so I went upstairs. I'd brought back a couple of old saucepans from my day at Oxfam; they'd come in handy as a start off when I moved. I intended to put them in the boxes stored up for my new life, but when I went into my bedroom they weren't there. It was all gone.

Everything had been pulled out from under my bed and gone through; there were bits of old letters and some shreds of photographs left behind but very little else. The cupboards above had been emptied and everything tidied up: the books were all in alphabetical order and had been dusted. It was almost clinical. I pulled out the Children's Illustrated Bible; this was where I kept my most important letters and bits and pieces. Jonah and the Whale hid my letters from Rachel and the flowers she'd given me; I'd carefully pressed and attached them to a piece of black card with her name at the bottom. They weren't there. None of the things I'd kept: the notes from Sophie and the bright white dreadlock which had fallen out of the back of her hair when we were messing about by the cemetery, none of it was there. No wonder she wasn't speaking to me. I buckled down on the bed and stared at the place where things used to be, expecting it all to reappear.

I sat for ages in shocked silence, listening to the sound of my Mother banging around downstairs, then the back door opening and closing.

'So, is she back then? The dirty sod. I've burned the lot. The books you found, that catalogue thing with the names of all those women: filth the lot of it. No daughter of mine is going to be like that. I won't have it,' he bellowed at her.

I could hear her muttering something in reply but couldn't make out what it was. There didn't seem any point in trying to listen anyway, knowing what was being said made little difference anymore, so I carried on looking round at the empty space. All I had left were a few novels deemed safe for me to keep, the books I had when I was a child, the old stereo I'd been given and the saucepans brought home that day. Not a great deal to begin again with.

Years later, when I sporadically visited my Mother, she would take me upstairs and show me the new additions to her tea towel collection. Whilst she was occupied with carefully folding and placing her precious items away for safekeeping I would stick my head round the door to the room that was once mine. The bed was long gone and it appeared there was no trace of the person who had once inhabited the space. Maybe that should have made me sad but, if the truth were told, I was only too pleased that that person was long dead and buried; the mausoleum to that old life had been turned into a store room for a freezer and a stack of suitcases.

All those months of squirrelling away pots and pans, bedding, cutlery and pictures had gone in the few short hours I'd been out of the house. When I set out for my shift at the charity shop all had been normal. I'd run my hand over the top of the box which contained a rather battered old feather duvet that a neighbour had given to Mother and she'd subsequently passed on to me. The feel of it had been comforting and now I mourned its loss acutely. The letters being taken hurt me more than any of it. All the things I'd kept and clung to which gave me a sense of having some place in the world had gone.

I had a notion of how it must feel to be completely free. Or did I mean adrift? I sat on the bed where, as a small child who couldn't sleep, I'd pretended to be aboard a boat that was drifting motionlessly on a calm sea. I used to find it comforting and safe. Now the sharks circled, they'd nipped in whilst I wasn't looking and devoured the things which made me myself. I was waiting for them to come back and take me too.

The feeling of being adrift had a strange effect. There was a sense of having no restraint. I no longer had anything to protect and almost a rising madness in the centre of my chest. It was like a mixture of anger and something else I couldn't quite put my finger on.

I could still hear his voice downstairs and the low murmurs of her replies. Then I heard footsteps approaching; the seventh step creaked when weight was put on it and then almost sighed in relief when the load was moved onto the eighth. The steady, climbing footfall stopped at what I imagined was the top of the staircase, then Mother called out, 'you'd better come down and get your tea.' It wasn't really a request, more a warning that it would be better to come down and face the music sooner rather than later. I stood up and walked out of the room, following her down the stairs. He was sat at the table clearly waiting for my entrance.

Usually I would've skirted around the issue, busied myself with the pots or boiling the kettle, but today I stood there and waited for the inevitable to happen. I could see the white of his knuckles as he clenched his fists and the back of his neck getting redder. He got up from the chair and turned to face me, eyes thin and piercing, burning into mine. I stared back at him. The fear that generally welled up inside was today being held down by anger, anger growing with every second he glowered at me.

Mother was trying to distract him. She tried her best but it didn't work, I could feel the heat in my face rising, and though I saw my stepfather's mouth moving, I couldn't hear what he was saying. It was as if I was in a soundproof booth. No booth could save me from the right knuckle that suddenly pulled back and appeared with such force against the side of my face. I reeled backwards and stumbled into the table. The corner of it caught my back and knocked the wind out of me. I gasped and stood up straight again, cheek bone stinging, burning with the pain of impact.

I could hear all the sound in the kitchen again, the kettle on the gas boiling wildly, spitting water onto the iron top of the cooker. Mother was crying and shouting for him to calm down; the dog whined at the bottom of the stairs; my stepfather ranted madly: 'If you don't stop messing about with them girls

327

you've been seen with I'll knock your bloody head off next time. No daughter of mine is going to bring shame on this family; your poor Mother's worried to death about it. Well, no more. You will bloody pack it in, I'm telling you now lady.' He was pulling his fist back to strike again.

This time I was ready. He lurched forward and I ducked to the side quickly. His fist missed completely and he punched the empty air in front of him.

'Why, you little sod! I'll teach you!' he bellowed, grabbing my arm so I couldn't move this time, raising his hand to attack again.

Before I knew the full extent of what I was doing, I'd pulled back my free arm and punched him hard in the stomach. He doubled up. Whether it was the shock of retaliation or the force of the blow I wasn't sure.

He staggered backwards, falling back into his seat. His face was a picture. He had no breath to start shouting again and, as my Mother was in a state of astonished stupor, I took the chance to have my say.

'How dare you take things out of my bedroom! How dare you think it's all right to go and take the things that belong to me and burn them! How dare you! And then you think it's all right to hit out as usual! I'm fed up with your fists, hiding bruises and all the other stuff you do, do you hear me? It isn't going to happen any more!' I'd started off quietly and finished up shouting at the top of my lungs.

Mother was crying loudly now and he was starting to get his breath back to answer my tirade. He stood up, stepped towards me and started to growl.

'This is my house. Your bedroom is mine and the things in it are mine. You'll do as I want in this house, do you hear me?' He threatened with the tone of his voice and the closeness of his face. I could smell the cigarette smoke, stale on his breath.

I stepped back and looked straight at him without blinking, quiet for a minute but keeping my eyes on his. After gathering my thoughts, I replied, 'well, if everything in this house belongs to you then I won't be staying here for much longer. I'm leaving at the end of summer and going as far away from

328

you as possible. You'll never be able to touch me again. My things will be my own and I'll never have to worry about you going through them or reading my letters or threatening the people I love. You've taken away so much from me over the years and I'm not going to let you take anything else. It stops right here and now!'

I turned my back on him and made a move towards my Mother who was now silently sobbing next to the sink. She looked at me and through the tears started to have her say.

'Just you apologise for thumping your Dad like that. He hasn't ever done you any harm. You don't know what side your bread's buttered on, honest you don't. You've got a good home here. Just you make it right now and we'll start again.' She paused for a breath, 'And if you don't then you'd better move out like you said, the sooner the better. I told you years ago we'd have been better off putting you in a children's home. You've been nothing but trouble.' With that she burst into tears again.

It was my turn to be astonished, not expecting my own Mother to turn against me. I thought she'd take my side against him, but no support came. I don't know why I was surprised; in the years since the fateful day she'd married him I'd always come in a poor second.

'Right then; if that's how it has to be, as soon as I can get out of here I will.' It was all I could manage without betraying myself by crying.

'Where will you go? You haven't got any money.' She seemed shocked and concerned at my reply, wanting me to cave in and apologise, for life to continue as it always had. But I couldn't and, more so, I wouldn't. I had made my decision.

I shrugged my shoulders and looked past her through to the open window. The air smelt fresh and calm and it called me.

'Well, I don't know. I'm waiting to hear about a place at university. The first one I get, well, that's where I'll go. Sounds as good a way of finding somewhere to go as any. And as for money, I'll manage. I've saved a bit up and I'll have to find a job when I get there. What did Gladys in the factory use to say? Needs must when the devil drives. I'll be fine and at least I won't be here with him. In fact I'll be more than fine.'

I picked up my coat and flounced out through the kitchen door. The air hit me; I suddenly felt dizzy and had to lean up against the wall to recover. I was cast adrift, on my own little boat again, and just had to wait and see where I would wash up.

I walked for a long time, standing to watch a flock of geese flying in formation over the edge of the river valley before slowly trudging home. Except this wasn't home anymore. In the next few months I would have to find my own niche in the world, 'A Room of One's Own', as Virginia Woolf expounded: somewhere I could belong.

Chapter 53

By the time Monday came around I was glad to get out to work, even though the hours standing at the machine seemed endless. Indoors, no one was speaking to anyone else. The house was quiet except for the droning of the TV, but at least it took the edge off the atmosphere and anything was better than nothing. I felt as if I was in a fragile bubble which was dangerously close to bursting. I didn't have an ally. I used to believe Mother would always be one no matter what, but I'd been proved wrong.

People get sent though, when you most need them. I've always believed that; if there's a need then someone will come along to fulfil it eventually. That's exactly what happened.

Along came George.

George appeared one Tuesday evening over the top of the sock-extruding machine. Well, more he stuck his head around the side of the funnel where the single socks tumbled out into piles ready to be toed and topped. I never saw the finished product, apart from in the factory shop; no matter how cheap they were sold Argyle wasn't a style I liked.

George was a knitter; he worked continental shifts: four twelve hour days a week. It suited him; he liked a lie in at the weekends, then to sit and watch telly and stroll round his garden in the afternoons. By the time it got to the evening he was ready to get out and see his mates. He had a standard size poodle called Eddie with a curly chocolate coat, and wherever George went so did the dog. Apart from when he was at work, then Eddie stayed home with George's partner Bob. Bob was retired, well before his time. He'd worked on the railways until he caught his foot in the rail as the points changed. The accident ripped the side of his foot open and severed an artery; the fire service and paramedics managed to free him, saving his foot from amputation before the train came and sliced his whole leg off. He'd walked with a limp since then. George said he was lucky not to be walking on a stump.

People in the factory laughed at George. They laughed at his jokes, at his wisecracks and daft antics. Then when he wasn't there or had his back turned they laughed at him, at his life and at Bob, though none of them really knew the slightest thing about either of them.

George was kind. He seemed to know when things weren't right, as if he could sense sadness. He would beam a smile over the machines at me, trying to brighten my day. At tea breaks, when his shift combined – collided he called it – with mine, he'd come across to our side of the machine room with packets of biscuits or bags of Pontefract cakes picked up from the corner shop on his way in. He had a sweet tooth and gravitated towards a like-minded soul.

'So then my little fruit, what's the matter this fine summer evening? The sun has been shining and the birds singing and all should be well with the world, though it clearly isn't with you is it?' He smiled a broad warm smile and proffered a bag of sweets.

I took one and sighed as I unwrapped it, then set about telling him the sorry story of the weekend's events. I'd gone past tears and managed to get the whole tale out without getting upset. He listened and nodded and got angry for me in the right places and, once I'd got to the end, he squeezed my arm and forced another sweet on me. He had to get back to his machine. He worked on the circular knitting machines, each re-thread was around an hour's job, so I had plenty of time to consider the fact I'd managed to blurt out about eight years' horror in less than ten minutes.

An hour and a half later he returned full of bluster with a big grin on his face. I'd started to believe that unburdening myself had put him off me; the spilling out of my life story and then him not returning as soon as his re-thread was finished had me worried. I'd kept my eye out, noticing he'd disappeared from the shop floor. People not being where they should always made me feel unnerved.

As it turned out George had nipped home to have a word with Bob and returned full of good news. I had no idea that the news was meant for me.

'Bob's got this flat; it was his Auntie Joyce's. She's long gone and the flat's stood empty for a good couple of years. It's above a foot place – you know what I mean – a chiropodist. It's not much to look at mind, but it could be made nice given a lick of paint and some curtains.' George stopped and grinned at me, though I had absolutely no idea why he was telling me about dead Aunt Joyce's previous abode. I smiled blankly back at him.

'So, what do you think then our kid?' He grinned again and seemed to be waiting for an answer, except I wasn't sure what the question was. Then it dawned that he was offering the flat to me.

'Where is it, the flat?' I managed to get out eventually after standing there for a few minutes in a bewildered fashion.

'It's in Nottingham love. Sorry, I thought I'd said. Not too far away but far enough to not be too close, eh! What shall I tell Bob then?'

I'd assumed it would have been in Belper somewhere. I'd been to Nottingham a few years previously to a family wedding but had no clue about what area it had been in. The only real memory of that day being the city seemed huge. Double-decker buses rushed past and the cars drove away from the city in three lanes of traffic: all bustle, rush and noise. It seemed exciting.

'I suppose I'd better tell my Mother that I'm going to live in Nottingham then George,' I grinned before he rushed around the side of my machine and squeezed the life out of me with a massive hug.

'You won't regret it. It'll be the start of a new life for you. Get away from here and start to live for yourself, eh?' He paused. 'You can get into that university there can't you?'

I explained that I'd applied through the school to go to lots of different places, Nottingham was one of them and I'd have to check up to see if they'd accept me. While I was speaking, my mind was already made up. I was going to go anyway, start afresh like George had said. It could be no worse than being here after all. Who could tell? Maybe it might be a lot better.

So, for the next few weeks messages went backwards and forwards between me and Bob, tenancy agreements were sorted out, and George gradually picked up bits and pieces that I'd managed to carry to work and took them to Nottingham.

The flat itself was filling up with my things and even though I'd still not seen the place I had a picture in my mind of what it was going to be like and how I'd live once I was settled. The thought of my battered second-hand saucepans sitting in the kitchen cupboard made me feel secure somehow.

I hadn't mentioned anything to Mother or anyone else about leaving, keeping a low profile and saying very little; it seemed safer. I had an idea that if people found out I was going to move away, and had already found somewhere to live, a way to put a spanner in the proverbial works would be found. I wasn't going to take any risks this time and decided to wait and not say a word until I had the piece of paper in my hand telling me I had a college place or, failing that, I'd saved enough money to keep myself for the first couple of months until I could find a job. Either scenario was fine. I really wanted to be able to go to university and sit for hours uninterrupted in the library surrounded by books and silence, with no one to bother me. But, equally, working in a shop would do just as well. I was finally going to save myself and that was what ultimately mattered.

Each day seemed to drag along at the slowest pace possible. I worked as much overtime as I could fit in and managed to pull in quite a healthy wage, half of it each week passing directly to George. This was for advance rent so that by the time I was to move, in the middle of September, I'd be paid up for at least two months. It was a good feeling to have control over my own destiny.

At the cottage things were very quiet. My stepfather seemed to be making a real effort to be polite and to start conversations, asking about work and what I'd been doing, talking about the plastics factory and his pigeons. Whilst

334

Mother was there I answered in short, equally polite sentences, still feeling it was only right to try and make life a bit more bearable for her despite it being the complete opposite for me. When she wasn't in I made no bones about the fact I didn't want to speak to him at all; his attempts at conversation were matched with silence.

Then a brown envelope arrived marked 'The University Clearing Office'. I whipped it up off the mat so no one would see, stuffed it into my work bag with my sandwiches, and pretended no post had been delivered that day.

On the walk to work I sat down on a low wall near Springers and opened the envelope; it was an offer letter. The offers depended on my grades and were alphabetically listed; near the bottom was the college I was looking for.

Nottingham Polytechnic. I needed a B-grade and two C-grade 'A' levels. I had them already without even waiting for the new results to come from my current studies. I wasted no time and posted off the letter of acceptance to the college board. It was all over. I was moving to Nottingham and my new life was to begin.

At work, through the whining and clanking of the knitting machines, I bellowed my news across to George. He took the letter, read it through, and with a misty look in his eyes, congratulated me on my success.

'Well girl, this is it isn't it? The great escape. Time to start digging the tunnels, eh! Have you told your Mother yet?'

I hadn't said a word so far; he was the first to know. Telling Mother would have to be at the weekend. It would be the first time I'd see her properly. I wasn't looking forward to it because despite everything I didn't want to leave her alone with him.

'It's you or them girl, remember that. If you don't go now then you'll spend the rest of your life here and get grey and old like the rest of us. You'll always know you could have had a different life and you'll never forgive yourself if you don't do it. Take it from a man who knows.' George, as usual, was wise.

I knew he was right. I had to take my chance to get away and change now, otherwise, as he said, I would indeed end up old and greying, walking the high street of Belper on a Saturday morning wearing a mushroom-coloured mac and rainproof head scarf. This was a fine tradition for Derbyshire women but it wasn't for me. I had to be brave and tell Mother I was leaving.

Chapter 54

The weekend came around quickly enough and I'd planned my words down to the last syllable, certain of what I was going to say. As long as I didn't give Mother a chance to get a word in edgeways I would be all right.

The atmosphere was still strained as I got up that morning. My stepfather was sat on the bottom step of the staircase smoking a cigarette; I had to squeeze past him to get into the kitchen. He wouldn't move. My leg pushed into his back as I stepped down, causing waves of revulsion to run through my body and set up home in the pit of my stomach. The feeling spurred me on, reminding me of what I had to get away from.

Mother was, as usual, at the sink with her arms up to the elbows in soapsuds. She was washing a pile of jam jars and lids, the jam kettle was on the stove and steam was billowing up to the ceiling, condensing into water droplets which were starting to drip down the walls and form tiny rivulets. She was making the first batch of strawberry jam from the garden crop and muttering about the fruits floating when they should be submerged. May Clarke's old cookery book was propped up behind the taps so she could read the recipe as she soaked the jars and cleaned off the labels. She'd made jam the previous year and had left the jar washing to my stepfather; for months afterwards, each time a tart or sandwich was made it had a faint taste of pickled onions and she vowed never again to let anyone help if they couldn't be trusted to do the job properly. She'd stuck to her word.

'Mother, I've got something I have to tell you about next weekend.' She continued to scrub at the jars with a scouring pad so I carried on. 'I'm going to Nottingham next Sunday morning. I have a flat that I'm moving into. It's all sorted out.'

Initially my announcement didn't seem to sink in. She carried on in exactly the same way; the rhythmic scraping of a rather tenacious marmalade label required concentration and patience. Then she stopped, took her hands out of the sink and slowly wiped them on the wet tea cloth next to her.

'Well, you can't just go like that. How have you got a flat? How are you going to pay for it? I'm not going to pay for it for you. You make your own bed if that's how you're going to carry on and you'll have to bloody well lie in it as well.'

The surprise as well as indignation in her voice was audible.

I was ready for her questions but not quite prepared for the anger she was showing. I'd expected her to be surprised, shocked even, but not angry.

'I have the money to put down three months' rent already. I've been saving it up at work with George. The flat belonged to Bob's Auntie. It's been empty for quite a while but it'll be fine with a bit of paint and some bits and pieces. I wouldn't expect you to pay for it. I know you don't want me to go but I have to: for me,' I blurted out.

My eyes started filling with tears but I wasn't going to show I was upset. Telling her I was leaving made it all very final, as if there was a definite end to my time in Belford and the clock had started to count down to the beginning of another life. The thought scared me more than I wanted to admit because, even though this life had been intolerable, at least I knew who I was in it and what went where. When this door closed I wasn't sure what the new one opening would bring.

Mother was standing staring at me as if she couldn't quite believe what I'd said. The last few weeks had shook her to the bones. She'd been used to a steady existence, knowing each day inside out. Since the incident where I'd punched my stepfather, the axis on which her life was based had somewhat shifted.

He fidgeted on the step as if wanting us to remember he was there, clearing his throat and making his voice heard.

'Well, if I were you duck, I wouldn't bother about her. If she wants to go then let her. She's never known where she's well off. Not many kids would've had the life she's had; she doesn't know how lucky she is. You mark my words: give her a couple of weeks and she'll be back, desperate to come home. You just see if she isn't.'

Mother didn't give him a reply so he carried on. 'Anyhow, it's about time she went isn't it? She's been nothing but trouble for the past few years, running around with them girls and not bringing a proper wage into the house. Now we find out she's been squirrelling away money instead of paying into the house. She's nothing but a selfish little sod! Well, I won't be begging her not to go and I won't miss her either.'

It took all my resolve not to reply. I wasn't going to give him the satisfaction. Inside though, I was furious, feeling slandered and hugely let down by my Mother, who again, said nothing in my defence.

'And I know that George she works with. He used to go into the pub where the pigeon club meets. Nothing but a poof he is; can't lie straight in bed just like that Brother of hers. It's no wonder she's hooked up with him. Christ Almighty, she's no better than she should be. Before we know it she'll be as bad as he is, just you mark my words,' he spat in my direction, eyes burning with hate.

I couldn't stand there any longer and listen to him degrading one of the few people who'd tried to help me, so I turned my back on them both and went towards the stairs.

'I think you should just pack your stuff up now and go today. We don't want you here anymore, do we Maureen?' He didn't let her answer. 'You go and live in Nottingham and good luck to you because, believe me lady, you'll need it. And I tell you this for nothing, don't you come running back to your Mother when you're in trouble, because you've burnt your boats with us.'

He had to have the last word and I let him have it. I was too upset to speak. In my room, behind the closed door, I burst into tears, allowing them to run freely down my face and onto the old shirt I was wearing. These would be the last tears I would shed in this house. I left them to dry on their own as I pushed the few decent clothes I had into a bag and bundled the last of the pots and plates into the top of a box.

Downstairs was quiet. The door hadn't opened or closed so I assumed they were still in the house, though no one was speaking. I walked out of my tiny bedroom for the last time. Downstairs I could hear the television blaring out from the front room, canned laughter from a comedy repeat.

'Right, I'm going,' I shouted. There was no reaction. Though the television was loud I knew they'd both heard. I stood for a couple of minutes waiting for any response, but the only sound was the television broadcasting to its silent audience. No reply came.

I swung the bag onto my shoulder, opened the kitchen door and stepped out into the bright mid-morning sunshine.

Chapter 55

Later that day I found myself sat in the living room of the cosy little flat which was to be my home for the next eight years.

After George and Bob had gone, I went from room to room, looking at the empty spaces and the view through the windows. The large London plane tree which stood in the front yard waved its branches in the breeze and the wind whistled through its leaves. The sound made me feel settled and secure. At home. As the night set in, light from the street lamp opposite sent a slight glow into the room. It was enough for me to be able to pick up a pen and write a letter, taking a sheet of old monogrammed paper from a now slightly battered satin-lined box.

Dear Rachel,

Well, here I am! We always said that one day we'd move away from Belper and life would be different. For me it starts now, in Nottingham.

How have I ended up here? It's been a long story since the last time I saw you and to tell it all in this note would take me all night and probably into tomorrow. So maybe if you get this and would like to meet up then please get in touch. It would be wonderful to see you again.

I think of you everyday.

Love always,
Caroline.

Two weeks later a hand-addressed envelope landed on the mat. Inside the note began:

Dear Caroline...